ALL HAIL
THE KING'S INDIAN

DAZZLING

"Gardner flicks back and forth between the comic and the tragic, Gothic parody and high seriousness, with the virtuosity of a lizard's tongue or of the rather satanic hypnotist . . . dazzling."

Chicago Tribune

EXCEPTIONAL

"Hooray for John Gardner . . . a double standard of excellence in comtemporary American writing . . . exceptional . . . one of America's finest fiction writers."

Milwaukee Journal

EXUBERANT

"Royalty and serfs, knights, monks, prisoners and jailers . . . Gardner uses exuberant creations in the service of a stern task: to sneak up on truth without startling it into sham abstractions."

Time

By John Gardner
Published by Ballantine Books:

OCTOBER LIGHT

GRENDEL

THE SUNLIGHT DIALOGUES

NICKEL MOUNTAIN

THE WRECKAGE OF AGATHON

THE KING'S INDIAN

FREDDY'S BOOK

THE ART OF LIVING AND OTHER STORIES

THE
KING'S INDIAN

Stories and Tales

John Gardner

Illustrated by Herbert L. Fink

BALLANTINE BOOKS • NEW YORK

To Nicholas Vergette

CONTENTS

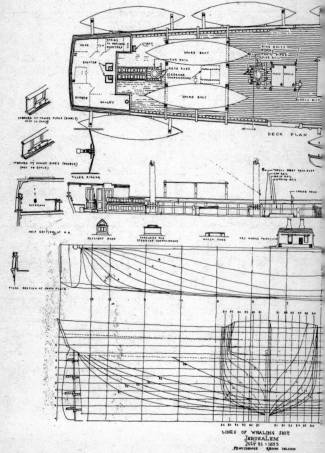

LINES OF WHALING SHIP
JERUSALEM
JULY 21 · 1833
PROVIDENCE · RHODE ISLAND

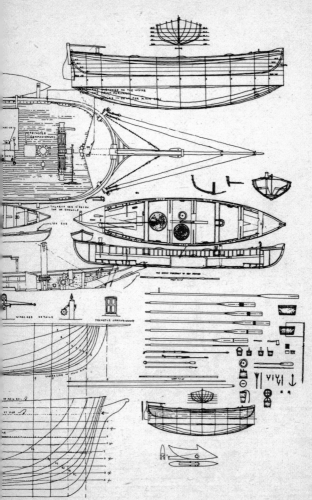

TOPGALLANT CROSSTREES

TOPMAST CAPS

SHARE NET

STAND DECK EYE
TO PIER RAIL

LINES OF WHALING SHIP
JERUSALEM
JULY 21-1833
PROVIDENCE RHODE ISL.

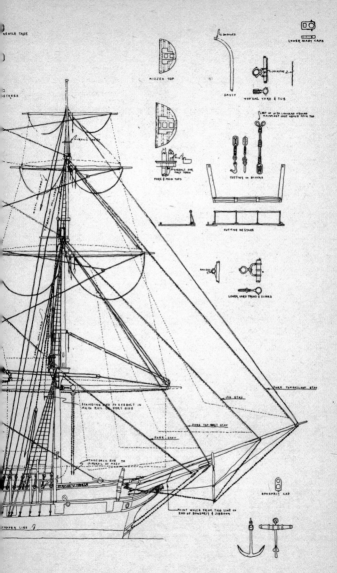

NESTLE TREE

MIZZEN TOP

DAVIT

LOWER MAST CAPS

TOPSAIL YARD & TUB

FORE & MAIN TOPS

CUTTING IN BLOCKS

CUTTING IN STAGE

LOWER YARD TRUSS & SLINGS

JIB STAY

FORE TOP MAST STAY

FORE STAY

BOWSPRIT CAP

COPPER LINE

Book One

THE
MIDNIGHT READER

PASTORAL CARE

1

I know pretty well what I look like in front of my congregation and how they're disposed to think of me. I'm not exactly dwarfish—a man of medium stature—but I'm by no means as tall as I would have been if anyone had given me a vote in the matter. I do have the freedom to wear my whiskers and hair as I please, and despite the pursed lips of certain members of my congregation I wear them longish, really from vanity, though I once preached a sermon which I think was true, as a metaphor at least, on my beard in relation to conformity, the death of religion. John the Baptist, I soberly observed, lived far from town as a religious ascetic, and society said, "He's crazy." Jesus, on the other hand, enjoyed people, all kinds of people, and society called him an encourager of immorality. Any denominational executive could have told them both that their behavior was stupid;

things would be ever so much better with the church if John would merely comb his hair and Jesus would try to be a little more discreet. . . . But however that may be, I do not deny that my square beard and the curls at my collar are to me a compensation for my failure to reach six feet. I stand, by habit, somewhat stooped; I must have recognized in early adolescence that I was locked forever from the joys of imposing height. But my shortness, my stoop, are not the worst of it. My gestures come more from my mother than from my father, a thing not especially unusual in my trade, but offensive to me just the same. Between genes and my early environment—my mother's love— I'm not left much room to move around in. Very well to read Spinoza and Tillich on Free Will. I am, for all their philosophy, disadvantaged. All this passes through my mind sometimes when I'm lecturing my flock, and I smile suddenly, to their consternation. Actually, I am richly blessed, it occurs to me. My failure to look truly distinguished keeps me honest, keeps me Christian. However righteous, however learned my explication of the Biblical texts, I can't forget that by ideal standards we're all of us silly-looking, witless geese; we'd better be kind to each other and trust in the Lord. So I stand, somewhat precariously balanced, on the footstool hidden behind my pulpit, and I gesture with my long white fingers like a lady choir director, and I give them the Word.

I tell them mainly, in a thousand different ways, the secret of shaking their foolish gloom, their dreadful and regular depression about things. They do not understand in the least what they're here for. The institutional church is not the church at all, I say to them, but a foul encrustation, a birthday party for a man who's left town and forgotten to leave us a forwarding address. I read them scripture: *"And the Lord said through his prophet Amos, 'I hate and I despise your feasts, and I take no delight in your solemn assemblies. . . . Take away from me the noise of your songs; to the melody of your harps I will not listen. But let justice roll down like waters, and righteousness like an ever-flowing stream.'"* They are

troubled by this, and they know where I mean to take them with it. To "the crisis in the church," the weather-beaten sign on my office wall, THE CHURCHES OF CARBONDALE WELCOME YOU—*memento* (*mori*) from the good old days, when building buildings was the glorious mission, which first meant building congregations, pulling in dollars, shanghaiing in the lame and halt, the fat-cat self-complacent and the crazy, letting them imagine that the purpose of the church is social respectability, support of the government, perpetuation of the old traditions, the proper maintenance of graveyards real and symbolic. They know I will bring up the church's involvement with William Sloane Coffin and the peace movement, John R. Fry and the urban poor. They compress their lips, avoid my eyes, and look miserable. Some of the staunch in my little congregation are nervously wiping their sweaty hands in their handkerchiefs. That above all brings trouble from the pulpit. I will tell them the Christian message is one of exuberant joy—"Christianity is a wide, smooth street where all the lights are green," I say. But how can my people believe such things? Not Christian worshipers but infiltrators, people never even informed about the strange Christian theory.

I wax eloquent, smile, show my large square teeth. I think of the stubborn, stupid sheep of Palestine, Christ's comic metaphor for all of us, and I butt them with quotations, roll my eyes, look wildly alarmed for no clear reason. "Cheer up!" I tell them. "God loves you, crazy as it seems!" I can hardly be surprised at their uncertainty. The older members of the congregation came up through a church that no longer exists, a church ruled mainly by spiritual guides who in the privacy of their sterile cells rolled frightened eyes and bleated in vain for the spirit, terrified by Hell. You encounter them yet, those clerical antiques: leftover dinosaurs angrily, confusedly hunting for the herd; mock saints in mortification chains; collectors of offerings for stained-glass windows. (Surely God loves, if not us, stained glass.) Against their influence I prate and howl and hoot.

"One of my favorite wealthy conservatives," I tell

them, "financed an edition of the letters written by pastors in Geneva during the period of Calvin's dominance. He thought they would show the church's distaste for political involvement. What they showed was that these early Calvinists were actively plotting the overthrow of the French government." I tell them, with ecstatic joy, of the revolutionary Wesley.

They look miserable. Hopelessly, absurdly unredeemed. The first four rows are completely empty. There are only four people, as usual, in the fifth—Dr. Grewy, who is for some reason my friend; Professor Watson, from the university, who has heard everything and maintains a coolly professional disinterest; his wife, whose present affair is with a dentist and who comes to talk with me three times a week; and old Elbert Finch, stone-deaf but a creature of rockfirm habit—a virtue I profoundly admire, though not a Christian virtue. In the rows beyond sit the clustered remains of the crisis. Once again I praise God for my ridiculousness. If I weren't ridiculous—balanced (*vanitas*) on my pulpit stool—I might easily grow scornful, indifferent to these people. And if my pitiful flock were not confused and unhappy, they would joyfully go out into the world and leave my church empty. We need each other. I give them a vision they only half understand, a vision vaguely exciting, though alarming. I explain for them words in Greek and Hebrew and they frown, beginning to perceive. One day, it comes into my mind for an instant, they will suddenly get it, and they'll rise as one man and shout Hosanna!, and I'll become supererogatory. Hastily I toss in something to confuse them: *kheseth,* the Hebrew for God's steady love. The Hebrews, I tell them, lived in a much less comfortable world than ours, and they assumed that pain and death were to be expected. For them, any break in the flow of pain was a matter for remark; the mere fact of survival was a miracle. Then hurriedly, slyly, I wind it up. "Thank God therefore for his goodness!" They purse their lips, give me a glance up-from-under like a bull, and bow their heads. I notice, near the back, a face I haven't seen before—a rather ghostly face, bearded, prophetically staring. He does not bow with the rest for the benediction. I lose my place, hesitate, repeat myself.

2

As I stand at the back of the somber, dark-beamed church shaking hands, the smell of furniture polish all around me, the church windows burning with autumnal light, my people become individuals once more, as I too become individual. I'm used to this change and approve of it, though it baffled me some, when I was younger—made me doubt my authority. I would not say to them, individually, the things I have told them—the things I have been free to tell them—from the pulpit. Poor old Miss Ellis, the piano teacher, whose house is crammed with massive, ornately carved furniture from Burma, where a dear, dear friend (I have never heard the dear friend's name) was a missionary. Miss Ellis hates Communists, destroyers of temples, and she does not like it that Jesus was killed for suspected revolutionary activities. Her bosom heaves and her blue eyes blink tears when she speaks of Foreign Missions. Once when a novelist from Kenya spoke to the Ware Class, gently but firmly explaining to those venerable ladies that the chief effect of Foreign Missions has been to soften up ancient cultures for colonialism and capitalistic exploitation, Miss Ellis nearly had a heart attack. Her mouth gaped, her face went pale beneath the paint and powder, her small, liver-spotted hands pressed hard against her heart. She was indignant, outraged, the man was an ungrateful beast. An animal! Miss Ellis spoke with tender passion of her friend's dedication. The man from Kenya was sympathetic, the soul of courtesy (although a heathen). He did not mean that missionaries were aware of their effect. They were saints; no one who had watched them could deny it. But their effect in Africa was history. Miss Ellis left the meeting shaking, prepared to cancel her pledge because we'd invited such a man. But three days later she sat weeping in my office. She was lost. The world was meaningless. She told how her mother, all her life, had given every spare penny to the Missions. It did not matter that Miss Ellis had done the same. It was not her own waste that broke her heart. She had her music, at least. But her mother had meant to do good in the world—a generous, warm-hearted, love-filled woman: Everyone who ever knew her had been devoted to her. "Think of it," she whispered. There was terror in her eyes, an emptiness dark as what astronomers call the coal-pocket. "Think of her lying there, in her grave in Philadelphia, and her whole life *nothing,* as if she'd never even lived!" She sobbed. I searched my wits for some honest comfort. She told of the death of her missionary friend during World War II in Burma. Her life, too, the friend's, was meaningless. Everything was. Everything!

I could have told her—I hinted at it—that that was the point of Christianity. All systems fail: psychologies, sociologies, philosophies, rituals. To believe in any firm system whatever, even Foreign Missions, is to be left—like Adam biting into the apple—with a taste of blowing ashes. Flexibility is all, the Christian's ability to respond, get up again, die if necessary, because everything is finally all right. We follow not a system but a man, I could have said. A conviction, a vital spirit. But who can say that to a piano teacher, for whom sharps and flats are the rock of ages, and goodness is not situational but metronomic? What I did—sighing, with a hasty private apology to God— was get down on my knees with her and pray. "Dear heavenly father have mercy upon us in our torment and confusion, for we are as children," etc., etc. Miss Ellis wept, her scaling, painted lips trembling, her white fists doubled at her chin. And it was true, I saw, that she was very like a child, like one of her own terrified students suffering through Bach in the aquatic light of Miss Ellis' front room with its oppressive oriental chests and red velvet drapes. I did not like the theology in which she was reared, but I was no missionary. Let her be converted on Judgment Day.

She sobbed, kneeling on the carpet beside me, her face turned up toward the sign, THE CHURCHES OF CARBONDALE WELCOME YOU. And it worked, of course—as how could it not? She accepted her bafflement and disillusionment, turned over her helplessness to Jesus, just-as-she-was-without-one-plea and so on. Exactly as a Christian would have done. I could have told her, if I'd wanted, that prayer itself can be idolatry—a confusion of the symbol and the fact. I didn't. I led her in a hymn. (The door was closed. My secretary, Janice, was in the back room running off mimeographs.) *What a friend we have in Jesus, all our griefs and pains to bear* . . . Our voices quavered uncertainly up to THE CHURCHES OF CARBONDALE WELCOME YOU. Miss Ellis caught my hand—hers was small, but her grip was as powerful as a monkey's. *What a privilege to carry, everything to God in prayer.* When we finished we stood up. "Reverend Pick, I don't know how to thank you," she said. Tears, trembling smile. I said, "Don't thank me, Miss Ellis, thank Our Savior." Callous, you may say. I prefer to view it as a momentary lapse from charity. Love is a difficult thing to sustain without hypocrisy on the one hand, stupidity on the other. I felt sympathy for her, but not enough sympathy to abandon my theology, accept her as an equal. Miss Ellis proves more generous. I sometimes think she no longer listens to anything I say in the pulpit: I'm a harmless lunatic, a dear, dear friend. But she does listen, strange to say. Heaven only knows what she thinks of it all. She tips her head now (blue hat, white berries), preparing her face for my greeting.

"Good morning, Miss Ellis."

"Good morning, Reverend Pick. Such a splendid sermon! It makes a person think!"

The strange young man I noticed earlier, no doubt a college student, comes up behind her. He's very tall. He has curly hair hanging to his shoulder blades, and wide blue staring eyes. He moves like a zombie, a creature in a dream. Gives me the willies even now. I reach up eagerly to shake his hand and inadvertently —unless *he* arranged it— catch hold of his thumb. He gives me a power-to-the-people shake. As he does so he passes me, speaking not a word, turning to keep his staring, drowned-man eyes on me. He turns the way a sign would, or a hovering object near the ocean floor. He backs out the door, still staring at me. Beyond all doubt a maniac, or else stoned. Or Christ come down to check on me. I feel a brief, sharp tingle of fear, a rising of the hackles, but it passes at once. I have no idea why the stranger rouses such feelings in me; but it's of no importance. They too, the members of my congregation—Miss Ellis, standing at the door, looking back—are alarmed by him. Their distress is in their eyes.

"Good to have you with us," I call after him.

As he backs past Miss Ellis into the too-bright October sunshine, I have a fleeting impression that it's the world, not the stranger, that's moving. In the arch that frames him, trees rise past his ghastly head like planets.

I reach toward Professor Stibitz, who catches my hand, squeezes hard, and smiles. "Very interesting sermon as usual, Reverend." A voice like a cello.

"Why thank you."

"Not at all."

3

John Grewy, M.D., is in the church office counting money from the collection plates. Janice, my secretary, leaves as I come in. She never leaves anyone alone in the office. A careful guardian. Gentle as a dove, you might think at first glance; but watchful, everlastingly there. Her devotion could unchain earthquakes. I'm sometimes a little afraid of her myself. Dr. Grewy has his coat off—it's on the back of his chair—and sits in his wide gray suspenders. He's a short man, a few inches shorter than I am, and equally ridiculous. Brown hair crookedly parted down the middle, gold-rimmed, thick-lensed glasses, a neck whiter than a lily. He'd do well to grow a beard, in my opinion.

Nevertheless, God loves him, and even I, I find, am glad, as usual, to see him.

"We rich as the Vatican yet?" I ask.

"Not yet." Belatedly, he smiles. His eyes, behind the thick lenses, are like hens' eggs.

I have in some way slightly annoyed him, made him lose his bearings. I don't worry about it, though I keep it in the back of my mind as I take off my robe and hang it in the closet. It comes to me at last that he dislikes jokes about the Vatican. By prayerful meditation—that is, by turning it over and over in his mind until the idea has become no longer shocking—he has adjusted to the ecumenical movement. Now here I am, casting aspersions on another faith. I shake my head and smile, and, the same instant, I catch my reflection in the glass of the photograph of Lake Geneva. I'm startled, as usual, by the beard. I remember the strange young man at the door, how alarmed I was by his oddity, his offensive foreignness. So my flock must have felt when I returned from my summer of study in San Francisco. Poor Dr. Grewy, for instance; a man of routine; a conservative. (I watch him light his pipe, stretching his lips like an infant at the nipple.) Dr. Grewy was chiefly responsible for, as he calls it, our physical plant. That was in the time of my predecessor, a silver-haired solemn old man with a lisp, or a whistle, to be precise, a sort of birdcall on the *s*'s of Jesus. Dr. Grewy was hurt, "deeply wounded," he said, when I first suggested, in some sermon or other, that the era of building in the forties and fifties was a theological error for which we must pay through the rest of the century. I gave him Kierkegaard's *Attack upon "Christendom,"* and he not only read it but made it the subject of his men's class discussions. I gave him Tillich, the letters of Bonhoeffer, and books on the work of inner-city churches. It gradually came clear in his mind that justice was more important than wine-red carpets in the lounge. Dr. Grewy was grieved, bewildered, obscurely ashamed of himself. He came to visit me one night at the manse. He stood in the twilight, two years ago exactly, clumsily buttoning and unbuttoning his suitcoat, looking vaguely around in his thick-lensed glasses at the porch ballusters, the mat that says *Hello!*, the stack of rotting wood for the fireplace, butt-ends from the Carbondale railroad-tie factory. I hardly knew him at the time—I'd been here in Carbondale less than a month—though I recognized him as one of my church officers. "Good evening," I said, reaching out for his hand.

"Oh," he said. "Oh yes! Oh." He looked down at the wood. "I hadn't realized," he said, "that you weren't unpacked yet. I was just—"

"Come in," I said. "Do come in."

The sunset was full of the smell of burning leaves.

"I'm Dr. Grewy," he said.

"Yes·of course. I recognized you. *Deacon* Grewy." I smiled, squeezing his hand with my right hand, cupping his elbow with my left.

"I'm an Elder, actually." He blushed. It meant much to him, I saw, this lofty position he was certain he didn't deserve.

"Elder. Certainly! What a stupid mistake!—Come in, Dr. Grewy, come in!" I guided, or rather pulled him into the dingy front room and encouraged him out of his coat. When he was seated I offered him wine. He looked alarmed, then confused. "I'm a teetotaler," he said. "Ah," I said. "Then coffee." "Yes, thank you."

We talked half the night. His soul was in torment. How absurd that a man like Dr. Grewy could possess a tortured soul! But life scoffs, as we know, at dignity. Behold what happens to the tallest oaks, the noblest elms. In poems, tortured souls are found in towering, deep-brained men, men with dark eyebrows that flare out like wings and legs firm as pillars from walking high windy cliffs, bare heaths, forsaken shores. They suffer, they see the Truth, and they overcome. Who'd need salvation if life were art? Dr. Grewy, whose sad habitation was life, was miserable.

He was cross at first, as if it were my fault that the Presbyterian Church had betrayed him. I told him—firmly, though without any rancor—that he was behaving like a child. He complained then about my predecessor. I told him he had no one to blame but himself. For forty-some years he'd been listening to sermons about Christian love, but when bombs went off in Mississippi churches, Dr. Grewy was tallying builders' accounts. He looked alarmed, wringing his fingers. I could not make out what made him stare at me. "Go ahead," I said rather sternly. "What's bothering you now? Come out with it!"

His lips were willing, but his voice was weak. On the third try he brought out, "Suppose—I lack—the *intelligence* to be a Christian?"

"Faddle!" I said. But I was sorry the next instant. He was dead serious, and the problem was real, and it had not been an easy thing for him to say. Medical doctors are intelligent by definition, yet here he was, baldly confessing . . . I was astonished. Intelligent or not, he was no ordinary man. His eyes swam in tears. I leaned toward him to touch his shoulder. It was a mistake. Or perhaps it was right, in the end. His arms jerked convulsively, and his tight face flew out of control, shattered into his hands, and he began to whoop, "God help me! God help me!" What was I to do? I jumped, exploded, up out of my chair—we were sitting more or less knee-to-knee—and reached down to hold him in my arms as I would a child, but I couldn't, standing over him, so I merely patted both his shoulders awkwardly, as though I were myself another child.

"Lost!" he whooped. "Lost!"

"Nonsense," I said gently. "Nobody's lost."

I tried to explain about Christian redemption. It all seemed extremely simple to me, but I've never been sure he got it. I tried to explain to him the Parable of the Talents. He sat listening carefully, looking bewildered. (He'd finished whooping now.) When I was sure I'd made everything clear as day, Dr. Grewy nodded slowly and thoughtfully, his many-times magnified eyes red and puffy, and he ran his hands back and forth on his legs, toward his knees, back again. "Welfare is ruining this country," he said, and nodded.

"Ah well," I said, "God loves us all. Probably."

Dr. Grewy puts the collection money in bags, sucks at his pipe, puts down numbers in the ledger. He glances at me, his eyes moving like fish behind the lenses. "It's none of my business," he begins, then falters. I let him stew for a moment. At last, he says: "You should be careful what you say. Overthrowing governments and things, I mean. What if someone from the FBI . . ." He glances at the office door. Sylvester Jones will be out there somewhere, sweeping, picking up scraps of paper, his face black as coal, his hair snow-white, a man old enough to be father of us all. "These days, you know . . ." He looks startled, as if by an abdominal pain. "You hear the news this morning?"

I shake my head, watching him.

"Someone blew up the Art Building." His face is as white as his soft, fat neck. His lips tremble. In a moment he'll be in a fiery rage against Communist Anarchists, dope addicts, Panthers. Though I mock him, I'm slightly infected by his fear. Someone once threatened to burn down my house. The memory's as much in my blood as in my mind: my sudden object-ness, imprisonment inside the whim of some unknown madman. I shake it off quickly. The world may control me, accidents of time and space and temper, but I needn't enchain myself with fearful fantasies.

"That's terrible," I say, and look at my watch. "But we'd better go, Dr. Grewy. Actually, I'm starving."

He closes the ledger, stands up, puts his arms in the armholes of his suitcoat.

I lock the office and start with him to the back door. We look up at the centerpoint of the arch above us. Behind us the wall is blue and red and yellowish green with pale projections of images in the new stained glass. All this is the work of Dr. Grewy and his build-ing fund. Though he believes now that adding on to the church was a mistake, he's proud, in spite of him-self, of the addition. It's a beautiful structure, modern, full of light; yet it harmonizes with the older part. I can hardly ask him to be sorry, whatever the stern opinions of the prophet Amos. I can disapprove of his love of wealth (I'd be ashamed to live in a house like his—a driveway that curves in for half a mile past shrubbery and pools; two white new pillars on the porch, set much too far apart, like a farmer's legs when he squats in the bushes to relieve himself), but I take men where I find them; they give me no choice. The church, they were sure, would grow larger and larger—even this new bank of sunday-school rooms would soon be totally inadequate. The rooms sit empty now, week after week, like the new wing the Methodist people put up, and like the Lutherans' new building. The Baptists unloaded their monster to the university. But all that is not Dr. Grewy's fault. He did what was asked of him, bowed down, humble and devoted, to the brass god Stewardship, and meant no harm. He donates time to the free health clinic; he cooperates, so far as his ethic allows, with the drug crisis center. He may not be exactly the salt of the earth, but he's as good a man as he knows how to be.

I watch him as he studies the stippled wall, the arch-frets yawing above us like the beams of a ship thrown upside-down. He glances at me, looks uncomfortable, puts on his hat. He toes out as he walks through the double glass door ahead of me, his hat as flat on his ridiculous head as an Indian's. I smile, let out a sigh. He pauses, waiting, while I lock the door. There's a scent in the air, delicate, elusive, and after a moment I place it, a smell like firecrackers. The Art Building, I remember. But the Art Building's more than a mile from here. Something else, then. Some fire in a vacant lot—dry weeds, old leaves. A larger, more usual apocalypse; another fall. Nearly all the cars are gone now from the parking lot. Marilyn Fish —pretty blonde in a fiery red coat—sits grinding on her starter. The motor catches, takes off like an explosion, and I wave to her. She smiles. I hear rumors about her. I mainly attribute them to jealousy and spite. She's active in social work, politics, the schools. But also, of course, she's a beautiful woman, and her husband travels a good deal in his work. One of these days she'll come into my office late at night and say . . .

"Lovely day," says Grewy.

Autumn trees flaming, white clouds, blue sky; as usual in southern Illinois at this time of the year.

Marilyn switches on her signal light, pauses—the motor roars—and, knowing no Dante, she turns left. "Praise God for his many gifts," I say. *Lead me not into temptation,* I think. So hour by hour I harmlessly recapitulate the fall. Dr. Grewy gets into his Cadillac, stares sadly through the window. I unlock the chain on my bicycle and meditate on *khiseth* and Marilyn Fish.

4

The front page, naturally, is filled with news about the latest bombing. Speculation is that it must have been an art student who planted, as they call it, the explosive device. The art students at the university have long hair and peculiar clothes. They live in shanties, with Negro neighbors, or they erect buckminster-fuller domes in people's woods, without permission. They smoke pot, drop acid (if that's still the expression), and engage in what the police call orgies. Also, they have keys to the Art Building. I study the pictures. Helmeted policemen guarding the rubble and smoke from a crowd of anesthetized bystanders. A girl with long hair and an Indian headband displaying the tattered and charred remains of what may once have been her paintings. She stares into the camera with gloomy indifference, like one who has happened into newspictures all her life. A policeman points with his nightstick to writing on a partly demolished wall; OFF AID! SHUT DOWN THE V NAM STUDY CENTER. It's not known whether the sign is recent.

I look again at the girl with the ruined paintings. I remember old war photographs. Starvation, despair, black smoke in the distance, charred trunks of trees like skeletal hands clutching nothing. I think again of Marilyn Fish's smile in the parking lot, the strange gray eyes alive with zeal and accomplishment. I shake my head.

The waitress refills my coffee cup, and as I glance

up, nodding thanks, I see Levelsmacher standing at the door, looking in. I look down again quickly, but he's seen that I've seen him, and he isn't free to pretend otherwise. I feel him coming over to me, jingling coins in his trousers pocket. I would rather converse with a weaving, dusty-eyed snake. As he reaches the table I look up, meet his heavy-lidded eyes. I'm struck by how wrinkled, even withered he is at forty. He seems unaware of it himself.

"Reverend Pick!" He hits me on the shoulder.

"Hello there!" I always make a point of addressing him as *there*. He makes a point of pretending I mean no offense.

"Meeting somebody?" he says. He makes it an insinuation.

"No no. Have a seat."

He swings a chair out, though he does not want to sit with me (Hypocrite Hippy, they say he calls me). He throws a leg over, pulls at the knees to preserve the press, and sits. His suitcoat is yellowish brown. "That's really something. Man!" He thumps my paper with his index finger and grins irritably, as if to say, if I had *my* way . . . There is no smile in his tiny brown eyes. His mouth jerks. A tic. I have a theory that all his smiles are lies, attempts to sell real estate, and the tic is his last touch of honesty.

"The people of this town are getting God damned tired of these guitar-playing crazies. Take my word for it, Gene." He calls me Gene at the end of every sentence. It's a memory device. I smile and take his word for it. The waitress comes. He asks for coffee and a grilled cheese sandwich, and he gives her a quick seductive wink. The tic gets revenge. He looks down. Then he looks at me up-from-under and grins. "You been getting any, Gene?"

I sigh, smile, and shake my head. He smiles, exactly imitates my headshake. *He* has been getting some, of course. He thinks of himself as supremely free, liberated by Christ. All is forgiven. Nothing is unforgivable. Love God with all your heart and soul and be kind to your neighbor's wife. (His own wife plays ignorant.) I glance away from him, remembering dowdy, fat Carol Ann Watson, his first, or the first I learned of. She sat in my office, comfortable but prim, plump knees together, her hands on her purse. "Reverend Pick, I'm having an affair," she said, "and the thing that makes me feel guilty is I feel no guilt about it." "Maybe you should try having two," I said. And we laughed, because it was all right, though perhaps a little stupid. Good for her ego, at least. It was *not* all right on Levelsmacher's side, or not all right with me, anyway. I catch myself and struggle once more to think better of him. He uses the church as a power base, it seems to me. Communion as contacts. But perhaps I'm mistaken. There's no man on earth, I tell myself, who doesn't feel remorse from time to time, and doesn't occasionally feel compassion. The sandwich comes. He talks as he eats. I pretend to listen, sipping my coffee, but in fact I pay no attention to him. The restaurant is full, families having sunday dinner out. A great hum, the clink of silverware, screech of children. His talk veers between women and the bombings, as if, without his knowing it, his heart discerns some connection between them. All at once I rivet my gaze to my cup. He speaks, leaning forward, talking intimately past cheese, about Marilyn Fish. I'm startled—amazed—at the intensity of my emotion.

As soon as he pauses, I glance at my watch and abruptly get up. "Good heavens! Excuse me!" I look again at my watch.

"Late for something?" He appears surprised, distressed.

"If my head weren't screwed on——" I say, and laugh. The laugh sounds hollow, a giveaway. I wave, excuse myself again, and take my check to the counter.

Outside, where sunlight explodes all around me, I pause, remembering that look of distress. Headlights, windshields on fire with sunlight stare at me, waiting to hear some opinion. The birds on the telephone wires are silent. A pigeon lights on the McDonald's sign, half a block away. 6 billion sold. A policeman stands watching through the Kroger store window, his fist on his hip, beside his gun.

5

When I hear her voice in the vestibule, I realize I've been thinking about her a good deal this past three days. I'm not ashamed, by any means, but I'm bothered by it. Who isn't childish enough to wish that Eden could remain forever pure? My feelings about Marilyn were innocent, once. We worked together on social projects—I got her appointed to the Community Conservation Board—we joked, told long stories when she happened to drop in and had half an hour to throw away. I cared about her, as the saying goes, and cared equally about her husband, her children. No, precision: I admired her hips and breasts, her walk; but there was a line I did not cross or admit the existence of. At the sound of her voice I'd think, *Ah, Marilyn!* and I'd go out to meet her. That is not how it is with me this moment. Poisoned by Levelsmacher's leer, bits of cheese at the corner of his mouth. My chest is sick with secretiveness.

Satan, shove off.

I'm concerned about her; that too is true. I do not want some creep messing up her marriage, least of all myself. Is it possible the things he told me were lies? I can hardly get Marilyn to talk to me about it, not unless she brings it up herself.

Janice pokes her head in. "Reverend Pick, Marilyn Fish is here."

"Send her in, by all means!" I jump up and move around my typing desk to meet her, as always. She appears, beads of sweat on her tanned and freckled forehead, a clipboard in her hand—no doubt one of her petitions. Her smile is, as always, childlike. She has the teeth you see in toothpaste ads.

"Hi Gene. Can I get your signature on this?" She leans forward for my kiss on her cheek as she speaks, as usual. My kiss is selfconscious. She notices—so it seems to me—but ignores it, smiling at my forehead. Marilyn greets everyone she's remotely fond of with a quick, light hug and kiss.

"What this time?" I say, mock-scornful, looking down at the half-filled sheet.

She laughs. "You want me to help you read it?"

I pretend to read. She turns away, goes over to the green leather couch below the Carbondale churches' welcome sign, sits down, takes cigarettes from her purse, lights one.

"Well ok," I say doubtfully. I sit behind my desk, reach for a pen, write my signature. I swivel back.

"Man what a day," she says. She looks at the photograph of Lake Geneva, the round-topped table with the green glass ashtray, assuring herself that all's well, all's clean. "What's happening with you?"

"Same old thing," I say. "Saving souls, writing sermons to ruin them again." I glance away from her, then back, and smile. "How's Don?"

"Terrific, at last report. We never see each other, but now and then we get a note through. He's in Chicago the rest of this week and all next."

It strikes me that she's not as happy about it as she pretends, and I'm glad. "He's there now?" I ask. I'm not sure why I've asked it.

"Tomorrow morning." She swipes her hair back. She breathes smoke deep into her lungs, lets it out through her nostrils. It bothers me. Mutability. In the back of my mind I'm aware of some unnameable wish. She pulls down her skirt, unnecessarily. It occurs to me that everything is all right between us. I feel comfortable with her, as she feels with me. I like her shape, high cheekbones, freckles, gray eyes, but what I feel now is pleasure in her company, not desire. I could laugh at Levelsmacher's sick-minded talk. She's one of the elect. I think again of the dead-eyed stare of the girl in the newspaper. I could have been a missionary, all right, like Miss Ellis' dear, dear friend. They say they've found the answer, these Children of Albion, with their communes and pot and devotion to

Art. But I compare their malnutritious faces with Marilyn's, their staring eyes with Marilyn's eyes, and I scoff at their claims of holiness and peace.

She says, "Say. Speaking of saving souls, you won a convert last sunday."

I raise my eyebrows, widen my eyes in amazement.

She laughs. "I sent him here to listen to you. A boy I met in the drug clinic. He's no druggy. He's 'into revolution,' he says."

"Ah," I say. Uneasiness goes through me. "I noticed him."

"He's all right," she says, reading my emotion as usual. "He's a sweet, gentle boy. A little crazy, of course." She laughs again, then catches herself, looks apologetic for laughing at a friend. "You blew his mind, he says. He wants to talk to you sometime."

I throw my arms wide. "Suffer the little revolutionists to come unto Me."

"I will, if you promise to be nice."

"I promise."

"I don't know that he'll come, of course. He's strange."

"Unlike the rest of us."

She pretends to be amused. I'm embarrassed for an instant. She tamps out the cigarette and gets up, graceful. "Gotta run, Gene. It's always great to see you."

"Come any time," I say, and get up to walk to the door with her. With my hand on the knob I say lightly, "Say, Marilyn, what ever happened to Levelsmacher? He hasn't been in church for a month or more."

"Levelsmacher who?" she says quickly, and looks at my forehead. Her whole face bursts into a blush.

I am sick, not because I've found her out; sick because I've frightened her, meddled with her life.

She puts her fingertips on my chest, lightly, and looks at them, mind racing. She decides to smile brightly and say, "Oh, you mean Bill!" She shrugs. "I never see him."

"I keep a sharp eye on attendance," I say, and pat her arm.

She laughs, then goes, remembering to say goodbye to Janice. When Marilyn is gone, Janice steals a quick glance at me over her typewriter. She knows the whole thing. I step back into my office and close the door.

6

He sits unmoving, calm as the center of one of our southern Illinois tornadoes. His bearded face is expressionless, even the huge, skyblue eyes that stare at me and never blink. His voice is gentle, neither friendly nor unfriendly, merely there—somehow unnaturally there, as if removed from time and space.

"Your sermon really blew my mind," he says. There is no smile, no ironic apology for the ridiculous language. I cannot tell whether he stares at me admiringly or in order to penetrate to the depths of my soul, discover what use he can make of me. I think of the words of the half-cracked Baptist, "*I am the voice of one crying in the wilderness, 'Make straight the way of the Lord.'*" Not a man; a disembodied voice, a once-flesh heart consumed by message. I cannot tell whether I'm afraid of him or eager to speak with him, perhaps argue points of theology.

"It was wonderful to have you with us," I say. He grants me neither smile nor gesture, merely stares at me. If he knows my words are hypocrisy he dismisses it. What are merely human faults to him? I know well enough what my emotion is now. I'm afraid, full of superstitious dread. His gentle, absolutely open gaze has eerie power. He's like a Renaissance painting absurdly, ominously superimposed on THE CHURCHES OF CARBONDALE WELCOME YOU. I have no way of guessing his origins, no way of placing him. Is he Jewish? Polish? Italian? Was his father wealthy—some Chicago doctor or lawyer, say? Was his father a mechanic? Whatever accent he may once have had has been swallowed up in the indifferent vortex, reduced to the language of the Children of Albion. Whatever his distinctive style of dress in former years, it is lost in the swampgreen of Army fatigues, a peace sign sewed where the stripes should be.

"I'm Reverend Pick," I say, suddenly remembering I forgot to tell him that earlier, when I found him this morning waiting with infinite patience by the church office door. "I don't believe—"

He stares at me and at last understands what I'm asking him, trivial-minded as I am. "I'm called Dow," he says.

"Tao?"

He does not smile or show interest. "Dow Chemical Company."

I laugh, for lack of something better to do. It does not seem to surprise him that I laugh. He even smiles slightly, to put me at ease.

"You're a student at the university?" I ask. I'm feeling better now. I have something to call him. I line up my pencils and pens on the glass of my desktop.

He answers gently: "I used to be a student. But I went over to Nam—they drafted me, like. So lately I'm into revolution. I bomb things." He smiles, the barest flicker, apologetic.

I don't believe him. He'd have to be crazy to say such a thing if it were true, and though he's strange, uncanny, I can't believe he's crazy. I'm overwhelmed, suddenly, by *déjà vu*. We've been through this whole conversation before, I know exactly what he's going to say next, but I can't remember how it comes out, what it means. I move cautiously, as though, despite my conviction, I believe he's dangerous.

"You really bomb things?"

He nods. "Not people. Things."

"Of course." I nod. I squint at him. I cannot seem to make the room come real, and I remember Carol Ann Watson's remark that that was how she felt the first time she found herself in bed with another man. It wasn't possible, yet here she was. It wasn't possible. She felt no guilt, no trace of fear. How could it be? I imagine Miss Ellis, bent over, wide-eyed, at the outer office door, all color drained from the rouged and powdered cheeks. A communist anarchist talking with the Reverend, and the Reverend going on as he would with a deacon he'd happened to meet at the Post Office. Lost again in a senseless, mindless universe.

"I'm not a Jesus freak," the young man says. For some reason it's important to him that I understand. "Not like some, I mean. I don't really care if there's a God or Heaven, and like that. But I dig the third temptation." Though he's otherwise motionless, his long, thick fingers move on his leg, extending a three.

I consider. "I'm not sure I know what you mean."

"Jesus in the desert." All this time he hasn't moved a muscle, except those fingers—he still has them raised like a weary blessing—and his lips. "The thing about coming to terms with world powers. I read a book about it, when I was over in Nam. And persecution."

I shake my head, admitting bafflement.

"Like Osiris and Cybele and all those other goddesses and gods. But when Jesus' religion hit Rome, they had to persecute. They were anarchists."

I think about it and begin to understand, despite the problem of his pronouns.

He says, "And I dig what you said about the true church, and how God hates the feasts. I wanted you to know I been thinking about it. You blew my mind."

I smile, slightly wincing.

"That's all. I just wanted you to know. And also the part about the fig tree, whatever." I try to think what, if anything, I said about a fig tree. Abruptly, gracefully, the young man stands up. "Far out," he says like a parting benediction. With these words he backs toward the door, keeping his face to me. It crosses my mind that he thinks I may pull a gun on him. But I'm sure it isn't that. Then he's crazy, simply, as Marilyn said. But it isn't that either. Still gazing at me, benign, inhuman, he backs away through the outer office. At the far door he gives me a peace sign and suddenly—amazingly—smiles. He has a beautiful smile. His eyes are like Brahma's. He vanishes. I shake my head. I have told him nothing, I haven't even contradicted him. The thing's impossible. And now all at once I see perfectly clearly that every word he said was true. I jump up to follow him, but when I've passed through the outer office (my secretary frowns at me, cross), there is no one there but old Sylvester, bending down to the vacuum cleaner. He cautiously rolls his eyes at me.

7

The meeting goes dully, as usual. As usual, I hardly listen. The treasurer's report goes on forever. We have a ditto we could read for ourselves if we wished, if my Elders weren't mindless ritualists. Let God forgive them; myself, I'm too tired. I've been dragged into meetings every night this week—City Planning Commission, Boy Scouts, Urban League. . . . The secretary reads, and again I don't listen. But something puzzles me. They're nervous. There's something going on at this meeting that I'm not in on. It's not the reports.

When it's over they do not stand around talking as they usually do. They button up their suitcoats, put on their hats, say goodnight to one another and, distantly, to me, and they walk, studiously casual, out into the warmth of the hushed fall evening, the smell of burning. I line up my pencils on the top of my desk, thinking, waiting for something, then snap out the office light. Someone clears his throat at the outer office door. I jump.

"Oh, I'm sorry," he says quickly. It's Dr. Grewy.

"You startled me," I say, and smile. He too smiles; falsely. The church is dark now, except for the light above the glass double door and the wash of gray light from the parking lot. Dead leaves blow past the arch, scrape dryly on the blacktop.

Dr. Grewy rubs his hands together as if to warm them. "Actually, Reverend—"

I study him. His distress is acute. He unhooks his glasses and clumsily unfolds his handkerchief to clean them.

"Can I take you home, Reverend?"

"I have my bicycle, John."

"Mmm. Yes." He continues cleaning his glasses. At last he looks up, takes a deep breath. "Reverend Pick, I hope you'll forgive me for saying this. I think you know how I feel about you. That is, how we all —" He pauses again. Lies are bad for the digestion, he once told me. He puts his glasses on, looks at me sadly. "I wish you'd be a little more discreet," he mumbles.

I wait. "About what?" I can't tell whether to laugh or be frightened.

He sighs again. "The other day . . . that is . . ."

"Come out with it, John."

He nods. He feels as stupid as I do. "That young man you were talking to, Gene, that bearded one . . . in your office." Again he finds it difficult to speak. "We're not prejudiced against beards in this congregation. You're proof of that. But for the sake of all of us—" Again he clears his throat. "Certain people overheard your conversation."

Memo: Fire Janice.

Memo: Also Sylvester.

"You want me to lock the door on him?" My anger's absurd; I realize it even as the anger flames up. I do not fool myself that it's righteous indignation. They are telling me what I can do and can't, and like any hot-headed, undisciplined child, I demand my egoistic will. But I turn it into righteous indignation, protecting my freedom with grandiose noise and smoke. "Is he not human, John? Is he not as good as a leper, a beggar, a woman taken in adultery?"

He's more miserable than ever. Even he knows my tactic is vulgar and unfair. "It's not what *I* think," he begins.

I touch his arm. "All right, John. Thank you. Sorry I blew up." We walk toward the door and through it. I lock it behind us.

"I really am sorry." He is shaping his hat now, sick at heart.

"It's all right," I say, and smile.

I am angrier than hell, beginning work already on my sermon.

8

My gaze sweeps the congregation. They sit docile and expectant, as usual, Not universally fond of me (here and there I see a friendly face, here and there a hostile one) but willing to be lectured, willing to permit me the license the pulpit between us grants. I hesitate longer than usual, I'm not sure why. It dawns on me that I'm looking for the stranger, the wild man who's "into revolution." I don't find him, and for reasons I don't take time to analyze, I'm relieved. I lean forward, precariously balanced on my stool. My voice trembles. It's not the tamest of sermons. There will be some—I have no idea how many—who will want to see me hanged for it.

I tell them:

"It's Passion time. Jesus has been saying he's going to be killed. He and his disciples have come up to the city—to Jerusalem—for the feast. They've been spending nights with friends out in the suburbs, partly as a security precaution and partly because it's cheaper. They are coming back to the city in the morning. It's early. Still cold. Jesus is hungry. He spots a fig tree by its leaves. He jogs ahead of his disciples to see if there's fruit. There is nothing. He curses the tree: 'Be barren forever!' By evening the tree is dead.

"It's a strange incident. Most Biblical scholars doubt that it ever happened, though both Matthew and Mark record it. Some treat it as an acted parable. But a parable of what? Proof that Jesus suffered psychological pressure like an ordinary man? Proof to the disciples of the power of faith? So Matthew reads it. But Matthew came late and was probably quoting Mark and trying to rationalize the grisly story.

"Consider the story from the point of view of the fig tree. Wasn't the curse unfair?

"First, it wasn't the season for figs. It was almost certainly Mark himself, not some later reviser, who wrote ὅ γὰρ καιρὸς οὔκ ἦν συκῶν — 'for it was not yet the time for figs.' It was remarkable, in fact, that the tree even had leaves on it. Wasn't it unfair to expect it to have fruit as well? And even if it were the right season for figs, the tree grew beside a public highway. Thousands of people passed every day. Jesus was surely not the first who spotted the tree and investigated to see if it had fruit. Perhaps the tree was remarkably fruitful but had generously given away all it had. And even if it was the season for figs and the tree produced none, even if the tree was barren, wasn't it unfair not to give the tree another chance? Maybe next year would have been better. Maybe somehow it would get fertilization, or someone would give it proper care. Knowing its unrealized potential, wasn't it terribly unfair not to give the tree one more chance? What kind of parable *is* this? The curse is outrageous—and final.

"The Bible is full of symbolic trees. For instance the Psalmist's symbol of the righteous—like a tree planted by the rivers of water, that brings forth its fruit in its season. Or there's Jeremiah's symbol of Judah: 'God once said you are a green olive tree, fair, with good fruit.' But the situation has changed, the prophet says. The tree has turned brown; the fruit, if there is any, is inedible. God will blow his breath on the tree, there will be a roar like a tornado as the dry branches burst into flames, and the tree will be consumed. Outrageous. Final.

"Think about it. The prophet's tree of Judah started well. It was valuable and healthy and produced excellent fruit. Only with time did it lose vitality and purpose. That happens, you know, with human institutions. Judah is not the only nation that went wrong. Any institution, life-style, program, can be vital at its inception but become, in time, an obstacle, a sickness. The tree of Judah has become, according to Jeremiah, 'unredeemable.' Like an elm with dutch-elm disease, there is nothing that can be done for it; it can only be destroyed with the hope that its destruction will keep the disease from spreading.

"Take another tree. The editor of the book of Jeremiah put together two pieces written by Jeremiah that have no relationship except that each uses a tree figuratively. One refers, as we have seen, to Judah. The other refers to Jeremiah himself. He is the ethical man trying to be right in an unrighteous society, trying to do what he can to redeem his culture—but his contemporaries, even his own family, hate him and plot against him, saying, 'Let us kill him and the world will forget him; let us destroy the tree with its fruit.' Again, outrageous. Not only is there no hope for the sick society, there's no hope for the righteous individual within it! The Psalmist, it seems, was overly optimistic. The righteous too are 'like the chaff which the wind drives away.'

"Whether or not Jesus actually cursed the fig tree, as Matthew and Mark report, the early church accepted the parable; and I think you can see how early churchmen understood it. Jesus began inside the church of his fathers. Though John the Baptist objected, Jesus demanded baptism of him, because John was, he knew, the last of the prophets, the last green leaf on the withered tree of Judah. Throughout the gospels we read of Jesus' grief at Israel's failure to catch up, recognize that the wait was fulfilled, the time was now. And if you still doubt that the fig tree represents dead, sham religion, authority grown sick, look at the *context* of the fig tree story.

"Immediately afterward in the gospel of Mark comes the story of Jesus' cleansing of the temple. Then come the lessons drawn from the story of the withered fig tree—the fundamental laws of the new religion: Have faith in God; do not pray if you cannot forgive. In other words, love God and man. Then comes the story of the wicked husbandmen, the men who betrayed their lord, stealing and wasting his vineyard, and were therefore executed. After that comes the question of tribute to Caesar. 'Whose image is on this coin?' (In Greek the word is *ikon,* implying holy image.) 'Render unto Caesar what is Caesar's,' Jesus says. If you have accepted something from worldly powers, confess the debt and repay it. But the saying admits of a more radical interpretation: If Caesar usurps the rule of God, decrees that immorality is moral, then resist him; blow up the Pentagon.

"You have heard before today that the early church was a trifle anarchistic. If one of those wild-bearded, fiery-eyed men were to enter our church this morning, we'd have considerable difficulty welcoming him. Unwashed, obstinate, indifferent to all we take comfort in. And perhaps we'd be right to hope he'd go away. But let us be careful about turning in righteous indignation on fiery-eyed radicals, resisters of government, blasters of fig trees.

"By the fruit we bear—if any—men shall know us.

"The barren fig tree, the vineyard stolen and wasted, brings a sentence of death. —Outrageous or not."

I pause, look solemn.

"Let us pray."

In the middle of my prayer I glance out over the congregation. My spine goes cold. The boy with the beard, the staring eyes, is watching from the vestibule doorway. I know pretty well how long he's been there, just out of sight, listening.

9

I do not claim that what I'm doing makes sense. For every move I make I can give two explanations, one more or less reasonable, one sick: I have fled to the wilderness to confront the Devil, think out what's right; or I have fled my responsibility. Outside the train window, the Amish farms of Ohio flash by: barns red as blood; ancient thrashing machines; gangs of workers—communists, pacifists—throwing antique shocks of wheat with handmade forks, talking together in the old-fashioned silence of steam. In the seat across the aisle from me an old Negro woman sits sleeping, indifferent to Eugene Carson Blake and his militants, indifferent to demands for reparations from the Presbyterian Church. In the front of the car a soldier, no more than eighteen at most, sings drunkenly of bottles of beer on the wall—ninety-nine tragic particulars in the vast array of emblems: Even pleasure, oblivion must pass, casually, senselessly fall in the endless chain of chance destructions.

The Carbondale newspaper lies on the seat beside me. BOMB DAMAGES POLICE STATION. I have no way of knowing whether or not the bomber was my admirer. Neither have the police; but the smaller headline reads: *Bomber linked to local minister.* I'd already seen it when I got Janice's note, "Call Mr. Leffler, Security Police." I did not make the call. How could I have helped them? I have no way of knowing where he lives, and neither does Marilyn—I know because I asked. And what could I have told them? His description, perhaps. Do I want them to have his description? How strongly do I disapprove of him? Or to put it another way, how sick is the tree of Judah?

No, I'm lying, of course. Nothing to do with politics. It has to do with responsibility, the dangerous freedom my pulpit grants. I told them what was true, or what I believe to be true (we are forgiven in advance for nonomniscience), and what it was necessary for them to hear. If I'd known he was listening I would not have spoken in quite the same way. I didn't know; but any effect my sermon had is nevertheless my fault. They know that too, my congregation. It isn't easy to stare down their stares.

I could weep and confess, like Dr. Grewy. Throw up my hands in despair, like Miss Ellis.

My mind flicks away from the idea as if burned.

I try to read the paper that I've already read three times. The light outside is green. It will be night soon. Abruptly I get up and start toward the club car. I can drink myself into a stupor if I please; there's no one here to be offended by the sight of his minister drunk. It's a curious feeling. If I meet some young lady who's willing, I can climb into bed with her.

Everything is possible. I think of Levelsmacher. What conceivable line can he have used on Marilyn Fish?

Though my own car is practically empty, the car behind is half-filled. Long-haired boys and girls in beads and rags; an acrid stench in the air, maybe pot. Legs and arms sprawl into the aisle. I carefully step over them. A beefy man in an expensive gray suit looks up from his magazine and nods as I pass. I nod back, though I'm sure I've never seen him before, and I continue down the aisle, steadying myself on seat-backs against the swaying of the train. I push against the pressure of the door; the roar of wheels assaults me. I push against the second door and enter the club car.

As soon as I'm seated with my drink I see him coming—the man in the suit. Alarm leaps up in me, then passes. It's impossible that the man's a police-man. Even if he is, what have I to hide? He stops, tips his head, smiles at me.

"Care for company, my friend?" Before I can answer, he extends his big hand. "Name's McGiver, Paul Anthony McGiver, M.D."

I'm not sure I believe him. His jaw is enormous, with creases like pits at each side of his mouth. He has similar cracks between his eyebrows and running from beside and below his eyes. His chest and arms are like a wrestler's, or maybe a weight lifter's.

"Have a seat," I say, and gesture across the table.

He accepts at once, sliding in, carefully holding up his large glass of bourbon. I consider telling him my name's Johnson, but, then, for no reason, I tell him the truth.

"A minister," he says. He studies me, then smiles. "I'd have guessed in a moment. I've got a good eye for things like that. Of course, with ministers it's easy."

I struggle not to be offended.

"I couldn't help but notice that paper you're carrying. It's a terrible business."

I nod. "Terrible." It occurs to me only now that I'm still carrying the thing. It's two days old.

He lifts one black eyebrow. "You heard the latest, I suppose?"

I wait, keeping calm.

"The crazy nut's blown up some church. I saw it on television."

Every line of the club car, the stranger's face, is suddenly too sharp, so precise as to seem unreal. I can't speak for a moment. I bring out, finally, "In Carbondale?"

"That's what they said on television. It's a hell of a thing!" He leans toward me. "You all right, Reverend?"

I suck in breath. He scowls at me as if furious, then leans forward, preparing to stand up. "Let me get you something. I've got my medical bag right back—"

"No no. I'm fine. What church was it?"

He continues to study me, not hearing. I repeat the question, and he relaxes a little, looks down at his glass, shakes his head. "I'm afraid I didn't catch the denomination," he says. "Maybe someone here knows." He looks around the car. Two soldiers playing cards; the conductor sitting in the corner, writing on a tablet; an elderly man in a straw hat, drinking beer.

"Never mind," I say. "It's not important. Please."

He scowls at me again, then decides to accept it. Suddenly, he smiles. "I gave you one hell of a shock there. Never crossed my mind how news like that would hit a minister."

I too smile, then notice my martini, and drink.

"It's a hell of a thing all right," he says. He nods, solemn. He takes out cigarettes and holds the pack toward me. I wave it away. "They just don't care about anything, those people. I've been watching them—those hippies up there in the car where I am. I don't mean they're evil, I don't mean they're all of 'em nihilists; nothing like that." He scowls at his drink waiting for the idea to come clearer in his mind. His huge jaw works and the heavy cracks in his face deepen. He looks furious, as if any moment he might leap up and smash things. When he speaks again I forget to listen. I feel again as if I'm falling endlessly through space. In a kind of daydream, I imagine

John Grewey coming into the club car, lips pursed, eyes distressed, perspiration on his forehead. Ever since I vanished he's been looking for me. He knows well enough what shame I feel, and he knows my arrogance—knows how impossible it would be for me to face them all. But a man can't simply drop out, he tells me. His fingers tremble and his eyes are wet. And so he's come seeking the hundredth lamb, bringing encouragement, concern, forgiveness. . . .

I smile, sickened. It is more blessed to give than to receive. They won't come after me. I have vanished from the face of the earth, fallen into freedom. It is nearly dark. In the west, a blood-red line. I sip the martini. It runs down my throat like lava. My fingers are already losing feeling. When you get used to martinis, like Marilyn Fish, like Levelsmacher . . . I suddenly understand something, but before I can firmly grasp it, it's gone. *Be barren forever.* For an instant the darkness hurtling by us alarms me, and I focus intently on the face across the table. The man is saying: ". . . of fatalism. Nothing is any longer evil to them, that's the thing. They 'love' each other—you've heard their talk—but they don't ask anything, they don't *expect* anything. If anything, in fact, they expect betrayal. The people they care about go through 'changes,' as they say, so they shrug and separate, have a smoke, a little wine. It's a strange way of life."

I nod. "Strange."

"Life's absurd, they say. Why fight it? So they put on funny-looking clothes, let their hair grow however it may, they abandon soap . . ." He shakes his head slowly, and the muscles of his neck bulge. He's outraged, if faces mean anything, but his voice is calm, as if weary. It comes to me that his leg is pressed against mine. I consider moving my leg but do nothing. If he hasn't yet noticed . . . Either way, embarrassment.

Suddenly he asks, "Do you believe in God?"

"Doctor, I'm a minister!"

"Yes of course. Of course. Forgive me." He's badly

flustered—and still, it seems to me, furious. I too am furious. Why, I wonder?

"I wonder if it matters," he says. He seems to speak more to himself than to me. His leg is pressed firmly against mine, and now I'm certain that he knows it. His right hand is under the table, in his lap. I could laugh, it's all, suddenly, so obvious. The weight lifting, the seductively serious talk.

Fruit, I think, and am back to the fig tree, to fruitless Pick. And if my life is fruitless, does it matter? Outside, the night falls endlessly. Where the darkness is heaviest I see for an instant the bearded, blue-eyed face. It does *not* matter. The truth explodes out of the night and the sound of wheels. The world is dying— pollution, old, unimportant wars, the grandiose talk of politicians, the whisper of lovers in cheap motels. The sentence of death is merely language, a pause between silences. *They* know, the Children of Albion asprawl in the aisles of hurtling trains. They have seen and understood, have abandoned all mission. I sip my martini, then on second thought drain it. As I rise to get another, I'm thrown violently forward, my head slams against the doctor's, then both of us are falling, clutching one another, shouting. The lights go off, then on again. The whole train jolts and shudders. We're standing still. People are shouting.

10

I have no idea what's going on. I stumble down the track with the doctor and the official, torches and lanterns all around us. Ahead of us, hippies in flapping rags, shouting, howling at one another. Behind us someone is ordering the passengers back onto the train. The stopped train—I glance at it over my shoulder—is grotesque in the enormous darkness. The red of the lantern on the rear platform is like light seen through blood. Beyond the cinders at the edge of the tracks there's a deep, dry gully on either side, and, beyond the gullies, old trees, barkless, strangled by woodbine now also dry and dead. We reach the silent group of people, faces out of some war photograph.

"Let us through, please," the official says. "This man's a doctor."

The crowd murmurs, opens up a path for us. I press in behind the official and the doctor. We come to a gigantic young man on his knees, bent over, writhing. He's crying and moaning something, I can't make out what. "This man's a doctor," the official says again.

The young man twists his head up, bearded, wild. His eyes are as tiny and crooked as a goat's. He shouts at us, enraged. "We don't need a doctor, we need a priest!"

"I'm a minister," I say, but no one hears me.

"Let us through," the doctor says.

The young man straightens up, shouting at us, crazy, and we see what he's been bending over. I look away, getting only a fleeting impression—an enormous pregnant abdomen in labor, a face smashed featureless, dripping hair, the dead stock of a tree.

"Christ," the doctor whispers.

"Is she alive?" someone asks.

"Get these damn people out of here," the doctor hisses.

The official straightens up, wipes his forehead, begins shouting. Everyone ignores him, staring at the body in the unearthly light of torches, red lanterns.

"She was stoned," someone explains to me, clinging to my shirt, driving the words in like hammer blows in hopes of being rid of all guilt. "She was stoned. Couldn't see where she was going."

"Get them *out* of here," the doctor shouts. His crease-chopped face is satanic with rage; his dry voice crackles with violence.

I back away; one more quick look at the body. Smashed, one leg turned backwards like a ridiculous doll's. Trainmen are pulling and pushing at the crowd. The great tall wildman with the beard and the crooked, goatish eyes is shaking his fists and shouting at us, or shouting at the sky; no one can tell. "Lunatics! Where were you? God damn you to hell!" He locks his giant hands together and wrings them, elbows going right and left, his torso cocked forward, his knees clamped together like the toes of his oversized shoes. "Damn them!" he wails. "God damn them! God damn you!" He flings his arms outward, rocks back on his heels. His rags fly crazily around him. Though the trainmen are hurrying the others along, no one goes anywhere near the enormous goat.

A thin-bearded boy takes my elbow, explains to me soberly, as if I might help him with his problem, "She was his chick. Back there." He searches my face.

The wildman keens, rocking backward and forward. "She's free of you at last, God damn you all. She's free, you hear me?" He laughs, shrill with pain. "She's free! She's free!" There's no doubt of it now: it's the stars he shakes his fists at—the indifferent shrapnel hurtling away from the darkness, black hole at the center.

I move a step toward him. I can't help myself, though I know pretty well what I'll seem to him. "Listen!" I call out. "Get hold of yourself!"

He stops, glares at me, his horrible goat-nosed face reddish-gray in the lantern-light.

"Let me talk with you," I say. "I'm a minister."

His head drops, his wicked eyes roll up, and for an instant I believe he really will charge me, in the blindness of his pain and rage. But there is nothing to charge. I am no one, for the moment; a disembodied voice; God's minister.

The wildman stumbles, drops to one knee, groaning, gushing tears. Cautiously, I touch his shoulder. "Trust me," I say. (The fall is endless. All systems fail.) I force myself to continue. I have no choice.

THE RAVAGES
OF SPRING

1

Life, I've often been inclined to believe, is preposterous. Witness, for instance, the fact that I of all people should be elected to tell this tale. I have, like other men, my virtues and defects—rather more virtues than defects, I believe (and I would say the same of any other more or less law-abiding man)—but I am not, have never been, the kind of being who causes great stirrings and swarmings whenever he sits or nibbles a pastry or puts his cap on. I'm as plain a man as was ever set to toiling and grieving on this godforsaken planet: a bachelor; a reader of dull books; a country doctor.

But perhaps the powers are wiser than they seem, choosing a common, unpoetic soul for a tale at first glance more fit for the author of "The Raven" or that even more curious masterpiece of feeling and thought caught in one great gasp, the "Ulalume." I am not, like Mr. Poe, a Platonist. (So he seems, at least, in the writings I've encountered.) I am, as I say, a country doctor, and what I chiefly know about absolute values is that they do not necessarily aid the digestion, but frequently impair it. Neither can I whole-heartedly share the Platonistic predilection for Eternity as opposed to Present Time. In my youth I used to ponder, in mixed discomfiture and annoyance, the remark of the famous chemist Davy, that when he had heard, with disgust, in the dissecting rooms, the opinion of the physiologists on the gradual accretion of matter, and its becoming endowed with irritability, ripening into sensibility, and acquiring such organs as were necessary by its own inherent forces, and at last issuing into intellectual existence —when he heard this atheist opinion, he remarked, a walk into green fields or woods, beside the banks of rivers, would bring back his spirit and feelings from Nature to God. I concluded, in the end, that Humphrey Davy was a perfect fool, though by no means mistaken. His pompous bray refuted nothing, but the walk was a piece of pure sanity. The mulch of the flowering spirit is under thy feet, neighbor!

All this may seem wearisome and irrelevant to you. Most people, I've noticed, are forever impatient, always hustling and bustling and darting their eyes around, now glancing nervously back past their shoulders, now craning forward in hopes of discerning in the mists of Time the outlines of things yet to be. I take no part in all that. I stand pretty firmly where I happen to be put, and I ponder things. I do not necessarily learn anything. But pondering is good for the constitution: it lends a wise calm to all bodily parts and lends to the mind and soul a special dignity, like that of an old Red Indian sitting in a tree. I like things done properly—even tortuously, when that's what's required—but done by a man who's got one ear cocked toward the infinite. It's for that reason I begin this tale with a few rather ponderous but needful remarks about myself.

It is difficult, however . . .

Hmm. Yes.

Perhaps I will drop that approach and attempt some other.

2

We always have tornadoes in the spring, down in southern Illinois. I've grown used to them, and thoroughly fatalistic. I feel, perhaps, a certain hesitancy about going out on calls on one of those mornings whose calm forbodes a twister. But sickness does not start up and stop as birdsongs do, depending on the weather, and so, despite the uneasy feeling, I hitch up Shakespeare, throw in my medical bag, and away we go. The weather darkens, as the day progresses; my uneasiness increases, and so does Shakespeare's. He glances at me as I come out from a call and loose the reins from the hitchingpost, and I throw a glance back at him, startled by some fear far, far below conscious thought. It's as if for an instant, we don't recognize each other, after all these years together. In a flash, that's past, the ear that seemed for one stroke of a heartbeat, to be flattening back like a warhorse's ear is erect once more, and the eyeball that seemed to have madness in it is merely my old friend Shakespeare's eye, long-suffering and possibly amused. I glance at the sky. So does he. "Getting darker," I say, and the old horse considers it, turning it over in his mind till he forgets what made him think of it. I chat on, riding down country roads, saying pretty much what I say to my patients to keep their minds off aches and pains. And the sky darkens further—blue clouds, almost black, coming over from south-southwest. The light burns green, slanting from the east, and the forested hills are suddenly beautiful: great, white syca-mores bursting through the blue-black and emerald green forest like heart attacks, and above us the thunderheads loaded and flickering with lightning like a dying man's brain.

At the crest of the hill, on this particular occasion—the occasion I've set out to recount to you—I tug at the reins, he resists, I tug harder, and we stop. I gaze at a world transmogrified: glowing green fields, wood-lots with trees as gray as bones, bright houses and barns, and, winding between them, the rich, gravy brown of the road. The horse turns his head. He thinks I'm a fool, and he's correct.

Then comes the wind. We can see it from ten miles away, coming at us, moving across the whole world like a thrasher's scythe. Where its cutting edge is, trees burst to life with the shudder of an infant first sucking in air, and behind, in the swath of the wind, even oak trees bend and buckle, and the willows are in motion like the sea. Then rain slams down on the hot, cracked earth. It kills more things than it nourishes, no doubt. Down in southern Illinois, whatever can make it through the ravages of spring to the time when the heavy, wet heat moves in, crowding every meadow and marsh with green—the time when the rattlesnakes come out on the rocks in dry, brown creeks to sun themselves (coil on coil, their hatchet heads lifted to watch you pass) . . . the deadly hot summer when farmers get up before dawn to hoe bottomlands, and work there only till the dew's off the ground, then quit, which happens when the sun's shoulder-high . . . in summer, I was saying . . .

The wind. Let me see.

We stood there in the road, watching, and it seems I fell into a momentary trance. The storm came plunging northward toward us, and it never even crossed my mind that I ought to seek shelter. Grass, birds, underbrush creatures around us were hushed and motionless, hugging the ground, waiting as they do when an eagle's been sighted. And then, not one at a time but simultaneously, like angels arriving out of nowhere in a vision, three enormous black cyclones appeared, maybe twenty miles away, and they came along, crazily swaying like wild black savages, dancing where the scythe had passed.

The world came awake, whispering alarm at the first little puff of wind, and old Shakespeare bolted.

3

In many ways horses are wiser than men, and so old Shakespeare proved that afternoon. He shot straight forward, downhill toward the storm, and just in the nick of time I saw what his plan was. Some fifty yards from where I'd paused to consider the beauty and grandeur of Nature in her rage—some fifty yards from where, no doubt, my absentminded stare would soon have plunged me headlong back into the buzzing, blooming confusion—stood two old gateposts of hand-hewn stone, which supported enormous black iron gates of the kind one sees mainly at the entrances to graveyards. The gates were wide open (they were normally locked with a padlock and a length of rusty chain), but, closed or open, no sensible creature in all southern Illinois, except a horse, would have ventured up that driveway. When I saw the turn coming, I threw myself violently left, snatching at the seat-rail and clinging, and somehow remained with the carriage, which remained with the horse. The world fell silent, as if we'd crossed from one sphere of reality to another. The carriage wheels, moving through deep, lush grass, made not even a squeak; old Shakespeare's hooves were the hooves of a dream horse: He might have been rushing past planets toward deepest space. Above us, huge beams of old trees interlocked, and what little light there was left in the world came in needles. So we rode for what might have been hours, silent as phantoms in that silent lane. It was not, of course, hours. Two minutes, perhaps.

I am not a man given to foolish superstitions, nor am I in the ordinary sense religious, though my father was a Presbyterian minister and I begin to suspect I will carry his habits of speech to my grave, for their inherent felicity if nothing else. Much less am I a person of easy credulity. I have heard too much gossip in my fifty-four years to give credence to even a little of it; and I have seen too often, in my chosen profession, the errors of other men's eyes and ears and chests. I diagnose on the basis of evidence, and that which I cannot understand I respect and ponder.

Nevertheless, as I have said, I would not personally have chosen that lane, even to escape a midwestern tornado. There were stories—nebulous, disquieting. Things had been seen, apparitions or whatever, which so bothered those who believed they'd seen them that they preferred to remain unspecific. I had treated certain patients whose physical condition suggested to me (though I would swear neither that it was true nor untrue) that something up there on that hill was decidedly wrong. I had no particular idea what it was and, believe it or not, no great interest in learning. Whatever evil the place entertained, it did not come aggressively out to us, but waited, quiet and contented, like a sleeping dragon. There were of course some who were more curious than I. Of those who went up to the house to taunt it, poke it with a stick to learn what unnatural anger they could rouse, some came back baffled, having learned and seen nothing; others came back troubled, uncommunicative. Some who swore they'd seen nothing whatever did not seem to me entirely convincing.

"Strange business," I'd say to myself, and I'd hook my glasses back over my ear, dismissing it. "Let him sleep with the lamp on, if the boy insists," I would say to the mother. "We must never be overly contentious in dealing with Nature." And I'd leave her with pills for the young philosopher's sedation.

Shakespeare, however, took a princely disinterest in my reasonable aversion or my reasons for it. Any port in a storm was *his* philosophy, and I (with the thunder now crashing above us, and the rain slamming down, bringing sticks and leaves) was in no real position to debate with him.

4

Then, ahead of us, there was a widening patch of sea-green sky full of lightning flashes—the world was howling, everything was churning, writhing, screaming, obscured to the vagueness of things seen under water—or things wrapped in fire—by the plunging, blood-dark rain. At the center of the patch of unnatural light stood the house we'd all of us heard of, and some, as I've said, had reportedly seen. Smaller, humbler than I would have expected. No work of evil men or devils is finally impressive compared with the vastness of the universe or the hopeful imagination. And yet it was a fine old house, for southern Illinois. Tall and morose, with heaven knows how many rooms, and a soaring, blunt tower that swayed like something alive in that violent wind. Beside the tower lay a graveyard, its tombstones crooked and skewbald as an old wolf's teeth. In the house there were no lights, no signs of habitation.

We hurtled silently toward it, alien creatures in the storm's loud tumult. I thought nothing, smashing my hat to my head, soaked to the bone like a drowning man. Then, little by little, I became aware of the horse's indecision. Not fear of the great, dark house, but simple bafflement. The house stood alone—one moment blazing like a jewel in the lightning's flash, the next moment invisible, a void. Alone! No barn, no shelter for four-legged creatures, however well-meaning their hearts or adept their minds!

I tugged at the reins and, surprisingly, he responded. The nightmarish gallop slowed down toward reason, and in a moment I was guiding him, controlling his terror. His headlong rush dropped down to mere hurry, then dropped down further to a considered trot, and finally, after a struggle of our two uncertain wills, to something resembling a walk. I snatched off my glasses so that I could help him see, folded them carefully away in my pocket, and guided him along the graveyard fence to a rough, natural wall, almost cave, defended by bedraggled hemlocks and pale, square boulders. There, where the wind whipped over us, harmless, and the rain, flying by, left us almost untouched, I jerked the reins with my stubborn human intelligence—whatever he might think, I was sure I was right—and he deferred to me and stopped. After a moment I got down. The earth felt strange, unnatural to my feet; my soaked trousers clung, chilly, to my skin; my rear end was bruised and sorrowful, and I could have drawn you, by feeling out my fiery pains, a scheme of the human muscle system. I went around to his head. He was wheezing like a steam engine, and crying. It's not generally recognized that horses cry; but I give you the word of a medical doctor and veterinarian that more than rain was streaming down those coal-black cheeks.

"Whoa, boy," I said, and stroked his nose. He stood swaybacked and suffering, remorseful. "No harm," I said, still stroking his nose. "You've found us a fine place to wait it out." He turned his head toward me and I moved it with my hand. I could hardly stand his sorrow. No doubt that will seem a mite strange to some. (Human arrogance is never spent.) Nevertheless, the horse was profoundly ashamed and grieved at the way he'd stolen the authority.

In the end he was comforted and accepted my decision. I then made another, which was not altogether defensible, but I had no reasonable alternative. It was a simple fact that I had seen those twisters, and even a fatalist must cling to common sense. High wind is one thing; a twister is another. The wind that tore through the trees around us was dangerous enough— it snapped huge branches, smashed lilac bushes, even tore out boulders and rolled them as much as ten feet from their places. We were safe in our shelter if no cyclone struck. But cyclones are fanatic. No shelter can save you but the shelter designed by human ingenuity—deep in the earth, Time's womb, as the evolutionists say. I've read about twisters that have raised whole houses up and sprayed human beings through four, five states. Whatever strange beings might live in that old towered house beyond the graveyard, if they were southern Illinoisans, they had a storm cellar. I couldn't save my horse if a twister came wrecking all life where we stood, but I could crawl to that house in the hope of encountering friendly spirits and perhaps be saved.

"Stay here, boy," I said, and I gave his wet, black neck a pat. "Do as I say. I'll be back for you."

No point recounting what terror I felt, crawling, clinging with both hands to the earth, fighting through the open space of unmowed lawn and tearing wind, toward the house that stood, stupidly defiant, on the treeless crest. Uprooted trees came lumbering toward me, slow and unnatural, like underwater creatures, snatching at me, and with them came smaller, swifter objects I couldn't identify. Something living struck me on its way to its doom—a woodchuck, a rabbit, I have no idea—and clung with all its power till I beat it away. The roar of the world was deafening, the dust and small stones blown like needles against my face made me cough and clamp my eyes shut. But, at last, by some miracle, I reached the porch, slippery as flesh with ancient paint, and, still lying on my stomach, I pounded at the door. I couldn't hear myself what sound I made. Bucking the wind, I reached for the huge brass doorknob—it was shaped like a gryphon's head—and turned it. The door shot open. I tumbled in, driven by a gust that caught me like the kick of a mule, and lay on the carpet gasping for breath. Then the room quieted. Someone or something had closed the door.

I lay there groaning, no wiser than a horse. Then I fainted.

5

I came back to consciousness on an old, damp horsehair couch. I was aware, at first, only of the couch and the wallpaper, both of them thickly patterned with flowers, dark as cave walls, and scented with cat or baby urine. Little by little, I remembered what had happened, and I heard, as if in dim memory, the howl of the wind—clattering shutters against old brick walls, whistling past cornices, cracking the limbs of nearby trees. As consciousness brightened, I came to understand that the wind, the couch, the dark, flocked wallpaper, rotted by years in this thick swampy climate, were real. There was a voice, a woman's. It had been going, like a voice in a dream, for some time. It sharpened now. What it said, I couldn't tell. I was dressed in warm, fresh-smelling clothes and had my spectacles on. Someone had cleaned them.

Then there seemed to be another voice, a man's. I opened my eyes (I had slept again), and a blurry face was craning forward, looking down at me. I was aware, at first, only of red, red hair sweeping out like some ludicrous halo on a sunday-school painting, henna-red hair as ferocious and unnatural as the hair on an antique ventriloquist's dummy. A sharp pain went up through my sinus passages and in a moment I recognized it: smelling salts. The voice said clearly, "He's reviving now." And then, without transition (as it seemed to me), I was sitting up, holding a glass of hot wine, and the redheaded man sat across from me, speaking, the wind still howling. On a low walnut table beside him an oil lamp flickered in the drafts that moved, indecisive and troubled, through the room. A figure all in white withdrew from us.

"A physician," he said. "Interesting."

I'd apparently been holding conversation with him, but I had, now, no memory of it.

He was silent for a time. Gradually his features came into focus. He had, I saw, no ordinary face. Enormous gazelle eyes as pale as glass, an uptilted nose above protruding, crooked teeth, and skin very nearly as ashen as dried-out clay. It was not necessarily an alarming face, though my first reaction was definitely alarm; but it was, emphatically, a kind of face you'd not expect to see twice on one planet. A vague uneasiness crept over me, or perhaps creeps over me now, the alarm of hindsight.

"I'm a physician myself," he said, "—or used to be." His smile was as quick and unsettling as lightning. "I gave up all caring for the sick long ago—stabbing deeper, so to speak. Driving my scalpel to the heart of things. If I could make sense of my terrible discoveries—"

Sudden as a genie, the woman dressed in white was there. I gave a little jump, in fact, she materialized so quickly. Yet her stance was casual, her pale, almost transparent hand seemed gentle and loving on his shoulder, drawing him back from me, calming him. "Surely our guest is not interested in that!" Her smile, false or not, was magnificent, transforming a plain, almost ghostly face into something radiant. Her hair was black, perhaps Italian, possibly Semitic, but some sickness (I suspected a cancer of the blood) had robbed her of the bloom one expects in Mediterraneans and had left her face moonlike, lusterless. She was twenty or twenty-five, not older. Her eyes, limpid brown, were startling if you happened to compare them with her husband's (if he was, as I assumed, her husband)—those large eyes as cold and intellectual as death. One did not need to be a medical man to see that my host was in an extremely unhealthy psychological state and that the woman meant, subtly, to protect him from himself and me from him.

I said quickly, in slight befuddlement, "Not at all, not at all! It's always a pleasure to meet a fellow physician!" And, a second too late, I gave a hearty laugh. It rang out demonic in the huge, dim room. They exchanged looks swifter than lightning bolts, and the man's lips parted and stretched back in a grin. His crooked, jammed teeth flashed. For no reason that I can explain even now, a shock of terror went through me, blasted like a deep-laid dynamite charge from my spine to my brain. And instantly, as if to confirm that warning from the pit, the ghastly little scientist hurled himself toward me and snatched my free hand—my wine went flying, and I gave, I fear, a ridiculous whoop—but then, through my terror, I heard him bleating: "God bless you, Doctor! You've no conception what this does for me!" Then, seeing the wine splashed all over my knees, he shrank back, eyes widened, like a terrified horse. "Forgive me!" he cried.

"No, no!" I said. "No trouble! Mere trifle!" The pounding of my heart was dangerous, and I gasped for air, but pretended, even so, to laugh it off.

"Mother," he said, "a cloth, quickly!"

She fled from the room. I stared after her, still clutching my chest. "That's your mother?" I said, and took my glasses off. The woman was unquestionably ten years his junior. Immediately I saw my mistake— or thought I did. A mode of expression, one parent to another. Nevertheless, the sudden light in the pale man's eyes was disquieting.

"All in good time," he said, and showed his teeth. The excitement in his voice was not comforting, nor was her shriek from a distant room, assuring us that she'd found a cloth. Mad as March hares, the both of them, I thought. I must step wary.

Now the woman had returned with the cloth and was dabbing at my knees and slippers, laboring quickly and shyly, her face tipped to one side, like an often whipped dog, or like one of those wasting saints in old, old paintings. I watched her narrowly. But that moment a great jolt shook the whole house, and I remembered—amazed that I'd forgotten—what I'd come for.

"Good heavens!" I said, "we must all hurry down to the storm cellar!"

They looked at one another in what I'd swear was panic, then immediately smiled, disingenuous as thieves. "Impossible!" they both said at once. The doctor leaned forward and, splashing out his arms as if trying to communicate in a foreign language, said: "Out of the question! The storm cellar's flooded!" *"Flooded!"* she squealed, a split second after him. They laughed, hard and sharp, as if at some ghastly gallows joke.

"Flooded?" I said. I studied first one, then the other. "I see." You may imagine that you, in my place, would have insisted. But I assure you, one can never be too careful with these people.

Now the woman had poured me more hot spiced wine. It seemed to me unnaturally dark and thick. On reflection I determined to leave it untouched, though without appearing to do so.

"But rest assured, Doctor," she was saying as she poured. "Our house is completely invulnerable."

I thought of the tower I'd seen teetering in the wind, and sweat popped out on my forehead. It seemed to me now that I could hear it creaking, rocking the whole house from side to side. The woman poured wine for my host.

And now once more the pale man hurled himself forward from his chair, his white hand flashing toward me like a knife. "Forgive me! I've failed to introduce myself! I'm Professor John Hunter."

I no doubt showed my surprise and, immediately afterward, my horror. "John Hunter the geneticist?" I asked, too casual.

"The same!" he said.

And so now I knew beyond a shadow of a doubt that he was dangerously mad—and mad as the true Professor Hunter, dead these thirty years and entombed with his victims. "I'm glad to meet you, sir," I said. "And I am—" I examined his face, decided to be cautious. "Dr. William Thorpe." We shook hands. He looked at me, clinging like a monkey to my hand, as if he would never let me loose, yet innocently smiling, and I knew—as surely doomed as a prisoner hearing the judge read his death sentence—that "Professor Hunter" had been through my belongings and was apprised that William Thorpe was not my name.

6

Who knows what drove him to talk to me? The woman did not like it, but there was nothing she could do. He sat leaning forward, his face in darkness, his red hair lighted by the flickering lamp. He talked to me of Gnostics, Albigensians. I have only the vaguest idea what he said or why the poor demented devil should be, as obviously he was, so outraged by long-dead heresies. At times, too excited to remain in his seat, the professor would leap up to pace, head and shoulders thrown violently forward, his nostrils flaring, his enormous pale eyes rolling in his head like my Shakespeare's.

All the world, he said, went stark, raving mad in the second century, when the Gnostics separated body and mind. And the bitter proof, perfect ikon of it all, was the twelfth-century Albigensians. His eyes grew paler and paler as he talked, or so it seemed to me, and the knuckles of his clenched fists went white, almost blue. To the Albigensians flesh was worthless and meaningless, he said. The inner circle, the old initiates, turned further and further from bodily delights, and eventually the chief of those wise old men starved themselves to death. Meanwhile, those of the outer circle, equally persuaded that flesh was irrelevant, gorged themselves and drank themselves blind—irrelevant—and organized orgies of fierce though unimportant copulation. So while the old men upstairs, in the inner sanctum, starved, indifferently abandoning life, the younger, downstairs, indifferently consumed it. Once the mind cuts reality in two, not all the king's horses or horsemen can reassemble it. I said the opinion was interesting. What else could I say?

He spoke very softly—now and then throwing me a worried glance—of his work in the field of genetics. He pitched his gaze just higher than my head (standing pressed into the corner now, as if someone in the room had driven him there) and he spoke with unnatural gentleness, as if to renounce John Hunter's history of laboratory murders—grave on grave of dead foetuses—or as if he had hope of appeasing the howl and shriek outside.

"But to men of true Imagination," he said—and cast his eyes toward the shuddering ceiling—"to men of Feeling and Intellect, the truths of the Ancients need not be exhausted! Suppose you and I should deny God's existence, crush the mad poets' idea of Soul. Would we not have at last made life whole again?"

"Wholly bad, I venture."

"Perhaps, perhaps! But then again, we might get a shock, don't you think, Doctor? Suppose all goodness is immanent, buried in matter—in animal spirits, the humours, in cryptarch, inorganic atoms—buried there since Time began, where it labors to be born? Suppose knowledge is a thing that can be eaten, as cannibals imagine—West Indian savages, for instance, who consume the shamans of rival tribes. Suppose, in other words, that knowledge is actually, in some way we can't understand, mere *meat*."

The anguished wringing of the woman's hands was dreadful to behold. My diagnosis was that the man's revelation of his mind's imbalance was profoundly unsettling to her sensitive soul. I'd have comforted the lady if possible. But I could hardly reach out and pat her arm to reveal my fellow-feeling. Hunter's eyes, paranoiacally rolling, missed nothing.

"The hypothesis would not be very *good* for one, it seems to me," I asked. "As to its ultimate truth or falsity—"

"Heaven knows, not 'good for one,' not *healthy,* I agree!" He blanched, lips trembling, and clasped his hands together. "Yet what is the intellect for if not to penetrate, dissect? There's your God, Dr. Thorpe! The human intellect!—God and Devil both! It creates and burns the crepuscular world with its own pale flame and leaves nothing in its wake."

I fidgeted. He was actually catching me up in his lunatic paradoxes. Rather than reason with a raving madman, rather than play my mouse's part in his mysterious game of cat and mouse, I would sit more heavily, arms pressed firmly to the arms of my chair, my spectacles rigid and low on my nose. I would cling to common sense as to an oak tree. "You say knowledge is meat. You would hardly call beefsteak crepuscular, a thing of twilight."

He leaned forward, squinting. "Nothing exists, Dr. Thorpe. We're dreams in the mind of a sleeping dragon. That's our hope."

"Thus I refute Bishop Berkeley!" I said, rather fiercely, and gave the chair arm a resounding thump.

He squealed with laughter, a noise indescribably terrible to my ears, as if the chair arm should suddenly have felt pain and should confusedly express it by a laugh. Then for a long time Hunter was silent, his frightened eyes riveted to me. The swaying oil lamp above us projected his shadow on the wall, a crouched, wild-headed animal. I received a strong impression that the poor man was trying to tell me something, flash me some warning or signal some desperate appeal. I glanced at the woman—small, dressed in white, like a virgin laid out for her funeral. Was it possible, I wondered, that *she* was the threat, and Hunter's nonsense all aimed, in fact . . . Sickly as she was in all other respects, her bosom was large, like a bosom of a healthy young wet nurse.

Puzzling. But the storm, baying, tearing with ferocious jaws at Time and Space . . .

I've lost my thread. Let me see.

He spoke of Lamarck's idea, in *Zoological Philosophy,* of the transfer, from male to female, of a complete but tiny man. The old idea was in part correct, he said, though in ways no one but he, John Hunter, had recognized. He spoke of the theory of inherent influences—the idea, now all but universally scorned, that a rifleman's child might be born with the overdeveloped shoulder of his father. That too, though greatly oversimplified, was true. And he told of some monk who had recently gotten some curious information from beans—or perhaps from peas; I've forgotten. I understood, alas, hardly two words out of three. It was all very technical, and even though I am, in a sense, a scientific man, it was beyond me. I set it down as gibberish, in fact. Mere fancy without judgment.

Perhaps he guessed that. He fell silent, studying me intensely. Suddenly, out of the blue, he asked: "Does the Greek word *klone* have any meaning to you, Doctor?"

I searched through what little remained of my Greek. Then: "It means 'crowd,' if I remember rightly."

"Exactly!" He smiled, then went still more pale. "Dr. Thorpe, I have discovered the secret of kloning animals—including human beings. I can turn one animal to an infinite number, every last one of them identical, a perfect duplicate."

"Nonsense," I said. I spoke sternly, to snap the man out of it; but one might as well have rebuked the storm.

"I've discovered a ray with strange properties—that is, I think it's a ray. Perhaps a stream of particles, or motes. In any case—" He glanced nervously at the woman, then, with sudden determination, crossed to a desk at the far end of the room, opened it, and brought out a daguerreotype. He looked at it a moment, as if screwing up his courage, then hurried over to my chair with it. He practically hurled it at me, snapping his lean, stiff arm at me, the daguerreotype hanging in his violently shaking fingers. "Dr. Thorpe, do you recognize this man?"

It struck me that I did, though at first I couldn't place the features. Then with a jolt I remembered the etching one comes across so often in old medical books. "Why, that's Hunter!" I said, and was immediately flustered. My host, he claimed, was this same Professor Hunter. But the man in the picture was in his seventies. His beard was trim, his bespectacled eyes were . . .

Hardly knowing, I . . .

Hardly knowing what I was doing, I put the picture away in my pocket as though it belonged to me.

"Don't you see?" he said loudly. His voice cracked.

"My dear fellow, I see *nothing!*" I shouted.

"That man is my father. Or, rather, that man is my identical self. And this woman—" He swung to point to her. "This woman is my mother, my wife, my sister. We're not *human*, Dr. Thorpe. We're *copies!—klones!*"

"Stark mad," I whispered, and clasped my hands tightly.

"Miserable, but not mad," he cried, dashing away from me, pacing in strides that would have been comic were they not so outrageously full of woe. "I can multiply my body and soul indefinitely—or any human being's. I've lived twice already. I have fleeting memories of people dead a hundred years ago. Imagine, Doctor! There could be a thousand John Hunters!" He laughed wildly at the horror of the thought. The laughter arched out toward the storm like a lost soul's screech.

I refused to be terrified. I did not believe him.

"You're incredulous," he said, "but I can prove every word of it, to the last syllable! I can show you my machines, my papers. Come!" He leaped at the woman and snatched her hand, dancing crazily past me. She threw me a wide-eyed imploring look, like a helpless animal in flight from dogs, but there was nothing I could do. I avoided his hand when he snatched at me.

I said firmly, forgetting all fear of him, "Hunter, you're mad."

"Yes, mad, God knows! But every word of my incredible tale is true. Mad as Faust—nay, mad as Lucifer! But I've told you no lies, if there's any salvation in that, sir. Follow me!"

The storm was growing worse. He stood stamping by the door like a lunatic child, his white hand clamped around the woman's. With every new gust, the whole house cracked and shuddered. I could swear there was flame in his eyes.

I said slowly, soberly: "Where *are* these machines and papers you mention?"

"In the tower," he answered, and his crazy eyes were triumphant, as if I'd conceded.

"Impossible, then! Unthinkable! There's no place in all this country less safe. Calm yourself! Show me where the storm cellar is, and I'll inspect your materials tomorrow—if there's anything left of them. I'll look, I swear it. I give you the word of an official, licensed physician and veterinarian."

But my sensible suggestion had no trace of effect. Some demon was in him, and nothing in ordinary humanity could any longer reach him.

"Dr. Thorpe, I beg you!" he wailed, and reached for my hand again. His whole body shook. Tears streamed down his cheeks. Even she—his mother, as he insisted on calling her—was wavering and surely in a moment would convert to his side.

Life, as I have said, is preposterous. Heaven knows what came over me. All my personal fear, all my life-

long good sense were overwhelmed by the pitiable
spectacle before me: They seemed all at once neither
human nor monstrous but merely outcasts of Nature,
clinging to each other, hand in hand, and looking up
to me imploringly for help. Before I could change or
even know my mind, I took one step toward them, and
in that step gave up and followed.

7

The door through which they led me—the woman
went willingly, eagerly—opened on a circular wooden
stairway with a rail worn smooth by many climbings
in the night, a pitchdark room as airless as dreams
of the grave. At what was perhaps the third turning,
I saw light above, frail and unearthly—the lumination
of the storm. It grew brighter, more ominous. I could
feel the giddying sway of the tower. But at last we
arrived, despite all that—came out into the world of
Hunter's ungodly laboratory.

It was not the machines I looked at first—great,
square, black boxes over operating tables, glass-walled
vats, cramped chemicals and tubing—though Hunter
ran to them immediately. Most of the room's south
wall was a window, and the spectacle that window
conveyed to us now is one I pray never to be witness
to again. The churning sky was the unholy purple of
glass balls on a lightning rod. The bloom of the
lightning was virtually continual: it was like watching
flames touched by cobalt and copper, but watching
from deep within them. The torches Hunter had lit
near his machines were a tragicomic mockery, a human shout against the fury of breakers on a rocky
coast. And Hunter was, I saw, shouting to me now.
I could hear, against the roar of the storm, not a
whisper. Sparks and reflections of sparks danced
weirdly in the room as he turned a great brass crank
on the largest of the two machines. I glanced again
at the window, then back at the machines and at the
stacks of journals and loose papers in the glass-doored

racks beyond. Suddenly, for no conceivable reason—unless imagination is the soul of judgment, and things in the world (black boxes, books) are the heart and soul of imagination—I believed him for an instant—believed he was, as he claimed, not human, and neither was she.

Then it came. All three of us heard the sound at once. My blood congealed. It was a noise like a thousand railroad engines, every one of them with its whistle blowing. It was the voice of the cyclone, or of God, as the woman fancied. I cannot swear that my eyes really saw what I think I saw when I turned to the window. I seemed to see not one cyclone but four, creatures more terrible than the Bible's Four Horsemen, close at hand now and moving toward us as if sentient: four black giants that towered above us to the beams of Heaven, swaying like witchdoctors, watching us, moving with terrible purpose toward our tower. I stood wide-eyed, stunned. Now the woman—she who'd said so little before—was screaming like a beldame directly in my ear: "They've come! The Hounds of Heaven have found us! Forgive us, Thorpe!"

I rolled my eyes at her, my feet rooted to the tower floor. And then for some reason my nightmare chains melted and without pausing to waste one word on her I bolted to the top of the circular staircase and threw myself headlong down into the darkness, my only conceivable hope. As I fell, the tower was already giving way, tearing free like a tusk being yanked from its supporting bone. I couldn't tell whether the violent blows were the stairs, as I tumbled down head over heels, or falling beams, or bodies, or bricks, or scientific equipment; but I knew the great roar was like an awesome silence, and my lungs—nay, my very soul—screamed to heaven for air.

I lay. . . .

The rest is confused. I have an image of papers and books rising up into the night like startled birds. So much for a lifetime's labor! But I can't have seen that, must have dreamed it.

I lay pinned under something, still conscious, it

seemed to me, though I cannot assert as a medical man that the consciousness was not illusory. I felt the draw of the cyclone's heel, and things all around me rasped like snakes in a pit, and writhed and stirred. Then, it seems to me, I was crawling, and I came upon Hunter and seized his legs, trying to drag him to safety—to the house, perhaps. Part of it held fast. But I felt his death tremor, his violent jerking as he fought his way to a better world—and I released him in horror. In purple-green light I watched him cringe one last time, and jerk, and die. Then, not exactly with amazement, with—what?—I watched the dying body separate. It became several small creatures, pink, blue, green. (All this was surely not real, mere nightmare; but for certain reasons which will soon be evident, it is necessary that I record all I saw or thought I saw, on the chance that something in all this may give some hint of what actually took place.) I studied the creatures, so it seemed—I could hold four or five in my two cupped hands—and then I apparently lost consciousness.

How long my unconscious state endured I cannot determine. I awakened to what seemed to be screaming wind, but when I opened my eyes the day was beautifully bright, very calm and peaceful, a day to give philosophers hope and artists new purpose. Shakespeare stood above me, looking puzzled and uneasy, still attached to what little remained of the gig. I had no idea where I was (I recognized at once that I'd suffered a concussion), and though I recognized Shakespeare as someone dear and familiar, I couldn't for the life of me recall his name. My head throbbed and my whole body ached when I tried to move; nevertheless, I managed to move my head sideways, and saw the storm's destructions. There was scarcely a brick or timber left of that once-proud tower, and the roof of the house had slid halfway off and lay cocked like a battered gray cap on a crumbling skull. It came into my bewildered consciousness that the screaming persisted, though it was not loud, and not wind. Slowly, painfully, I got my poor frame into a sitting position, then managed to get over on my hands and knees and drag myself, groaning and grimacing, in the general direction of the noise. Shakespeare watched, suffering for me.

At last, some forty feet from the ruin, I came to the open storm cellar by the graveyard fence. Inside it I found three small, wet, bawling children—boys. They were all of them red-headed, buck-toothed, and pale as ghosts.

8

How I got home again is unimportant. I have been told by kind neighbors that it was the circling of vultures that signaled our distress. Despite their aversion to Hunter's house, the neighbors steeled themselves, knowing what harm that storm had done throughout southern Illinois (the town of Murphysboro was almost wholly wiped out; Boskydell, Jonesboro, and Anna were all severely damaged), and so, guided by our sheriff, they came to the ruin and rescued us—myself, the horse, and the children. No trace was ever found of the scientist and the woman nor, so far as I know, his books. The children were placed, for a month or so, in the home of a well-meaning, though stern and rather too-otherworldly old woman, a widow, sometime midwife. I recovered very quickly from my trivial discomforts—a dislocated shoulder, scratches and bruises like a newborn babe's, and a concussive bafflement that for two or three weeks blanked out all memory of the events of that night. The bewilderment I felt in that one connection had no serious effect on my performance of my duties. I walked, perhaps, more deliberately than formerly, as if feeling my way like a child; and at times I was conscious of a certain difficulty in remembering simple medical procedures that were normally automatic.

The situation with the children was more serious. It was a difficult case. I visited them three, four times a week—an eight-mile ride in each direction, which fact I mention not to show my diligence but to suggest my concern and puzzlement. (We physicians are all too often maligned by those who confuse objectivity with callousness. We're as much like artists, it seems to me, as like scientists. Can any man of sober judgment assert that Mr. Poe, for example, does not vividly experience the anguish he so forcefully—and so objectively—portrays?)

Discounting the obvious evidence of shock—blue nails, staring eyes—I could find nothing physically wrong with them. There was no vomiting, no bruise or bump to suggest that they were lost in the timelessness of skull fracture. Yet their eyes were full of terror, as if witness to things too monstrous to be recalled. Like the Albigensian initiates of old, they refused to confess to any feeling of pain or pleasure. They would recognize neither the old woman nor myself, indeed, seemed not even to recognize their own reflections in the mirror.

The old woman stood hunched at the bedroom door, her crooked frame draped in Bible-black, her dim eyes like nests in a dying tree. Outside their window it was bright, breezy June. Shakespeare stood nibbling at the leaves of a magnolia, turning his head now and then to discover if I were coming. I sighed, lips pursed, shaking down the thermometer, snatching in the back of my mind for something I'd known once, some long-forgotten trick like Meno's multiplication. Their temperatures were normal, except that they were identical —for some perfectly natural reason, no doubt, though it was queer, in fact, damned eerie. The old woman's white, arthritic hand gave a jerk, and I glanced at her over my glasses. It jerked again, the crooked index finger raised as if signaling me near. Still frowning, I left the three staring redheads and went over to her.

"Mab!" she whispered, or perhaps she said *mad*. Her toothless gums left the word uncertain.

I nodded, merely thoughtful, not necessarily indicating agreement.

She whispered something like, "My sister's baby was mad, over thar in Missoura." She dabbed with a wrinkled gray hanky at her mouth.

"I'm sorry," I said. My mind was still on the case,

not her words. The old woman smelled of cabbage and crabbed age. They can't help these things, the elderly. But I was eager enough to be rid of her, and shut of her opinions.

"Cured it," she said, and beamed at me.

Again, meaning nothing, I nodded. I glanced back over my shoulder at the children. They lay as before, motionless as corpses beneath the frayed gray sheet, their red-rimmed eyes staring, full of terror. The old woman said something more to me, snatching at my sleeve as a child would, but I did not catch the exact words. "Yes, good," I said impatiently.

I took a small vial of pills from my medicine bag on the chair. Sedatives. It was the souls of those three lost children that were unquiet, not their bodies, but I had no medicine for the human soul; a doctor must treat what he can get to. I gave the pills to the widow, along with instructions, then nodded, said good-day to her, along with a word to the children—"Obey Mrs. J—, I'll be dropping in again," or some such—and I left.

I said nothing whatever to Shakespeare, riding home. I drove to the barn, unharnessed him and fed him, gave him a solemn pat on the neck and nodded as I'd done to the old woman, then walked back over to the house, reaching in my pocket for my key as I went. It was not in the pocket I expected, and I reached inside my coat, pausing on the porch now and gazing absently over the hills, bright green—a thousand shades of green. My groping hand came to the picture I'd gotten that night from Professor Hunter, and alarm shogged through me before I even recognized what it was my fingertips had brushed. "Klones!" I whispered. The hills were suddenly a mockery— joyfully, meaninglessly green, an ironic comment on the dreadful abandonment of those awful creatures in the bed. I didn't need to think to perceive their situation, or lack of it: They were, all three of them, John Hunter cruelly resurrected.

I should of course have known it at once, from the instant I first laid eyes on them. But remember, to me they were not words on a page, as they must be to my

reader, who sees all this more rationally, from a distance; they were children—flesh-and-blood lambs of God. My spirit shrank back with every particle of Christianity in it, and I fumbled through the rest of my pockets, sick with anxiety, as if, if I could not find that key to my door . . .

I found it, of course. Was it merely my imagination that the sky had gone darker, lost luster, as if . . .

No matter. I was not put on earth to be physician to skies. I understood perfectly well now the terror in those unnatural, hunted eyes; understood it and was impotent to deal with it. How he'd done it was unimportant to me. Let scientists deal with the mechanics of it, if any there be who care so little for their immortal souls.

Like any man in a daze, I groped to the chair where normally I spend my evening with poets, with philosophers, occasionally with my father's beloved theologians, long-dead creatures exactly like myself—or dead, nonexistent till my eye revives them—and I charged my pipe, took my shoes off . . . He had spoken of memories, phantoms of his own former life. She'd wrung her hands, I remembered. No wonder.

For there was no mistaking the cold evidence of the daguerreotype. The short, neat beard of the original John Hunter and the wild streaming chaos on the second one's chin, the dimpled white chins of the three small children—they did not hide that unspeakable identity of eyes, nose, teeth. Gruesome outcasts, fiends in human shape!

The night was sullen and overcast, a night, I'd have said, to furbish the unhealthy souls of Mr. Poe or the author of *Macbeth*. My horse was irritable, indignant, but I drove him cruelly, forgetting all former good will, never permitting him to slack, old and weary as he was. His hooves rang out in the bandoned darkness. He got his second wind; his mane and tail streamed out like those of a younger or infinitely older horse, the terrible black the Devil drives. Where the road went under trees, the night was so dark I had nothing to tell me the horse was still there but the clatter of the gig that stiffly, clumsily connected us.

And so, near midnight, we came to the widow's house.

There were no lights, no sounds of life. I hesitated, getting down from the gig, checked, it may be, by something deeper in my soul than mere justice or charity. But I overcame the debate going on, unheard, in whatever must pass for the heart of man, and, snatching my whip from its rack (I have no idea why), I hurried to the old woman's door. I knocked twice, loudly, with the butt of the whip, then paused, listening, then knocked twice again. (I did not relish that terrible silence. We weren't yet shut of tornado season.) Again I knocked, and this time, the third, a voice called out, and soon I heard the creaking of a door, within, and her shuffling, slippered feet. It was a sound like hard, irregular breathing. She fumbled with the latch, got the wooden bolt back, and with a little whimper tugged the door inward. She looked up at me in alarm, knotty hand on her bosom. In her other hand she had a candle.

"I've come for the children," I said.

"Oh, it's *you*, Doctor!"

"Whom on earth did you expect?"

She seemed to try to remember, then shot me a cunning look. I looked past her, searching the dim and flickering room. I knew, suddenly, that something had happened. I'd stood here before, peering over the old woman's shoulder, sweeping my gaze over kitchen pump, crockery, table, wired-up chairs . . . There was some object on the table, a ghastly gray thing like a shriveled head, and there was string, a butcher knife, several pieces of damp cloth. I pushed past her and stepped to the table, my boots loud as thunder on the hollow floor. It was a root, a mandrake. I turned in rage. "What have you done with them?"

Her gnarled hand trembled like a tree in high wind, and her cracked face was yellowish-green in the candlelight. She gave a moan, a kind of wail with words in it, jumbled, anile, helplessly tumbling. I stalked past her, making sure the three children were not in their beds (though I knew they were not; I'd been through this before). The bedroom window was open, screenless. I leaned out, trying to remember what to do, and

in the almost-perfect darkness—no moon, no stars—
I found a center, a patch so dark it had to be an
object—yet I knew there was no tree in that place. My
heart thudded at the walls of my chest with such
force that I couldn't stand upright. And then the black
thing whinnied—Shakespeare, much closer than I'd
guessed, standing next to the wellhouse. Suddenly I
remembered what had lain there struggling in the back
of my mind—the old woman's mumble on my earlier
visit; the Indian mandrake cure.

"Witch!" I whispered, turning from the window. I
was angry enough to have struck her with my whip,
but no time for that now. I stormed past her and out
into the darkness and over to the well's stone wall.
After a moment my groping hand found the crank,
and, slowly, as carefully as you'd handle a scalpel, I
brought up what hung below. The old woman stood at
my shoulder with the candle, whimpering for forgiveness, as they came in sight. Three staring children, all
mad as the moon, fiercely gagged and tied in the copper washing tub that was to support their difficult
journey from the world of demons to the world of
men. I swiftly untied first one, then another, and
started on the third when my hand paused, swifter
than my mind. He was dead. I felt the same shock I'd
have felt if he were human. I looked up at the widow.
She too had seen it. Her mouth gaped, and the fist at
her bosom opened and closed convulsively. It was not
my savage wrath she was afraid of. I carried the children, the living and the dead, to the kitchen, and laid
them on the table.

"I need more light," I said.

She went weeping and quaking away to some dark
recess and emerged a moment later with a lamp. She
placed it on the table and lit it. As the flame leaped
up, I reached toward the two who were living, to move
them away, a little, from the corpse. As my hands
drew near, their tiny mad eyes snapped suddenly into
focus and their hands reached out to catch hold of me.
I jerked back as I would if those wrinkled white hands
were snakeheads. The old woman bent close—watching me, not the children—and though tears ran down

her cheeks like rain, the evil, toothless mouth seemed to be smiling. Shakespeare had his head in the open door, silently urging me to hurry, there was very little time. A tingle of fear came over me, one that I remembered. I glanced around the table as if to see what I'd spilled or disturbed, but there was nothing, which faintly puzzled me. I concentrated again on the pitiful creatures. Their hands were raised, waiting, and their eyes had me nailed as a cat's eyes nail a mouse before she strikes. My mind was full of wind, reeling and shrieking, but the whole world outside was calm, waiting without hope or plan, with the vast and sorrowful gentleness of a deathly sick horse.

Then, very slowly, I lowered my hands toward the children. Their fingers closed around my wrists—fingers weirdly unawkward for their age—and when I'd gotten my hands around their backs and raised them to my chest, they clung to my ears, my glasses, my nostrils, as if no tornado on earth would shake them free. When the leering old woman reached out to them, joyful, they shrank, sucked in air, and screamed. They were out of the woods.

The widow helped me to bury the dead one in a grove behind the house, with whippoorwills for preacher and only the sunken place in the ground as memorial. Then I loaded the living ones, wrapped in old blankets, in the back of the gig, and we started home. It was dawn, deathly calm. All the birds had stopped singing, and the sky was green. I spoke with old Shakespeare, as he guided us along, of animals, and monsters, and the nature of things.

THE
TEMPTATION OF ST. IVO

1

God forgive me, I hate Brother Nicholas. I hoe in
silence, sweat pouring down my forehead, catching in
my gristly eyebrows, dripping from my nose, washing
down my neck inside my cassock, and down my shoulders and belly, my legs . . . My feet grow slippery in
my sandals. My arms ache, my heart pounds, and
despite my labors I can't stay ahead of him. Without
raising my head, since I know he's watching, I roll
up my eyes for a glimpse of the village, still half a mile
away, beyond the wall—stone houses, slate roofs, here
and there at the edges of the village, thatched huts;
above the rooftops, lindens and maples and great dark
plane trees, and above the trees the three-pronged
local church, like Satan's pitchfork reared against the
clouds—and I see my helplessness, whatever the issue

of my senseless flight. I know his hoe must surely overtake me before I can reach the monastery wall, and if it doesn't, I must turn down the next row of beans and must face him, pass him, and as I pass hear his whisper, shrink from his trawling, ferreting smile. Where we meet, where he attacks me, will be his decision. He's younger than I am, and stronger, for though we weigh the same (he's nearly two feet taller), his weight is all in his muscular thighs, his chest, his shoulders. I am old. Fifty. My weight's in my miserable belly. My arms and legs are like a sickly old woman's, as white as potato sprouts under the cassock, and as flabby, as jiggly, as buttocks. I spent all my years—until lately, when Brother Nicholas made that life intolerable—at books, serving God with my hand and eyes. I drew, as he did, zoomorphic capitals—beasts eating beasts in the universal war of raging will against raging will: dragons, bears, birds, rabbits, bucks, all coiled, unwitting, in the larger design of an *A* or an *O*. Decorations for sacred manuscripts. I was said to be a genius along that line. All the glory be to God. But then one day there was Brother Nicholas, long-nosed, eagle-eyed, his flowing hair more black than a raven's, and he was whispering, brazenly defying the rule—whispering and whispering, and glancing at me slyly from time to time as if daring me to respond to his whisper or report him to the keeper of the cell. I'd do neither. The scheme of providence demands of us all that each man humbly perform his part, sing his own line in the terrestrial hymn, as the planets are singing, unheard, above us, and with charity forgive those to left and right when they falter. That may sound pompous, simpleminded, but it's true, or anyway I hope it's true. A man can go mad, discarding all tradition, reasoning out for himself the precise details of celestial and terrestrial law. I've been there. Live by rule, as all Nature does, illuminating the divine limits exactly as ink fills invisible lines. Put strife aside. Shall blue contend with gold, or gold with crimson? We are merely instruments, and he who denies his condition will suffer. The world is a river, and he who resists the pressure of Time and Space will be overwhelmed by it.

Surely I am right and Brother Nicholas wrong! I could not answer him in words—the rule of silence forbade it—but I told him in every way I could that I had no wish to contend with him. I gave him gifts, touched his shoulder gently as I passed. He hissed at me, eyebrows lifted, "Ha! Homosexual!" I changed to a carrel far removed from his, smiling meekly to let him understand I intended no offense. He smiled, jaw thrown forward like a billygoat's, and moved to the carrel directly behind my new one. I prayed for peace of mind. I put all my energy into my work. But I can hardly deny it, that endless, malevolent whisper was distracting. Malevolent. Why should I shrink from the charge? He meant me to hear it, meant my soul to be offended by it. I can see him now, tall, his long hair black as midnight, his careless, undisciplined brush moving swiftly, making swoops and arcs, his tiny pig's eyes rolled to watch me, his thin mouth wickedly smiling as he whispers. But I would not break the rule of silence, not for any provocation, and after a moment his eyes would slide back to his work. He's a fiend, I would tell myself. I tried to believe, and to some extent succeeded, that it was not Brother Nicholas himself I hated, but the devil within him. For there *is* a devil within him: So both doctrine and common sense maintain. He willfully, pointlessly strikes out at me. He scorns all rule, defies all order for mere anarchy's sake. I will not deny that I begin to be alarmed. There's no question now: He's pursuing me. Though his craft is mediocre, he had a position many brothers might envy, in sinful secret. He sat in comfort in the cool of the high-arched sunlit hall, merely filling in lines with his weightless brush, while out where rain makes a cassock hang heavy and sun burns the forehead and nose to a crisp, men less gifted—lay brothers of the order—were pitching manure behind the monastery stables, or hauling, shaping, and emplanting stone, or throwing their weight on the blunt iron plow and stumbling along after oxen. You've no idea till you've tried it what that means. They don't dawdle, those beasts. Even Brother Molin, whose father was a giant, can't muster the power it would take both to hammer the plowshare in and jerk back the rein that would slow the lead ox to a walk. So we see on every side that he who pursues his individual will, in defiance of providence and common profit, will be dragged, will-he, nill-he, where the oxen choose, but he who will put all his back into plowing, merely guiding direction, and will let oxen run as the Lord inspires, can carve out furrows that feed not only the monastery but passing knights and the prisoners in town as well. When I asked to be transferred to the fields, pleading that God had called me there, to serve with the humblest of our lay brothers, mortifying my puffed-up heart—for I had no wish to put the blame on Brother Nicholas; it was not his mysterious hostility toward me but my own infernal inclination to wrath that endangered my soul—Brother Nicholas at once asked for similar transfer. I think I need not set it down to sinful pride that I interpret his transfer as pursuit of me. He does not whisper, at least not notice-ably, when others are nearby. In fact, when I mentioned his eternal whispering in confessional, and spoke of my unholy reaction to it, my confessor was unable to believe me. He's new, this confessor, and doesn't know me well. I was not much surprised or disappointed. As one grows older, one sees with increasing clarity, and no great sadness, that finally one cannot take one's troubles to other men. They have troubles, limitations, of their own. Gently, kindly, the voice behind the dark curtain said: "Brother Ivo, pray for perception in this matter. Open your heart to God, and consider in your mind, with the freedom and pure objectivity God's grace can give, that the situation may not be as you think. You work at a pitch very few maintain. You do not sleep as many hours as the rest of us. All your brothers have noticed and have worried about it, and have prayed for you. Meditate on this: that the mind and body are interdependent, so long as corruptible flesh enfolds us. The strain on the body which heightens your gifts may heighten, also, your soul's susceptibilities to influences darker than those which illuminate your art. As we grow older, my son, we become increasingly prey to the powers that begrudge us our celestial destination." Ah, how rich with self-satisfaction that sleepy, maternal voice! It's not easy to believe he was ever shocked awake with an image burning to be realized, an image so fierce in its holiness and beauty that it lifts you, as if by the hairs of your head, and condemns you to pace from wall to wall in your room, stalling its terrible energy, until at last, praise God, you hear Vigil ring and can plunge, after prayers, into diligence. But it was not my place to condemn my confessor. He too is God's instrument, unless all Brother Nicholas whispers is true. If my case is special, not because I'm nobler than other men but because my endowment is in certain ways freakish, not easily understood by confessors created to treat more usual ills, I must suffer in charity the measure of loneliness involved in my call. "Thank you, Father," I said, resisting the anger of frustration. And in the days that followed I made an honest effort to believe it might be as my confessor, and all who observed us, supposed. Most widespread errors, I have come to see, contain an element of truth. I prayed for sleep, and I slept. But the whispering continued. And watching my brothers shrewdly—pretending to struggle with an interlace figure round a serpent's head —I discovered with a shock that, in point of fact, they *knew*. They'd glance up, startled, from four great sun-lit windows away when Brother Nicholas' whispering began; and then, quickly, they'd look down again, denying the knowledge. They were far enough away that they might be mistaken (though they knew they were not). Also, he was not whispering to them. So I fled to the fields. He followed me, smiling, tall and hollow-eyed, his affected meekness sinister. And now his hoe is some six feet behind me, swiftly, casually tearing up the earth, still gaining on me, and I begin to imagine already that I can hear his whisper. *Brother Ivo, your rules are absurd! The order of the world is an accident. We can change it in an instant, simply by opening our throats and speaking. Brother Ivo, listen!* The sound is so distinct I glance back past my shoulder without meaning to, and I see I'm not wrong. His eyes meet mine, sharp blue cones of fire beneath his coal-black brows. He smiles, shows his teeth. *Brother Ivo, I've decided to murder the Phoenix. I've discovered where it lives.* I jerk my head around, continue hoeing, stabbing fiercely, resisting the temptation to work sloppily and escape him again. *You don't believe in the Phoenix, Brother Ivo? I give you my word, you're the only man who can save the beast.* "Fool!" I could tell him, "do you take me for a blear-eyed, bull-necked serf, who places his trust in mere outward signs, allegorical apparel—phoenixes, salamanders, fat-coiled dragons? I've been painting the shadows the truth casts all my life!" But my heart quickens and a tremor of fear runs through my veins. I almost spoke! I have underestimated my enemy again. Why is it so important to him that I break my vow and speak? What will he have proved? That one man can be corrupted? Surely he must know that any man can be corrupted! He continues to gain on me, whispering. The blade of his hoe strikes two inches from my foot, jerks backward, strikes again. He will soon come even with me. *I leave tonight, Brother Ivo. As soon as they're all asleep, after Compline. Up there on the mountain, that's where it is. A cave just under the outcropping rocks. There's a goatpath goes up to a hundred yards from the entrance.* "You're out of your mind," I could say. "There is no Phoenix." But it isn't true, in any sense I understand, that Brother Nicholas is out of his mind. He comes even with me, his sleeve brushes against mine, mock-seductive. I jerk myself away. I pass no judgment on those of my brothers who are homosexual—except for their blatant hypocrisy. They furtively touch one another in the fields, exchange little glances while kneeling to receive Our Lord's blood and flesh, stand closer together than necessary at the urinal; yet they claim, faces innocent, even dripping pretty tears, that they cherish the Church and all her laws and doctrines. I do not like to be confused with such men. Sin of pride, no doubt. The Lord knows what's true and false about me; what matter what my brothers believe? And yet I'm enraged, tempted almost beyond resistance to turn on him with my hoe. (In a fight he could easily kill me.) I flash him a warning glance, struggling to do it with the dignity befitting a superior; he smiles, head tipped, flaps a womanish hand; and suddenly I see how grotesque I must look, head drawn back unnaturally, pursed lips pompous, a small fat man twisting his head around, manfully struggling to stare down his nose at a man who's taller. Again, he's made a fool of me. I turn, facing him, but swallow my shout. He studies me coolly, leaning forward over his hoe, as detached and cold-blooded as an alchemist studying iron, and I am certain (if ever I doubted it) that Brother Nicholas is no homosexual: He is merely shameless, cut free of all anchor, and will use whatever he can find to make me uncomfortable. I control myself. My rage turns to fear. The shadow of the forested mountain has reached the western edge of the village. All the valley to my left is in ominous shade. He leans toward me, whispering. *Do not be too hasty in judging my project, Brother Ivo. Many notable authors have spoken of the Phoenix, and holy men among them. Cyril, Epiphanius, Ambrose, Tertullian.* He hisses straight into my ear, spraying spittle. *Illum dico alitem orientis peculiarem, de singularitate famosum, de posteritate monstruosum; quem semetipsum libenter funerans renovat, natali fine decedens, atque succedens iterum Phoenix. —And what of the ninety-second psalm?* He rolls up his steel-gray eyes, mock-pious. *Despite all that, you deny the bird's existence. Very well! But it exists, nonetheless, and I have found it, and I mean to murder it. Prevent me if you can!* And now, without a backward glance, he strides forward, hoeing. I stand watching, baffled by the turmoil of my emotions, until he's chopped his way nearly to the monastery wall. He's like a monstrous crow, bent forward, black hair streaming down over his shoulders and the black of his borrowed habit. Dirt flies, bits of plants. I press my hand to my chest, calming the rush of my heart, and, after a moment, I look down again. A trickle of sweat runs down the handle of the hoe.

2

I can find no escape from this dread that has come over me. I have walked from end to end of this place so calming to my soul at other times: I have tried to lose myself in the majestic schemata of stained-glass windows, the gargoyles' brute anguish, high above me, or the noble beauty of groups of monks in silent fellowship, their white cassocks sharp against the dark of groves or shadowed hillslopes, like delicate white flowers in cedar shade. I have considered the old, symbolic walls, the ascent of shaft on sculptured shaft toward finials blazing in the sun's last light. Image of the whole world's hunger for God, this gem of abbeys. I have fled like a tortured ghost from one green courtyard to another, have stood on the bridge looking out on the mirror-smooth lake where two old monks sit fishing and a heavy old serf, a lay brother, black-robed, sits sleeping at the oars. Swans move, silent as grace, toward the darkening shore. I have knelt in prayer at the place where the river divides in three, in the shadow of oaks and walnut trees, but no prayer came, my eyes were too full of black arches and pilings, the dark, honed oblong of the infirmary, home of the dying. My eyes go, sick with envy, to the third-floor room of scribes and illuminators, the room where, not long since, I was master. Pride, envy, wrath . . . My soul is bloated, weighed down, with sin. It fills me with panic. He has only begun on me! In a matter of days . . . I pray for understanding. If I could grasp what drives him, I could elude him, I think. I could pity him, look for the good his hostility toward me obscures. I could feel charity. Is it envy that drives him? Envy of my skill, perhaps? Intuition would leap, cry out *yes!* if it were so. I remember when he looked at the Phoenix with which he makes fun of me now. A design as perfect—I give thanks to God—as anything I've done. Interlace so complex as to baffle the mind as God's providence baffles, his mysterious workings, secret order in the seemingly pathless universal forest. Twelve colors, the colors of the New Jerusalem. And in the feathers of the bird, ingeniously, almost invisibly woven, the characters RESURREXIT. Brother Nicholas studied it, holding the parchment to the light, at arm's length, frowning. I could see that he understood its virtues—the reverence, the integrity of mind and emotion, the tour de force technique. Then he turned to me, gave me a queer, bored smile, and handed the parchment back. It was not feigned, that smile. One knows what one knows. He whispered, "Excellent," and I saw that what he said he meant, but also that the excellence was a matter of total indifference to him. Then if ever I might have spoken! A man cannot be a master artist if he lies to himself, settles for illusions; and I do not fool myself that my vow of silence is as important to me as God's gift to me of skill. But I said nothing. If I were to break the vow, it should be in the name of another man's need, not my own. I had known from the first time I heard him whisper that one clear possibility was that Brother Nicholas was reaching, in devious fashion, for help. If he mocked religion, mocked all divine and human value, it might be with scorn born of anguish. I was by no means sure that he wasn't a far better artist than he seemed. It was perhaps despair that made him careless, indifferent. What if I, a fellow artist, was his soul's last human hope? What selfishness, then—what spiritual cowardice—that I refused him what he asked, a companionable voice! But the choice was not by any means that easy. Far into the night I would pace in the black of my windowless cell, from bench to wall, from wall to bench, wringing my fingers, straining for clarity, wrestling with the problem. I would pray on the cold stone floor until my knees felt crushed—they could hardly support my weight, next day—and still no certainty came. This was the thing: None of my brothers is free from sin, any more than I am, as I've always admitted; but how lax our order has grown in these, the world's last days, is alarming to me. Many brothers here keep hounds and hawks, though all the councils have forbidden hunting, *causa voluptatis,* as a mortal sin. They not only go out with hounds and hawks, they mount horses and join in noisy, drunken hunting parties, chasing headlong after rabbits and deer and outrunning the hounds themselves. They show no shame about feeding their packs from the possessions of the poor, so that slender greyhounds fatten on what might have kept children alive. They know well enough how little I approve, and how little I favor their costly meals, their wrestling matches, their frequent absence from prayers, their indifference to the chants. Though vengeance is the Lord's, I know, not mine, I can't very well keep secret my irritation, nay, scorn. I fight for humility, but surely it is true that either you believe in the code and traditions or you don't, and, if you don't, you ought to get out. And so the question is this: How can I be sure that Brother Nicholas pursues me from need of me, not from hatred of what he thinks my foolish, old-fashioned rigidity? How can I know he hasn't sniffed out the anger certain others feel, know that his purpose is not, in fact, to play their master of the hunt? How do I know it's not barbaric joy that drives him—the joy of the kill? I can say this: He whispers to me of freedom. He tells me he's freed himself of all restraints—religions, philosophies, political systems. He tells me he means to so use up life that when death comes it will find in him nothing but shriveled dregs. He looks in my eyes as he says this (it was weeks ago, but I see the grim image more clearly than I see the abbey spires, now dark in the shadow of the mountain). *You understand this,* he whispers. *You're a man of keen intelligence, though afraid of life.* I do not answer, but my heart beats quickly. "You're wrong," I would tell him. Not wrong in mere doctrine. Even if there were, as he claims, no Heaven or Hell, he would be wrong. A terrifying error. So this: Suppose it's zeal that drives him, the passion of a mad ideal. If so, he will be merciless. My vow of silence will be a minor detail. Having broken down my defenses there, he'll press on, break down my further defenses—teach me gluttony, lechery, sloth, despair. He'll hammer till I'm totally free, totally abandoned. I cannot know, nonomniscient mortal that

I am, whether his pursuit of me is a devious plea or a murderous temptation. And even if it is indeed a plea, I cannot know that the plea won't press me further and further, exactly as demonic temptation would do, and in the end demand, absurdly, my crucifixion, last proof of love, complete forgiveness, And so I cling to my creed, my rules, my traditions. If God is just, despairing man's cry will be answered. If not, what hope for any of us? So I reason it through for the hundredth time, and am no more satisfied than ever. Like a man hopelessly lost in a wilderness, I search the darkening sky, the pitchdark woods for some sign, and there is none. In the abbey they are singing Compline now. Who would guess from the sweetness of their voices that they are mere men, fallible and confused and perhaps at times terrified, like me? *Dear Lord,* I whisper . . . But I find myself moving, plunging back toward the bridge and across it and up the wide stone steps toward the chancel door, hardly aware what it is that I've decided. I wait there, listening. It scarcely bothers me that I've missed supper, missed the service. Compline ends. For a few moments longer they will kneel on the floor in silent prayer, then begin to get up, one here, three there, then more, padding softly away to their beds. The confessor will be last to leave, as is right and traditional.

3

I am surprised at how patiently he listens tonight. I pour out my sins, worst of all, my faithless terror. Strangely, the fear does not diminish, here in God's sanctuary. Behind me, beyond the confessional door, the great room is dark except for one red flame above the altar, the burning heart. I cannot see where the ornamented columns attach to the ceiling: For all my eye can tell, they may plunge upward forever, into deepest space. "Father," I whisper, "I am afraid. I believe in the Resurrection, believe that God has redeemed us all, made mankind free—all these things

I've believed since childhood. But I seem to believe them only with my mind. My heart is full of fear."

His voice is gentle, mysteriously patient. I would feel better, somehow, if I could see his face—lean on his humanness until my trust in God comes back. I have a childish fantasy that he might not be a man at all but an angel or demon, perhaps a fox with slanting eyes. I have done too much drawing, too much looking at drawings; my mind is infected by shadows from dreams. He says gently—the huge room echoes around him from window to window and beam to beam: "You believe Brother Nicholas is the Devil."

"I do," I confess. "It's madness. I know that. And yet I need some help against my fantasy."

"I understand, my son."

"Father, I haven't imagined these things. I realize it's difficult for you to believe, but he does whisper. Constantly. It's like a serpent's hiss—he means it to be, to frighten me. And he follows me. There's no denying it: He followed me out into the fields. He follows me everywhere, teasing, tempting, tormenting me . . ."

"I know."

I look up, startled, at the black curtain. The room grows ominously silent. At last I whisper, "You know?"

"I know, yes. I have thought and prayed on this matter of yours, and I have watched. I witnessed it myself this afternoon."

My heart races, full of joy. Only now do I recognize that I have actually begun to doubt that Brother Nicholas whispers. "He's not homosexual. That's one of his acts. One more trick to destroy me—a way of forcing me to wrath. He's cunning, Father, and shameless. He believes in *nothing*." I tell what he's said to me of freedom. Behind the dark curtain the confessor seems to listen. I tell him of the lunatic joke about the Phoenix. The confessor stops me.

"But that's absurd," he says. "Surely Brother Nicholas knows you take no stock in dead mythologies!"

"Exactly! But you see, that's his cynicism. It's like a certain kind of madness, but it isn't madness. Sometimes madmen, to avoid the dangers inherent in human contact, will retreat to gibberish. They communicate yet don't communicate. So Galen writes, and many other ancients are of the same opinion. But it's not fear of human relationships that drives Brother Nicholas. It's scorn, Father. He speaks, as if earnestly, of things he knows to be nonsense, and thus he mocks all earnestness, exactly as he mocks all love in his feigned homosexuality." I wait eagerly for his reaction. I'm not sure myself that I am right. It seems a full minute before he answers.

"Scorn," he muses. A tingle of superstitious terror runs through me. I fully understand only now how dangerous my enemy is. My confessor says: "But wait. Perhaps we're proceeding too quickly. He told you he was going to murder the Phoenix—told you he would leave the monastery tonight, after everyone was asleep."

"Yes, he said that." I do not grasp what my confessor is driving at.

"And if he *does* leave?"

"Why should he? He knows perfectly well—" But a chill in my spine tells me that my confessor is on to something.

"If he does in fact leave, what will it mean? Is it possible that his absurd warning is in some way a code? Could he possibly have meant—" He pauses, thinking. I wait. I am afraid to make the guess myself. "There are numerous possibilities. If he's as satanic as you think, he may mean he's resolved to kill some child or virgin—a Phoenix in the sense of unique innocence and beauty. Or he may mean the Phoenix as figure of man's immortal soul—his own, perhaps . . . or yours. Then again, the Phoenix may be a symbol of Mary, as we read in Jerome, or of Christ Himself, as in the poem we ascribe to Lactantius. But what he can intend, if that's his meaning—" He pauses again, and his silence, as he thinks the question through, expands in the room, makes the shadows seem darker—crouched animals, demons with burning eyes. I concentrate on the curtain between us, black as the pall on a coffin. "Our best course, no doubt, is to wait and see if he leaves."

I snatch at it. "Yes!" But I know, instantly, that it's a hope of fools.

"If he does, of course, you'll have a terrible choice to make."

I am suddenly aware that I am bathed in sweat, as if I'd been hoeing for hours in the sun, except that the sweat is cold. "But there's this," I say. "It would be a violation of rule for me to leave the monastery. If he makes me break one rule, he'll make me break another. Rules are my only hope against his nihilism."

"True, if it's nihilism. On the other hand, as you've suggested, if all his acts are a devious plea for help— if his terror in an abandoned universe is as great as your own this moment—then surely you'd be right to break the rule. It would be the act of a saint, a soul whose purity is beyond the rules that protect and keep the rest of us."

For an instant it seems that he too is a tempter. I have seen no visions, worked no miracles. "I am no saint, Father."

He seems to consider it.

I try to think, make out what he is telling me. But all the time, despite all his kindness, my dread is building, a monster independent of my conscious mind. I whisper, suddenly remembering: "There's no slightest sign that his behavior is a plea, Father. All the evidence points—"

"You forget, my son. He told you, when he said he would murder the Phoenix, 'I give you my word, you're the only man who can save it.' Surely that means you *can* save it, whatever the meaning of the symbol."

The room is full of fire, the demons in every dark corner are real. "I didn't tell you that," I whisper. With a violently shaking hand I snatch away the curtain between us. In the darkness, I can just make out his features. "Brother Nicholas!" I whisper—

He bows, solemn. "The question is, can you trust the promise I've given you." He smiles, then turns, his robe silent, and he goes into the darkness.

4

I abandon hope. I have lost Brother Nicholas, though I'm by no means confident that he has lost me. The woods contain no glimmer of light—interlocked beams like a roof above me, the boles of the trees twelve feet apart. All sounds are muffled; I can scarcely hear the cry of birds or crickets, much less the snap of a twig that would tell me my enemy is near. I have no opinion what the outcome will be. I am afraid, sick unto death with fear. I have no faith that the universe is good, as I have thought. Yet I am here. I have no choice. Men hunt wild boars in these tomb-dark woods. It is pointless for me to be afraid that I'll startle some ancient loner and be murdered by it. Nevertheless, poor shameless, mindless creature, I am afraid. There are also wolves. (If they're circling me now, bellies close to the ground, eyes light, ears turned toward where I whimper to myself, I have no way of knowing.) I stumble on, perhaps going in circles, laboring forward through hawthorne and oakmoss, in the absurd hope of coming on some path. But no, there *is* a sound. A sort of creaking, a clank, and something else. For a second I can't place it, but at last my heart leaps: the snort of a horse! I move toward it, pushing through the underbrush as fast as I can, splashing out my arms in the darkness, groping, kicking with a sharper whimper through nettles, tangled vines like limp wet snakes. Suddenly there is open sky above me, and stars, then the darkness of trees again. I've come out on a grassy road, a few wisps of fog in its hollow, and fifty feet away, loping toward me, an enormous horse, steel-visored and skirted, and on the huge beast's back, a knight. I scramble out onto the road and kneel. "Mercy!" I cry out. "My lord, help me!" The horse rears, crazy, and faster than the eye can see, the knight's steel hand has the sword out, raised above his head, prepared to come down on me and split my skull. An eternity passes. I peek up past my hand.

He's inhuman, gigantic in his shell of steel, no expression but the pitchdark slit of his eyes and the slightly moving plume on the top of his helmet. And then, deep-voiced inside the visor:

"Who are you?"

"Brother Ivo, from the monastery." I raise my hand to point, but I don't know the direction.

He doesn't believe me. "What are you doing in the woods, monk?"

"Looking for Brother Nicholas," I say. I try to think.

"Brother Nicholas."

I nod.

At last, doubtfully, he lowers his sword, raises his right hand to his visor and lifts it. In the darkness I cannot see his face. There might be nothing inside. (I am maddened by art, I recognize again. Perhaps his face is an evil monkey's; perhaps it's a death's head. My mind has lost control: The rules, techniques of a lifetime devoted to allegory have ruined me.)

The voice becomes less forbidding. "He's a friend of yours?"

I try to think. I am tempted to laugh a little wildly. "I don't know."

I have a sense of something moving behind me. I jerk my head. The horse shies violently and rears again, and again the knight has his sword out, the visor snapped shut. I throw myself down on the ground in terror, hands over my ears. Nothing happens. Two minutes pass. I look up, cautiously. The knight is bent forward on his trembling steed, scanning the darkness of underbrush with those slanted black slits. At last he straightens up, lets the sword drop a little.

"What was it?" I whisper.

Another minute passes. He is listening to the woods. No sound but the breathing of the horse. At last he tips up his visor again and studies me. "Stand up, monk," he says. I obey. He says, "Turn around. Over there in the moonlight. Press your clothes flat to your skin. That's right." It comes to me that he's looking for weapons, a dagger, say.

"I never carry any weapons, my lord." I look up at him, earnest. No knowing what he thinks, that shell of steel sitting huge and still as a castle in the thin, frail moonlight.

"Maybe not." He continues to scrutinize me. Finally, with a movement surprisingly quick, considering the weight of the armor he wears, he slips the sword into its scabbard and reaches down to me. "Climb up."

I cling to his gauntlet and lift my foot up on top of his spiked iron shoe and he pulls me up behind him. The smell of his sweat hits my nostrils, stronger than the sweat of the horse. I reach around his waist to hold on, and faster than a striking snake, the iron palm of his gauntlet nails my wrist. I cry out, and the horse shies in terror. I nearly fall but he holds me. He realizes at last that I had no intention of snatching the dagger he wears on his thigh, and he relaxes, though he still says nothing. He throws his weight forward slightly, and the huge horse takes three steps, then pauses, shaking like a leaf.

"There's something in there," he whispers, and closes his visor. We peer into the darkness. It seems to me that I see Brother Nicholas standing motionless in the blackness of the forest eaves. He stares straight at us, smiling his mysterious, scornful smile.

Nothing means anything, the figure whispers.

Faster than lightning, the dagger has flown from the gauntleted hand. We do not hear it strike, consumed by moss, dead trees, the darkness at the heart of things. *Nothing means anything,* the forest whispers. The knight is trembling. The face still seems to smile at us. But it is not a face, we know now—some trick of light—and the voice is not the Devil's voice but some heavy old animal in its lair, unable to sleep because of age.

"Mistake," my defender whispers.

"It's nerve-wracking business, knight-errantry," I say, and wipe sweat from my forehead.

"Keeps you on your toes," he says, and laughs. "Sooner or later they get you. It's a hundred to zero."

He leans forward. The horse begins to move. I

cling to his waist for dear life. His strong legs are locked around the horse. We're a strange image, it crosses my mind, floating through moonlit mist down the silent, grassy lane, plumes bobbing, steel armor on the knight and horse like the pale recollection of unreal fire. . . .

THE WARDEN

1

The Warden has given up every attempt to operate
the prison by the ancient regulations. Conditions grow
monstrous, yet no one can bring them to the Warden's
attention. He paces in his room, never speaking, never
eating or drinking, giving no instructions of any kind.
He dictates no letters, balances no accounts, never
descends to the dungeons or inspects the guards. At
times, he abruptly stops pacing and stands stock-
still, listening, his features frozen in a look of vengeful
concentration. But apparently nothing comes of it. He
looks down from whatever his eyes have chanced to
fix upon, his stern and ravaged face relaxes to its usual
expression of sullen ennui. (I speak not of what I see
but of what I used to see, in the days when he occasionally called me in, in the days when sometimes

he would even smile grimly and say, "Vortrab, you and I are the only hope!") After a moment's thought he remembers his pacing and at once, doggedly, returns to it. His pacing has become a kind of heartbeat of the place. Even when I'm far from here, lying in my cottage in the dead of night, I seem to hear that beat come out of the stones, then ominously stop, then at last start up again, the old man walking and walking in his room, like a gnome sealed up in a mountain. I, his mere amanuensis, am left to do what little I can to keep the institution functioning. I pay the guards and give them encouragement; I visit the cells and arrange for the changing of straw and the necessary burials. When we lose personnel, which happens often—sweepers and grave-diggers loading up their satchels with government equipment and slinking away like wolves in the night—I go to the village and find, if possible, replacements. It's a touchy arrangement. They all know I have no authority. They doubt that they themselves have any. It seems to me at times that we have nothing to go on but our embarrassment. That and the money that still comes, from time to time, from the Bureau of Correctional Institutions. I have a subterfuge that I've fallen into using, though I doubt that anyone's convinced by it. I tell the guards and supervisors that the Warden has commanded so-and-so. I say, for instance, "The Warden is concerned about the smell down here. He's asked me to organize a clean-up detail." At times, when morale is unusually low, I pretend that the Warden is angry, and I give them stern orders, supposedly from him. They look down, as if afraid, and accept what I say, though they do not believe it and certainly stand in no awe of me— a small, balding, fat man forever short of breath. It gives them a reason to continue.

How long this can last I do not know. Let me set down here, for whoever may follow, a full report of how things stand with us, though none of this touches on the cause of our troubles—a thing so complex that I scarcely know how to comprehend it.

Some weeks ago, finding one of our older and more loyal guards asleep at his post, and being, perhaps, a trifle edgy and self-righteous from worry, lack of sleep, and irritation at being required to do more than I'm trained to do, I stepped briskly to the sleeping man's side and shouted directly in his ear, "Heller! What's the meaning of this?"

Heller jumped a foot, then looked angry, then sheepish. "I'm sorry, sir," he said. He's a small man, narrow-chested, with a thin, nervous face like a comic mask—large-eyed, large-eared, beneath the long nose a beard and mustache, and, to the sides of it, rectangular spectacles. He was obviously distressed at his lapse of vigilance—at least as distressed as I was, in fact. If I'd been fully myself, I'd have let the matter drop. But I couldn't resist pressing harder, the way I myself am pressed.

I jabbed my face at him. "What will the Warden think of this?"

He lowered his eyes. "The Warden," he said.

I said, "What will happen if some prisoner got into the corridor?" I came close to shaking my fist at the man. He looked past me, morose. They always know more than you do, these Jews. You see them shuffling along the roadside, hats sagging, beards drooping, eyes cast down as if expecting the worst. They tempt you to swing your team straight at them, let them know for once how matters stand. No doubt that's what Mallin would have done—the man we had here some time ago. A nihilist, destroyer of churches, murderer of medical doctors.

At the thought of Josef Mallin, I pretended to soften, but it was really from cruelty not unlike his, a sudden wish that the accident had happened. "You wouldn't be the first guard killed by his own reckless laziness, Heller. You know what they're like. Wild animals! Whatever touch of humanness they may ever have possessed . . ."

Heller nodded, still avoiding my eyes. He refused to say a word.

"Well?" I said. I struck the stone floor with my stick and stamped my foot. The idea of Mallin, even now that he'd been dead for months, made my indignation seem reasonable. Guards *had* been murdered, from time to time. And there *were* certain men so bestial, so black of heart . . .

Heller's eyes swung up to mine, then down, infinitely weary. Immediately, I was ashamed of myself, slapped back to sense and sick to death of the whole situation. I turned from him in stiff, military fashion, though I have nothing to do with the military, and started away. I knew well enough that he had no answer. No one has an answer for a question, a manner of behavior, so grotesque. But as I started up the dark, wet stairs, self-consciously dignified, full of rage which no longer had anything to do with Heller, he called after me: "Herr Vortrab!"

I stopped, despite myself. I waited, squeezing the handle of my stick, and, when he said nothing more, I turned to look at him, or turned partway. The tic which troubles me at times like these was jerking in my cheek.

"I'm sorry to have troubled you," he said.

His foolish, weak face made me angrier yet, but for all his meekness he managed to make me more helpless and ludicrous than ever. Nor was it much comfort that in the flimmer of the lamp he too looked childlike, clown-like, absurdly out of place. The flat, heavily initialed stones glistened behind him, wet as the bedwork of the moat. He had his hands out and his shoulders hunched, like a scolded tailor. It was impossible to meet his eyes, but also impossible not to, in that ghastly place. The corridor winding through the shadow of chains and spiderwebs toward increasing darkness was like a passage in a dream leading endlessly downward toward rumbling coal-dark waterfalls, sightless fish.

"You haven't talked to them, sir," he said.

I stared at him, eyebrows lifted, waiting.

He raised his hands, the center of his forehead, his narrow shoulders in a tortuous shrug, as if pulling upward against centuries. "I *do* talk to them," he said. "If they're animals—"

"It's forbidden to talk with the prisoners," I said. I squeezed harder on the handle of my stick.

He nodded, indifferent. "Doesn't it strike you that we—we, too, are prisoners? I go home at night to my wife and children, but I never leave the prison. —That makes no sense, I suppose." His shoulders slumped more.

"It certainly doesn't," I said, though I understood. I too go home every evening to the same imprisonment. My senile father, who's ninety, paints pictures in the garden, thoroughly oblivious to my worries; amused by them. My two small children cackle over jokes they do not explain to me, watching as if through high windows, great square bars. My wife . . .

"Heller, you need a vacation," I said.

His smile, for all its gentleness, was chilling. Centuries of despair, determination to continue for no clear reason, some ludicrous promise that all would be well though nothing had ever been well or ever would be. A brief panic flared up in me.

I took a step down, moving toward him, then another, and another. The panic was fierce now, icy, irrational, a sense of being led toward ruin and eagerly accepting it. "What prisoners do you talk to?" I asked.

Again, this time more thoughtfully, he looked at me, his fingers on his beard. With a slight shrug, he turned and moved down the corridor, then timidly glanced back, looking over his spectacles, inquiring whether I'd follow. At the first turn, he lifted a lamp from its chain and hook, glancing back again. I nodded impatiently. He held the lamp far forward, at eye level. Rats looked up at us. We came to the worn stone steps leading downward to the deepest of the dungeons. The walls were so close we had to walk single file, the ceiling so low that even a man of my slight stature was forced to walk cocked forward like a hunter.

At the foot of the steps, the cells appeared, door after door, dark, iron-barred crypts. Most of the barred doors supported great silvery spiderwebs like spectral tents, their sagging walls gaudied by moisture drops that shone in the glow of the lantern like sapphires and rubies. The stink was unspeakable. Old straw, human feces, old age, and the barest trace, like some nagging guilt, of the scent of death. At the fourth door on the right-hand side, he held up the lantern, and, obeying his gesture, I cautiously peeked in.

What I saw, when my eyes had adjusted to the gloom, was a naked old man seated in his chains—seated or propped, I couldn't make out which—in the corner of the cell. Beside him lay a pan of uneaten food and his lumpy, musty sleeping pallet. He was a skeleton awkwardly draped in veined, stiff parchment. His hair and beard, which reached to the floor, were as white as snow, or would have been except for the bits of straw and dirt. One could see at a glance that his luminous eyes were useless to him. His hands, closed to fists, were like the feet of a bird; his wrists and ankles were like crooked pairs of sticks. I could not tell for certain whether or not the man was still alive, but my distinct impression—the smell perhaps—was that he wasn't. I thought I felt something behind us and turned to look. There was no one. A flurry of rats.

Heller called out, "Professor, you have a visitor." The words were distorted by echoes running down the long stone corridor and bouncing from the lichen-covered walls of the cells. The prisoner made no response. Heller called out the same words again, more slowly this time, as if speaking to a child hard of hearing. And now it seemed to me that a kind of spasm came over the face—not an expression, not even a movement of features suggestive of human intelligence, but some kind of movement, all the same. I watched in horror, pierced to the marrow by the sight of that dead face awakening. Then—still more terrible—the skull of a head turned slowly to the right, straining, perhaps, to decipher some meaning in the echoes. Heller called out a third time, leaning forward, hand on beard, calling this time still more slowly, and, as the echoes died, there came from the creature in the cell or from the walls around him a windy, moaning syllable almost like a word.

"He's saying 'Friend,'" Heller whispered, at my shoulder. Then, to the prisoner: "Professor, tell the visitor your crime."

Again the prisoner seemed unable to grasp what the guard was saying. He swiveled his head like an old praying mantis, translucent white. But when Heller had asked the same question three times, the prisoner brought out a series of noises, hoarse, reedy grunts— his stiff, dark tongue seemed locked to his palate— and Heller interpreted: " 'No crime,' he says. 'Was never accused.' " Heller studied me, looking over his spectacles, trying to see what I made of it. But I had no time to consider that now. I was beginning to understand, myself, the prisoner's noises. I needed to hear more, test my perceptions against Heller's. I struggled against distraction. I had, more strongly than before, the impression that someone was behind us. Except when I looked closely, I was aware of a bulky, crouching shadow. No doubt it was merely a trick of my nerves; at any rate, Heller was unaware of it. I nailed my attention to the prisoner.

"Why do you call him 'Professor'?" I whispered.

The guard looked away from me, annoyed by the question, then changed his mind. He asked the prisoner, "Professor, tell us of Matter and Mind."

The prisoner sat perfectly still, as before, but it did not seem to me now that he was struggling to make sense of Heller's words. He seemed to consider with his weakened wits whether to respond or relax his attention, drift deeper into death. Then, little by little, I saw him laboring back toward thought. He began to speak, if you could call it speaking, and Heller interpreted word for word until, by my touching his arm, he perceived that I no longer needed his assistance.

I can suggest only faintly and obscurely what I felt, listening in darkness to the tortuous syllables of that spiritless old man. The lamp threw the shadows of bars across his body, and I had a sense—a conviction related to his words—that insubstantial shadows alone were sufficient to pin him in his place.

"There is no immateriality," he said. "Mere word. Mere sound." He ran his thick, dry tongue around his lips. His eyebrows lifted, part of an attempt to get his jaw muscles working. For all his difficulty in expressing himself, it was plain that he had his words by heart. He'd delivered the lecture a hundred—more like a thousand—times. Not merely to students; to himself more often; to the rats, the spiders, the bats, the darkness and emptiness around him, perhaps to neighboring felons, while they lasted. The lecture was doubtless the anchor of his sanity, or had been once. Such tricks are common among prisoners. As long as he could still put the words in order, still grasp some part of their significance, he was himself, a man, not yet reduced to the level of beasts, whose suffering, if not unconscious, is soon forgotten. I could see by his pauses and the accompanying expression of bafflement and panic that the power of the magic was draining away. A ghostly pallor lay over his features, his voice trembled, and his blind eyes stared fixedly, as if he were listening intently to every word.

I no longer recall the exact phrasing, but I remember very well the general argument—that and the terrible struggle in his voice, like the labor of the prematurely buried. As Heller and I have reconstructed it, the lecture went as follows:

"There are gradations of matter of which man knows nothing, the grosser impelling the finer, the finer pervading the grosser. The atmosphere, for example, impels the electric principle, while the electric principle permeates the atmosphere. These gradations increase in rarity until we arrive at matter unparticled; and here the law of impulsion and permeation is modified. The ultimate, unparticled matter not only permeates all things but impels all things, and thus *is* all things within itself. This matter is God. What men attempt to embody in the word 'thought' is this matter in motion.

"There are two bodies, the rudimental and the complete, corresponding with the two conditions of the worm and the butterfly. What we call 'death' is the painful metamorphosis. Our present incarnation is progressive, preparatory, temporary. Our future is perfected, ultimate, immortal. The ultimate life is the full design.

"But of the worm's metamorphosis, you may object, we are palpably cognizant. I answer: *We,* certainly—but not the worm. Our rudimental organs are adapted to the matter of which is formed the rudimental body, but not to that of which the ultimate is composed. We thus perceive only the shell which falls from the inner form, not the inner form itself. Yet consider. In certain states—in states of entrancement, as, for instance, when we have been Mesmerized—we perceive independent of rudimental organs: We employ the medium we shall fully employ in the ultimate, unorganized life.

"Only in the rudimental life is there any experience of pain, for pain is the product of impediments afforded by number, complexity, and substantiality. That is not to say that the rudimental life is bad, however painful in a given case. All things, after all, are good or bad only by comparison. To be happy at any one point we must have suffered at the same. Never to suffer would be never to have been blessed. But in the inorganic life, pain cannot be; thus the necessity for the organic."

I have no idea how long it took him to get all this out, nor what I thought of his opinions at the time—though I've had fearful occasion to think back to them since. I stood motionless, clinging to the square iron bars as if the slightest movement might shatter his delicate hold on sense. Heller, too, stood motionless, staring at the floor, his hand closed on one end of his mustache, his bearded chin pressed firmly to his chest. When the lecture broke off, the guard shot a glance at me, then moved the lamp closer to the bars and peered in at the prisoner. The sudden alteration of the shadows was alarming, as if something alive had slipped closer to us. Then, without a word, the guard stepped back from the door of the cell, gave me a nod, and started toward the stairway we'd come down.

When we reached the relatively less dismal passage above—a corridor six feet wide and eight feet high, lighted, every twenty feet or so, by flickering, smoke-dulled hanging lamps and etched, like all our prison walls, with the initials of a thousand miserable souls long since departed—Heller dropped back to walk beside me, his head bowed and his long hands folded in front of him.

"So now you've seen," he said.

I nodded, not certain what it was that he meant I'd

seen. My mind turned over the Professor's ideas—those and the irony of his present condition, his whole life of pain grown remote, unreal, a cold refutation of his optimistic theory.

"The man's innocent," Heller said. "A keen, metaphysical mind; and yet through all these years—"

"On the contrary," I said, "we've no notion whatever of his innocence or guilt. He was no doubt legally sentenced to this dungeon."

The guard stopped and looked at me, holding the lamp up to see me more clearly—exactly, I noticed with a shudder, as he'd held up the lamp to inspect the old man. "Why would he deny his guilt at this stage? Surely he's aware—"

"Habit, perhaps." I said it too sharply, as if for the benefit of the darkness behind us. I could hardly blame the guard for his quick little shrug of exasperation. I looked away, toward the steps that would lead me to higher, wider corridors and at last to my chamber, remote from this graveyard of the living. The guard waited, not even bothering to scoff at my suggestion. Again I could hardly blame him.

"I must speak to the Warden about this," I said, clipped and official, and looked over his head. The guard leaned toward me with a jerk and a bewildering smile, and caught my arm. "Do!" he whispered. His fingers dug into me. (I have seen it before, the guilt the men feel about the horrors they help to perpetuate.) Though I know the importance of keeping the forms in a place like this, I did not shake Heller's hand from my arm. "I'll see to the matter at once," I said. My voice was accidentally stern.

And so I left him, my step as metallic as an officer's, my walking stick a weapon. As I passed the guards in the passageways above I gave to each of them a crisp salute. Some responded, looking up from their half-sleep, their dice games, their lunch baskets; some did not. I let it pass, secretly listening already for the sound of pacing that would prove that the Warden had been all the while in his chamber and knew nothing of our breach of regulations.

And so I came to the Warden's door and stood

listening. My knock brought no change to the rhythm of his step. I knocked again, and then again. It was unthinkable that the Warden couldn't hear the banging of that great brass knocker—the figure of a lion with eyes worn blank by a century of hands. But the Warden continued pacing.

2

The sky ahead of me, as I walked home that evening, was a thing of sublime and fearsome beauty. The sun was still high—it was the middle of summer—and the weather had for weeks been alternating between hot, dense, muggy days and twilight cloudbursts. Mountainous thunderheads towered all around me, some miraculously white, where the sunlight struck them, some— the lower clouds—glowering, oppressive. The sky in the glodes between masses of cloud was irenic blue, and down through some of them came shafts of light that transmuted the ripening wheatfields, the pastures, the plane trees, hedges, and haycocks to images from a dream. Here and there on the horizon, sheet lightning flickered.

I hurried. The rain was not far off. I might easily have gotten transportation if I'd wished—with one of the guards relieved of duty; with the lumbering, creaking supply wagon that went back each night from the prison to the village; with some kindly stranger in his touring carriage; or even with one of the farmers bringing in hay. But I preferred to risk a soaking; I valued, almost superstitiously, the long walk home, transition from the world of officials to the world of men. Tonight especially. I hadn't yet shaken the image of the wasted, enfeebled "professor" or that ominous burden on my soul, the Warden's self-confinement.

The land was becalmed. Shadows lengthened almost visibly, and the light grew fiery green. Moment by moment, the landscape around me darkened more. The river vanished, then the hedges, soon all but the hills. I would hear now and then the low warble of a bird, a sound that seemed to come from all directions, like sounds heard under water. Gradually, even the hills sank away. All the more impressive, even awesome, then, that directly above me stood a window of somber sky, its frame edged by moonlight, and in the infinite depths of that sky, three stars. Despite the warning of thunder in the distance, I stopped in my tracks—as stirred to wonder as my father would have been, a foolish old man, but one with all his sensibilities refined by landscape painting. Something of what the old prisoner had said came back to me. Not words, exactly. A sense; an impression. I had a feeling of standing outside myself, as if time and space had stopped and in one more second would be extinguished. As quickly as the queer impression came it passed, faded back into shadow like a fish. And for some reason impossible to name, I was left with a feeling of indescribable, senseless horror, a terrible emptiness, as if I'd penetrated something, broken past the walls of my consciousness and discovered . . . what? But perhaps the cause was above me, not within. The walls of the open, moonlit glade were collapsing violently toward one another, blotting the stars out, tumbling downward like a falling roof. I seemed to hear a step, and I turned to look back. In all that darkness there was nothing to be seen—neither on the hills nor on the road behind me—nothing but the smoldering torches on the prison walls.

3

I do not ordinarily mind the burden of my father's senility. It provides distraction from those other problems I have no power or authority to solve. In any case, I'm the dutiful, respectful sort. If I'd meant to question or judge the old man, I'd have done so long since. He has his opinions, and I have mine. I let it go at that. On this particular evening, however, his whimsy took an extraordinary turn.

We had finished supper and were seated in the

parlor, except for my wife, who was washing dishes. I've told her time and time again that the children are old enough for that, if only she'd give them some discipline. But she prefers to do all the work herself. She enjoys work, no doubt. It frees her from the rest of us. So tonight, as usual, they lay scribbling, gouging great holes in the paper, on the floor, beside my father's shoes. Every now and then they would glance through the window, keeping watch on the storm like creatures in secret league with it. My father was sorting through old canvases—paintings of craggy precipices; huge-boled hickories, walnuts, oaks; sunlight bursting through chasms, orange and purple. Whatever the quality of the paintings—I'm no judge—the old man certainly had the look of an artist, erumpent white hair ferociously shaggy, eyes deep-set as two caves in an overhung cliff. When he clamps his mouth shut, the tips of his nose and chin come together. You'd think, from the looks of him—the heavy-veined temples, the glittering eyes—that the old man misses nothing; but not so. One can have no notion, from moment to moment, where his mind will surface next.

He jerked his head up, cracked lips pursed, staring at me as if angry in his attempt to remember what it was that, a moment earlier, had occurred to him. I lowered my treatise—the *Discourse* of Descartes, I think it was—and at last, with another little jerk, abandoning the paintings stacked beside his chair, he said, "Ah! So you're executing Josef Mallin!"

I was so startled I nearly dropped my book. There are times when his senility seems purposeful, malicious. Worse than that, there are times when, for all his confusion, he seems to see with perfect clarity what troublesome thoughts are astir at the edge of your consciousness. "Mallin's been dead for months," I said sharply. The tic came over me, flickering like lightning. I covered it with my hand.

"Impossible!" he snorted, but the next instant he looked unsure of himself, then cunning. "An interesting man," he said quickly and firmly, like a good liar shifting his ground. He leaned toward me, bent-backed, slightly drooling, and in the lamplight it seemed his head grew larger. His eyes were like a tiger's. "A man could learn a good deal from that Josef Mallin," he said. "Tried to burn down my studio once."

It happened to be true, though how it fit with the subject at hand was impossible to determine unless, like my father, you were addled. He suddenly jerked still nearer to me, as if he'd hit on something. "He's an atheist!" he said.

I sighed, still covering the tic, then sadly nodded to prevent his continuing. I did not appreciate (to say the least) his insistence on bringing Josef Mallin back to life. The period of Mallin's imprisonment, first while he awaited trial, then while he awaited execution, was a terrible strain on all of us. He was a brilliant devil, black-haired and handsome and deadly as a snake, so cunning at bribing or persuading his guards that at last the Warden himself took charge of holding him. It was shortly after his death that the Warden began that interminable pacing in his chamber. Mallin's execution, I might add, was unpleasant. His crimes were the worst of the three main kinds of which the laws speak, so that, after the decapitation, his head was thrown to the sawdust in the village square, to be eaten by dogs, as the law requires.

But my nod did nothing to check my father's babblings. "He claims the Bible is a pack of lies," he said, squinting, tightening his fists to get the thought exact. "The man's not merely indifferent to religion, he *hates* it, heart and soul!" He struck his knee with his fist, as if some great point were scored.

I could not help but glance at my children, sprawled on the floor with their coloring papers and candies. One of these days I must force them back to their Bible lessons. My wife, unfortunately, can see no reason for reading the Bible if one does not like it. She enjoys it, herself, and she merely laughs—as she laughs at everything I stand for—when I insist that religion is no natural impulse but a thing to be acquired. (I know only too well. It's a thing I myself never properly acquired, despite my father's love of Scripture and his labor, when I was a boy, to make me study it. I could profit by religion's consolations, I think, if only I'd reached them at the proper age, the age when trust is as reasonable as reason. If I'd known what troubles this world affords . . .)

"I admit," my father said abruptly, "that I've never seen a ghost myself, that I know of." I blinked, grasping in vain for the connection, and I felt my heartbeat speeding up. Needless to say, I'd said nothing to my father of my foolish idea, in the dungeon this morning, that something was watching us. My father continued soberly, "But I know a little something of states of entrancement. Sometimes when you're painting, a kind of spell comes over you, and you know—you positively *know*—that there's no chance of erring with the picture at hand. You're nailed directly to the universe, and the same force that moves in the elm tree is moving your brush." He nodded.

Again I nodded back; I hardly knew what else to do. I'm always uncomfortable when he speaks of himself as a master craftsman. His paintings in recent years have been clumsy and confused as a child's. Not even kind old ladies buy them. I listened with the back of my mind to my wife in the kitchen, rhythmically washing and rinsing plates. She works, always, in a pleasant daze, humming to herself, her mind as empty as a moonbeam.

My father said, "He hates Swedenborg, too, and the politics of Spinoza. 'The essence of life is suffering,' says he."

Once again I gave a start, thinking of Heller's pathetic "professor"; but my father didn't notice, engrossed in the pleasure of pontificating. "Says Mallin, 'I can say at least this for myself. I have steadily resisted illusion.'" My father smiled wickedly, as if he'd just made some vicious joke at my expense. I pursed my lips, watching him closely, but, of course, the whole thing was lunatic. I took off my spectacles and sighed.

Now both of us listened to the kitchen sounds, and the sound of the children's chewing. After a time, he began nodding his head. "It will be a great blow to the Warden, no doubt. The minute the axe comes down on Joe Mallin, the Warden's life will go *fssst!*" He grinned.

I was positive, for an instant, that the old man knew perfectly well that Josef Mallin, "Laureate of Hell," as he called himself, was dead. I suspected that he brought the matter up just to torture me, remind me of my worrisome troubles at the prison. But then, as before, I was unsure. I saw—so vividly that I winced away—the image of Mallin's head rolling from the block into sawdust, spraying blood. The mustached lips were curled back, furious, raging their pain and indignation even now, and the black eyes—small flecks of sawdust hung on them—stared, now, full of hatred as ever, at the clouded sky.

My father looked down, disconcerted for some reason. "The prophets leap backward and forward in time," he said loudly, and slammed the arm of the chair with his fist. "There is no past or future in the grammar of God."

The children looked up at him and laughed. There was candy between their teeth. I felt giddy, pulled crazily in diverse directions. I was suddenly reminded, looking at my children, of those bestial creatures at the prison—your usual criminal, I mean; not "the Professor," as Heller calls him, and not some outraged philosopher-poet like Mallin. They live, the more usual criminal lot, for nothing but pleasure, like animals. They wallow in their food; when you let them together, they attack one another sexually; when you let them out into the exercise yard they snap at the sunlight, roll in the mud, and provoke horrible fights, even killings. I must have been fond of my children once, but, if so, I had now forgotten it. They were completely out of hand. I had tried to correct them— I'd tried many times—but my wife and father undid all my labors, she because she saw no point in correcting them—"Let them be, let them be!" she'd say lightly, with that foolish, carved-wood smile. As for my father, he disapproved of my *mode* of correcting them. He preferred tiresome argument to switchings. What time have I for argument, a man overworked, in an impossible situation? Between my wife and my father, I was hopelessly walled-in.

He was about to speak again—he was raising his hand to shake his finger at me. To sidetrack his ravings I leaned forward quickly and began telling about Heller's "professor." He closed his mouth tight and listened carefully, his heavy white eyebrows so low they completely hid his eyes. While I spoke, he turned his head, apparently looking out the window, not at me. I too looked out.

It was a violent, sternly beautiful night. A whirlwind had apparently collected its force in our vicinity, for there were frequent and severe alternations of wind, and even the brief illumination the lightning gave was sufficient to show the velocity with which the great black tons of cloud careened and collided. When I'd told the whole story, including as much as I remembered of the lecture on Matter and Mind, my father nodded, his eyes screwed up tight, and said, perplexingly—"Some poets get to the heart of the matter. Most just fool around with language." I could not help but wonder, that instant, who was more lonely, more desperately helpless—the prisoner whispering in his pitchdark dungeon, or myself.

Fortunately, however, our conversation ended there. My wife came in, wiping her hands together, smiling vaguely, passing her eyes like a casual benediction over all of us. "Father," she said, "it's bedtime. The same for you, children."

My father looked hard at her, thinking about whether or not to consent, then got up, stiffly, and shuffled toward the far end of our cottage, where he sleeps. Halfway there he paused, noticing his violin, and, as if he were curious, discovering some object never seen before, he bent to pick it up off the table. The children, meanwhile, had for some reason decided that they too would obey, and had started in the direction of their bedroom. They too, however, found some pretext for changing their minds. Though she still went on smiling, two lines for consternation appeared between my wife's eyebrows. "Children, *do* go to bed," she said. They did nothing, of course, and she merely put the tips of her fingers together. "They're just like

Grampa," she said to me, and smiled, exactly like a picture of a hangdog saint. I studied her thoughtfully, saying not a word.

My father told her, raising a trembling arm and pointing, "They're not like me at all. They're like *you*."

It was not strictly fair, of course: My wife is the soul of diligence, and she's sensitive besides. She prays nightly; she cooks, cleans, darns our stockings for us; she has a remarkable natural feeling for music. Nevertheless, I was perversely delighted at hearing him speak so crossly to her. I closed the volume over my finger, rose from my chair, and bent down to pick up the children's horrible scribblings.

"Good heavens!" my wife cried, staring out the window. Her face had gone white. I straightened up quickly. I had an impression, for an instant, that there was a man out there—a man in a great black coat and black boots, someone I would know, if I could make myself think calmly. But we were both mistaken, for the next instant there was nothing; it was merely an illusion manufactured by the storm. Yet, when the children squealed, an instant later, my first thought was that now they too, had seen it. It turned out to be nothing of the kind. The little girl was trying to pull down her brother's trousers. Without a word to their mother (I had never spent a more miserable evening), I went after the little criminals, spanked them soundly with my shoe, and put them to bed. I now felt much better. My father's look of outrage had no effect on me. My wife's alarm was a pleasure. I stood at the window, smiling out at the storm with satisfaction. But there was a flaw in my comfort. I could not seem to rid myself of the feeling that he was still watching us, standing behind some tree, perhaps, or peering in from the darkness of the shuddering grape arbor. I watched for some time but saw nothing in the least suspicious, neither on my grounds, nor on the rain-slick road, nor on the serpentine lane beyond the stone gateposts, rising past lindens and maples toward the old church.

4

The situation at the prison grew desperate. Though I tried repeatedly, I could get no response whatever to my knocks at the Warden's door. It was a case altogether without precedent, and so, though I knew the risks in appearing insubordinate, I wrote to the Bureau of Justice. After two weeks, I had still received no answer. At even greater risk to myself, I wrote a second letter. I might as well have dropped my complaints into a cistern. I closely questioned the courier— a man I have always found, in the past, to be dutiful and efficient. He spoke of an iron-studded door in an unlighted hallway, a huge brass plate bearing the single word JUSTICE, and beside the door a bill of instructions, among them instructions for the delivery of petitions. These last had a deadly simplicity: *Deposit petition in slot. No exceptions.* I studied him, looking severe, no doubt. "Could you hear anything through the door?" I asked. "Nothing, sir," he said, and touched his cap as if in sign that he must leave. "Not a *sound?*" I said. His blue, button eyes stared straight ahead. His turned-up nose was like a halt signal reared in my roadway. "Do not press me, sir," the nose seemed to say. "It's none of my affair." I couldn't help but compare the man with my troublesome friend Heller. Heller, too, knew what was his business and what was not, but he never put that knowledge in the way of his lugubrious humanity. However, I sent the courier on his way, and I did not trouble myself about sending more letters. As a matter of fact, I'd heard before of the inefficiency and corruption of the Justice people. It was one of the Warden's chief complaints. He, luckily, had strings he could pull.

Meanwhile, we had one near-calamity after another at the prison. The cook was found murdered. All evidence suggested that the murder was the fruit of a long-standing feud between the cook and his assistant. Being unable to rouse the Warden, I took action myself, placing the assistant in confinement to await his trial. I did this, of course, upon no legal authority; but I could see no reasonable alternative.

Hardly was that ugly matter resolved, and a new cook installed, before a second crisis struck. A sizeable group of the guards revolted. I asked, in the absence of any other authority, for a conference with their spokesman. The meeting was arranged, a ridiculous melodramatic affair, since the leader of the rebellious faction was convinced—surly, double-dealing peasant that he was—that my intent was to get him alone and unceremoniously shoot him. I scarcely bothered to protest the opinion, but met him, as required, at the prison front gate, at the hour of noon, with all the guards loyal to him on one side, their guns aimed at me, and all those loyal to me on the other side, training their guns on him. Even if we'd met as friends, it would have been a dreary spectacle. The guards' uniforms were faded and threadbare, here an epaulette missing, there an off-color elbow patch. Coats lacked buttons, trousers and boots were no longer standard; if treachery came along, it was doubtful that more than a few of the rifles on either side would fire.

Clownish and base as all this was, I sweated profusely throughout that meeting. What assurance could I have that men so disloyal would not hazard a further disloyalty, and shoot me for their sport? The rebellious guards' demand was simple. I must double their pay. "Impossible!" I said—as it most certainly was. If I hadn't been so frightened, I might have laughed. My opponent declared the meeting ended; he would speak no further except with the Warden himself. I found a delaying tactic: I would relay to the Warden the rebels' demand and would meet them in twenty-four hours with the Warden's response. With some mutterings, they accepted. The guards on each side lowered their rifles, and I went briskly back to my chambers next to the Warden's. I did not bother, this time, to knock on his door.

As I was unlocking my own, a hand touched my elbow. I jumped. It was Heller. "Good heavens!" I said. He nodded, his bearded mask-face smiling sadly down at me, and he took off his cap.

I'd been avoiding Heller, I need hardly explain. I had given my assurance that I would speak to the Warden about his so-called Professor, and for reasons outside my control (though I could hardly admit that to Heller), I had not done it. I was certain, now, that he was here to ask what the Warden had decided with regard to his friend.

"Come in, Heller," I said, and cleared my throat. "I've been meaning to speak with you."

He must have known well enough that that was untrue. I'd been ducking and fleeing at sight of him for a week. But he nodded, still smiling sadly, and stepped ahead of me into the room.

"Very elegant," he said, pretending to look around for a moment, then staring at his cap. Though it was plain that he wasn't much interested, in fact, in the elegance of my chambers, I seized on his remark to stall the embarrassing question I expected. "So it is," I said. "In former times, the prison used to have important visitors. In those days cases were in constant review. In certain situations, the chief justices themselves would come down. But of course it's no longer practical. With the seat of government so much farther away . . ."

Heller nodded. I saw that he relished our meeting as little as I did. I too now fell silent, knowing there was no escape. We stood like two miserable children gazing apprehensively around us. I remembered my own first impression of the place. Though smaller than the Warden's, the central chamber is enormous. Exactly as in the Warden's chamber, the windows are long, narrow, and pointed—situated so high above the black oak floor as to be altogether inaccessible from within. Feeble gleams of encrimsoned light fall from the trellised panes to warm small patches below. Ancient, dark draperies hang on the walls. The furniture is sparse, comfortless, antique. The general effect, I felt at the beginning and I now felt more strongly, was one of oppressive, irredeemable gloom. One has an occasional, rather eerie sense of something moving in the corners of the chamber—an effect, perhaps, of cloud banks passing between the windows and the sun.

Heller drifted toward the far end of the room, hands behind his back, head tipped forward and to one side. When he came to the bust of Plotinus on its high black marble base, he paused and looked at it. I waited, perspiring, wringing my hands.

He turned and said, "Do you know why the guards want higher pay?"

"Do you?" I asked. Again I waited, rigid and official to hide my uneasiness.

"They lose everything they make through gambling. Stop the fellow who empties their pockets, and all the rest will resolve itself."

"You're quite certain of this?"

"I can show you," he said.

I agreed at once, and Heller led me down the great dark stairway to the first of the lower passages, and thence to a large, communal cell which had not been in use for many years. At the back of the cell a large stone had been removed, as I saw at once by the reddish light breaking through from somewhere lower. At Heller's direction, I stepped to this patch of light and looked through it. Below lay a windowless room without furniture of any kind, an abandoned cell whose door was directly beneath us, out of sight.

Four guards in shirtsleeves hunkered on the floor, shooting dice. It was clearly not one of those ordinary games, the kind I break up in the corridors. All four were sweating, their shirts pasted to their chests and backs. Beside each man stood a small pile of pebbles. One man's pile was slightly larger than the others, but not significantly so.

"Keep your eye on the fat man," Heller said.

I nodded.

The fat man—a guard named Stuart, a man with hair longer than regulations allow, and a neatly trimmed beard, small fingers like a woman's—threw the dice several times and lost. He seemed unconcerned. On the other hand, those who took his money, represented by the stones, did not seem as cheered by their success as one might normally have expected.

The others threw, sometimes winning, sometimes not. I began to feel Heller was wasting my time. He apparently sensed it. "Keep watching," he said. I did so, mentally telling myself that after five more rolls of the dice I would insist upon leaving.

Then something happened. The guard named Stuart began to glow. Call it hallucination if you will, a trick played by the oil lamps around them, but I *saw* the glow, and so did Heller, whose hand immediately tightened on my arm. The fat man was glowing like a lamp-chimney. "Stuart can't tell you himself how it happens," Heller whispered. "All he knows is that for four or five minutes he knows exactly what the dice will do."

He stared at the dice now, white as new bone against the lamp-reddened floor. He patted them, smacked them, fussed with them as a mother fusses with a baby. Suddenly he snapped them up and flung them the length of the room. "Five and two!" he yelled while the dice were in the air. Five and two came up. The other three gasped. Once more Stuart fidgeted with the dice, then flung them. "Hard six!" he yelled. Two threes showed. The others were trembling.

"Get out of the game, fools!" Heller whispered.

But it was impossible.

Next Stuart called out eleven and made it. Then four. Then nine. I felt a weird urge to go down to them, join in.

"Come away," Heller whispered.

I resisted.

"Come at once."

That evening I called the fat guard to my chamber. Simply, brutally, rapping the table with my walking stick, I gave him my imperative—which I attributed, of course, to the Warden. He would return all his winnings to those he had robbed and would depart the prison forever, or I would jail him. He expressed indignation, outrage. I was firm. He wheedled, spoke of "divine gift." I said nothing. Heller sat across from us, toying with his pistol. Stuart whimpered, begged, called me irreligious. I read him the regulations on gambling in the prison. I did not mention that I had no authority to confine him to the dungeon. The simple truth was in any case that, authority or no authority, I would do it. At last, he was persuaded. And so the second of our near-calamities was averted.

5

Less than an hour after my meeting with the spokesman for the rebels (the second meeting by the prison gate, the meeting which resolved our differences), Heller came to my chamber, where I lay resting a moment, and, when I answered his knock, expressed a desire to speak with me. I met him more guiltily than before, since now I felt that not only had I failed to fulfill my promise with regard to "the Professor," but had failed him though owing him a favor. When I'd ushered Heller to an old tattered sofa and had seated myself across from him, he brought himself immediately to the point—that is to say, to the first of his points. Looking sadly at his knees, he said, "Have you spoken to the Warden, Herr Vortrab?"

I could see no alternative but to confess the truth. "I'm afraid I have not. The plain fact is, I can't get to him."

His eyebrows went up in an inverted *v*, but despite that, he did not seem surprised. "He refuses to listen?"

I held back for a fraction of a second, and then came out with it. "He refuses to answer his door," I said. I felt so curiously relieved at having unburdened myself of that dreadful secret that on an impulse I told him more: "In fact, Heller, I haven't laid eyes on the Warden in months!"

The guard was stunned. But the next instant, to my astonishment, he laughed. "Why, then," he cried, "what makes you think he's there?" Almost merrily, he threw out his hands. I could hardly account for his look of joy. It was as if my revelation . . .

But I said firmly, "I hear him pacing."

"Impossible," he scoffed. "What does he eat? Does he sneak away for supplies in the dead of night?"

I had gone, of course, too far; I must now go all the way. "Believe what I say or not," I told him, bending toward him, my hands raised, fingers interlaced, to hide that infuriating tic, "but the Warden never leaves his room—at least not by the one door I know of."

He stared at me as if convinced I'd gone mad. At last he said, "How can you be sure?"

After a pitiful flicker of hesitation, I rose, keeping my face turned away, saying, "Come, I'll show you," and led him to the great studded door, showed him how firmly the door pressed down on the smooth oak sill, and directed his attention to the undisturbed dust. He studied it all with the fascination of a scientist. At last, with another queer shake of the head and that same odd smile, he said, "Apparently it's all up to us, then."

I was at the point of agreeing when I sensed something left unstated in his words. He glanced at me and saw my hesitation. He smiled, more lugubrious than usual, and shrugged. "The prisoner you met—the Professor—has passed away," he said.

I made no attempt to hide my embarrassment. "Poor devil," I said, and snatched off my spectacles and bit my lip. "I'm not surprised," I added, merely to be saying something. "It's a miracle he lasted so long."

Heller nodded.

As I turned back toward my chamber, he said gently, "We must give him a proper burial, sir. We must, so to speak, put his soul at rest. He belongs in the churchyard, where he would have gone, as a Christian citizen, if it weren't for this terrible judicial mistake."

I saw that he was serious. I might have laughed at the outlandish idea if I did not already owe so much to Heller—and if, moreover, I had not just now placed myself in his power by my ill-considered admissions. I said, at last: "Only the Warden can order such a thing."

He looked down, rubbed his mustache. "But it seems the Warden has abandoned us."

It brought me to my senses. "Not so!" I said. "Listen!" Catching his arm a trifle roughly, I led him back to the door and bent my head to it, indicating by a gesture that Heller do the same. For an instant, I heard nothing. Then, listening still more intently, I caught the faint, familiar sound of the Warden's footsteps pacing the carpet, louder as the Warden came near, then softening as he retreated to the further wall. "You hear?" I said.

He listened, neither convinced nor unconvinced. His ears, unfortunately, were considerably less acute than mine. After a time, he said, thoughtfully studying me, "I don't hear a thing." A flurry of panic swept through me, and I pressed my ear tighter to the door. But there was no mistaking it: He was there, still pacing. At times, as he'd done in the old days, he would pause—I remembered again the way he would stare, fierce with concentration—and then he would begin to pace again. "Take my word for it, Heller, he's in there," I said.

For a long moment he looked at me, absent-mindedly smoothing his beard. At last he accepted it, or seemed to. "Then we must rouse him," he said. Before I knew he would do it, he snatched up the lion's-head knocker and banged it on the iron plate with such force that it rang like a blacksmith's maul. I did nothing to check him, though I was sick with fear. Obviously, he had no memory of the Warden's wrath.

When he stopped, I bent, trembling all over, to listen at the door. The Warden had stopped pacing, but he did not come to us. The longer we waited, the greater my apprehension grew. Heller said: "You see? It's up to us." He smiled again, but his thoughts were far away, his long, thin hand still mechanically moving on his beard.

I agreed in haste and, catching his arm, virtually hurled him away from the door and back to my chambers. Almost unaware that I was doing it, I allowed myself once more to be guided by Heller. As soon as we were secure, I pushed the door shut behind us and locked it, then immediately crossed to the brandy closet, where I poured a glass for myself and one for Heller. When I'd taken a sip, which did not calm me, I turned to my conspirator. "What are we to do?" I whispered. It no longer mattered to me, in fact, that if we did as Heller wished we were throwing the ancient regulations to the winds. I had no more authority to grant a pardon than to flap my arms and fly. Indeed, formal pardon was out of the question. But we could perhaps entomb Heller's friend, if we were circumspect.

Heller sipped his brandy and ignored my agitation. "My people," he said, "have a long history of dealing with absurd situations. Leave everything to me."

"Gladly!" I said, and gave a laugh as hollow and despairing as Heller's own.

He sat stroking his bearded chin, looking up over his glasses at the shadows in the room's dim corners, as if reading there, in indefinite shapes, the outline of his plan. At length he said, "This evening a large parcel will be delivered to your cottage. From there it's only a stone's throw to the churchyard."

"Whatever you say," I said helplessly. I drank off the brandy and returned to the closet for more. My whole chamber rang, it seemed to me, with the sound of the Warden's footsteps.

"A· burial detail," my friend said then, with the same queer smile, "will meet at your gate after sunset."

The footsteps paused. I was sure he could hear every word we said.

"Good," I whispered. "I agree." We shook hands in haste, guiltily, and parted.

6

What anxiety I suffered, waiting in my cottage that evening! My family seemed determined to drive me mad—the children quarreling endlessly, my father more fantastic than I could remember ever having seen him. Shortly before sunset, I caught sight of the great black supply wagon coming from the prison to the village. I tried to show no particular interest as it lumbered down toward my gate, drawn by four gray horses ruled more by mindless habit than by the sleepy old peasant who held the reins. The wagon listed on its broken springs like a foundering ship, and with every pothole the wooden wheels struck (the road has been in shameful disrepair for years), I was sure the whole hulk would topple, and our secret come clattering out. I fixed my eyes on whatever tract I was pretending to read—my father had his fierce eyes fixed upon me—and I did not look up until the clumsy structure paused in front of my gate. The nearer horses nibbled at my tulip tree. The driver slept on. And then, as if of its own volition, the wagon started up again. I cleared my throat, closed my book as if casually, and ambled toward the door.

"Smells are strange things," my father said.

My heart leapt; but I was sure an old man could not smell, from this distance, the corpse that now lay, I knew, beside my gatepost. I strolled out onto the porch and down to the road. When I glanced past my shoulder I saw my father, my wife, and the children peering through the window. Perspiration poured down my inner arms. Heller would feel no such guilt, I was sure. I was determined that before this was over I would learn his secret.

When I reached the road (the sky was now red, and evening birds had begun to sing), I found an old, innocent-looking trunk, its clasps unnaturally gleaming in the decaying light. The stone wall beside the road and the long-dead climbing roses hid it from my family's view. I drew it into the shadow of the wall, holding my breath against the stench. I hastily covered it with branches and leaves, then hurried back up to the cottage. My father was sitting in the kitchen, tamping his pipe with a nail.

"It's a beautiful evening," I remarked as naturally as possible.

"It's a *good* evening," the old man said, pursing his lips and squinting at me, wicked eyes glittering.

My panic increased by the minute. I'd be a very

unsuccessful criminal! I remembered Josef Mallin's ungodly calm, the smile of scorn, the self-righteous conviction that was visible even on his decapitated head. Halfheartedly, I made conversation with my palely smiling, abstracted wife as she prepared our supper. She was later than usual, which alarmed me. If Heller's burial detail should arrive while we were still at table, I had no idea how I'd escape my family's watchfulness. Between dreary, absentminded remarks to my wife and father, I asked myself a thousand questions. Was I right to trust Heller to arrange the detail? Obviously I'd been out of my wits! It was a hundred to nothing that sooner or later one of the guards he'd persuaded to help would disclose what we'd done. But it was no use thinking about such things now. In my agitated state, I felt downright relief when my father turned, for no discernible reason, to the subject ordinarily more distressing to me than all others.

"I'll tell you what it is with Josef Mallin," he said. He drew in pipe smoke, savored it, and let it out again. I actually leaned forward, eager to hear him. "He's convinced all ideals are a flight from reality. The unpleasant facts of life, he claims, charge the human soul with longing. They drive a man to make up a world that's better than ours. But that better world is mere illusion, says Mallin; and illusion, being false, a mere cowardly lie, is as foul as actuality. So he goes at the universe with dynamite sticks. —It's a natural mistake." He leered, showing his crooked, gray teeth. His eyes came into me like nails.

"Well, he's paid for his mistake," I said too loudly.

My father nodded, presumably to keep peace. He lit another match, and held it over the cracked, black pipe bowl. He said, "The Warden, now, he *believes* in the mystical experience. But, unfortunately, he's never had one. He wastes his life anticipating. It's a terrible crime. A mortal sin, I judge."

"That's true," I said eagerly, senselessly. But it did not persuade the old man to babble on. He fell silent, as if everything were settled.

At just that moment, my wife announced supper. I went to the parlor to call in the children. They came at once, not from obedience, of course; from hunger. As I was about to follow, I glanced out, hardly thinking, toward the lane. They were there—Heller's burial detail! I could see nothing but their shapes, dark blocks against the gray of the road, standing motionless as tombstones, waiting. A curious feeling of calm came over me, a mingled indifference and determination that reminded me of Heller. Without a word to those expecting me for dinner, I stepped to the door, opened it, and went out.

7

My mind was curiously blank, as I climbed, with my walking stick, up the old stone lane toward the churchyard; and blank as I took my turn at the shovel. We would have been, to a passer-by, a curious sight. Of the dozen or more of us, only I myself was beardless, the rest of them shaggy with orthodoxy. Two of them at least must have been rabbis; they were not only bearded but wore tattered robes. No one spoke. They were a company born for undertakings, sad-eyed, stooped shouldered, all their faces the mirror images of a single expression: shrugging surprise and mild pleasure that they too were not dead. They worked in rhythm with one another, or stood harmoniously silent. It was as if they were performing a religious duty—though the churchyard was Christian and the man we were burying certainly no Jew. The night above us was immense, majestic. Except for the graveyard itself, all the grounds of the church were shrouded in darkness, shadowed by the interlocking limbs of chestnut trees and oaks. Above the open space of the graveyard, the full moon shone serene, mysterious. The grave was chest-deep when, panting heavily, sticky with sweat and slightly dizzy from my unusual exertion, I handed the spade to the old man seated in the grass above me and prepared to climb out for my period of rest. A hand reached down out of the group to help me; I accepted it. When I was free of the grave I recognized

Heller. "Thank you," I said. He said nothing. He led me to a crooked, low tombstone wide enough that both of us could sit on it. The old man who had taken my place shoveled steadily, his upper teeth closed on his bearded lower lip, three younger men standing above him, waiting their turns.

"He was a strange man," Heller said. I merely looked at him, too winded to comment. "He never ate," he said. He took a deep breath and looked up into the night. "It's amazing he lasted as long as he did."

I nodded, a trifle reluctantly, glanced over toward the grave-diggers.

Heller frowned, silent for a moment, then at last continued: "I think of something he used to say: 'In the inorganic life, pain cannot be; thus the necessity for the organic.' There's the secret of the man. He relished his pain because of, you know, his mysticism." He looked away from me, down at the grass, then sighed deeply and looked up at the moon again. "He hated life, you know, yet delighted in it, because of what its horrors would do for him later."

Something my father had said crossed my mind, flitting softly, like a bat at dusk, almost too swift for me to catch it.

"Perhaps he was guilty after all," I said.

Heller turned his face toward me.

I rose from the tombstone, less giddy now, though still short of breath, just perceptibly light-headed. He, too, rose. I walked, hands in pockets, down the aisle between graves. Neither of us spoke. At length, we came to the slope declining to the moonlit pool. The shadow of willow trees lay on the water, motionless, snatched out of time. We could hear the faint crunch of the spade behind us. On the opposite side of the pool the old stone church stood brooding, as patiently still as its reflection. Beyond the church, where the dark trees began, there was motionless fog. We stood for a long time saying nothing. At length, following some train of thought of his own, Heller said, "It was a terrible injustice."

I said nothing, watching the reflection of the church.

"He clung to his pain, but in the end he lost all sense of it. If there are angry ghosts, envious prowlers in the shadow of the living—" He stared across the pool, smiling thoughtfully, perhaps unaware that he was smiling. It was not, I saw, a matter of great importance to him. Merely another of life's ironies. I felt a queer irritation and found myself squeezing the handle of my cane. I calmed myself, listening to the rhythmical crunch of the spade.

"There's no such thing as a ghost," I said suddenly.

"I don't believe in them either," he said, "but I'm afraid of them."

I moved closer to the water, head bowed, musing. He followed. We looked at the dead-still reflection of the church. No one had used it regularly for years. Doors hung loose, some of the windows were broken. People who came to the graveyard would repair it, from time to time, for the sake of the dead or for those who were yet to be buried here, but the repairs were pitiful at best. A wired-up sash, a softwood patch where the door had been broken, a supporting stake to prop a sagging iron fence. Heller said: "Or is it the Mallins of the world who come back—the enemies of 'illusion'? Maybe the unexpected fact of their survival —maybe it makes them more furious than before at the particled world of sticks and stones, the obstruction blocking—"

"*No* one comes back," I said, and struck the ground with my stick.

He smiled, looking at the grass. "No doubt you're right. Not the Mallins, at any rate." He sat mechanically nodding. "How could a man like Josef Mallin live more intensely than he did?—boiling like a cauldron from the cradle to the grave!"

Nothing, it seemed, would drive him from the subject. Why it was important that we speak of other things, I could not say; but it was. I felt as I'd felt on the road, walking home from the prison that night— that any moment I might slip outside myself, become no one, everyone, the drifting universe.

"Enough of this," I said, and gave a false little laugh. "Heller, this is hardly the time or place—"

I let it trail off. I was thinking suddenly: *Which is more appalling, the crude stone church on land or the one upside-down in the pool?*

Heller touched my arm and tipped his head down to study me. "You're in earnest," he said.

"We're grown men," I said, and laughed again. "Talk of ghosts is for children."

He too laughed, watching me. His teeth, in the darkness, were misty white. "Come now, Herr Vortrab. Look at the fog in the trees, the glitter of stars in the windows of the church. Surely such stubborn realism does them an injustice!" But he paused, seeing my agitation. "Well—" he said. He turned his hands palms up, a harmless tailor once more.

Behind us, the crunch of the spade, old men's voices, the black hole awaiting the world's latest victim, persuading him to rest.

"What man can say what he really believes about these things?" Heller said lightly.

I felt unwell. I'm too old, too fat to be shoveling graves. My heartbeat was a little wrong somehow; my tongue was dry.

Heller said, downright merry now, "No one comes back, of course. You've convinced me, Herr Vortrab! Neither the unfeeling nor the hypersensitive, neither idiots—"

I touched his arm.

Everything was silent. The pool was so still the night itself seemed dead. The gravedigging was finished and Heller's burial detail stood across from us. I counted them. Eleven.

I gazed at the upside-down image of the church. Tangled vines crawled down toward the steeple and pushed against the windows. The still air was wintry, not as if cold had come but as if all warmth in the area had lost its vitality, decayed. I was aware of someone standing to my right, and I glanced over, casually. It was the Warden, standing with one hand in his pocket, the other cradling a revolver. He stood with one highly polished boot thrown forward. I saw, without alarm, that a part of his forehead was blasted away, as if by some violent explosion. He noticed my glance and nodded, severe, withdrawn—laboring despite some inner turmoil to be sociable. Dried blood from his wound lay over his left eye and cheek. "Good heavens," I said, with a quick, no doubt somewhat obsequious smile, and leaped back a step. I threw a look at Heller. When I turned to look back at the Warden, he was walking away, moving hurriedly around the rim of the pond in the direction of the church. Heller was touching his beard, looking over his spectacles at me.

"Impossible!" I whispered—probing, perhaps, to learn for certain whether Heller too had seen it.

But Heller had no answer, as silent as the eleven across from us, watching—all twelve of them watching: grim, moonlit jury.

"We're finished here," I said abruptly, my voice rather shrill in that midnight stillness. I pointed with the tip of my stick toward the gravemound.

Heller nodded, still not commenting. What was I to do?

Stiff-legged, ridiculous, my back still tingling, I led them past headstones to the iron gates and down the pitchdark lane to my cottage, where I left them with a crisp good-night and a click of my heels. No doubt they smiled at that later.

What was I to do? I too had my laugh. From the darkness of my parlor I peeked out at them, trudging down the road, the rabbis' skirts dragging, the younger men clinging to the elbows of the old.

That is how things stand with us. I no longer bother to deny that I am frightened, hopelessly baffled, but neither do I pretend to believe that sooner or later he will answer my knock. I need rest, a change of air, time to sort out my thoughts . . . but each day provides new calamities. . . .

We no longer go home nights; it wouldn't be safe to leave the prison in the hands of the guards we have now, except, of course, Heller.

A fool came to visit me, to sell me a book. It began, as I remember, *Modern thought has made considerable progress by reducing the existent to the series of appearances which manifest it. Its aim was to overcome*

*certain dualisms which have embarrassed philosophy,
and to replace them by the singleness of the phenom-
enon.* . . . I drove the man out with my walking stick.
Heller looked on with his cap in his hands, mournful
of eye but not altogether disapproving. He thinks I'm
mad, of course. Each new regulation I bring "from the
Warden," each new pardon or death sentence, increases
his despair. I understand his feelings. I do what I can
for him. "If Order has value, you and I are the only
hope!" I whisper. He nods, mechanically stroking his
beard.

I worry about him. Late at night, when he should
be asleep, I hear Heller pacing, occasionally pausing,
deep in thought.

JOHN NAPPER SAILING THROUGH THE UNIVERSE

1

My Joan drives slowly, as she always does after those drunken parties, clinging to the wheel with both small, blue-white hands, her jaw thrown forward. Her beauty in the darkness makes me faint: white cheekbones high as an Indian's, red copper hair, gray eyes. An apparition; an apprehension of weirdly lighted crypts in a mist-hung grove.

I stare through the windshield, through my clownish reflection, and though I've forgotten my behavior already, I am full of wrath, remorse. Ah, how I've made that poor girl suffer! Woe, woe! My reflected mouth twists. Then I smile (so does it), gloomier than ever, and pull down the brim of my old black hat till it meets with the collar of my overcoat. She'll forgive me. Poor Joan understands my plight, and hers; the plight of the universe. Lightless; mere shell of its former self. We've survived a good many trials together, my Joan and I, poor suffering artists (a composer, a poet). The years have made us like a couple of sly old outlaws, shriveled and testy, holed up in a cave. We dress in black.

The car lights myopically grope down the road, past old drunken telephone poles, dead barns.

Then we're home, the house and chickenhouse stark as tombstones under the zombie glow of the security light. She parks the car—hangs it up by one fender on the sagging fence—comes around to my side and helps me out, and we lean on each other across the lawn to the steps and up into the bone-white house, empty, too big for us two tonight, the children sleeping with friends in town. I suffer a black premonition of sad old age. Two husks in the doorway. Pictures of children, grandchildren. I play with the idea, walking stooped now, testing my lips in search of teeth.

"I b'lieve I'll go set in my chair, heh, good ole chair," I say to my love, old joy of my life, and wring my fingers.

"Come to bed," she says.

I give her a look. There's a time I'd have knocked her on her ear, but we've grown old. I obey. She pauses at the top of the stairs to catch her breath, one hand on the newel post, the other on her heart. (Tick tick. Ah, woe!) She was beautiful once. I watch her looking at the painting of our daughter. She glances back at me, a thought in her mind (she too, our Lucy, will grow womanly, beautiful; but time will blast her, her flesh will sag like an elderly dog's— they too have their flicker, their hour as art, like Snow White's stepmother, Cleopatra, Eve). She looks down, silent; a kind of snag in Time. At last we continue on our arduous way, come huffing and blowing to our room—cracked plaster—and, fumbling, helping each other as we must, we get ready for bed, take our teeth out. I'm ninety-two. The planet is dying —pestilence, famine, everlasting war. The nation's in the hands of child molesters.

She says in the darkness, "I miss John Napper."

I grunt, swimming back, unwinding time, and I

smile, foxy. I pat her hand. I have half a mind to get up and write letters, give all my enemies heart attacks. I am sober, as still as midnight, full of joy.

2

He was a huge old man, wild gray long hair and shabby clothes—clothes that transcended shabbiness, became a kind of magnificent mess, a flight of wild chickens and Chinese kites that filled the whole room, filled continents: the last and noblest argument for monarchy. He was full of joy, mad Irish. His pleasure in life was ridiculous, like a bear reeling home with a honey tree, and I, even I, was impressed by it. He had an absurdly beatific grin, even when the songs he sang were sad (he was a singing painter). When he sang of the death of Hiram Hubbard, grinning down like a snowcapped mountain at his steel guitar, he was Brahma himself, standing outside, behind, beyond, creating the world out of nothing, with luminous eyes. My banjo, above his calm, sang rackety glee.

"It must be hell to be his wife," I said, sitting in my corner, bloodshot, hunched. His admirers hadn't considered that. They looked startled, pursed their lips, troubled, and gloomily shook their heads like a roomful of crows.

But his wife was brave. She would smile absently, hearing him sing, or she'd help him find the lost pieces of the tape recorder when he wanted to tape the goats outside their bedroom window or the roar of a passing train. Day and night, through that year, they'd have visitors over—"Come anytime! Marvelous!"—sitting on the floor of their shell of an apartment, and John Napper would hold forth, wide-armed, beaming, on the general topic Everything, and his wife, Pauline, amused and sly, would hunt for the coffeepot cord he'd misplaced (for all his care) and would eventually work out a toggle for him. "Perfect!" he'd say, the soul of happiness. Happiness is stupid, dangerous; but there was some mysterious trick in his, some ingenious sleight of wits. I watched them, brooding, hatbrim over my eyes so they wouldn't suspect.

Sometimes, absurdly, the campus police would arrive at his sessions, hands on their nightsticks, sniffing for pot, ears cocked for time bombs, watching the bearded guests as they would tarantulas. John Napper's smile was so gleeful I could hardly believe, myself, that we were innocent. When they left he would say, "Incredible! Simply incredible!" He looked it. "Balance is everything," he'd whisper, and give us a wink.

I wrote in my notebook: *A tricky old man.*

I wrote:

> *When people with violently opposed opinions attack each other in John Napper's presence, he has two main ploys. One is to say, "Exactly, exactly!"—soberly, thoughtfully—to everything said on either side, until the people debating grow slightly confused; the other is to resolve the thing by an appeal to higher principle, for instance: "Welsh music and Irish music are both marvelous, both marvelous! But personally I hate Welsh music, and I love Irish music."*
>
> *Ridiculous or not, everybody shifts to the side of the Irish. It's a fact, however, that Welsh music is superior.*

I watched and waited. My sense of world sorrow, black-hearted rage, took increasing concentration. I'd go home from parties melancholy, half-convinced that all my poems were false, I'd misunderstood the universe.

"How happy they seem," my wife would say, leaning on her elbow, jaw thrown forward.

"Shut up," I'd say with a furtive glance upward, my hand on her knee. "I'm working on it."

His stint as visitor among us ended, and he went back to Paris, to his studio. He was replaced by a typical important artist—crafty, charged with familiar opinions. He scoffed at John Napper, couldn't play the guitar, and talked like a commoner of "masterpieces." I wrote the new man threatening letters signed Auber, or The Arrow, or *KKK*, tipped off the police on his sexual perversions, and avoided him. He was crazy. A German. As for myself, my writing turned darker. I could think in nothing but hexameters.

Joan stopped composing.

"I can't," she said. The children, supposed to be doing their homework, were hiding behind the couch, making flags.

"Write!" I told her. "I'm the wolf at the door." I clawed, made a horrible face. I meant it.

"No use," she said. "I've lost conviction."

"The planet's dying," I said, "the nation's in the hands—"

She turned to me, slowly, the way blind people turn, or cranes at dusk, at some whisper no one else hears. "Why can't we go visit the Nappers?"

"In Europe?" I howled. I banged the piano. "We're poor! Have you forgotten?"

"Poorer than you think," she said—smug, full of woe. The children peeked over the back of the couch.

I wrote grant applications, working down cellar by candlelight. I cackled. They were brilliant! They worked.

3

The only paintings of his that I'd seen were brochure reproductions, mostly black and white, for a show he'd had in New York while visiting America. Landscape with flowers, people with flowers, flowers with (barely visible) cats. I'd smiled, lugubrious (*memento mori*), and thought them pretty—decorative, tasteful, good at least in this: They were the work of a warm-hearted, gentle old man. For what that's worth.

When we reached his Paris studio, in a famous old house full of studios, La Ruche—dark, roundish house, octagonal, gloomy in its cavern of trees as the House of Usher, but tamed by dogs, kids, half-dead vines, here and there bits of sculpture and auto parts collected and abandoned by generations of Left Bank artists—the Nappers weren't home. They'd loaned the place to some friends and had gone off to England. We drank wine with the friends—a beaming American of twenty-two and a girl who was pretty, carefully considered, but invisible against the gray-white walls—and after a while, from out of the closet and under the bed we dragged some old John Napper paintings. They were a shock: dark, furious, intellectual, full of scorn and something suicidal. Mostly black, with struggles of light, losing. He'd been through all the movements, through all the tricks, and he thoroughly understood what he was doing—a third-generation master painter. Understood everything, it seemed to me, but why he kept fighting instead of slitting his wrists. No sense of the clownish in the universal sorrow. No sense of dressing up, putting on gray spats, for the funeral. I hadn't looked with sufficient attention at the pretty pictures of flowers in the New York brochure.

"Amazing, eh?" the American who was using the studio said. Looking helpless, innocent, maybe slightly alarmed, pulling at the ends of his big John Lennon mustache. A cartoonist. He had eyes like Orphan Annie. He played bass jug in a jug band back home, which was how he'd met John Napper.

I nodded, peeked out past the brim of my hat. Joan smiled, superior, looking over some mosaics by the wall. We drank some more wine and talked about Paris. There used to be two famous places like La Ruche. The other of the two was blown up in the riots, just after it was given to the Government. The friend had been told by the white-bearded sculptor who lived in the darkness downstairs with his dying wife.

When we arrived in London, I called up John. He invited us over. Third-floor apartment upstairs from a sensitive elderly lady who was, John assured us, "Marvelous! Marvelous!" We'd seen her peeking through the curtains at us. We went down to his second-floor

studio with our Scotch and tea—my Scotch, their tea
—and we looked at the picture he was working on
now; also some others, all of Pauline, that he'd recently finished. The new one was large—not enormous,
the size of the studio stopped him—but large; generous. A lady in flowers. You couldn't tell much. He'd
just roughed it out with thin, thin colors, almost
invisible. Crafty, eyeing him sideways, I mentioned
the paintings in his studio in Paris.

John Napper became still, towering above me in his
bare feet, big belly protruding, his hand—behind the
uplifted nose—radiating wild silver hair, Christ's head
(slightly mystical, cracked) in polished wire. He
smiled, a confirmed and satisfied maniac. "Amazing,
isn't it? I was mad!" His hands clapped. "Totally
mad!" He was ecstatic, awed, like an old-time pirate
reviewing, long after conversion, his shocking deeds.
I leered, sharp-eyed, and John Napper said, "But
that's nothing. Nothing!" He made a dive, a terrifying
swoop, at a huge stack of old canvases and photographs under the table where he kept his brushes. He
started sorting them, scattering the things into, loosely,
piles. Joan and our children—Lucy and Joel—and
John's wife, Pauline, went after the ones that drifted
away to the corners of the room, the fire-bright patches
of light by the windows. He showed us his history—
what survived of it. He'd lost more work than most
artists do: a random bomb on an English house; a
musty, dark cellar in a French gallery, once a Nazi
torture chamber, where mold and murderous ghosts
ate the paint. (John Napper's view.) When he'd sorted
out what he wanted us to see, we looked, heads touching, at the Napper retrospective. Ghoulish faces, fuliginous lump-people, terrible previews of Hiroshima,
mournful cityscapes the texture of, roughly, dried
blood. Here and there, there was a scraggly flower, a
crushed bit of light. "Amazing!" he kept saying. Joan
smiled, moved away with Pauline, talking.

He had, among other things, some portraits. At one
time portraits had kept him alive. One was a commission portrait of the Queen—Elizabeth II. Idealized.
"The critics all said I should be hanged," he said.

"They wanted her dumpy." He grinned, eyes bright as cornflowers. "They love her exactly as she is," he said. The grin turned into a laugh, pure joy at the ridiculous goodness, deep down, of patriotic critics. He said:

> *"Lecteur paisible et bucolique,*
> *Sobre et naïf homme de bien,*
> *Jette ce livre saturnien . . ."*

Lucy said, "John, will you draw my picture?"

He looked thoughtful, half-imp, half-grandfather. "How much can you afford, Lucy?"

She thought about it, an eight-year-old not indifferent to money. She got out her purse and counted. She said: "Seven pennies." Sly. She pushed back her hair; her mother's gesture.

John Napper beamed, eyes brilliant and wicked. The sly shall inherit the earth. "Perfect."

Joel watched, envious, and made his face a mask.

We agreed to meet at the Wallace Collection, where John could introduce Joel to the armor and, after that, sketch Lucy. Then Pauline, my wife, Joan, and the kids went upstairs to the living quarters, to look at Pauline's mosaics. (Gloomy things, as mosaics go. The things from her youth were bright, full of warmth.) I hung around John's studio looking at the photographs. The morose early paintings, deadly intellectual, furious; the realistic portraits, expert, professional. Neither kind was, I thought, great art, though they were obviously good. There was something I felt myself at the edge of (peering like a raven, round back hunched). It had to do with light. Beyond—deeper than—all the technical facility, all the spearheading or riding of movements, there was something obsessive, obscurely frightening, in the light.

"Isn't it amazing!" he said happily, as if all that were a thousand years ago.

I nodded, glanced away. Smoky, dead yellow sunlight came in, pushing down from a slate-gray sky past the chimney-loaded houses west of the studio. It crept toward the paintings as if drawn in by them, like Grendel.

4

We met at the Wallace, and John showed us the armor. He stood huge and wild-headed, an enormous bird with diamond eyes, his sportcoat tattered like an anarchist's. He pointed out the ornamentation on swords and pistols, so finely wrought that it might have been carved by intelligent spiders. Sometimes he'd bend over, bringing his huge beak an inch from the glass, like a nearsighted eagle in front of a mirror, his eyes screwing up like a jeweler's, and he'd say, "Exactly!" Not to us. "It's marvelous, the work of human hands! Do you realize the people who wore this equipment—all those glorious heroes—are dead, all vanished!" He laughed, pure joy, examining his hand. It was long and powerful, lighter than a wing. The armor stared at us, faceless—abandoned husks, old crusts of creatures. We noted the Christian solemnity of German artists, the change in the English when they'd once seen the work of India. We smiled, paternal, at the clever French. He kept glancing at the window, and at some point, for reasons of his own, he said, "Good. Exactly!" and snatched Lucy's hand and walked with her, smiling and bowing like a courtier leading a princess—but hurrying, subtly; gently and firmly propelling her down the long hall counterpaned with slanting light and out to the courtyard, the fountain, where he meant to do the sketch. He seated her on a bench in the shade and sat down cross-legged on the ground with his pad and pencils— he, too, was in the shade, wild-haired, the fountain in sunlight—and started. He got Joel to tell him a long, made-up story ("Something about castles and princesses," John said, and Joel obliged). He listened to the story as if with total concentration as he drew. Then he finished, shot a glance at the sky, and said, "It's going to work," and smiled—something cunning in the smile, as if, by an old and ingenious trick, he'd outwitted a dangerous enemy.

We left the place, John subtly hurrying, propelling us, and caught a taxi. John dropped us off at our hotel and hurried home.

He came back that night to our hotel, rags flying, his hair eloquently insane, face jubilant with light. He'd brought his guitar. I got out my banjo and we went down together to the hotel pub—a splendid place. The hotel was the house where Edward VII kept Lillie Langtry—a place full of hand-carved balconies, rooms with paintings on the ceilings (old rapes and wars), marble-topped tables, sculptures of centaurs, malevolent cherubs, a dying stag. What was now the pub was her private theater, complete (still complete) with her royal lover's box—appropriately gloomy, set back from the lamps. (The whole pub was gloomy, or all but the frosted-glass mirror, indecipherable swirls.) John Napper had been there to parties before the house turned hotel—the Inverness Court. It was run now by Irishmen—grinning young bellboys, Lucy's friends; bossy colleens at the main desk and back in the dining rooms; a manager built like a pigeon, with curly black hair. We sat at a table on what used to be the stage—the bar girl turned off the television, some American thriller—and we played as we'd done in John's apartment in southern Illinois. The manager bought us drinks and sang. Obscene or sweetly plaintive ditties on love and death. "Lovely," John kept saying. My glasses were misted over with tears. Soon the pub was packed with Irishmen, singing in the darkness, playing tin whistles. I sang a dirge or two in Welsh, old mining disasters, modal hymns from the bottom of the sea. The Irish were polite. John sang the rare old American song he'd picked up on his visit. "Hiram Hubbard." His voice got quieter and quieter as he approached the end, the execution. "And his body shrank away." The Irishmen wept. Someone mentioned Belfast. The police were shooting people now. After that we played some more, but the Irish didn't sing. Laughed; threw well-turned phrases like darts. It was late, 2:00 A.M., and our singing was illegal. The Irish began leaving, a few at a time, and my Joan took our sleeping children up to bed. The colleen at the desk was astonished, furious. We had a last beer, John Napper smiling, gazing down at the table top, not talking except to say now and then, "Amazing." I went to the door with him and watched him walk away, majestic old giant in his flowing tatters, to hunt down one of those big black hearselike taxis. At the Bayswater corner he turned and waved his huge guitar case, gray hair bright as the sunlight coming through whitecaps in a dream, and then he disappeared into the blackness beyond the lamp.

5

I was working on an epic poem, the Jason story. A ridiculous project, but you write what the spirit tells you to, whether the spirit's responsible or not. I decided to drop by John Napper's with it. I knew that when he paints he listens to music, the radio, anything at all to distract him.

He was ecstatic, enthralled—too enthralled to be read to. "An epic!" he said. "Marvelous!" We debated how long it had been since the last one. He told me stories from the Táin Bó Cúailnge, the Ramayana, the Mabinogion. He told me how Punch, as in Punch and Judy, came down from Shiva, the god of destruction —from Indian *pansh,* meaning "five," the five senses. Around noon a former student came, a girl he'd taught in Paris. She pawed excitedly through his old and new paintings and told him excitedly all about her life. He was radiant, listening. He asked her about people they knew, the divorced and the dead, and we all drank tea, wine, Scotch (I the Scotch). He told her, with a crazily majestic gesture, that I was writing an epic—the first in a thousand years! She was thrilled. "You must hear it!" he said.

She looked alarmed. "How long is it?"

"How long is it, John?"

"Long," I said.

"Marvelous!" he said. He bent double, clapping. "*Marvelous!*"

The girl looked excited, quite honestly excited, it seemed to me, but it was midafternoon, there wasn't time.

"Hear just a little," he said.

But then someone else came—the American he'd loaned his studio to in Paris. The boy stood grinning, pulling his mustache. John Napper leaped to the door and hugged him, then saw the small, shadowy wife in the doorway behind her husband (she's been sick, it had made her prettier), and he hugged her, too. They shone like angels. "Pauline!" he called up the stairs, "you'll never believe this! Come down!" He made them stand out of sight so that when she came she'd be surprised. Pauline threw up her hands, head tilted —gesture from a Chinese dance—and smiled.

I went back the next day, and this time I managed to read to him. He was delighted, painting quickly, thoughtfully, his bare feet long as shovels. He talked, when I finished, about Holman Hunt, how the music of the Beatles was exactly the same; he talked about Picasso, the pompous old ass, how his work reminded him of Franklin D. Roosevelt's Victory Speech. I was tingling with excitement, not all from the Scotch. My gaze wandered over his paintings as I listened. The gloomy, suicidal old ones, the big bright new ones, among them the painting of Lucy just now taking shape on the easel—Lucy among flowers. A chill went through me.

On the wall there was a huge, dark seascape. A transitional work in the Napper career. It had Turner things in it—illusions of movement, sultriness, light seen through cloud, the faintest suggestion of a ship, small in an enormous sea and sky. The ship was in trouble. The universe was churning. Turner, I remembered John's telling me once, had two different lives, two different wives: He was Captain Something in one of them, a man of the sea; he was Dickens' model for the character Scrooge, though in fact a secret philanthropist.

In the pretty flowers, the pretty face, my daughter's eyes were calculating.

He said, that evening, "I love it that the Celtic god of poetry is a pig." He wrinkled his nose on the word *pig* and magnificently became one.

"Pigs understand what the wind says," I said.

He smiled, delighted. "Yes, so they *can!*" We knew the same old songs. "But that's not what I love about it. Artists truly *are* pigs. *That's* what I love! When I was young—" He wrinkled his nose again, unspeakably, divinely revolted by his youth. "That's my chief pleasure in growing old. One can work with fewer and fewer periods of swinishness, rooting and rutting." He reveled.

I poured more Scotch from the bottle he'd bought. For me he'd bought it. John Napper never drank at all when he was working—and very little at other times. Not even much beer, by Irish standards. I was making up for his sobriety today. ((Balance is everything.) I looked at the big picture by the wall, the new painting, Pauline among flowers. It was good, no picture a young man could do. It was full of planes, not the changing depths of perspective but something else. Figure seated against tree on hillside, flowers everywhere; birds, lights, shadows. She gazes—strangely like the seated figure in an Egyptian tomb—toward a valley, a sudden openness, a kind of gasp in space, dark and in some unliteral way mysterious. Everything in the picture, every dart of light, moves, grows, corrupts before your eyes. The figure even breathes: an optical illusion from the paisley of her dress. And at the center of all that joyful movement that shadows away toward not quite joyful—the face hangs perfectly motionless, holy.

"I understand you," I said, and smiled.

He smiled back, waiting.

Poetically drunk, I understood all sorts of things. He'd gone to the pit, in those Paris paintings, fighting for his life, squeezing the blood from this turnip of a world to hunt out the secret life in it, and there was none there. He'd hounded light—not just visual light—straining every muscle of body and mind to get

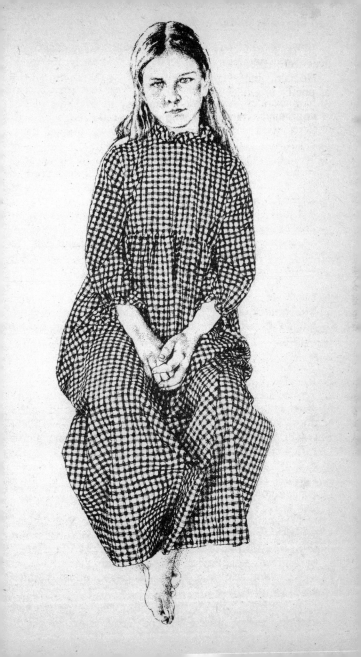

down to what was real, what was absolute; beauty not as someone else had seen it but beauty he could honestly find himself, and what he'd gotten was a picture of the coal pocket. His wife had seen it too. Her mosaics went dark, as morose as anything of his, and maybe more so. And then, at the edge of self-destruction, John Napper had, I saw, jumped back. He would make up the world from scratch: Let there be light, a splendid garden. He would fabricate treasure maps. And he'd come to believe it. How could he not, seeing how it lighted his sad wife's eyes? It was majestic! Also nonsense.

I told him all this and he beamed, wicked—a mirror image, it seemed to me, of me. "Exactly! Exactly!"

Pauline called down to us, to ask if I could stay to supper. I told her I was meeting Joan at a restaurant —she'd been working all day on a thing for flutes— and when I looked at my watch I saw I was half an hour late already. I got up, fell down, got up again, the room spinning out like Einstein's planets, and I hunted for my old black coat. John Napper looked alarmed. "I'll come with you," he said. Pauline was at the door. I found my coat and fumbled into it— also my lugubrious old black hat. They talked. "Wait, John!" John Napper called. "We're coming with you. We insist!" They were glorious with joy. It was the finest idea they'd had in years. Pauline hovered at the door, so tall it was awesome, her hands tentatively reaching in case I should stumble again. She stood with her head tipped, smiling widely, like that figure in those ancient Indian carvings: maiden kicking tree. Fertility symbol. She had fiery wings. John was down on his hands and knees, hunting in the corner for his shoes. He snapped his fingers, got up and went past me. Then they were dressed, Pauline elegant, towering to heaven, John in a black suit, blazing white shirt—neater, more dignified than Edward VII, majestic as Jesus Our Savior returning triumphant.

We went to find a taxi. We talked about Mahler and metaphysics.

When we got to the restaurant, Joan had eaten. She looked beautiful and outraged, red hair falling down her dark blue dress like swirling fire. "You look beautiful!" I said. *"Pig!"* she said. I winked at John. "Marvelous!" he said, and launched a tale. I got, despite Joan's frown, a drink. Before long—I'm not sure how it happened—someone picked a fight with me. About Samuel Beckett, if I remember. Joan fled, weeping. Pauline flew out into the street behind her.

And then I was alone with John Napper in a taxi, square black chariot in desperate flight. "Damned ridiculous Welshman!" he said. His hair was like a halo. His nose was the whole Platonic idea of royalty. "Did I win?" I said. My lip was bleeding. "You were marvelous! Marvelous!" John Napper tipped back his head and laughed. I shook my head, hunched up in the darkness as if I were waiting out a mine shaft cave-in. "You're crazy," I said affectionately. "Always see the best in everything."

"But it's *there,*" he said, as if it were the most obvious fact in the world. "It's wonderful to fight it, be blind to it. I admire that! But a man gets old, you know—loses his piggish stubbornness. . . . Ah, to be young again! Violent!" He looked young, violent.

"You're crazy," I said.

"Exactly!" he said. He leaned forward, towering above me in the seat, Chelsea running by like a dream outside the taxi window (Turner had two different lives, two different wives: He was Captain Something in one of them, a man of the sea; he was Dickens' model for the character Scrooge, though in fact a secret philanthropist).

"Exactly," he said.

"Exactly!" he whispered, his wide eyes glittering, his smile thrown forward in the darkness like a spear.

Lucy bought the painting for seven pennies. Not American pennies. The darker, more formidable English kind, the kind you lay on dead men's eyes to prevent their gazing back.

Book Two

TALES OF
QUEEN LOUISA

QUEEN LOUISA

1

Mad Queen Louisa awakened feeling worried and irritable. That was by no means unusual for her. It had been happening since she was a little girl, or, as she sometimes clearly remembered, a lizard. She fanned herself with the fingers of one hand, anxiously searching, as she always did for the first few minutes, for the deeply buried secret of her soul's unrest. She was not afraid of rape or poverty or death. She'd established these facts beyond a shadow of a doubt many years ago—she'd long since forgotten precisely how, but one cannot keep plowing the same old ground. As for lesser fears, suffice it to say that she'd read all the books in the royal palace—not only those in Slavonic and Latin, but those in German and French as well, and one in English, sometimes reading in her character as queen, sometimes as a huge and sleepy-eyed toad in spectacles—and she'd systemati-

cally crossed off all possible causes of distress from
anorexy to zygomatic fever. Despite that, she always
woke up worried and irritable. Her solution, which
was simple and brilliantly effective, once she was
awake to remember it, was to find little nothings to
attach her deep, vague worry to. The lady-in-waiting
seemed peaked, out of sorts; some trouble with her
husband? Or the castle's north wall had moss on it.
Do moss roots run deep? Could they loosen the
stones?

She opened the curtains of her huge gold bed. (The
king always slept alone these days. He said it was the
wars. Had he taken some mistress?) Already the chamber was alive with light—the chambermaid always
threw the windows wide open at six o'clock. Orderly
details make orderly days, Queen Louisa believed.
Also, toads like the early morning damp. Every surface, every plane or flange or lozenge of the furniture
gleamed, almost sang, with light. The combs and
brushes on her dressing table were so bright she had
to blink.

Carefully, she slipped her toes into the cold, then
her shins and knees. The floor, when she reached it,
was deliciously icy. She'd catch her death of pneu-
monia, she realized, and hurriedly felt left and right
for her slippers.

The door flew open, and the chambermaid rushed
in. She was supposed to be here when the queen
awakened. Queen Louisa felt a catch and thoughtfully
narrowed her large and luminous (she knew) eyes.
What had the chambermaid been up to? she wondered.
The girl looked flushed. She was fourteen, no older.
She looked—the queen touched her bosom in alarm
—she looked pregnant!

At Queen Louisa's moan, the child rushed to her
and seized her hands.

"Are you ill, your majesty?" On her cheeks, two
bright roses. Her eyes were gray.

"*I'm* well enough," the queen said very cautiously.
Her mind raced over whom it might be. Not the page,
certainly. He was fat as a pig and reeked of old cider.
She did hope not one of those trumpet players! It

couldn't be one of the knights, of course, because of the wars—unless perhaps one of the wounded ones. Her mind fixed with horrible and vaguely pleasurable fascination on the thought of the chambermaid creeping to the infirmary, slipping into bed with some great gored creature with a six-month beard. She secretly whispered a prayer to protect her from salacious thoughts.

"I just stepped out for a minute, your majesty," the chambermaid said.

Queen Louisa was sick with worry now. Perhaps it was no one from the castle at all. Perhaps the girl's father, some peasant from the village.

"Help me with my dressing-gown," the queen said weakly.

"Of course, your majesty!" She bowed very low and went pale for an instant. A sign of pregnancy if ever there was one! But the queen said nothing. Mad she might be—so everyone maintained, though they did not seem so all right themselves, in her opinion—but she was not a person who poked into other people's business. A little cry escaped her. The lady-in-waiting who'd been fighting with her husband should be here now too. Was she off with the great dog, the chambermaid's father? The girl was studying her, alarmed by the cry. Queen Louisa smiled gently, and the girl was reassured. Queen Louisa extended her arms for the golden sleeves.

"Is his majesty at breakfast?" Queen Louisa asked. It was important to keep one's servants at ease, keep their minds occupied.

"He left in the middle of the night, my lady. The wars, you know." The child's voice sounded so apologetic you'd have thought the wars were all her fault.

"Well, no matter, my dear," Queen Louisa said. "I'm sure we'll manage."

"I do *hope* so, your majesty!"

Queen Louisa froze. There was no mistaking the distress in the voice of her chambermaid. It was something beyond any personal distress. (Mad Queen Louisa had a sense about these things.) She moved toward her gold and ivory mirror, lacing up the front of her dressing gown. Very casually, she said, "Is something wrong, my dear?"

Suddenly, touched off by the tender concern in her majesty's voice, the chambermaid burst into tears. "Oh, my lady, my lady, how dare I reveal it?"

Queen Louisa frowned, profoundly worried, then hurriedly smiled, for fear she might shake the child's foundations, and lightly patted the chambermaid's hand. "Tell me everything," she said, "and Queen Louisa will fix it."

The child required no further encouragement. Clinging to her majesty's hand, she said, "A witch has appeared on the mountain and put all the hermits to flight. The peasants are so frightened they can hardly speak for shuddering. What are we to do? Oh, your majesty, your majesty! The king and his knights are a hundred miles away!"

Queen Louisa sighed but refused to tremble. She put her arm gently around the poor girl and sadly gazed into the mirror. Her great heavy-lidded eyes gazed back at her, and her wide, sad toad's mouth. The golden dressing-gown clung tightly to her thick, rough, swampgreen torso, though the sleeves were loose and a little too long. "Never mind," she said. "Queen Louisa will fix it." And she would. No question. All the same, it was inconsiderate and irrational of the king to leave his kingdom in the hands of a queen who was insane. Fleetingly, she wondered who his mistress might be. *Not* her own lady-in-waiting, surely! But the moment the thought occurred to her, she was certain she was right. (These hunches of hers were infallible.) —But if so, then his majesty was the chambermaid's fat peasant father, who was sleeping with the lady-in-waiting because of her troubles with her husband; and the peasant's child, that is, the king's, her little chambermaid, could be only—her own lost daughter! Queen Louisa smiled, feeling wildly happy, but said nothing for the moment, biding her time. She felt warm all over, and strangely majestic. She was soon to be a grandmother.

2

"The Court is now in session," Queen Louisa said.

The judges looked befuddled and a trifle annoyed, which she could well understand. But the facts were simple, and nothing makes a trial run more smoothly than simple facts. It was not, of course, the business of royalty to explain itself to mere judges of the realm. ("Never complain, never explain" was Queen Louisa's motto.) And the facts were these: that the king and his knights were all far away, except for the knights in the infirmary, and there was no one at home to deal with the troubles but the Royal Court. Therefore Queen Louisa had assembled the Court.

The chief justice looked over the tops of his spectacles, holding his wig away with the back of the fingers of his hand, partly for the sake of seeing better, partly for the sake of hearing. He looked from the empty defendant's chair to the empty benches where the various lawyers and their witnesses should be. It was a tense moment, and the chambermaid glanced in alarm at the queen. The lower justices, one on each side of the chief justice, pretended to study their copious notes and copy them over more legibly, though the queen suspected they had nothing written down in the first place. Queen Louisa could easily forgive them, however. Indeed, she'd have done the same herself. Surely they'd never encountered a case quite like this before.

Timidly, but with a hint of irritation, the chief justice said, "Where is the defendant?"

The lower justices smiled as they always smiled at every question he asked, as if saying to themselves, "Very shrewdly put!" Their smiles emboldened him to ask it again, even letting out a little smile himself: "*Your majesty, where is the defendant?*"

Queen Louisa smiled too, though she pitied them, really: dependent as children, hopelessly shackled in rules and procedures, wholly unprepared for the rich and strange. In their long white wigs they looked like sheep. In fact, when she saw how they held their pencils—poked between their pointed hooves—she became half-convinced that they *were* sheep. With the greatest possible dignity—to set a good example for the chambermaid, since a kingdom where the honor of courts is forgotten is a kingdom in trouble, and also because sheep are people, too, whose feelings can be hurt—but mainly because she had a vague suspicion that only by speaking with the greatest possible dignity could she prevent her words from seeming ridiculous, even to a sheep—Queen Louisa said: "You ask me where the defendant is. *That,* my lord justices"—she paused dramatically—"I leave to the wisdom of this Court."

They looked at each other, and the chief of the justices paled a little and glanced at the clock. Again he peered down at the empty benches where the defendant, witnesses, and lawyers should be. He cleaned his spectacles. "Your majesty," he said at last, like a creature completely baffled . . . but he let his words trail off.

Queen Louisa said nothing, merely patted the chambermaid's knee to show that all was well. The child, of course, never having been in a court before, had no idea how long these things took. She too kept glancing anxiously at the clock, wringing her hands, and pulling at her kerchief till it was so twisted around one could hardly see her face.

Meekly, the justices began to make guesses. "Is the defendant somewhere else?" asked the one on the left.

Queen Louisa pursed her lips and thought. "You're warm," she said at last. She exchanged winks with the chambermaid.

"Somewhere outside the castle?" asked the one on the right.

"Warmer!" said the queen, and squeezed her hands together.

"He's having his coffee!" the chief justice cried.

"Cold," snapped the queen.

"Poor devil!" they moaned. They had no real understanding of trials, she saw, or else they weren't really trying.

"In my opinion," the chambermaid whispered, "this Court's getting *nowhere*."

"Trials are like that, my dear," said Queen Louisa. "But if you insist, I'll give their honors a hint."

"Would you?" begged the girl.

Queen Louisa rose and extended her long-sleeved arms for silence. "My lord justices," she said, "let me give you a hint."

They accepted eagerly, all three of them waiting with their pencils poised.

"Our business, I think you'll agree," said the queen, "is justice."

The justices furtively glanced at each other, as self-conscious and timid as newts. For no clear reason, she was suddenly filled with a profound sadness. Still the justices waited, hoping for something more and scratching their foreheads with their chewed-down eraser ends. ("Justice," the chief justice kept mumbling, picking at his lip. He wrote down: "Just Ice?")

Queen Louisa continued, watching them carefully for a sign they'd got it: "You've perhaps heard that our hermits have been frightened from the mountain by an alleged witch." She paused, startled, rather pleased that she'd thought to say *alleged*. It was the first real clue. The witch was perhaps in fact *not* a witch, in which case, of course, the whole trial . . . She glanced suspiciously at the chambermaid, then remembered, in confusion, that the child was her daughter. The child glanced suspiciously back at her. But still the judges' faces were blank. Queen Louisa sighed and worried that she might be spoiling everything by revealing too much. She continued, however: "Since the king and his knights are all away, it seems to me our bounden duty to investigate this matter. I therefore suggest that we ride to the mountain and investigate."

"Hear, hear!" the judges cried wildly, all three of them at once, and glanced at each other.

That must have been the answer (though Queen Louisa had to admit she'd gotten lost somewhere), because the poor little chambermaid was trembling all over and clapping her hands and weeping.

3

There was some difficulty with the queen's horse. In the end, they all rode in the royal carriage. The chambermaid huddled in the shadow of the queen, contributing nothing to the conversation, no doubt partly because, sitting with the queen, she was wedged in tight.

"I was born of simple, honest stock," the queen narrated. The chambermaid looked up at her eagerly, from the seat beside her. Outside, the landscape was glittering white. On the castle wall, now far in the distance, the gored knights from the infirmary were all waving colored banners and shouting. The three old sheep sat leaning far forward, for Queen Louisa was speaking very softly, harkening back. All three had their thin hooves folded on their knees and their bowlers in their laps, for the ceiling of the carriage was strangely low. She was reminded, and spoke of, the ceiling of the cottage at the edge of the forest where her parents lived. (She sat with her knees pulled tightly together, despite cramp and discomfort, but even so she could give no more room to the chambermaid. As she spoke, Queen Louisa kept her hands carefully in front of her great green wattles, merely as a kindness to the others. Personally, she rather enjoyed her appearance. "A queen with a *difference,*" she liked to say, winking coyly.)

"It was a marriage no one believed would work. Mother was Irish, and Father was a dragon. Except for a very few dear friends, they were cut off by both communities. But the cruelty of people who had supposedly loved them served only to intensify their love and deep respect for one another. I was the youngest of the children, of whom there were sometimes seven and sometimes four, depending."

"Depending on what?" the chief justice broke in,

not at all urgently—in fact tears were streaming from his large, pink eyes.

"Depending on our parents," Queen Louisa explained, and realized now for perhaps the first time how profoundly true that was. "We were poor but extremely proud, you see. —Of course it was difficult for Father to get work." She remembered with a pang how he'd sit by the fireplace pretending to read the evening paper, though in fact, as everyone in the family knew, it was a paper from last year. A tear ran down the side of Queen Louisa's nose. "It was difficult," she said once more—merely to find her place again— "for Father to get work."

"It would be, yes," said the sheep on the left, "being married to a Catholic."

Queen Louisa brightened. "But poor as we were, we had each other!"

"Perhaps that's why sometimes there were only four," the chief justice said.

She had a curious feeling, which she couldn't in the least explain to herself, that the conversation was losing direction. She decided to leap forward. "When I was nine, there was a fire in the old wooden church in the nearby village. Naturally, Father was blamed for it." She paused, frowning, though she was secretly flattered. "Excuse me," she said to the chief justice, "are you writing all this down?"

He looked up, startled, still weeping profusely, then immediately blushed. He held the paper toward her, on which he'd been writing, in large block letters, with the greatest imaginable concentration. The paper said: JUSTICE ST. JUICE CUTE JEST [crossed off] SUITE SITE TIE IS US USE

Queen Louisa mused, the chambermaid peeking around past her elbow. "IST!" Queen Louisa said suddenly in German.

"TU ES," cried the chambermaid in French.

"JE SUIS," cried the sheep on the left.

They merely looked at him.

Queen Louisa sighed. "Well," she said, "they took Father away. I remember his parting words to us. He was a poet at heart, I've always felt. It was a wintry morning very like this one." She gazed sadly out the window. "He gazed sadly out the window, a policeman standing at each side of him—he had only his old singed overcoat on, and I remember the tears were coursing down his cheeks—and he said:

> "*'My loves, do not blame the authorities for this.
>   Who can swear
>   that his own apprehension of reality is valid? There
>   are certain insects—
>   I forget which ones—that have no apparatus
>   for determining
>   that other insects of their own same kind exist.
>   Such is
>   our lot. Have faith! Love even those who bring
>   sorrow to you!'*"

"Hexameters—loosely," the chief justice said.
She looked at him with new respect.

There, unfortunately, she was forced to discontinue her narrative. They'd arrived at their destination.

4

The monastery gates were open wide. Queen Louisa discovered, descending from the carriage and keeping the chambermaid's hand in hers to give the poor child courage, that in the monastery yard there was no one at all, not even a footprint in the snow to suggest that possibly someone had been there, or at least someone's shoe. She tiptoed softly to the monastery door, leading the child, and the three old sheep came audiculously behind her, huddled close together and holding their bowlers on with both hands, as people would do in a windstorm. There was, of course, not a breath of wind, but logic was not their strong point (she thought fondly) and, also, the bowlers were new. The inside of the monastery was also empty. She tried the back door.

"I'm frightened," said the chambermaid.

"Call me Mother, if you like," Queen Louisa said.

The chambermaid looked at her, then looked away, sucked in her lower lip, and seemed to think about it.

Queen Louisa laughed gently. "You young people!" she said.

In the snowy back garden they encountered a truly amazing sight.

The garden's stone walls were encased in ice, as was every tree and shrub and leftover flower stalk. But in the center of the garden there was a glorious rosebush in triumphant bloom, such bloom as would hardly be natural on even the warmest summer day. And beside the bush there was a horrible ugly old witchlike person who was trying to cut down the rosebush with an axe. With every swipe she took, the trunk of the bush grew wider and stronger, and the roses bloomed more brightly. At the feet of the ugly witchlike person, an old red hound lay whimpering and whining.

Queen Louisa stared in astonishment, believing for an instant that her whole life had been a terrible mistake. But somehow or other she collected her wits and called out in a stern and commanding voice, "Stop!" —for she was capable of such things, if driven too far.

At once both the witchlike person and the dog looked up at her. For an instant the witchlike person was thrown, but only for an instant. "Never!" she cried, her lean lips trembling and her eyes so ferociously green with evil that Queen Louisa was fearful that the chambermaid might faint. Immediately the witchlike person began swinging the axe like someone in a drunken rage, and the old dog whimpered and whined in such awful and unspeakable misery that even the Royal Court was moved to tears. The rosebush, of course, grew stronger by leaps and bounds.

"Stop her! Do something!" the chambermaid hissed, clinging to Queen Louisa with trembling hands.

But Queen Louisa thoughtfully narrowed her eyes, pursed her lips, and calmed the chambermaid by patting her hand. "Be quiet, Muriel," she said very softly. "I don't think we've quite understood this situation."

"Muriel?" said the chambermaid.

"My dear," said Queen Louisa in a stern but not

unfriendly voice, signifying by a look that she was addressing the person swinging the axe, "every stroke you strike makes the rosebush stronger."

"Good point!" said the judges, frantically searching through their trouser pockets for their notebooks.

"Get away! Be gone!" said the witchlike person.

Queen Louisa smiled. She said, "Dog, come here."

With an awful groan, the old red hound got up and came timidly toward her. It settled at her feet and closed its eyes like a creature enormously embarrassed.

"Muriel," Queen Louisa said out of the side of her mouth, "meet your ridiculous father."

The chambermaid looked at the dog, touching her chin with three fingers. "How do you do," she said at last.

The witchlike person was perspiring now. Her black robe clung to her armpits and back, and her nose and chin (which were as blue and as pointed as icicles) dripped. She stopped swinging and leaned on her axe, panting. "I'm not beaten," she whispered.

Immediately, as if at a signal, a hundred wolves in the robes of pious monks came bounding over the garden wall and crouched, growling, with their ghastly fangs bared, in a semicircle around Queen Louisa and her friends.

The witchlike person laughed. "You see, my ancient enemy," she cried, "your whole life has been a terrible mistake! The forces of evil do exist! Ha ha!" Words cannot describe the unearthly horror of that final "Ha ha!" She raised the axe in one hand and brandished it. "We're cosmic accidents!" cried the witchlike person. "Life is gratuitous, it has no meaning till we make one up by our intensity. That is why these gentle monks have joined me in seeking to wreak havoc on the kingdom. Not for personal gain. Ha ha! Ha ha! But to end the boredom! To end all those mornings of waking up vaguely irritable! Ha ha!" She sidled toward the queen. "I have seduced your husband. What do you think of that? I have filled him with the feeling that life *is* meaningful, if only because it can be thrown away. I have—"

Suddenly Queen Louisa heard, behind her in the

formerly empty monastery, a thrilling crashing and
clanking of armor. The witchlike person went pale with
fear. "Strike now!" she exclaimed to the wolves.
"Strike now, and quickly, before it's too late!"

But the wolves stood trembling and wringing their
paws, too terrified to move an inch. And before you
could say Jack Robinson, the door behind Queen
Louisa opened and a thousand gory wounded knights
came out, pushing into every available space in the
garden, saying "Excuse me" as they passed Queen
Louisa and her friends, and they raised their swords
to execute the wolves.

"Stop!" cried Queen Louisa.

Everybody stopped.

Queen Louisa walked with great dignity and calm
to the miraculous rosebush, her webbed hands grace-
fully crossed across her wattles.

"You've all misunderstood everything," she said.
"Or else I have. But no matter, since I'm the queen."
She could have explained, if she wanted to, how sorry
she felt for the wicked of this world, who couldn't
even cut a rosebush down. Though she'd admit, in all
fairness, that perhaps the rosebush *was* cut down,
since she was insane and could never know anything
for sure, and perhaps the whole story was taking place
in a hotel in Philadelphia.

"Watch!" said Queen Louisa. She closed her large
and luminous eyes and concentrated. A gasp went
through the monastery garden, for behold, Queen
Louisa had changed from an enormous toad to a
magnificently beautiful redheaded woman with a pale,
freckled nose. Her white, white arms were so delicately
dimpled at the elbows that neither knight nor wolf
could refrain from licking his lips with desire.
"Mother!" cried the chambermaid. "My beloved!"
cried the king—changed that same instant from the
dog he was before. The witchlike person was reduced
in a flash to the lady-in-waiting. She sat weeping and
groaning at her monstrous betrayal of everybody, and
especially her husband. The leader of the wolves said,
"Let us pray." The rosebush, being of no further use,
withered to an ice-clad stick.

Queen Louisa extended her soft white arm to the chambermaid. "My sweet," she said, "it's natural that youth should be rebellious. I was rebellious myself. But I want you to know that if you want to come home, your father and I agree, you're welcome."

Neither demanding nor expecting that the others would follow her, lovely Queen Louisa turned, with a gentle bow, and went back into the monastery and through it to the yard and on to the carriage. She got in and, with a thoughtful frown, turned back into a toad. Immediately the three sheep got in, and after them Queen Louisa's daughter, Muriel, and then His Majesty the King and Her Majesty's lady-in-waiting. The wounded knights lined up behind the carriage to follow it home. With two extra people beside them now, the three sheep were so crowded they could hardly breathe. Yet they smiled like madmen in their joy at the king's proximity.

Queen Louisa said—the child looked up at her with admiration like a gasp—"Don't blame yourself, my sweet. It's true, of course, that your dramatic leaving gave your father ideas. The poor old fool was in his forties then, and, I'm sorry to say, all people in their thirties and early forties have this awful lust—this ridiculous hunger for experience, so to speak. And the pretty way you mocked him, of course, and flirted with him—"

"*I* did all this?" the chambermaid said.

Queen Louisa smiled sadly at the look of dismay and bafflement in little Muriel's eyes. Then, with the carriage gently swaying and the snow falling softly from the pitchdark sky, Mad Queen Louisa told her beautiful newfound daughter the story of her life.

The boy beside the coachman said: "Isn't this a marvelous tale to be in?"

The coachman, who was silver-haired and wise, gave his nephew a wink. "You barely made it, laddie!"

KING GREGOR AND
THE FOOL

1

Another thing that can be said about King Gregor is that he dearly loved his work, and he was good at it. That was why he spent too much time at it, as the Fool kept pointing out, and tended to neglect his family. No doubt it was true that it was because of his neglect that Mad Queen Louisa spent more and more of her time these days as an enormous toad, though in her natural shape she was the most beautiful queen in the world. And presumably it was why his daughter—if it was true that, as Queen Louisa insisted, he had a daughter—had run away from home and only recently returned, having gotten herself into trouble and having no one to turn to.

King Gregor nodded, his dark brow deeply furrowed.

"Yes, true, all true," he muttered to himself, stroking his long black beard.

Which, however, did not resign him for one instant to the Fool, or to the whole institution of Foolery. The man wouldn't give him a moment's rest, carping and carping, prating and prating, often in spontaneous rhyme so terrible it set King Gregor's ears on edge. "Surely," King Gregor thought, pressing the back of his hand to his forehead, "an exception should be made in my case! Isn't it enough that I'm married to an insane queen? Do I have to put up with a Fool besides?" No one knew how he suffered. No one understood. Queen Louisa, of course, was the life of the party, the one everyone adored. Bold King Gregor (as he liked to call himself and as he'd tentatively suggested from time to time that he might not unfittingly be called, but it had never caught on)—Bold King Gregor was always the straight man, cruelly upstaged by the magnificent Louisa. He loved her, yes, of course. It can safely be said that no king who ever lived was more devoted to his queen than was Gregor to Louisa. But it was not easy, being the ruler of an important kingdom and the husband of a madwoman, everlastingly rolling the same old rock up the same old hill, like Sisyphus of old, straining to introduce into the kingdom, in his own small way, some trifling note of sense. Did the Fool understand this, criticizing, criticizing?

No the Fool did not.

King Gregor glanced back at the battle on the plain below and saw that his men were getting too far to the left, where they could easily be surrounded, if the enemy thought of it. He reached over to his trumpeter and poked him in the arm with one finger. "Trumpeter," he said, "blow 'Advance to the Right.' "

"Yes sir. Thank you, sir," the trumpeter said, and smartly lifted his instrument, banderoles streaming, and blew the call. King Gregor's knights, down on the plain below, stopped and looked up, raising their visors to hear better, got startled looks as they realized their situation, and hurriedly scurried some distance to the right. King John, on the mountain beside King

Gregor's, hammered his hand with his fist and stamped in fury. King Gregor smiled.

But almost at once he began frowning again, and stroking his long black beard first with one hand and then with the other. He'd had a stunning idea about getting rid of Fools and had written a long rather eloquent letter to all the kings in the neighborhood commending his idea to his colleagues' attention. The idea was this. A Fool, in the final analysis, is merely a kind of safety valve for the feelings of the people who are ruled by the king and have no right to disagree with him, except through their supposedly mad, and therefore not responsible, spokesman, the Fool. Why not establish a new relationship between kings and their subjects, a system in which everyone voted on everything, so that Fools were no longer needed? The disadvantages of this, he would readily grant, were dreadful to contemplate, but there was one overriding advantage: Once Fools were no longer of value, the kings could round up the Fools and chop their heads off.

In the end, as so often happens, his fellow kings had rejected the idea not because it was unsound—they could never reach agreement on that—but because, as someone put it, "The old ways are the best ways." This, in King Gregor's opinion, showed a gross ignorance of history.

"In the old days," he sourly pointed out, "armies fought with clubs with huge spikes sticking out. Surely our modern swords and lances and catapults are a vast improvement."

The argument had no effect except that several of the kings went back to equipping their soldiers with huge spiked clubs.

King Gregor shook his head, slowly and thoughtfully stroking his beard. It wasn't easy to be sane when the whole wide world around him was crazy.

"Excuse me," said the trumpeter. "Here comes King John."

King Gregor sighed and nodded. On the plain, the armies broke for lunch.

2

"I nearly had you there. Admit it, you old devil," King John said, punching him merrily. "Nearly caught them fifteen miles off base." His tiny blue eyes twinkled happily, and his yellow mustache twitched with his twitching cheeks.

"You should have jumped us sooner," King Gregor said glumly.

"I should have, that's a fact," King John agreed. He bit off another large piece of blue cheese. Down on the plain, the surgeons were bandaging the knights' wounds. King John tucked the bite in the side of his face and said, "How's Queen Louisa?"

"She's fine, just fine," King Gregor said. Then, for politeness, though his heart was heavy, "How's Hilda?"

King John winked obscenely.

King Gregor sighed.

For a long time after that, neither king spoke. The two trumpeters, who were playing cards, looked sadly at their masters. At last King Gregor said, "Life is very baffling, it seems to me."

"Never admit it! That's the secret!" King John said, and chuckled.

King Gregor went on eating his apple. He had his crown off; he'd set it casually on the grass beside him. His stiff black hair stuck up oddly, with a tight ring around his head where the crown had rested. His enemy studied him with a look of sympathy, then abruptly looked down. His eye happening to land on King Gregor's crown, between them, he reached out and lifted it up, tossed it gently on his hand to weigh it, then brought it up level with his eye to examine the jewels and the Latin inscription.

"Maybe it would help if you talked about it," King John brought out, not glancing at King Gregor.

"It's nothing specific," King Gregor said. "It's just

that I feel—" He narrowed his eyes and pursed his lips. "I feel old," he said.

King John smiled gently. "I know what you mean."

They watched the two dukes winding up the path toward them, talking together as they came. As the two dukes came nearer, the trumpeters stopped playing cards for a moment and looked at them. The two dukes approached the two kings and saluted. They presented the morning's list of dead and wounded. Both kings shook their heads, not commenting. It seemed to King Gregor that his enemy was blinking back tears. Some mad, unheard-of question came drifting into King Gregor's mind but timidly fled before he was able to identify it. The kings handed the lists back to the dukes and saluted. The dukes returned the salutes, turned sharply on their iron heels, and started back down the path, clanking. The trumpeters returned to their game.

Suddenly King Gregor said, "My wife and daughter will be coming out to watch, a little later in the day. I told them they could."

King John's eyes popped wide open and the crown tumbled from his hands, but all he said was, "You don't say!"

"I get a lot of criticism, you know, about never spending time with the family."

King John eyed King Gregor in a manner that suggested some doubt of King Gregor's sanity.

"I don't feel I owe you an explanation," King Gregor said in a way that sounded, even in his own ears, peevish, "but I will say this: You don't understand the strain I'm under, living with a bunch of lunatics. Oh, I know, it's only Louisa herself that's truly crazy. But there they are *with* her all the time, you know, and they get used to her behavior, get to playing to it, so to speak, and pretty soon the line between sense and nonsense is a little indistinct. For example—" He was suddenly speaking rapidly, in the way in which one speaks to one's confessor sometimes, when one knows that one has sinned but has a feeling that the case is unusual and the normal definitions don't perfectly apply. "For example, one hour after supper last night, Louisa said in a bright, sweet voice—she has, you know, a lovely voice; it's difficult to believe that a voice so sweet, so full of gentleness and goodness, could be uttering nonsense. . . . She said, as I was saying, 'Listen! I've got a marvelous idea. Let's everybody go skinny-dipping!' Before I could even catch my breath she was disrobing herself. And so were they! All of them!—even my pregnant daughter and that horrible troublemaking monster my Fool. Even Tcherpni, my Minister of Economics!" King Gregor laughed, then remembered his unhappiness and stopped himself. "The next minute, off they all went through the palace, reaching out like swimmers and slowly bringing their arms back and reaching out again, and sometimes giving a little kick with one foot, except for old Tcherpni's wife, who was doing the dog paddle. My Chief Justice almost drowned, but someone swam out and saved him and put him on the dinner table, where he was safe."

"You poor devil, Gregor," King John said, moved.

"Actually, it wasn't so bad, in some ways. Queen Louisa, as you know, is a woman of extraordinary attractiveness, even with her clothes on." He narrowed his eyes and rubbed his knees with the palms of his hands, laboring to think it through. "And, of course, the whole business may not have been as mad as Queen Louisa pretended. We do, after all, have a pregnant daughter to marry off, by hook or crook, and in situations like these . . . in situations like the event I'm describing . . ."

King John studied him suspiciously.

"All I'm saying is, it's difficult to keep one's sanity, in a household like that."

The blond king nodded. He asked, without seeming to put excessive weight on it, "And did *you* join the fun, on this curious occasion?"

"What could I *do?*" King Gregor said, suddenly perspiring. "I was their *host*."

3

The afternoon's fighting went badly for everyone. King Gregor had difficulty keeping his mind on his business, so molested were his thoughts by curious emotions and wordless intuitions, and one in particular, though for the life of him he couldn't make it come clear—some feeling of fundamental error, perhaps some error of his own, perhaps some error of all mankind. Again and again as he tried to concentrate, his mind would suddenly be filled with an image of Louisa naked and unspeakably beautiful, with her fiery red hair flowing softly behind her as if the palace really were filled with water. And then sometimes he would remember Her Majesty's lady-in-waiting, Madame Logre, who had practically no breasts at all but who, nonetheless, had an unnerving appeal in King Gregor's eyes. And now and then he would suddenly blush and clamp his eyes shut, remembering little Princess Muriel, with her pitifully thin white thighs and her gently paggled six-months-pregnant belly and those lovely gray eyes, lovely in spite of the ugly dark circles, eyes that shone, contrary to reason, with saintly innocence. He'd been conscious of wanting, as he walked slowly through the palace, thoughtfully stroking his beard with his right hand and swimming with his left, bowing to his grave and gallant knights as they swam by arm in arm with their elegant ladies, or throwing a word of encouragement to some elderly minister who was puffing hard and looking very doubtful that he'd make it as far as the safety of the stairs—he'd been conscious of wanting to embrace them all, both the beautiful and the ugly, and cling to them as a sweet uninhibited child clings for dear life to his parents. "My people," he kept thinking. "My people. *My* people!" It was a wonder that he kept from bursting into tears.

As for blond King John, he paid scarcely more attention to his army than Gregor did to his. The dark king's words had made a profound impression on him.

He had always thought of his enemy as a man with his feet firmly planted in the world, a man who knew his mind and could get things done. Sometimes King John would find himself chuckling. "That old devil!" he said from time to time. But at other times a great, wordless sorrow would well up in his breast, and he would be forced to wipe his eyes with his sleeve.

The armies, clumsily striking out without plan or supervision, gored each other fiercely, knocked each other's horses down, and sometimes found themselves lost in the woods a mile from the plain where they thought they were. Tempers were frayed, chivalry was forgotten. The horses, badly guided, as confused and angry as the knights who rode them, savagely bit and kicked each other. A veteran knight who was known far and wide for his skill and courage sat crying like a child in the mud and tangled grass.

It was at this stage of the battle that King Gregor's faithful trumpeter tapped him on the shoulder and pointed down the road. With a sinking heart, King Gregor's sad eyes took in the glittering banners of Queen Louisa's entourage. When he glanced over at King John's mountain, he saw that his enemy was also aware of the queen's approach. The blond king was miserably shaking his head, looking down at the horrible travesty of a battle.

King Gregor paced back and forth, feeling suddenly furious. It was all her fault, he clearly understood. As for her sweet and notorious madness, he didn't believe a word of it. She'd plotted the whole thing to make a fool of him. No doubt she'd had a private word with the Fool, a creature as cold-bloodedly sane as she was. No doubt they'd had a good laugh, yes! King Gregor seized two great hanks of hair, one with each fist, and yanked at them, trying to pull them out, but though it hurt a good deal, no hair came out. The queen's entourage kept coming, gleaming.

"Make everyone stop fighting," he shouted suddenly to his trumpeter as though the trumpeter, too, had been privy to the plot. With a look of alarm the trumpeter snapped up his instrument and blew first the retreat call used by King Gregor's army and then the retreat call King John's army used. The armies looked up in confusion and then, looking puzzled, began to back away from each other.

"Clean this mess up!" King Gregor shouted through his cupped hands.

King John, who at once saw the wisdom of this, began shouting the same.

The knights climbed awkwardly down from their horses and lumbered behind the lither yeomen to the middle of the plain and hurriedly snatched up dead men by the legs and began to drag them away to the woods. They tied ropes to the hooves of dead horses, then tied the ropes' other ends to the saddles of their battle steeds, and began dragging the dead horses' corpses away.

"Now everyone line up for the attack!" cried King Gregor and King John at once.

The yeomen helped the knights back up into their saddles and the two armies went to opposite sides of the plain and lined up, feeling suddenly excited and cheerful, for a whole new attack. The standard-bearers cleaned up their flags as well as possible, then hastily took their accustomed positions. The horses trembled with excitement and confidence, so that their armor rang and their bright skirts glimmered like water in a brook.

King Gregor could hardly stand still. He kept hitting his hand with his fist and smiling wickedly, showing his huge square teeth. "That's more like it!" he kept saying. Over on his mountain, his enemy was jumping up and down like an idiot. King Gregor grinned like a wolf about to strike. "You've met your match, my friend, in Bold King Gregor!" he yelled.

And now the queen's entourage had reached the top of the hill. The horses lined up on the battlefield stood with their heads turned to watch her, and they were smiling exactly like King Gregor and King John. The knights sat with their visors up, smiling, too. Slowly, awesomely, they raised their lances into charge position, the butts of the lances cast firmly into the fewtre-supports.

The queen and her entourage had now reached the flat elevation where King Gregor stood. A page took her lily-white hand and gently helped her down from her dapple gray. Another page helped the princess down. The Fool got down alone. His gray-bearded dwarf's face was twitching and quivering with what might have been malicious disgust.

"Are we late?" Queen Louisa excitedly whispered. Her beautiful red hair flew out bravely in the breeze.

"Mother, hush!" cried the princess.

King Gregor said, heart pounding with excitement, his bearded lips trembling with violent emotion, "Just in time, my queen!" He raised his arm smartly and smartly brought it down. With a grandiose flourish the trumpeters played *Charge!* At either end of the battle-field the knights snapped their visors shut like a thousand iron doors and their steeds reared up and arched their necks like dragons in jubilant war with the universe. From the knights on the right side a great triumphant shout went up: "For Bold King Gregor!" and from the left came an echo like a mighty reboation from crystal cliffs: "For Just King John!"

And now like earthshaking thunder or the rumble of a vast, dark flood came the deafening rumble of the horses' hooves as the armies came plunging with bright lances lifted to strike at each other's throats. Horses neighed, demonic, stretching their powerful legs for more speed, and the quarter-ton lances came grace-fully dropping from nearly upright position toward the deadly straight-on position of the hit. Violently, bravely, down the field they came roaring, their flags wildly whipping, and suddenly, louder than a moun-tain exploding, Queen Louisa yelled: *"Stop!"*

The horses skidded in alarm. The lances dropped past hit position and stabbed into the ground and lifted up the knights like pole vaulters and left them hanging straight up, kicking wildly and trying to let go.

"What have you done?" King Gregor screamed.

"Grotesque!" cried King John, and beat the ground with his fists.

Queen Louisa said with a baffled look, her white

fingers trembling, "Listen, they could have *killed* each other!"

"That's the *idea!*" King Gregor screamed.

Queen Louisa tipped her head, seemed to think about it. Slowly, she turned her lovely face to examine her husband's face, which was contorted with rage and awful humiliation.

"Gregor," she said, "you people are all crazy."

4

King Gregor lay alone in the other bedroom, clenching and unclenching his fists and biting his lips and weeping. "Damn her, God *damn* her," he kept whimpering, clenching and unclenching his fists. He would divorce her. His decision was unalterable. He had thought at first he would lock her up in the dungeon, but he'd known from the beginning that he couldn't really do it. Why couldn't she be crazy like other people's queens— setting fire to the curtains of the palace, for instance, or wringing her fingers and moaning like a witch? King John, no doubt, would never speak to him again, nor would any of the other of the neighborhood kings. He would trudge past their presence like a stupid, black-bearded old peasant, never lifting his eyes to theirs, his hands pushed deep in his trousers pockets and his crown fallen forward like an old drunk's hat. Dogs would come piss on his shoes and he wouldn't have the courage to object. He laughed bitterly, a dark laugh which ended in a sob. "Old ways are the best ways," he thought. He'd made himself a laughingstock. His own knights would scorn him. All this for his pride, for his insisting on marrying the most beautiful queen in the world, crazy or no crazy. He thought of her soft white shoulders and clenched and unclenched his fists.

Was he secretly wishing she would come to him and apologize?

He sat up abruptly, furious at himself, and snatched off his nightcap and threw it on the floor.

"I am wishing no such thing!" he said. "I wish—"
He suddenly got up and began to pace.

Outside his door there was a footstep. He almost
called out "Yes?" eagerly, but caught himself in the
nick of time. He waited, wiping his hands on the sides
of his nightgown and angrily sniffling.

"Your majesty?" a voice said.

It was not the queen.

"Go away," said King Gregor.

But the door creaked open and the princess came in.
"Your majesty," she said again.

"Go away," he said again, but not convincingly.

"Your majesty," she said, "if only you'd just *speak*
with her. She just lies there, sobbing and sobbing and
sobbing, and everybody's just horribly upset. Even the
Fool says—"

"Don't mention that creature's name to me!" King
Gregor yelled.

"I don't even *know* his name," said the princess.
"Everybody just calls him the Fool."

But King Gregor saw he was on to something. He
stopped pacing and pointed at the princess. "Listen
here," he said. "Is it or is it not true that the Fool
keeps all the time saying:

> *'You think I'm small because I'm lazy;*
> *But big brave knights get killed. That's crazy!?'* "

"Why, yes," said the princess, "I suppose he may
have said that."

"Exactly! So that's where she got it. From the Fool!"
He smiled wickedly and rubbed his hands. "Get the
Fool in here."

"It's after midnight, your majesty!" the princess said.

"Call him!" roared the king.

The princess backed away with her fingers on her
chin. A moment later, she returned with the Fool,
who was wearing a nightcap exactly like the king's,
which was infuriating.

"Fool," said the king, "I've decided to chop your

head off. That poem of yours is what gave the queen the idea to come ruin my war with King John."

The Fool blinked like an owl. "Really?" he said. He was not as confident as usual just now. His knees knocked together and the twitching of his gray-bearded face was anything but scornful. He was cunning, though; you had to give him that. He said, "Which poem, your majesty?"

King Gregor told him.

He contrived to look puzzled, though still shaking like a leaf. "But that's from the Bible," he said.

King Gregor stroked his beard, looking at the princess to see if it was true. "Is it really?" he said.

"I'm not sure, your majesty," she said.

"Get me an expert on the Bible," said King Gregor.

The Fool shook his head and wrung his hands. "Impossible, sire," he said timidly. "The only expert on the Bible for miles around is—"

"Get him for me!" roared the king.

The Fool finished his sentence, kneeling now, so awful was his terror of King Gregor: "The only expert on the Bible for miles around is Just King John."

"Get him!" roared the king, then had second thoughts. "Is he really?" he said.

The Fool nodded, cowering and raising his arms as if fearing King Gregor might hit him.

King Gregor thought about it, sucking at his cheeks. It crossed his mind that he rather liked the way the Fool showed so much fear of him. It was natural, of course. Everyone agreed he was the most fearful king in miles and miles. At last he said, though feeling he might possibly be making a mistake: "Go get King John."

"At this hour of the night?" the princess said.

"I'll get him!" squealed the Fool, glad of any excuse to escape the terrible glance of King Gregor. And before King Gregor could answer, the dwarf had fled.

"I may have judged that Fool a bit too hastily," King Gregor said.

The princess nodded.

5

Just King John was red with indignation. Even after his six-mile ride he seemed still half-asleep, spluttering like a man who had been rudely awakened by a splash of cold water. "King Gregor, you're crazier than *she* is!" he said.

King Gregor was seated in the throne room, Queen Louisa beside him. He was not speaking to her yet, but he was, as everyone knew, a fair man, and if she was to be exonerated, because the sentiment on which she'd acted was from the Bible and thus not open to mere intellect's antilibrations, however insane one might privately think it, then she had, he supposed, a right to know. Also, he hadn't been able to stand the thought of her lying there crying and making her face puffy. He felt much better now, partly because he was doing the right thing, the manly thing, and partly because, whereas he and Queen Louisa had on their crowns, King John had come away in his nightcap, which, like his nightgown, was red with white flowers on it. He looked, in point of fact, like a silly idiot, a king beneath the dignity of Bold King Gregor, so that it was foolish, in a way, for King Gregor to bother making war on him.

"We have summoned you here, sir, for one simple purpose," said King Gregor. "We understand you are an authority on the Bible."

King John glanced suspiciously around him. Queen Louisa looked supremely solemn. So did the Fool and princess. At last King John said, "I may have a certain acquaintance with the Book." He casually picked a speck of lint off his sleeve.

"Then you will not object, I presume, to being put a simple question."

King John closed one eye, looking at King Gregor very carefully with the other. "I might not seriously object to that," he said.

"Excellent, sir. Then the question is this. Is it the

case, as certain persons have alleged, that the following quotation is Biblical?

> *'You think I'm small because I'm lazy;*
> *But big brave knights get killed. That's crazy!'*

Answer yes or no."

King John tipped his head down. He covertly glanced at the guards he'd brought with him, then at the assembled crowd, then at Queen Louisa.

Queen Louisa said, "He's not called Just King John for nothing," and smiled.

"Yes or no?" said King Gregor, leaning forward.

"Hebrew," said King John, "is an ambiguous language, naturally."

"Ha! You don't actually know, then?"

With a casual wave, King John sent the idiotic question away. "Of course I know," he said.

The throne room was absolutely silent. Everyone was leaning forward, waiting. King John glanced at his guards again, then at Queen Louisa. King Gregor had the distinct impression that Queen Louisa winked.

"Yes!" said King John triumphantly. "The passage is distinctly Biblical. Loosely."

Pandemonium broke loose. Everyone whooped and threw their hats in the air, because the war was over, and the Fool jumped up and down on his stool as if he thought he were a monkey. The princess sobbed and threw herself into the arms of a gored and wounded knight, and the queen, leaping up ecstatically, suggested that everyone go skinny-dipping.

"We'll do nothing of the kind!" King Gregor roared. "Who's running this kingdom?"

A great silence fell.

He liked so well the impression he'd made that he said it again, beaming and majestic, his eyes like fire. "Who's running this kingdom?"

Everyone was looking in the Fool's direction. It crossed the king's mind that the Fool looked suspiciously innocent.

"*You* are, my dearest!" Queen Louisa cried with shining eyes, and threw a scornful—indeed, a quite withering—look at the gray-bearded dwarf. Everyone shouted and (King John having quickly passed glasses around) drank a health to King Gregor. "To Bold King Gregor!" they shouted one and all.

Queen Louisa said with a sly look, "My friends, it's bedtime."

Another thing that can be said about King Gregor is that he dearly loved his family.

MURIEL

1

The best thing about suddenly having been turned into a princess was that Muriel escaped all those tiresome and ultimately dangerous ideas that her friends imagined it was necessary to maintain. Granted, there were other advantages. One of them, for a while, was her wardrobe. Actually, the reason for the dark circles under Muriel's eyes was not so much her pregnancy as the fact that every night, when everyone else in the castle was asleep, she would slip out of her golden four-poster bed and light all the candles in her great stone room and creep over to her wardrobe, which took up one whole wall, and try on more dresses. If she lived a hundred years, it seemed to her, she could never try on all of them. (This turned out not to be true.) With some of them came long pointed hats with trailing veils. She would walk back and forth,

looking sideways at her mirror, the silver or crimson or yellow or blue shimmering softly in the candlelight, and she would find herself so deeply moved that she could hardly whisper, "Hello there! How are you, Count?" or, "Aren't you sweet to *say* so!"

Another of the other advantages was the class of people one encountered as a princess. In her former existence, she had never so much as spoken to a knight, though sometimes, looking up from scything wheat (she dimly remembered), she had seen them riding past. They weren't like people at all: They went by, on their glittering, armored horses, like statues made of iron, or ominous machines. Their metal-cased elbows and knees, their steel-plated hands and feet never moved. The ostrich plumes fluttering on their helmets were no more signs of life than flags affixed to coffins. She'd almost come to imagine, without for a moment really thinking about it, that the dark suits of armor balanced on King Gregor's horses were empty shells. She didn't even think of them as tricks on the enemy—empty armor ensaddled to make the army seem larger. She dismissed them, peasant that she was, as merely one more inscrutable fact of government. A way of transporting suits of armor, perhaps.

Imagine her surprise, therefore, when she spent her first night in the castle (she'd been brought in as a chambermaid; it wasn't till next day that she was discovered to be the princess) and heard the trumpets sound and, running to her window, saw the drawbridge lowered, giving access to fifty of those battered suits of armor (and some goats), and saw the armor, assisted by pages, get down from the huffing, bleeding horses, pat the horses gently and wearily on the rumps, then stagger in across the flagstones to the central hall. She ran lightly down to watch. Even now, with a part of her peasant mind, she thought them mere automata. But as they reached the dais where King Gregor and Queen Louisa sat, they began lifting off their helmets. Their long hair fell flowing free to their shoulders and in some cases down to their tight, girlish waists. Some were old, with gray hair like shimmering silver. Some were young—a few were mere boys, in fact—with hair of chestnut brown, or black as ravens' wings. Some were blond; some had youthful hair like snow. They were not beautiful, those knights, in the normal sense. Some were ruddy with exertion, and some pale as ghosts from the long day's fight. But they certainly were, no question about it, men of a kind she had never seen before.

She had felt, at that moment, like a mortal raised to heaven for a precious glimpse. But the following day, when Mad Queen Louisa had decided that Muriel was her own lost daughter Muriel (Muriel would have said, except for the conviction of the queen and all her court, that her name was Tanya), it became necessary that Muriel, or possibly Tanya, see those magnificent knights as equals, or, indeed, inferiors. Her real mother, she dimly remembered (or anyway the toothless peasant woman who'd said she was her mother), had warned her many times that she must never judge things by outer appearance. "You're as noble as you think you are," the old woman used to say, ferociously greasing the carriage wheels of strangers who broke down on the road past the farmhouse. "People will come asking you for certain things," the old woman said with a significant look. "You remember who you are." Muriel, or Tanya, had puzzled over this since the age of eleven, when the old woman first began mentioning it.

Whoever she might be—she'd given up seriously worrying about it—it was an amazing thing to find herself suddenly in the company of knights, receiving love poems from them, as near as she could tell (they were full of hard words and obscure comparisons, and she had learned, after the first few awful embarrassments, to accept the paper with a polite, aloof smile, the way the other courtly ladies did, saying "Thank you very kindly," and folding the paper and slipping it down into her bosom to puzzle out later, when the others were in bed). It was a war of obscurities, each knight struggling to outdo the rest and furious when he saw that another's phrase was more befuddling. Muriel had, hidden under her huge silk pillow, a dictionary which Queen Louisa's minstrel had given her,

and whenever she found herself too exhausted for trying on clothes, she would get out the minstrel's dictionary and work, till she fell asleep, on the poems
from the knights. It was exciting at first, though she
could never make heads nor tails of half what they
were saying, not that it mattered much, probably. But
the poems came in so much faster than she could
unscramble them that the work became depressing,
finally, so that now, for the most part, she pasted them
into her scrapbook unread. In the beginning, it had
made her feel inferior, all that trouble she had with
modern poetry, but Queen Louisa had fixed that, as
Queen Louisa fixed everything. Muriel had said, in
such a casual way that no one could possibly have
suspected it was personal, "What does it mean, exactly,
when one says, 'Your eyes are like mystic pantarb
suns'?" Queen Louisa had looked up sweetly and
fondly, combing her fiery swirls of hair. "Oh, that'll
be Sir Clervel," she'd laughed. "Don't let him near
you!"

But the chief advantage of being changed into a
princess, at exactly the right time, in exactly the right
way, was that Muriel escaped the ideas of her low-
born former friends. She discovered this by a curious
accident, though the deeper meaning was perhaps
still a little uncertain. It came about as follows.

2

One day as Muriel was being driven about the coun-
tryside in an open carriage, with a lady-in-waiting on
either side of her, a rumble of thunder was heard in
the distance, and Muriel, looking at the sky in alarm
—for neither she nor her ladies-in-waiting were dressed
for rainy weather—cried to the driver, "Please, my
good man, turn around and drive us home at once, as
our dresses and hats will be ruined."

The driver obeyed and put the horses into a gallop
in the direction of the castle, but, for all their haste,
Princess Muriel saw that the rainclouds were amassing

far more swiftly than the horses could run. They gathered above her like black, churning mountains, shocking silver at the edges where the sun's beams shot past. They rose higher and higher, growing darker and darker, as if gathered together by sorcery, till soon they reminded her of monstrous wild horses that were rearing up crazily to strike with their hooves. "Faster! Faster!" cried Muriel, and the ladies-in-waiting cried the same, but with voices that sounded, in that weird, greenish weather, like witches' voices, hideous and mocking. They were, of course, anything but witches. The lady-in-waiting on Muriel's right was Madame Logre, lady-in-waiting to Mad Queen Louisa herself, for Queen Louisa had had a premonition that something terrible would happen to Muriel today and had wanted her own faithful servant to be with her. It was a general rule, Queen Louisa had noticed, that when terrible things happened Madame Logre was always there. Where general rules were concerned, Queen Louisa was conservative. It was to Madame Logre that the driver now turned with a pitiful look, tears running down his red, coarse face, stretching out his hand as if asking for mercy, but Madame Logre said only, "Faster, my good man!" and pressed a small bag of coins into his hand. With a moan of fear and agony, the driver turned back to his horses and whipped them to still greater effort. They were at this moment entering a deep, dark wood. No sooner were they inside it than the rain came hissing down, pushing past the oak leaves—it was now late spring—and pasting Muriel's clothes to her skin.

"Look out for the bump!" cried the ladies-in-waiting in the wood's profound darkness.

The next instant, so suddenly that she couldn't make out what had happened, exactly, Muriel found herself sitting in the middle of the road, alone, the sound of the carriage wheels and galloping horses fading in the distance.

"I've been jolted out!" thought Muriel, "—and so abruptly that no one has missed me!" The next thought that came was even more alarming. This was no place for a princess, or even for the peasant girl Tanya. No one ever came to the great, dark forest but rapists and anarchists and outlaws. She shuddered.

Then, taking courage, because, as the peasants she'd lived with used to say, "It's always darkest before the dawn"—which, oddly enough, was only sometimes true, but never mind—she got up off the road and walked over to the bole of the nearest oak, where she thought she might be more sheltered from the rain. Imagine her terror when, reaching out to touch the oak, her fingers came, instead, upon a human hand, which quickly closed on hers in a viselike grip. Muriel screamed.

"So we meet again!" cried a cruel voice.

"Vrokror!" Muriel gasped, and fainted.

3

She did not wake up, as she'd expect she would (for having been once a peasant girl she never fainted without planning ahead), in the smugglers' cave in the great black cliff, but in the basement of the village church, among all her old friends. She sat up blinking and looking around her. Fat, freckled faces smiled back at her, apparently delighted to see her. There was Djubkin, who'd kissed her in the barn one time, and there was Pretty Polly, about whom everyone was always writing sad or naughty songs ("So stable your horses and feed them some hay" Haw haw haw!), and there was Dobremish, the tinker's daughter, who'd once been Muriel's dearest companion. The whole of the candlelit room was filled with smiling friends. She greeted them all with hugs and kisses and could hardly believe her happiness, until she remembered, and cried out: "But where's Vrokror?"

They all looked embarrassed and guilty. "Don't think about him, Tanya!" they all said, patting her and kissing her cheeks. "It's so wonderful to see you."

But Muriel drew back from them, fearful and suspicious. "Where is he?" she said.

"Oh, Tanya, Tanya," dear Dobremish said, trying to smile, despite a frightened look.

She narrowed her eyes, considering. "My name's Muriel," she said.

Their faces fell.

Suddenly Djubkin slid his floppy cap off and crushed it in both fat hands at his chest. "We thought you'd be glad to see us, Tanya." In half a minute they'd all be crying.

"I *am* glad to see you, certainly," she said, "though my name's not Tanya—that is, not anymore. My name's Muriel the Long Lost Princess, and my parents are not mere farming people, as you all supposed, but His Majesty King Gregor and Her Majesty Mad Queen Louisa."

"Sure, we all know that," Djubkin said, with an ingratiating little wave.

"Good," said Muriel, feeling better all at once and momentarily forgetting her grounds for suspicion.

"Tell us about life in the palace," Pretty Polly said. She was a very pale and elegant girl, quite pregnant at the moment by heaven knew whom. Her hands were as lovely and frail as white flowers. She would have made, Muriel couldn't help but confess, a simply beautiful princess. But fate was fate, she consoled herself, and smiled.

"First," she said, "we all have thousands of dresses like this one." She glanced down and saw that someone had taken her samite dress and put an old, coarse peasant dress on her. "Well, not exactly like this one," she amended. She described the dresses in detail and at length, until all her friends' eyes were shining with happiness and Djubkin, without even knowing it, was moving his fingertips on Muriel's knee. Gently, she brushed his hand away. "And the knights write you love poems," she said then, and laughed. She quoted them some of the stranger ones, pretending she perfectly understood them, and everyone held his sides and laughed except Pretty Polly, who looked nervous.

"And what's Queen Louisa like?" they all asked, speaking eagerly, but still with a guilty look that puzzled her.

Softly, devotedly, she told them about Mad Queen Louisa. "When she's herself," she said, "she has ravishing long red hair and the palest, loveliest face in the world, with freckles on her nose. Everyone agrees she's the life of the palace. She tells songs and sings stories and sometimes when everyone's feeling low she explains her philosophy of life. When she's not herself —no one knows quite why—she turns into an enormous, gentle toad. The first time or two you hardly see any difference, she looks very much as she always does, except for the expression of the eyes and mouth, but gradually, as you learn to look more closely, the difference becomes as clear as day. She gets very short arms, and an enormous swamp-green belly, and her placid smile goes from ear to ear—you really have to see it to completely understand. She's a very fine person, in whichever shape. She organizes great charity balls and calls off wars and heaven knows what. She's majestic, really. I believe she's a kind of saint."

All her friends' eyes were misty. Then Djubkin said, "Is that all they do—just try on clothes and write meaningless poems and have charity balls and wars and things?" He didn't seem to mean it offensively.

"Well, they're royalty, you know," Muriel explained.

Djubkin nodded. He seemed to be more or less satisfied.

Frail Pretty Polly was nodding too, as though she completely understood and agreed. As if more or less to herself, she said, "I wonder how you *get* to be royalty."

Muriel looked away uncomfortably.

"Someone comes along and they recognize you," dear Dobremish said loyally, "the way they did Muriel." Her brown eyes sparkled and her cheeks got redder, as if the implied insult to Muriel were an insult to herself.

Everyone nodded instantly. Dobremish had a terrifying temper.

But the blacksmith's youngest daughter, Luba, said, with an apologetic glance at Dobremish, "Still, you know, it's an interesting question. I've often thought

my mama would perhaps have been a saint if it
weren't for us fourteen children. I mean, what has
Queen Louisa got to *worry* her, if you know what I
mean? What has she got to make her swear or want
to kill somebody, or tempt her to steal?"

"If you suppose for one moment—" Muriel flashed.

"Oh, where's your sense of humor?" Djubkin said.
All her friends started laughing. Muriel thought about
it, listening to that laughter, and felt suddenly lonely.

"Lots of poor people are saints," Dobremish said.
"A person doesn't need wealth and leisure to be gentle
and loving. And I'm sure lots of people of means are
cruel and petty." Her eyes were sparkling more dangerously now, and her black hair glittered.

"Exactly!" said Muriel, and everyone instantly
agreed.

"Still," said the blacksmith's daughter, Luba, "it
seems unfair, somehow." Everyone looked nervous.
"It's not as if they were handsomer than we are.
Dobremish, for instance, is the prettiest girl I ever
saw, even if she is a little pug-nosed. And when
Pretty Polly's not pregnant she looks simply adorable."
Luba paused and blushed. "I don't mean you're *ugly,*
Muriel—" But even Muriel could see she had a point.
Luba added in haste, "And it's not as if they're more
intelligent than we are. I never knew anyone as quick-
witted as Djubkin, though I admit he can be stupid
with girls. And for that matter, if intelligence were the
point, they'd make Vrokror a prince—if they could
catch him." She laughed, then went pale, seeing the
outraged look on the faces of her friends.

Muriel burst out sobbing, and Dobremish said,
weeping bitterly, "You stupid, stupid little horror,
Luba! Look what you've done!"

But Muriel was sobbing as if her heart would burst,
and in their anguish everyone soon forgot about
Luba.

"I swear to you, Muriel," Djubkin said, "that man's
name will never be mentioned again or *my* name isn't
Djubkin!"

"Who knows if your name's really Djubkin!" sobbed

Muriel. "Who knows anything about anyone? What am *I* for instance?"

All her friends bit their lips and wrung their hands, but in her awful shame and loneliness she trusted no one anymore. She remembered that the cries of the ladies-in-waiting had sounded to her like the laughter of witches, and remembered, at the same time, how all her dear friends had laughed to trick her when Djubkin said something was a joke which was not. Was anyone who ever lived more abandoned and miserable than she? Was anyone ever more lost and helpless in a senseless and lawless universe?

No.

Muriel said, "I believe you're all in league with him. Otherwise why would he bring me to you—he, wicked Vrokror, whom you all have pretended to scorn as a rapist and anarchist?"

She sobbed and sobbed, tearing her hair and noticing, in the back of her mind, that the peasant gown was itchy; otherwise her sorrow would have been perfect, as in a legend.

Dobremish leaned over her, weeping, trembling, her love for Muriel so great that she would joyfully have died for her. "Dearest, dearest Muriel," said Dobremish, "we are *not* in league with him. We saved you from him. But since that awful subject has come up, tell us what happened, I beg you, and perhaps you will feel better."

"I fell out of the carriage," Muriel said.

"No, not that, Muriel. What happened *before?*"

Muriel gasped, wringing her hands, and after a moment sat up to tell the story.

4

"Snow was softly falling past the lighted barn windows," Muriel related. "I was milking the cows. As I stepped into the milkhouse with a pail in each hand, I was suddenly and horribly accosted from behind. One hand caught me by the waist and another clamped tightly around my mouth, preventing me from screaming. I carefully set down the milkpails, which hadn't spilled, luckily, and allowed myself to be dragged—since I couldn't resist, naturally—to a coach that was parked in the darkness at the foot of the driveway. There, bound and gagged, I was forced to proceed with my unknown assailants to an isolated place on the seacoast above the rugged cliffs. The coach stopped in front of an abandoned farmstead, and my assailants, muttering unspeakable oaths, pulled me roughly from the coach and forced me, by pokes and prods, to the darkness of the barn. You can well imagine my paroxysms of terror, my pathetic whimpers, through the gag, for mercy, and the intensity of my devout prayers for deliverance by the powers above.

"But my fears of immediate molestation were ill-founded, as luck would have it. Hidden in the barn there was a large trap-door which opened, to my utter astonishment, on a stairway leading interminably downward. I was ordered to descend. The stairs, which had every appearance of having been fashioned in some former century, were crudely hewn out of the rock itself. Before we had descended a hundred steps, the soughing of the night wind above us was no longer audible. When we had descended approximately a thousand steps, I began to hear the crashing of the sea. Soon after that, opening a studded iron door, we emerged into a comfortable, though by no means lavishly appointed, room—a chamber, as I quickly realized, of a partially man-made cave. We passed quickly through this chamber, of which I got only the most fleeting impression (several paintings, a tea set), to a smaller room which appeared to do service as an office. At the end of this room was a fireplace, with a roaring fire, and in front of this fire, with its back to me, sat a rocking chair with a man in it.

" 'Thank you, that will be all,' said this unknown personage.

"Instantly—I couldn't help but mark the alacrity with which the stranger's commands were obeyed, though uttered in a voice quite gentle, unmistakably cultured—my assailants released me and retreated in the direction of the secret stairway.

" 'Come here, my child,' the stranger said.

"I have neglected to mention, though perhaps my narrative inadvertently makes it obvious, that though my mouth was gagged and my hands were tied, my feet were free. Horribly trembling, my knees violently knocking together, I approached the man in the rocking chair. I was not such a fool as to imagine I might overpower him. Relaxed and off guard as he seemed, I knew him a desperate man. When I had come up beside him, he slowly turned his face to me.

"That face! No poet, no painter or sculptor, indeed no nightmare of the most fevered brain, could portray the agony and malevolent beauty of Vrokror's face! (For Vrokror it was, as I'm sure you've guessed.) He was a man of no more than twenty-six, but he had suffered more anguish than have most men of eighty. He had neither beard nor mustache, and his curly hair, which once, I surmised, had been golden brown, was prematurely gray. Over his left eye, behind his spectacles, he wore a black patch. His mouth was thin and sensuous, his nose aquiline, his jaw firm, but by no means excessive. His adams-apple was prominent, but not offensively so: One might have known even without hearing him speak that his voice was deep, with the timbre of a viola da gamba and, of course, not a trace of vulgarity. He wore a ruffled white shirt and an elegant purple smoking jacket with gold brocade. At his waist, beneath the smoking jacket, he wore a cumberbund, with a sag to the left, where his dagger hung. His fingers were long and, one would have thought, gentle—the fingers of a lutist, which indeed he was, he later informed me. His feet, clad in purple velvet slippers, were long and delicate, like a beautiful woman's but with a masculine character. But his face! How can I, how dare I, describe it? It was a face radiantly beautiful yet evil. The face of a man who has suffered to such a degree that he has left to him no choices but tragic suicide or maniacal rejection of the world that had brought him to this pitiable pass.

"He extended his arm to me. 'Tanya,' he said,

'they've gagged you too tightly! How can I ever forgive myself?' Then, rising quickly and gracefully, snatching his dagger with a motion exceedingly natural and habitual, he seized the back of my neck with his left hand and cut the gag with the dagger in his right. I meant to scream, but before I could draw breath, his lips were on mine. 'Tanya!' he exclaimed, 'Tanya, my angel!'

"I struggled free. 'I believe we have not been introduced,' I said.

" 'I have always known your name, my priceless Tanya,' cried Vrokror.

"I was hardly myself or I would have seen through his demonic machinations. Vrokror's kiss had shattered my wits, I'm afraid. I had been kissed once before, but never by a man like Vrokror. I was beside myself, if I tell you the truth. My whole being was on fire. I felt suddenly starved, violent, terrified. I felt like a fledgling first falling into flight. My heart beat fiercely, my white bosom heaved—"

Muriel blushed. All her friends looked down in embarrassment.

She continued, soberly:

"Vrokror, unless he was a consummate liar, was as shocked as was I by what had just occurred. He looked away, in an agony of embarrassment, and said timidly, 'May I untie your arms?'

" 'I'd be very grateful if you would,' I said.

"Vrokror did so at once. As he drew the rope away he turned from me, profoundly agitated, and said: 'Tanya, I cannot forgive myself for what I've done. How you must have suffered! How terrified you must have been! But permit me to beg you to understand: I have lived half my life as a rapist and an anarchist. Not by choice, I assure you, but because of unfortunate circumstances. One morning just after my latest ingenious escape from hanging, I happened to see you mowing hay, and as I watched I felt my sanity slipping. "I must have her," I thought. You could hardly miss the irony, that I, who had been privy to the beds of the noblest ladies of the modern world—I confess it with shame—should be spiritually ravished by a twelve-year-old maiden.

" 'I threw myself heart and soul into my work, raping and murdering and destroying kingdoms, but nothing could drive your sweet image from my heart. I pretended otherwise, pretended I'd lost that insane fascination, and on your fourteenth birthday I disguised myself as an elderly priest and came to your party to prove to myself that my insanity was cured. You know, perhaps, the pathetic result.'

"I did, as soon as he mentioned it. I remembered a poor old parish priest, from the kingdom to the west, who'd had a heart attack and had to be carried away by his companions. I mentioned this incident.

" 'That was I!' cried Vrokror, *'That was I!* Nor was the heart attack feigned, I assure you. It took the best doctors in the kingdom to save me. Thank God, I could easily afford it.'

"The story reduced him to tears, and it was some time before he was able to continue. 'I knew then, Tanya, that you must one day be my bride. I resolved to make myself worthy of you. I dismissed all my assistants and sought honest employment. For three full weeks I hunted work, but it was hopeless—hopeless! I reassembled my former friends, and—alas—here you are.' With a convulsive shudder, he came to the point. 'Tanya, dear Tanya, I cannot dream of asking you to lower yourself to my depraved and bestial desires. Indeed, I will not ask it of you, for it would lower your virtue in my esteem. But I'm a miserable criminal with no hope in life, for all criminals at last become crows' food, dangling from the gallows. Perhaps you could do only this for me: Pretend, for one night, to be my wife. Lie with me in bed, talking to me softly, as a wife would do, and between us I will place a deadly sharp sword, so that I cannot possibly give offense.' "

Muriel's friends were looking at her, full of avidity. She said, "Friends, if you trust me at all, you will believe that any normal well-brought-up girl would have done as much as Vrokror asked of me. No man on earth was ever more beautiful and tragic, though certainly he was possessed by the Devil. At any rate, I complied with his request. We undressed (behind screens) and went to bed. True to his word, he put a sword between us.

"I can hardly describe the beatific peace of that hour in which Vrokror told me all his anguish and I told him in return my aspirations and fears. It did indeed seem as if we'd been married for ages, so gentle was Vrokror's hand on my stomach and so sweet was the feeling of his chest to my fingertips. The candle burned lower, and his face grew gentler. At last he fell asleep. I was filled with a strange tranquility. Though I admit I was aching with affection for him— why should I deny it?—what I felt most of all was a profound satisfaction. Someone loved me deeply, no doubt about it. And I loved him in return. I, too, fell asleep, or almost asleep.

"I will not blame on Vrokror, guilty as he is, the shameful calamity that was really my fault. As I was drifting off, I put my hand on the sword and nearly cut myself. Almost without thinking, knowing that Vrokror was safely asleep, I slipped the sword from between us and put it on the floor beside the bed. Then, indescribably happy, with my arms around Vrokror, I softly fell away into sleep.

"I awakened with Vrokror on top of me, a poor helpless victim of his shameful, sinful passion. What should I have done? I knew, of course, that it was wicked—oh, insanely wicked—but Vrokror looked so happy, so wolfishly happy, for once in his life! And *I* was happy. How can I deny it? It was wonderful— wonderful! And I loved him so much! I could have screamed my horror and righteous indignation, I know. I honestly thought about it. No one would have heard me, down here half a mile below the surface of the world, but I could have screamed in horror for my dignity's sake, and possibly I could have made him stop. But, oh, oh, oh, it was so beautiful. He kept apologizing like a choirboy, though I knew he'd been affectionate with hundreds of ladies—and I believed every word he said, though you may laugh, and suddenly it was over and we lay gasping and laughing and blushing at our sin.

" 'Tanya,' Vrokror said, rolling away from me and shaking his elegant fist at the ceiling to hide his profound embarrassment, 'within our lifetime I will destroy all governments, all ideas of station. Peasantry I will make an obscure, archaic word.'

" 'Vrokror,' I said, still panting and blushing, 'go to sleep. I forgive you.'

"He said, 'Tanya, I wish you would try to understand me. I have penetrated the grotesque stupidity of things as they are. I want you to be at my side in my hour of triumph.'

" 'Vrokror,' I said, 'you're a prerogative fool!'

"He looked at me sadly and strangely and said nothing more. Gently intertwined, we at last fell asleep.

"The next morning I asked him to take me home. He got up, put his clothes on, and called the two ruffians who had brought me to his den. 'Take her home,' he said, turning his face from me and suppressing a sob. They instantly obeyed. And so I was returned, safe and sound, to the farmhouse. It was two months later that I discovered I was carrying a child by the desperate Vrokror."

5

In all her little audience, there was not a dry eye.

"And now," said Muriel, "tell me how it is that you saved me from him."

It was Dobremish, her childhood friend, who spoke. "Nothing could be simpler," Dobremish said, weeping. "He captured you, with inside help from the castle, and when King Gregor and his knights came out in search of you, Vrokror became panicky and brought you here, with a thousand apologies, and here, until the moment you opened your eyes, we have watched over you."

"Then you are not," said Muriel, "his accomplices."

"Certainly not!" said Dobremish.

Luba, the daughter of the blacksmith, added quickly,

"Though we don't necessarily disagree with his opinions."

Djubkin told a joke which made everyone laugh till he could hardly see. Then Dobremish said, "It's true, dear Muriel, that it's not exactly clear to us why some people have to work all day and night while others do nothing but try dresses on, and it's true that we feel, as *you* once felt, that Vrokror isn't really as bad as the posters say he is. But we wish, heaven knows, no harm to you, or to anyone you love. We feel there's been some horrible breakdown in communications, as Vrokror says. In fact we think—"

Dobremish looked groundwards, unable to continue. Djubkin touched her arm. Bravely, timidly, Dobremish continued: "We wonder if, perhaps, in your favored position, you couldn't, perhaps, discover that we're all really royalty, like you."

Muriel's eyes widened, but she said as gently as Queen Louisa could have said it, "My dear friends, you *are* in alliance with Vrokror! Since that is so, I must ask you to take me to him, and we'll see what we shall see."

Though her friends feigned astonishment and injured innocence, it took her no time at all to wrest the admission from them. She had a firmness of conviction and a steadiness of eye that those of lower station simply could not match. It was Dobremish herself who led Muriel to the secret door. With Muriel holding the candle, Dobremish unlocked the door, but before opening it kissed her friend on the cheek, saying, "Tanya, or Muriel, whichever you please, do not judge us too hastily. Think it over carefully if you care at all for Truth. For perhaps we really *are* all princes and princesses." With that, she pushed the door open and stepped back.

6

"Dearest Tanya!" cried Vrokror. He too held a candle. It threw its feeble light to the cobwebbed corners of the room, which contained a bed, a table, two flimsy chairs. "How weary you appear, my love," he said. "You must come to bed at once!" He turned from her to fluff up the pillows on the bed.

That would have been happiness indeed, for Muriel, but raising her pale hand she sadly declined. "Not this time, dearest Vrokror. It appears we have much to discuss, you and I."

He gazed at her admiringly. How she had matured! he seemed to be thinking, and he was right, she felt. She took his hand and led him deeper into the room, out of earshot of the others. She indicated the two flimsy chairs, and when Vrokror had drawn them up side by side, she and Vrokror sat down.

"Vrokror, my dearest," Muriel began, "you have poisoned the minds of my former friends. You have turned all those happy and contented peasants into smoldering revolutionaries who can never again know their former contentment. I cannot tell you how that grieves me."

Vrokror nodded solemnly, adjusting his glasses with two fingers. From his one good eye, a tear fell.

"You warned me, of course," Muriel continued, "of your demonic purpose, destruction of all government. Now I find myself your helpless captive, and no doubt you will force me against my will to aid and abet you in your fiendish scheme."

All her childhood friends, she noticed, were crowded around the open door, peeking in and eagerly awaiting the outcome of their battle of wits. How ironic, she mused, that a twist of fate should pit two such lovers against one another in inexorable conflict. She sighed.

"I understand your reluctance to assist me, my dearest," Vrokror said, wringing his long fingers. "I was a prince once myself, as you may have surmised."

"I did, actually," Muriel said.

"Then no doubt you will also have guessed my plot. Using you as my hostage—O hateful necessity!—I mean to bring about the death of Queen Louisa, undermining the morale of Gregor's kingdom, after which I will throw the whole kingdom into war. When the knights are at their weakest the people will arise to my battle cry." His gentle eye shone in the candlelight as he looked past her head at his vision of the future. "Everyone will be equal. We'll all crowd into the palace, somehow——" He broke off abruptly. This was no time for idle conversation. "I will show you the letter I've written," he said. He nodded to Djubkin, who came hurrying from the door, drawing the missive from his waistcoat pocket. *"Dear Queen Louisa,"* the letter said, *"Princess Muriel is hidden far away, but I, a kind priest with your best interests at heart, can tell you where she is if you come to me alone at midnight and meet me in the village church. Sincerely yours, Father Plodza."*

Princess Muriel trembled as she read.

"She'll come, of course," said Vrokror with a cruel smile, "and that will be the end of her."

"Vrokror, have mercy!" cried Princess Muriel. But for all his tender affection for her, he answered only with an ugly twist of his handsome mouth.

"Soon we'll all be princes and princesses," said Djubkin, rubbing his hands together.

"And I'll be the queen," said Dobremish sweetly, "unless Muriel wants to be."

Muriel looked left and right in horror. How had he so tainted the minds of her friends? "Do not be persuaded by this madman!" she cried. "Think of Queen Louisa's great beauty and gentleness. Think of the valuable charities she runs!"

Luba the daughter of the blacksmith came to Muriel and kneeled before her, clasping her knees. "You haven't understood at all, dearest Tanya. Only *you* can stop Vrokror from this horrible treason. Simply recognize us as your long-lost brothers and sisters, princes and princesses."

Muriel's eyes widened. She threw her hands up in dismay. "No one would believe me! The idea's absurd!"

Her friends all stared at her solemnly. She was the princess; it was up to her. She closed her eyes, one hand pressed to her bosom, the back of the other to her feverish forehead. She thought of the wardrobe torn to shreds, thought of the inevitable decline of poetry. And with that thought she suddenly formed a plan.

As if in anguish she said, "I cannot recognize you as what you are not, for princesses do not lie. If Vrokror is adamant, I am powerless to prevent him." She turned her wan face to Vrokror, miserably weeping. "But I will say one thing. You've addressed the queen improperly in your letter. She'll tear it up in fury and throw away the pieces, which will wreck your whole plan."

Vrokror looked puzzled.

"One doesn't say 'Dear Queen Louisa,'" she said scornfully. "That's crude and barbaric. You address her as 'O mystic pantarb Sun.'"

Vrokror looked at the letter. "I clearly remember from when *I* was a prince . . ." he began uncertainly.

"Well, I've given you fair warning," said Muriel, and blew her nose.

After much discussion with Djubkin, Luba, and Dobremish, Vrokror made the change, and the letter was sent.

7

I set down the sequel with a trembling hand.

Queen Louisa, believing the letter was some kind of poem from Sir Clervel, took it to the minstrel to see if he could make heads or tails of it. The minstrel carried it straight to the king, seeing that the letter was a fiendish trick.

At midnight, King Gregor and his knights rode out stealthily and surrounded the old stone village church. King Gregor wore, on top of his armor and long black beard, a long white dress and false red hair and, over his visor of steel, a lady's veil. Thus disguised, he entered the church alone, his hands hidden in his long white shawl. Meekly, timidly, he approached the robed and hooded priest. When he was five feet away, the priest turned to him, threw back his hood, and cried fiendishly, "Surprise!"

"Surprise your*self*, Vrokror!" cried the king, throwing off his veil and wig and shawl and swinging his sword up to strike.

At this signal the knights all came crashing in through the church door and windows.

"Betrayed!" howled Vrokror, turning to flee. "Rise and defend yourselves, downtrodden peasants!"

Out of every shadowy corner came Muriel's childhood friends, armed with pitchforks, candlesticks, carving knives, fenceposts, whatever lay at hand. They leaped at the knights with the fury of wild beasts, though they must all have guessed the futility of it.

"Surrender!" cried Gregor, but they refused, of course. King Gregor gave the signal and his knights began swinging their enormous two-hand swords, coming down with great whonks on the revolutionaries' heads. Muriel, peeking from behind the altar, wept and sobbed. Down went Djubkin with a defiant cry. Down went Luba the blacksmith's daughter, valiantly hurling a pitchfork as she fell. Down went elegant and frail Pretty Polly, and soon after, casting a last sad look at her dear friend the princess, down went the tinker's daughter, Dobremish. Only Vrokror escaped. He snatched up the veil and red wig, threw the shawl around his shoulders, and fled into the night. At the end of the fracas, the church was so filled with fallen peasants, some of them bleeding horribly, that the knights could hardly walk without slipping and falling with a crash.

"Vrokror, see what you've done!" cried Muriel, insane with anguish.

It was then that Mad Queen Louisa arrived, Madame Logre just behind her. As the queen hopped through the church door, the church fell silent. She stared, wide-eyed in such shock and indignation that she couldn't tell whether to be the queen or a toad, and kept shifting helplessly from one to the other. At last, hands clenching her temples, she brought out, "My children! My long-lost princes and princesses! Gregor—monster!—you've slaughtered all our children!" She sank to her knees, shuddering and distraught.

King Gregor said, horrified, pulling with both hands at his long black beard, "Our children, Louisa?"

"Poor princes, poor princesses," wailed the queen. Madame Logre smiled, showing her pointed teeth, and hugged herself. The knights hung their heads and the king shifted nervously from one foot to the other.

"It was all my fault," cried Muriel, coming from her hiding place.

"Not at all," said Queen Louisa, trembling. "It was the fault of tiresome and ultimately dangerous ideas."

Everyone was puzzled to hear her say something that appeared to make sense.

"Mystic pantarb suns indeed!" said Queen Louisa.

This was so confusing that everyone felt more or less secure again; so much so, in fact, that the beaten peasants began regaining consciousness, rubbing their sore heads and groaning. Though many would have to go to the castle infirmary, none of them was seriously wounded or dead.

When Queen Louisa saw them getting up she was beside herself with joy, but she was also stern, as was necessary. "People with tiresome and dangerous ideas should be switched," she said, and sent out for a willow switch. She did the switching herself. Everyone but Muriel and King Gregor was switched, even Madame Logre, though she loudly protested.

"I never did a thing!" cried Madame Logre, and wholeheartedly believed it.

"That," said Queen Louisa, "is the most tiresome and ultimately dangerous idea of all!" and put the switch to her in earnest. Madame Logre did everything she could to escape. She turned into a mouse, a huge green serpent, a poor sickly old lady. All in vain.

Then, chastened, they all limped back to the castle behind Queen Louisa, who carried her willow switch in front of her like a flag, and Dobremish (who was always her favorite) in her lap. King Gregor and Muriel, who hadn't been switched, kept glancing at each other furtively, wondering what it was they did right. It was sunrise.

Meanwhile, on a nearby snowcapped mountain, Vrokror was watching the procession through a spyglass and muttering oaths and imprecations. "Maniacs, maniacs, maniacs!" he kept hissing, stamping his foot in childish rage.

"All error begins," Queen Louisa said, "with soreheads."

Book Three

THE
KING'S INDIAN

A Tale

I

"Hoaxes! Don't speak to me of hoaxes, sir! I was part of the worst that was ever dreamt up in all history, and not free of it yet. Two old gnomes from Nantucket, some years ago . . . Gnomes. Hah! Cracked checkerplayers, that's nearer the mark! Beelzebub and Jaweh! Never mind . . . interminable damned . . . Hoaxes. Hah."

He hunches up, cunning, a crafty old loon with his left eye cocked to the northwest corner of the universe. He is teased toward some barest possibility. He purses his lips. He looks both sly and apprehensive. His long, lean nose is the cutting edge of outlandishness.

"I could tell you a tale, if ye'd understand from the outset it has no purpose to it, no shape or form or discipline but the tucket and boom of its highflown language and whatever dim flickers that noise stirs up in yer cerebrium, sir—the boom and the bottle we chase it with—fierce rum of everlasting sleep, ha ha!—for I won't be called a liar, no sir! not when I speak of such matters as devils and angels and the making of man, which is my subject, sir."

With dignity, an angel enters, golden-winged, and places spirits on the table between the mariner and his guest (apparently a city fellow). The guest uncomfortably picks his lip. Except for the angel, the mariner's voice, and the guest's self-conscious ear, the room is empty; yellow. The guest is as yet only half-aware of the angel's wings. Blushing slightly, uncertain who is supposed to pay, the guest glances over his shoulder, adjusts his tie.

" 'Tell on, old loon!' yer supposed to say."

"Tell on," says the guest.

"God bless yer generous soul, sir, that I will!"

II

Says he:

"There never was a nobler sight in the world, nor like to be, I incline to think, than a brig in full sail out of some far-off foreign or American port, riding in a wind that knows its business, neither blustering like a fool nor slacking off. (Take a drop of the whiskey, sir.) And there never was a nobler sensation, God knows, than riding in the rigging of such a ship, the decks all gleaming with varnish below you, and the smell of unlimited futurity stinging your nosedrills. I'd aspired for years to such a ride, but always one thing had deterred me from it. I'm not a good man for taking orders or letting my soul be boxed in, so to speak. I never was good at it from the day I was born —an event I remember, believe it or not, with some clarity. I felt pain in my head, and then immediately a sensation of drowning, and I clawed and screamed, not from pain so much, though the pain was titanic, as from outrage and moral indignation. In time I came to forgive my parents for the inconvenience they'd afforded me, but be damned if I'd ever let another man take a similar advantage. Say all you like on 'Ain't all men slaves, either physical or metaphysical?' —myself, I like to preserve split-hair distinctions.

"I may as well mention another experience that came when I was young and impressionable and which served to support my predilection for keeping out of other people's clutches. Boston was a great place for mumbo-jumbo—magicians, clairvoyants, mediums who could fill up vast theaters with the shivers and shrieks of religion. There was many a murderer smoked out on stage, many a family miraculously reunited. There was schools in Boston that would teach you telepathy and the reading of minds for your greater success in business, and there was solemn narrations in the Boston papers of trips among vampire bats and prehistoric monsters, in search of Eldorado. It was a town fit to set beside any that ever was heard of to prove man's capacity for bunkum. The end of the world was close at hand, it was generally acknowledged. Man was entering his final age —the age of his psychic awakening. Those who scoffed at all this spirit-crepitation were such patent cynics, such mean-eyed, low-browed habitual doubters, they looked to any unprejudiced man like mightier fools than the mediums.

"Well, sir, as I was saying, when my father was home one time from whaling—he was a Nantuck whaler who'd been riding the swells from before he could remember, he used to boast—my parents took me to a mesmeric demonstration by the infamous Dr. Flint. Flint, as you know if you ever seen him, was a great gray craggy Adirondack of a man, with eyes like steel beneath that grandiose top hat, and a manner so forceful his magnetic passes made the tails of his coat fly out in pure dismay. His most striking demonstrations (not counting his more illicit ones, like the time he stole the King of Sweden's crown, and not counting one I saw years later, the strangest I ever saw on earth) were those involving his wispy little golden-headed daughter Miranda. One snap of his fingers and she's deep in a trance, standing stiff as a pine tree and heavy on her feet as a Post Office. Four burly men from the audience can't lift her—so Flint makes it seem. Laid between two upright chairs, this innocent, lovely-eyed child of just seven who surely can't weigh, in her normal state, more than forty-some pounds—this child, I say, can support the weight of six great Yugoslav acrobats, part of Flint's troupe. She can suffer being sawed clear in half inside a box. She can lean way off balance, supported by nothing but magnetic rays. She can float in the empty air like a duck on a river.

"I marveled at these things, ye may well believe—marveled far more than I ever did at displays of clockwork automatons or those crafty Paris memory experts. I marveled and shrunk back in horror, yes sir! and not all my father's ingenious explanations of how the trick was accomplished made a particle of difference. (My father was no mean sleight-of-hand man himself. He kept in practice to drive away the boredom on a whaler, so he claimed. I suspected from the first there was more to it than that. He couldn't eat a meal without causing his spoon to disappear two, three times, and he carried a false beard in his inside coat pocket—I never found out why, though now that I'm old and have seen a few things, whenever I drive into the village I do the same. He was a storyteller respected far and wide, and the wider the story was, the better he could prove it. He'd sported with a mermaid off Gibraltar one time, he told us once—the neighbors all gathered in the parlor as usual—and he made it so convincing my poor mother went into a secret rage and a decline that nearly ended her. With a pack of cards he was a dangerous man, and the way he snatched nickels out of empty air you'd have thought we'd be living in a mansion. 'Chicanery, my boy, pure chicanery,' says he. 'That's the whole secret of a long, rich life!' His grin was exactly like a monkey's; but I digress.)

"More than all the rest, the thing that set my soul atremble was old Flint's taking that girl back in time, demanding in a voice like a spelling-master's—as if human history, for all its shocks, was a voyage more or less easily remembered, but dull, so trivial it had slipped our minds—that she tell him whatever the audience demanded of Roman antiquity, or Egypt and Babylon, or the lost gold cities of India. The house-lights dimmed. The piano played softly. Her white dress shone like a moonlit cloud, and her face, with its oversized, mournful eyes, was like the moon reflected in the wine-gray sea. She told, in her sweet little tinkling voice, of floods, wars, famines, of endless destructions in forests and the shadow of temple-domes. The Professors of History, brought to judge, were dumbfounded. I struggled for breath. He took her back still farther. Every word she spoke—solemn as a voice from a Chinese jug—made images rise in my mind more real than the theater walls, the red velvet curtains, the eerie music of Flint's silver-turbaned piano player. He took her back to the earliest dwellings of man, the dripping caves. She talked of savage anthropophagi, half animal, half human, hunched around bonfires and whispering in terror of snakes. I began to feel something going wrong with my vision. I clung to my parents. Great gabbling birds flew all around me, purest white, darting, dipping, plunging, screeching, their wingtips stretching from wall to wall as they warred, all eyes, steel talons, and beaks, with the writhing serpents on the balcony around me. I screamed. I had seen all my life (I was then about nine) queer shadows at the edge of my bad left eye. Fraud though Lord knows he had to be, Flint had made them solidify a little. I was now convinced those shadows were real as the Parthenon, and a man like Flint, if he ever got his claws on me, could populate my world with such creatures. I'd have none of it! Those endless nightmares in which I confronted my father's whales—not to mention things worse, such as ghosts and green-haired, golden-eyed mermaids—was bad enough! I became that instant a desperate man, a fanatic. No mystic voyages for Jonathan Upchurch, says I to myself. No fooling around with those secret realms.

from whence deep thunders roare,
Must'ring thir rage, and Heav'n resembles Hell!

And so, as I say, I screamed. Flint spun around with his arms flung out and his coattails flaring—so people told me later—his terrible glittering face full of glee at the effect he'd produced, and he stared straight at me to improve on it a little, but then he saw I wasn't looking at him or at the girl neither, and he turned to stare, like a man alarmed, at where *I* was staring. The girl did the same, then swung her eyes toward me again, and then she too began to scream. Within three seconds the whole audience was hooting and throwing its hands up and pushing toward the aisles as if the building was on fire, and Flint was yelling with all his might, 'Gentlemen, I implore you!' and my father beside me was gleefully beating his fists on his knees, saying, 'Lunatics!' smiling like a lunatic himself, my poor mother trying to catch hold of my hands and comfort me. It was Bedlam—on all sides of me the rushing of those birds and the roaring and shoving of the crowd gone berserk—but like Shadrack meeting the eyes of the angel in the fiery furnace, I saw none of that, saw only the eyes of the golden-haired girl and screamed straight into them for mercy, and the girl screamed back.

"What it all meant I had no idea, though for years after that the name Miranda Flint had a dire effect on me, robbed me of my reason, made me sure that in a minute I'd suffocate. I was a cursed man. Whenever I heard Dr. Flint was in town I'd haunt the dark alleys of whatever shabby hall he was playing in, hoping I'd maybe get a glimpse of the two. A thousand times I fancied I saw them, or turned some corner and believed they'd trapped me, and my heart stopped dead as a mackerel. But little by little, of course, the spell weakened. Their pictures on theater bills grew foreign (she grew thicker, less appealing; his mustache grew scraggly) and at last they lost their power to frighten and draw me, suck me out toward unearthly things. Finally, the Flints' names dropped from the circuit, and I believed I was free of them. Dr. Flint was by now a wanted man, and as for his little Miranda, rumor had it she'd died somewhere in India. I'd escaped by a hair, I was pretty well convinced. That one encounter had proved there are deadly, enslaving attractions that might laugh at even winds and tides, unhinge the swing of planets. Such was my opinion and—because of my father's tales, no doubt—the old gray sea was involved in it.

"For these reasons, despite the proximity of my home to the port of Boston, despite my father's scorn and my mother's grief (she'd misgivings about the whole universe)—despite, even, the silent yet thunderous appeal of those powerful-masted merchantmen, gunboats, and whalers, sails pregnant-bellied as the noise of French horns, banners aflutter like fanfare trumpets—I kept to landside, working like a devil to stir up sufficient capital to go west to Illinois and try out farming.

III

"I had read in books about southern Illinois. It was a violent country—land of Mike Fink and Dan'l Boone and the blaspheming, murdering Harpe brothers—a country of mountains and rivers and endless hardwood forests; in the spring, a place of amazing greens—there's more kinds of trees there in southern Illinois than in the whole of Europe—and in both spring and fall it's a great broad highway to floods and tornadoes, the mightiest in the world. Not *northern* Illinois, you understand—flat and mathematical, staring like an idiot at endless sky and pasture. A whole other kingdom, this southern Illinois, dark with timber and bluffs and the slide of big rivers. I had to go there, that's all. Let other men hunt the squinting whale, or wait in dark upstairs rooms for spooks, the new age aborning, the exploded mind. Give me a southern Illinois big flood—silent, omnivorous, as unallegorical as butcher's bones—and give me a safe, high cabin to watch it from, with a woman beside me, some witchly Miranda Flint grown saner. The water swallows up the noise as it does the bottomlands, hurrying yellow. Where the current's strong there may be a humming, a gurgle now and then, or the hissing of friction by the red mud bank; and up the branches there may be a crashing as the yellow-brown wall comes down the slopes with its cargo of pigs and prairie chickens. But there's no sound, nothing, where the big flood rolls, the Ohio conjoining with the Mississippi: a burden silent, swollen, sinister—the idea of evil as pure physicality, with animals peeking from their high rock caves and Indians watching, silent as the waters, from the blufftops across from mine. There, no place but there, I would hack out my freedom.

"It was a place and occupation that appealed to me not only for the majesty in it, the liberty it afforded (I had a great-uncle, a bookish old hermit, who farmed in upper New York State), but also because, I may as well confess, it would take me close to wild Indians. Where I got this attraction, Heaven knows. I've been all my life a rapacious reader, much to my mother's and our minister's consternation. They believed the poor best that could be made of me, given the danger of my turning into a philosopher, was a schoolmaster—which, at age sixteen, I became. Perhaps it was some poem I'd read in my boyhood, or a half-ridiculous, half-mystical picture on a box of cigars. As for flesh and blood (discounting harpooners, who were a separate breed, their eyes cool reflections of the eyes of whales), I'd seen no more than a half-dozen Red Men in all my life—Vermont or York State rural Indians who'd drifted to Boston in deerskins and peculiar shaggy slippers and hats as formal as a Congressman's. Their eyes stared through you like the eyes of a long-since-beaten Assyrian, or a man brought back from the distant future, who knows your obsessions and's been told he must not interfere. They were eyes that had seen things that I, for all my books, had not—tornadoes, the tumble of buffalo, the light on forest floors after rain, the mesmerizing eyes of old, sick bear. All God's gifts we'd wasted, I knew by certain books. Caught up in a destinal vortex somehow of our own mad construction we'd intellected Eden to a soot-dark Foundry, a universal stench of codfish oil. We must check the spiral—'Haul in, haul in!' as the whalers say—and no white man I'd talked to (abstract as geometry) knew the trick of it. Indians knew things —or anyway so I'd read somewhere—without thinking, without learning. It was my settled conviction that they were, though a threat to my egotism, my spiritual betters, and for better or worse I was determined to make the acquaintance of these strange men, if they were men.

"Hence my project.

"Early mornings and again late evenings, when I'd finished my war on ignorance and returned my scholars to their rested-up homes, I took odd-jobs work of all descriptions. I was strong as a cart-ox but also, at least by reputation, sharp-witted. I hauled trunks and sea-chests, rolled whale-oil ashore, kept accounts for my mother's younger brother, a pharmacist, and even served, briefly, as odd-jobs man to the Reverend William Dunkel, our minister. His hair was iron-gray, as smooth and sociable as candlewax on top, but on his chin anarchistic with kinks and curls and darker patches. He wore no mustache, being vain for some reason about his long upper lip and the great, fierce English nose that crowned it. He worked me unconscionably, in my opinion, but that was by no means the worst of it. At every excuse, he labored to improve my character.

"'Upchurch, my boy, Discipline is a word full of hardness,' he said once, bending to catch my eye as, furiously, panting like a prophet, I split chunks of oak beside his cellar chute. He wore, as always, the dusty black suit which he'd got in New York and which inclined me to believe he was richer than he cared to let on to us. 'Discipline is a word full of hardness, I say, abounding in disagreeables, till we learn to peer beyond its hideous shadows and behold its weighty results.'

"'Yes sir,' says I. I set up another block and attacked it. He straightened up, slipping his thumbs into his coat pockets and squinting a trifle, protecting his eyes from chips. He made his face still soberer.

"'My earliest ideas of Discipline,' he said, 'were that it came through dark closets, half-hours spent in cellarways, a refusal of a mother's kiss, a teacher's ferule, a stand on the dunceblock. Later it came through an unwilling obedience to college rules, a binding of the will that took away the "do as I've a mind to." It came through studying lessons with a headache on a hot summer's day, or a nailing down to duty while green fields, balmy airs, and fleecy clouds all sang aloud for me to join them. After this, Discipline came to me in visions, and I saw her subjects standing in the stocks, with limbs swollen and lacerated, and hands always suppliant, or driven by force into glowing, fiery furnaces, or led against their will to the stake for burning. I shuddered at the word, for it always meant *endure,* and *endure* only. Now I speak the word with reverence, for, however it comes, it is wrapped up in glory.'

" 'Yes sir,' I said, and paused to wipe my forehead with my sleeve. Reverend Dunkel could go on in this orotund fashion for days—for all I knew, centuries. His chin, almost hidden in the imposing beard, was less than awesome, but his smile was the sternest I ever saw, except one time in Brazil on the face of a head-hunter. He wouldn't harm a fly, my mother maintained, and I must grant, in all fairness, I never saw him go out of his way for a kick at a rabid dog. He had, all the same, a devilish streak as bad as Flint's. He used to send articles on sin and damnation to monthly magazines for young ladies.

"He raised his eyebrows. 'You understand what I'm saying, boy?'

" 'Up to a certain point,' I said.

"He nodded grimly and lifted his long square hand to his nose. 'That's how it is with this life,' he said. 'The part we understand is irrelevant.'

"I soon took hire less troublesome.

"My new employer was a butcher, a red-faced Dutchman who rarely spoke. I did so well for him that I was soon transferred from delivery boy to carver. My project was proceeding splendidly—I seemed to have Midas' golden touch. While others my age were shipping on whalers, breaking their heads on windstruck booms and their hearts on foreign-tongued prostitutes, I (puffing severely on a pipe of clay) was laying up my treasures on earth, as Reverend Dunkel would have it, but from my point of view, my ransom. My luck was uncanny. On two separate occasions, in addition to my wages from the school and the butcher (whose name, by the way, was Hans van Klug), I found money in the street—sixteen dollars the first time, four the next. Though I knew well enough what civilization calls right and wrong, I'd heard sufficient of my father's tales of pirates and gold-crazy pirate hunters that I made no great effort to return what God had sent me. The very idea would have seemed to me then as mad as the ritual dances of African savages, of which I'd read lurid descriptions. I was not, Heaven knows, a democrat. The man who invented the wheel, I thought—with no little pleasure in my almanack wit—was a hermit on a mountain. Had he consulted the mass before setting to his work, they'd have persuaded him to think up the clothespin.

"Then, quite suddenly, my fortune turned. By an act of spectacular folly I lost all I had. Say it was the draw of the universe—the powers that laugh at winds, tides, planets. Say it was . . . whatever you please. Truth—what's known as 'plain fact'—is profoundly mysterious.

IV

"I had at this time seventy-five dollars, enough, by my pretty-well firm calculation, to reach Illinois and buy thirty to forty good acres. On a clear and cold October night, one of those nights when the sky seems bottomless, falling away from you even as you watch, I decided, on impulse, to have supper out. I'd worked late with van Klug, the two of us carving and packaging meat in the fuliginous silence we both preferred— indifferently lopping off arms and legs, joints, rumps, and shoulders, sorting the martyrdom of nature into piles and putting prices on it—and I knew my mother would be asleep long since. She had despaired a good many years ago of ever making me a gentleman. I'd made no secret of my plan to go West, and what could she do but accept, with some whooping, my abandonment of her? At times she'd play sick to keep me near, but I understood her tricks. Even if, good as her word, she had died of apoplexy, I doubt if I'd have felt much serious remorse. Is it Christian charity to be chained up in other people's foolishness? We occupied the house as if each of us lived there all alone, like two holy stylites on neighboring pillars—my father consorting with ice-caps and whales, serenaded by ghosts and mermaids, watched by demons, if the tales he told were true—and we seldom spoke, except that now and then she'd whine at me, or cry at her prayers, taking care that I overheard her.

"For convenience' sake, I decided to stop at the Buried Treasure Inn, on Front Street. It was a grizzly two-storey place with a bad reputation, barbaric with the whalebone-jagged speech of Nantucketers and the misanthrope dealings of 'privateers,' but the smells falling out into the crisp night air were persuasive enough that I swallowed my natural distaste for company, especially the company of drunken Long Toms, and pushed through the pitch-black, gable-topped door. The roar of their talk and the wall of smoke from their carved bone pipes crashed over my soul like a breaching wave, and along with the noise and smoke came the stink of their rum, like a whiff from a charnelhouse. The entry-way was crowded from wall to wall with sharp-beaked, red-eyed creatures alarming as rats in a breadbox—whalers: too lean, too garishly maimed, too wrinkled with crowsfeet to be mere pirates, yet more alarming than pirates: giant-killers. I had half a mind to turn homewards and make do with cheese. Yes sir. The walls, what little I could see of them in that thick brine-green, primaeval dark, were hung with outlandish clubs and spears—a thing very strange, it seemed to me, in a place notorious for drunken brawls. But what was life or death to them, those riders of whale-humps? Nevertheless, as I stepped up toward them they crowded together, polite as Presbyterians, and allowed me to pass. I went on up to the public room, equally crowded, and after I'd gotten a word with the landlord, pressed to the lighted room adjoining, where he'd promised to bring me supper. As I sat on my settle, uncomfortably glancing at the sea-dogs around me—not whalers these, if sulphurous fire in the eye is a sign (so it seemed to me at first), but still not unhumanized cripples neither, and dressed like gentlemen, or at all events like well-to-do gypsies—a genial fat old man leaned toward me and sociably called out, 'Ye don't drink, do ye sonny?'

" 'The devil in hell I don't!' says I.

"The whole long table roared with what sounded like drowned men's laughter. I was ashamed enough to kick a mule, being young and somewhat priggish (and having blushed bright red), but there was no mule there any sensible man would discomfit. They were tall as trees, and even their parrot, walking back and forth on the shelf above us like a suspicious and hot-tempered ports inspector, looked more than a wise man would tangle with. Their captain, a great, sleek shark of a fellow, at the end of the table, a man his crew called Pious John, slid an empty mug in my direction, and a man seated halfway between us— they called him Lovalie Will—gently pushed me the dented brass pitcher. The genial fat man who'd spoken to me first, a man with an eyepatch and sharp red ears, filled up the mug and slid it to me, a liquor that looked like water but was, I knew the same instant it touched my lips, raw gin, pure fires of torment. I doubt that I made a very noticeable face, but the table laughed, leaning forward, encouraging. It was a laugh just a whit less offensive now. As I gave it some thought, I inclined to believe it was almost downright friendly. 'Fine lad there,' says sleek old Pious John to his neighbor. I took a longer sip. For all Reverend Dunkel's ferocious sermons, the gin seemed to have no particular effect—a warmness, perhaps; a tranquility like that which old Reverend Dunkel, with bony fists clenched, was eternally recommending. I took an even longer sip and they smiled their approval. I saw they intended no evil whatsoever, whatever an ignorant stranger might suppose. I was picking up their society's ways. The landlord came in then, smiling like a Trojan in a field of Greeks, dished out meat and potatoes, and disembarked. His fear of them surprised me, and when he peeked back with furious button eyes I thought again of righteous Reverend Dunkel, and I very near laughed out loud.

"I ate supper hurriedly nevertheless, looking them over from time to time with my wall-eyed glance—an affliction I've borne with a tolerable patience since that first dreadful hour I've spoken of. They asked me questions, their red, weathered faces twitching like horseskin, their eyes as aglitter as eagles' eyes. I was tempted to pretend I was going to sea, but thought better of it. I wouldn't put it past them to shanghai a man, genteel as they might appear. They pried on, as men do—whether pirates or dentists or stone-masons —and I gave them at last, since I had no choice, a crude map of my mizered individuality: I told them of the Jonathan Upchurch farm in Illinois (as it said on the barn that was not yet built) and the seventy-five dollars I'd saved up toward its purchase. The mug was empty. Someone filled it.

" 'It's a damn sight better'n bein' et by the whales,' Pious John called out, and raised his mug to me. He slid his eyes toward the door, then back at me, eyes like a viper's, but with no ill-will. 'And better'n the life privateers put up with,' he added in a whisper, 'cutting men's throats for the pay of eternal damnation.' A muscle in his cheek twitched, a brief, sharp tingle, and he struggled to suppress some painful emotion.

"As if it were a signal, the whole dandy rout of them looked my way with approval and envy, turning their bright-black-eyed heads toward me, and hefted their mugs toward the rooftree. 'To southern Illinois!' they shouted.

"I drank. They talked strangely, like maniacs, of farming. Most of their fathers had been farmers, they said, but adverse fortune . . . 'Once ye've turned pirate there's no turning back,' Lovalie Will said, his long nose slick with tears. 'It's a sickness,' he confided. 'A terminal illness of the spirit.' I was startled by their candor, but I thought I understood it. I'd heard my

father speak more than once of the lonely, necessarily secretive life of the buccaneer. They had a code all their own, those universal outcasts living off the world without a soul's by-yer-leave, and though some were no better than poisonous snakes, there were some that were true-born gentlemen. They draped their arms around each other and me, quoted snatches of verse, and remembered fondly the smell of new hay off Mongolia. The yellow room glowed.

"Things got queerer and queerer. The room swam, as the saying goes (yet swim it did, sir). I pounded the table with the best of them, arguing hogs. They proposed a trifling game of chance. 'I'll have none of it!' says I, not yet their coney. The whole crowd thanked me. If I'd wanted, I thought, I could have converted the whole blamed pack into Christians. They then proposed some other entertainment, which I didn't quite catch, though I more or less agreed, all slack-jawed smile, and in an instant all of us were leaving the inn (old whalers' claws reaching, plucking at my coat) and we were rushing down the middle of the dark street, hooting—I reeling, falling down yet miraculously balancing my mug as a slow-winged gannet balances, asleep on a sailyard, and I roared in the night like Beelzebub with my pirates. Ah, communion!

"What happened for a span after that has vanished from my mind like smoke. I have a ludicrous image of my mother in her nightgown, a skinny arm stretched like a frantic wing, holding up a lantern at the top of the stairs, her mouth wide and trembling, her thin knees violently banging each other. I believe I spoke tearfully of my love for my father. Then darkness; and then, much later, this:

"I stood, somewhat dazed and extremely unwell, on the old decayed wharf by the abandoned lumberyard of Pankey & Co., gazing at a sailboat by the name of the *Jolly Independent*. She had a halfdeck or cuddy and was rigged sloop-fashion. I've no idea what her tonnage was, but I imagine she'd hold eight persons without crowding. I'd had an idea I was in southern Illinois, but when I looked out over the midnight ocean the truth burst over my spirit cold as Iceland.

The sons of seawhores had sold me the sailboat! As for my pirates, they were gone, vanished, more at random in the world than I was by seventy-five dollars.

"I carried on some, I hardly need tell you. Never was a mortal alive more foully swindled! I was persuaded long afterward, by my friend Billy More, that I may have been somewhat a party to the cheat. The mind runs deeper than its schemes, could be. But I knew none of that, that night on the wharf, banging my fists on the planking, performing my tantrum. 'Trust not, want not,' my hermit uncle used to say, looking sternly at his pipe, not at me, as if giving plain notice.

"How long I went on in this childish fashion I've no idea, though I can tell you I enjoyed it. I wept like a baby, profoundly conscious of my cruel and total abandonment in a world of ungoded sea and sky, on the shore behind me the bankrupt, fenced-up lumberyard. The one thing missing in my paroxysm of grief was some loving Miranda to observe my suffering and be filled with admiration. It was no doubt that that made me stop and sit up, legs dangling, elbows on knees and chin on fists, and commence to reconsider.

"The weather was changing, a warmish breeze coming up from southwest, and little by little my stomach seemed to be stabilizing. I looked at the name, laid in gold on the bow, the *Jolly Independent,* and the irony made me burst out laughing. It was a self-regarding Byronic laugh, soul-tortured and metaphysical, at first. But even as I laughed a change came o'er me. Two things came stealing to my mind at once: the sea-dogs had sold me someone else's boat, so it was mine and not-mine, like the whole of Creation —that was one of them—and the other was that, gazing out toward the eastern horizon, feeling the motion of the waves and wind, I wanted to be there, with Plato and Plotinus, despite all my sensible talk about southern Illinois. In landlessness alone lies the highest truth, shoreless, indefinite as God! thought I. Better to perish in that howling infinite than be . . . something or other. (I forget my phrase.) The boat seemed trying to tell me something, thumping her side on the rough wharf logs. Before I knew it, I'd climbed aboard and was bailing her—she was nearly half-filled. I hoisted the jib and mainsail the way I'd seen others do, and, keeping full, set boldly out to sea.

"The wind, as I've said, was blowing freshly from the southwest. The night was clear and cold, though warmer than earlier. I took the helm—a more difficult matter than I'd expected, but I soon got the hang of it. We flew like a seagull, riding the breast of swells. The mast, sail, and ropes, the bow and bowsprit bobbing like the head of a galloping horse, were as sharp in the moonlight as images in a dream. I sailed in a kind of drunken trance, wildly jubilant, as if I thought I'd been born indestructible. But the waves keep hoisting and heaving at the tiller, and when I glanced down once and got a look at my hand—it was paler than marble—I came sober of a sudden, and my joy edged quickly towards terror. Something had gone wrong. The wind had increased, and I was fast getting out of the lee of the land. Birds wheeled around me—screeching purveyors of lunatic advice. I tried to veer larboard, grabbing ahold of the tiller with both hands. Nothing happened; it felt like a whale had the rudder in his crooked teeth. I went faint, terrified, and suddenly the sea was no longer mystical nor I some floating inviolable spirit but both of us as real as ice-cold spray, fierce jolts, shrill wind, and the thumping, creaking, careening yaw of the sailboat. I felt myself falling, passing out, and then I was scrambling, gasping for air in the bilgewater. I got hold of myself and screamed for help though there wasn't a mortal in hearing range. I sucked in air and pulled myself back to the tiller arm. It was like a miracle, the strength my terror sent. But even that eerie strength wouldn't prove much comfort, I knew. A fierce southern wind and a powerful ebb-tide were plunging me straight to destruction. When I looked back over my shoulder the whole of the west had gone black—black as a pit but for the flicker of gulls. A storm was gathering. I had no compass, no provisions, and soon I'd be clean out of sight of the land. My thoughts seemed to rush as the sea rushed past, but, for all their bewildering rapidity, they went nowhere. The boat was moving at a terrible speed, full before the wind, no reef in either jib or mainsail, her bows completely under foam. I have no idea why she didn't broach to—my hands on the tiller were as influential as two sparrows on a fence. But the boat kept steady, and gradually, despite my terror, my thoughts grew saner. The wind was increasing. Whenever we rose from a forward plunge, the sea fell combing in over the counter. My hands, my legs, my face, had lost all feeling. Nevertheless, abandoning the tiller, I stumbled to the mainsail and let it go by the run. It flew over the bows and, weighted by water, snapped the mast off short by the board. The accident saved me, for the moment, at least. Riding under the jib alone, I boomed along before the wind, shipping heavy seas but surviving. My heart now pounded as hard as it had at the peak of my terror, but pounded for a different reason: I believed I had a chance.

"So I believed—overweening son of Adam, Reverend Dunkel would have said. For just then a terrible scream came down from directly above me—a shriek like the rage of a thousand demons. I twisted, screaming back, and had a fleeting impression of a great black monster, swiftly bearing down from above my head, indifferent, apocalyptic as a falling planet. My hair stood on end, my blood congealed, and I swooned again into the bilgewater."

V

The angel presses his fingertips together. The guest is befuddled.

"Hah! Damned philosophical," you'll say. "Ha ha! The mariner catches his guest by the trembling ear, and Heaven itself attends the two, and what can the mariner think of to tell? Why, nothing! Nothing!—as usual! A cunning tale! A crafty fabulation!"

But I answer boldly: "Fiddlesticks! There is more to these overblown tunes than you apprehend, sir." I am scheduled to hang, as so are you, though in my case the terrible hour is certain. (Barring accident.) I will not think of it (tugging my beard in panic, thinking. Tongue out, eyes bulged, swaying in the wind. Better the wind than the corpse that sways to its music! And . . .)

These halls are filled with ghosts. Take notice. They pass with unechoing steps outside my door, dragging soundless chains. See how they gape like stranded fish, how the midnight sockets of their eyes stare nowhere, meaningless. I people the darkness with undersea green —transform it to gray, hang spiderwebs. They approach me trembling, as if hungry to speak, but they remember they have nothing to say to me, no fears, no projections. Unmeaning'd, they're merely there, thinned out to vision; nowhere. Ten thousand thousand generations of hanged criminals. Think of it, Inspector! I strain my wits toward them, my own bleak future. We have nothing in common. Onward forever the dead come, soundless and staring. In me they exist, not "back there in the past" because there is no past, there is nothing in all this universe but the razor's edge between my memory and imagination, the instant's perception between things dead, unlimbed forever, and yet to be born . . . or yet to be borne. My very existence one second ago is banished out of life eternally. Second by second the world falls shut like a coffin-lid. Does nothing survive but the discipline ghosts have imposed on ghosts—the rock-firm shackles of dead ideas, steel wire on the New Lamb's testicles? There's energy for you! There's man intense!

"Ha ha," cries you, "there's paradox, there's quagmire!"

Not so! Let us speak of great works of art, or even foolish ones; brute objects decayed as old mountains, eternal instants. —But time's too short for that, I agree with you. Tack alee, then, mate, away from the maelstrom, away from the Coal-pocket, upward in all directions, home to Visions!

"You're *serious!*" says you with a look of dismay.

No no, just play; all play. Sit down.

(Serious in the manner of a sand castle, or an old

woman fashioning a paper rose. Whoever found out
reality with sand, old secondhand tissue?

'Tiss*you*, my lord!

'Tis who?

Sh! Sh!)

The guest now notices the angel's wings. He looks
mildly puzzled. He's no fool, however. Keeps his own
counsel, awaits some clarification.

"You were speaking of a hoax," the guest remarks.

"Ah, that," says the mariner, with a look both delighted and cunning. "I see yer a rationalist!"

VI

"She that overran me and picked me up was the whaler
Jerusalem bound from Nantucket on a three years'
hunting voyage, and a sorrowfuller ship never sailed
on the planet earth. As soon as the jolly-boat was
hauled aboard with my half-drowned body, and the
mate had signaled I was still alive, the Captain, assisted
by a man with white hair, retired in silence to his
cabin.

"I lay on a berth in a coal dark stateroom trying to
sort out the borders of reality, unscrambling dream
and recollection. My impression—dream or not (it
turned out to be not, in its main particulars)—was of
rigging awesomely arching upwards, rat-lined, storm-
lit, chalk-white-sailed, lifting tyrannic and overpower-
ing as a turreted castle. The ropework swung like a
vast spiderweb of Jacob's ladders, hung here and there
with sou'westered angels of dubious aspect, their skirts
flying out like fearful wings, and high above them in
the rain-black night the ghostly, pale-glowing battle-
ments ringing the crowsnests. Short-bearded men gazed
down at me like judges. 'He's coming to,' says one.
Lantern light colored his eyes bright red. He bent
down nearer my face. 'A drunkard.'

"I rolled my head left. Negroes barebacked as plantation slaves ran knee-deep in deckwash, silently dou-
ble-lashing longboats down. I managed to bring out

my thanks for the rescue—I could pretty well see how much trouble it had been, managed while the ship was still trimming for the storm—and I begged to be taken back to land.

" 'Not likely,' said one—the second mate. The grave-robber's humor I heard in his laugh made me struggle in anger and fear to rise up on my elbows and peer into his face. A pain went through me, the sky went spinning, and despite my clenched fists, my holy indignation, I collapsed to the deck again, senseless.

"When I next came conscious I was down in the stateroom, a whale-oil lamp burning dully above me, swinging, creaking on its chain like a crooning hag. As I turned my head for a look at the man standing over me, the pain was there again, a cat-o'-nine-tails wrapped round my chest. I went motionless, then yelled, less from pain than from anger at my chance captivity, and the man said gruffly, as if with amusement, 'Avast! Ye've got ribs broke. Lay as ye be!' He told me the name of the ship and her captain and the nature of their business on the seven seas. I could call back none of it to memory now. I remembered only this: When I asked where the ship would put in, he answered, 'Heaven if we're lucky; more likely lower.' He raised his hand—to the lamp, I suppose, for the stateroom went dark. 'What d'ye mean?' I asked him. He answered from the darkness, the voice of a minister discoursing on Hell, or a hanging judge when he talks of Heaven—'Yer destiny's set ye a perilous venture, but a far nobler venture than some, it may be. Ye're landless, landsman, and like to remain so, circling the watery wilderness now till Doomsday.' The rough sea rumbled in the bulkhead beside me, howling, infinite, like the grumbling of the Devil in his chains. The man went on speaking, or I dreamed he spoke. I imagined him with leathern wings and jagged sharksteeth, telling me lies and taking demonic delight in it. 'The omens are thundering bad ones, lad—except for, it may be, yer wall-eyed gaze. Ye've jined with a company of deadmen, ye see; deadmen pursuing a deadman down into his grave and, could be, through it.

Rest up, I advise ye. There'll be no more bringing the *J'rusalem* hard alee!'

"The ship pitched and rolled like a planet cut loose of gravitational moorings. I lay with my two hands clinging to the berth, and for a long time—some hours—that was all I knew, the slow endless rolling and the pounding of the storm, and below me a crashing like wrecks tumbling over on the ocean floor. But then I was aware of a further sound, an out-of-tune music that seemed to come ringing from the *Jerusalem*'s beams. It was a sound almost human, I imagined at times; at other times it was animal—the rumble of a tiger—or worse, the growl of atoms. I strained my ears, breathing more lightly than my broken ribs required. I caught a few sounds that were almost words—then scraps of melody, hymnlike. But the hymn was far darker than any Presbyterian hymn I knew: Music charged up like a lightning rod. It died away, sank deep into the storm. I began to believe I'd imagined it. But then—though the storm was as loud as ever, crashing all around me and whistling overhead—I heard it again, like the moaning of spirits, tormented demons so used to flame they transformed it as if automatically to musical wails. The sound was maddening; I'd never heard the like. But there was something far graver than that foreignness about it. The sound was freighted with a kind of accusation, a promise of revenge.

"Like them, as I imagined them, I learned numbness to pain and, flame or no flame, dropped my feet over the side and climbed up to a sitting position. There I remained for some time, all my weight on my arms. My waist, I learned by feel in the darkness, was tightly wrapped in canvas—old sail. Raising myself by the bulkhead chain (by the bulkhead chain and by will power), I got on my feet and, with hardly a pause, pushed forward toward the passageway. The ship rolled hard, like a thing malevolent and aware of my purpose, but I kept my balance and made it to the passage. I could see a dim lampglow, far to sternward. Though my whole body screamed and I was bathed in sweat, I lunged toward it. Ten feet from the hatch, my destination, the ship lurched again and I went down on the decking. The moment I struck I was unconscious.

"How long I lay thus I do not know. I awoke with the music all around me, lapping at my pain, and I crawled forward to the light, which came up through a trap. In the hold below me, in a room full of kegs, pumps, chain-cable, and patching timber—a clutter stacked tight as a family attic—some twenty-five big-shouldered black men sat, two or three of them shackled and chained. All the Negroes were young, between sixteen and thirty. I stared at them, more astounded than afraid. Gold-ringed savages singing their eerie, ungodly chants in the swaying lumination of an old brass lamp, their music summoning an answering music as eerie as the noises at a Boston séance—what was I to think? It was a whaling ship—so all signs showed. A whaling ship, yet here in the hold, a Slaver!

"*Slaver!* A word more smoky, more darkly ambiguous than Egypt's creator-destroyer Sun-god, to a man from Yankee Boston. We did not speak much of Slavers or the men who shipped on them. The whole institution was a cosmic inexplicable. Take the feeling you have when you see a butchered bear in van Klug's front window—hung upside down, like Peter on the cross, with the arms and shoulders and chest of a man—multiply that feeling ten thousand times, and you have, it may be, some feeble image of the superstitious dread in the heart of a Christian Boston man when, straying from the usual routes of his evening meditational walk to wynds more somber, he comes upon the dead-count bodies laid out on the wharf—black females, babies, stunted males—from a Slaver just berthed from Africa. Right enough, they're not human, you may say in your soul, and may support the opinion with a thousand cyclopaedias. But doubt bedevils you—those dead hands unnaturally like human hands, the misery frozen on the dead black face, perfect counterfeit of yours or mine in that sorry last hour. Quickly they cover the bodies with tarpaulins and march the cargo still salable to the wagons. (The living ones, too, could fool you for a minute, wringing their fingers and complaining to the skies, more religious than many a Christian pope—or weeping silently, like whalers' widows—or showing no trace of emotion whatever, like Cato the night of his suicide, reading his book.) It was known in Boston that the Lord smiles here on earth on His elect. So Calvin maintained, or so I'm told. And whether the captain of a slaving ship walked home chin on chest without muttering a word, or greeted his family with a shout and a smile, pulling out his pipe for his children's kiss, it was known that the captains of Slavers were well-to-do beings. These things were indisputable, however dubious. So that persons confident of their theological position shrugged, though uncertainly, at the sorrow of slaves, or at most pursed their lips as they would at the humanlike whimperings of injured dogs. But mainly we did not go down to the docks when a Slaver was in, but were checked by the same inexplicable dread (much multiplied) we'd have felt beside the carcass of a butchered bear, outlandish country brother. The institution was legal and right, but we were metaphysically uneasy. Though they would have denied it (studiously callous as men always are when the crowd condones what a decent man alone would feel leery of) the slave ship crews were themselves uneasy. Pirates, when they meet on the high seas, pause and greet each other. 'How many skulls?' goes the merry cry. But Slavers pass in silence.

"So, gazing down at the mournful singers, I was shocked, hardly able to credit my sight. A whaler, to any man born where I was, was a vessel above ambiguity, an emblem of pluck, sly Yankee craft. She was the soul of big business, industry, initiative. She was oil—light and power—vialed ton upon ton: egalitarian, winch-and-cable key to boundless Empire. A whaler with a hold full of slaves was a flat impossibility, as if Michael, Raphael, and Gabriel should conspire to get Satan a comfortable hotel. —But then it came to me I'd made a mistake. No women, no children; so she wasn't a Slaver. But the shackles, the chains . . . enigma!

"There was a noise behind me, the scrape of an opening hatch. I looked back, stiff-necked for fear of

another blast of pain. There was no sign of light, but
I could hear someone coming. I doubted I had time
to return to my stateroom. For some reason I didn't
even try to understand, I was filled with alarm at the
thought that I might be discovered where I lay—
premonition, no doubt, of the violence charging all
hands on that ship—and instinctively, whimpering,
still on all fours, I scuttled away like a crayfish. There
was a wavering film of light now, behind me, gleaming
on varnish where the passageway angled. I continued
backing off, clumsily quick-footed. Tears streamed
from my eyes; my clenched teeth ached. And then, in
the darkness, my right hand, following the bulkhead,
struck empty space. I jabbed in further. It was a narrow companionway leading toward sky and rigging.
I started up. Pain shogged through my veins with every
heartbeat. In a minute I was crouched in the lantern-
slanting dark of the foredeck. No one in sight. I eased
myself forward to the shadow of the windlass—movement was somewhat less difficult here, though the
deck was slippery from the wash of waves—and here
I lay still.

"The southern blow was as stiff as ever, but the
rain had passed on. Overhead there were clouds out-
lined by the moon to make silver-edged, teratic faces
—a few cold stars like wild horses' eyes—in all lateral
directions, the rolling, white-capped sea. The hatch I'd
just now come through lit up, then dimmed as the
man with the lantern moved on. I breathed easier, still
shallowly. It was a game, one man against the universe,
like my spree on the *Jolly Independent*. But as before,
the game abruptly ended. The hatch I'd come through
lit up once more, and this time the light did not dim
but grew brighter. The man came hurrying up the
companionway. Before his head emerged I was bowsward of the windlass and laid out flatlings on the forecastle head. The man with the lantern was shouting
something. His movements, his voice, were like those
of a machine. Wolff, he was called, I'd find out later.
The second mate. Another shout came from the watch
on the bridge, then another from the stern. ' 'E's away,

sir!' 'All hands!' For all the wind, the hull laid-to against churning seas, the masts trimmed tight, the deck was suddenly aswarm with men, their lanterns swinging, reflected brighter than diamonds in the foam, and the salt-spray air was alive with their ringing yells.

"In all that noise it should have been impossible to hear what I nevertheless imagined I heard—what by all the laws and traditions and above all superstitions of the sea I could not have heard—a woman's voice. It chilled me, threw me into panic like that of a periodic madman when he feels the faint tremble of his sickness coming on. It was a voice you might've heard in a school for young ladies, or a nunnery perhaps. Around and above me hung the stark gray whaler, professional killer, stern tool of industry lifting and plunging on a violent sea; on the deck below me and on the bridge above stood shouting men with lanterns. Nevertheless clear as day I heard it—the voice of a cultured young lady. Someone answered her, a voice muffled, maybe drunken, and I caught a name: *Augusta*. I held my breath, straining to hear any further word the girl might say. It was a voice that shot through me, magical, unearthly. (I was struck the same way years afterward by a woman singing in a field down in southern Illinois; a voice that made time stop, prepared for a mystical opening of the skies—a common enough thing, but powerful in its moment.)

"That same instant, the Captain emerged from his cabin and tottered to the rail like a man either deathly sick or drunk, his glinting eyes jumping the length of the ship to the windlass. I shrunk back into the darkness behind me. Where there'd been nothing before, there was now interference. I looked up. A black harpooner with a bone through his nose stood barefoot but steady as a steeple above me—a thousand feet tall and as wide as a gleaming stone mountain, he seemed. His harpoon lay casual as a hiking staff in his richly bejeweled and braceleted hand, as if I, no whale, were unworthy of his skill. I gave out a squeak, like a mouse in the shadow of a hovering eagle. The harpooner showed his enormous white teeth and chuckled, a sound like jackals chuckling on the Syrian coast, and his hand came down, very gently, and closed on my elbow."

VII

"This does concern a hoax?" the guest inquires.

"A hoax, sir. Aye."

The angel smiles, draws his pipe out, stuffs it. He stares out the window, his wings drooping, and absently pats his pockets, hunting for phosphor-sticks.

VIII

"They kept me locked up more carefully thereafter— locked up body and mind like a dangerous maniac, though I was freer than they guessed. They'd tell me not a word about the blacks in the hold or who it was owned that female voice. When I asked the first mate, Mr. Knight, about these things—it was the first mate himself that brought me food—he'd take a look of consternation as if he feared for his safety in the range of such a lunatic. But he never would flatly deny that I'd heard what I claimed I'd heard. He'd stand looking guilty, head forward, horselike, his shoulders drawn inward like those of a man who hears footsteps behind him in an unlighted alley—it was all he could do to keep from peeking past his shoulder—and he'd grumble gloomily, 'Who ever heard of black slaves on a whaler?' and would laugh, then throw me a sudden sharp look, as if hoping for an answer. Whatever the ins-and-outs of it, I saw I was less the ship's prisoner than he was, and I'd smile knowingly. 'Eat yer supper,' he'd say then. When I'd done so, he'd check my bandages and leave, all as quick as he could manage. I could see I had nothing to fear from him, though he never forgot to lock me in when he left me. He was a tall man, broad-shouldered as a chest of drawers, firm-muscled as a statue, but his leathery face was cracked deep beside the ice-pale eyes and again at each side of his wide, thin mouth with laughter lines. He was not a man built for ponderous meditation. Even if you saw him at home in Nantucket, sitting in the Methodist church in his tight black Sunday suit —a man with enormous feet and hands and a long, long neck with a small head perched on the top like a crowsnest—you'd have moved him in an instant to his proper setting, balanced at the stern of a long-boat shouting to his oarsmen, teasing, joking, cajoling, occasionally throwing a dare-devil taunt or wild curse at the whale. He was a creature designed for roughneck adventures and tales of them later to his numerous, healthy, pious family; but the design had gone awry. Something—something more troublesome than whales—had turned him speculative. Sometimes looking up from my plate of beans, I'd catch him staring at the bulkhead like a man looking thoughtfully off at the horizon. He was a man with grave responsibilities, and the longer I watched him, the surer I was of my natural advantage. I formed a plan.

"I said to him: 'It's no use pretending it's otherwise. I've been taken aboard a mystery ship, and I've penetrated enough already to be dangerous. God help us all!' I wrung my fingers, pretending I was greatly distressed by it.

" 'Then ye've penetrated more than I have,' says he, with his eyebrows up.

" 'That may be, Mr. Knight. That may well be.' I took hold of the sides of my head and pretended to close my eyes, but in secret I kept a bead on him. 'I hope you don't think it's for myself I endure this anguish,' I said. 'Not hardly, Mr. Knight!' I gave out a mournful laugh very much like Pious John the Pirate's.

"Mr. Knight pursed his lips for a minute or two, then tipped his head. 'It ain't?' says he.

"I laughed again, like an undertaker. 'I'll tell you the truth, though you may find it hard to believe at first. When you hauled me aboard, you hauled in more than you bargained for. Did you ever hear tell of the pirate Jonathan Upchurch?'

"He picked at his chin. 'I know a whaler named Upchurch.'

"'No relation,' I say quick as a rattlesnake. 'My father raises hogs in Tennessee.' Since he looked a little doubtful, I described the place in elaborate detail. His eyes got glassy. 'But woe's me,' I continued, 'I abandoned that heaven-on-earth and ran away to sea and became a pirate.'

"'Ye didn't!' says Mr. Knight, and takes his black wool hat off. His eyes, when he widened them, were about the size of two dimes.

"'I did, more's the pity. Turned to a life of throat-cutting.' I clenched my fists and heaved a terrible deep sigh.

"'I be damned,' he said. 'Young fellow like you! Well, I be damned.'

"'But you ain't altogether grasped the point, Mr. Knight. He's no ordinary pirate, this Jonathan Upchurch that sits here before you. It was gentlemen I sailed with, men of learning and refinement, and I was one of the highest respected of them all. Don't be fooled by my youth! A wild young boy that's got no sense, no fear of death, can be a dangerous character, and a boy that knows Latin and Greek and what have you, and's been taught smooth manners—such a boy can be a formidable character indeed. I've got friends from one end of this globe to the other—people of some importance, I can tell you: the King of the Zulus, I might mention, for instance, and the King of Niroona, who I helped one time with some underhand business off the Gold Coast. You'd be surprised what people a young man as wealthy as I can get near to —Congressmen, lawyers, governors, actors, stage magicians (I might mention Dr. Flint and the incredible Murdstone). If some misadventure was to happen to me aboard this ship . . . not that I'd personally care, understand . . . What has a miserable pirate like me to look forward to, except death and the hope of the Lord's forgiveness?—'

"I'd overdone it, could be. Mr. Knight reached down

for my dish with the look of a man out of patience. 'Avast,' he said, 'if you're a pirate I'm President Lincoln. Ye never been a mile out of Boston in yer life.'

" 'Believe what suits you,' I answered, and shrugged. I licked off my fork the way my mother does, elaborately genteel.

"He pointed a finger like a fencepost at me. 'What's Singapore look like? Who's the Captain of the *Great Silver Nail?*'

"I smiled sadly and let him press me awhile before I gave him his answers (my father's ballyhoo was worth gold just now). Mr. Knight got to looking exceedingly uneasy. He turned away, scowling and picking at his chin. He said, 'Gentlemen of learning and refinement, was they?' and grinned, about to leave.

"I lay back and put my hands behind my head. 'We used to talk Latin on the ship, to keep our brains in tune. Sometimes our Captain would drill the whole crew on logarithms.'

"He went out and locked the door.

"That evening he brought in a leather-bound volume of Boethius' *Consolation of Philosophy* in Latin. As if casually, I took the Boethius, opened it, and settled at once to reading, absent-mindedly forking in food. When I stole a glance at Mr. Knight, he was standing bent forward at the waist, head tipped, his bright little eyes screwed up like a watchmaker's, trying to make out if I was really reading or just pretending to.

" 'Perhaps I ain't really a pirate after all, Mr. Knight,' I said. 'Perhaps I'm, say, a schoolmaster.' And I let him see a smile just exactly like Pious John's.

"Mr. Knight tipped his head to the other side, one eye tight shut, studying the smile the way a robin would study a cast-iron worm, then picked up the plate, which I wasn't yet done with, and abandoned me without a word.

"The next morning it was a man named Wilkins who brought me food and checked the bandages. He was not exactly a pleasant person, to say the least, though adequate enough in his role as physician. Anyone on a whaler can set a bone, stanch a wound, or hook up an artificial limb. It's as much a part of a whaler's trade as stepping new masts on the shores off Japan when the ship's former masts have been blown to Calcutta. Whereas Mr. Knight was reserved, as befits a first mate, Wilkins, who was only a common seaman, would chatter your ear off, jerking his flat face close to you, his red bandanna clamped tight to his scalp, his muscles all twitching, his body thrown forward like à Chinese wrestler's, his hand on your elbow, your shoulder, the nape of your neck, as if intending no good to you. He was a man struck with lightning, unable to ground it, the flicker of it still in his eyes. He was a half-breed, or multi-breed (black-Chinese-Indian, or Lord knows what), with a thick-lipped, eternally smiling mouth and a sharply slanted squint, eyes black as coal. Where he got hold of the name of Wilkins is more'n I can tell you. Fact is, half of the crew called him Java Jim, and there was others that knew him as Quicksilver Nick. He answered my questions with a wink that belied his disingenuous words, denials that the hold contained slaves or that a woman had ever set foot on the *Jerusalem*. It did not take me long to guess that he'd once sailed with pirates and had been sent here to see if he recognized me. On the passageway bulkhead, outside my state-room, I could see Mr. Knight's long shadow, bent over, spying.

"I saw right away that even with Wilkins I maintained my advantage. He was one of them, involved, caught up in complexities, considerations. Mr. Knight had sometime befriended him, perhaps. Or the Captain had saved him from the gallows for the sake of his poor mother. As even Boethius had understood—though he'd turned it rather pious—a man like myself was outside the web that entrapped their kind. I was dependent on them, that might be so (I was not yet prepared to eat the passageway rats); but I was indifferent and, being unknown, I was possibly danger-ous, hence invulnerable.

" 'Yer lookin',' I said, 'to see if I'm a pirate ye recognize. Look hard, mate! Look hard!' and I pushed my face up close to him.

"He leered—not a genuine smile but a leathery

mask-expression, no expression at all—but the trick was one I knew. I gave back the smile like a mirror.

"He looked thoughtful, though he kept the leer. 'You're a pirate, yes indeed; that's plain to see. But you ain't any pirate I've met with.' He winked.

" 'Yer a fool, Mr. Wilkins. I'm a riverboat magician and part-time preacher.' I gave him back the wink.

" 'That's so,' he said. 'Yer a preacher-magician as plain as day. That's how ye met with Dr. Flint, must be.'

" 'Ah yes, Flint,' I said. It worried me a little that they'd fixed on that. The very idea of that devilish magician brought the sweat to my forehead, which is no doubt the reason his name had popped into my mind when I'd talked to Mr. Knight.

" 'Deadliest trickster in the world, people say. Or was till he vanished.' The little man's eyeslits were looking at me hard. I felt panic going up and down my back in cold shocks. I was sure there was some kind of trick in what he said, though heaven only knew what the trick might be.

" 'Vanished?' says I, looking blank as a hensegg.

"He laughed and tipped his head. Soon after, he left me.

"That very afternoon—my ribs were by this time pretty well mended—Mr. Knight came and issued me seaman's garb and, without so much as a word of explanation, put me to work with the scrubbing boys. Since I knew I couldn't do the work exactly right— as I would if ever I'd shipped as a pirate—I worked with exaggerated clumsiness, like a man hiding a familiar skill. Sometimes for good measure I'd step into a pail, as if by accident, and get my bare foot wedged. A time or two I got myself and my fellow workers all tangled up in rope. Mr. Knight and Wilkins watched from around corners—with my cast left eye I saw every move they made—and looked dubious, pulling at their chins. The following morning I was graduated to labor for the cook, a big, fierce-looking one-eyed Chinese, smoky from the furious galley stoves and testy from the grill's everlasting hiss. The cook, from the moment he saw me lay hand on a butcher's cleaver

—an instrument I took up with some relish, I must say, a little like Odysseus picking up his bow—was scared out of his wits. By noon he'd hid all his knives large and small. I took to playing little games with the masher and the rolling pin, and sometimes whispering to myself. He spoke to Mr. Knight, who picked at the tip of his nose and looked thoughtful, and I was shifted to the rigging, where I hung, terrified, clumsily tying and untying knots. In awe, sick and dizzy, I watched more experienced seamen like Wilkins dance on the royal masthead or leap like gibbons from stay to stay or swing out hand over hand on the yardarm. There was no possibility of clowning up here, no way on earth of exaggerating my clumsiness. All I could do was hang on for dear life. Even so, they rubbed their chins and seemed uncertain.

"That night, still under constant watch, I was issued a footlocker and shifted from my stateroom to less comfortable quarters, the crowded habitation of sailors before the mast. It was there—luckily, as the sequel will show—that I made the acquaintance of a smiling, freckled red-bearded seaman by the name of Billy More.

"He was sitting in the glow of the swaying lamp, on the bunk that stood end to end with mine. For the purpose of keeping them guessing about me, I struck up a conversation.

" 'It's no work for a butcher's apprentice,' I said, 'sitting up there on the rigging like a dad-blamed sea-gull.'

" 'Yer a butcher's apprentice, are ye then?' he asked with a grin so innocent and friendly I felt threatened a little.

" 'That's what I was back in Albany,' I said. 'Poor Grandma. She'll wonder what's become of me. I just left her for a moment, to feed the chickens, ye know—' I shook my head.

"He shook his head too and smiled a little sadly, thinking, I suppose, of his own grandmother. That too made me feel a trifle partisan with him and I quickly changed the subject. 'Strange that we never see the

Captain,' I said. 'What sort of a man might he be, I wonder?'

"Oh, ye'll make his acquaintance pretty soon, like as not. Curious gentleman, our Captain is.'

" 'Curious, is he?'

" 'That he is,' says Billy More. 'He's a highly cultivated man, is old Dirge. Speaks God only knows how many languages.'

" 'Ye don't say!' I said.

" 'Ye'll see for yourself, if we come within hailing of a stranger. Anytime we meet with another whaler and draw up tandem for news and mail, our Captain Dirge talks the stranger's lingo. It's point of pride with 'im. He's a scholar, ye might say. Got books about history and natural philosophy and Lord knows what-all.'

" 'Well, I declare.'

"He sat nodding to himself, thoughtful, as if going over what he'd said word by word and giving his approval. He got a troubled look then and started pulling at his fingers, making knuckles pop. 'Very changeable man, though, is Captain Dirge.' He nodded some more.

" 'Changeable is he?'

" 'I've known him to set after whale like a man with a devil in him. Last time I sailed with him, he'd send no boat in ahead of his own, him riding there high on the gunnels at the stern, and his eyes red as rubies. No pitch of the sea could throw old Dirge nor even draw his attention. Face was like a lantern. That was last time. This time . . . Well sir, he's a curious man.'

" 'He's not so eager this time, eh?'

" 'Not for whale. But then of course, his sickness—'

" 'He's sickly, ye say?'

"But Billy More had said all he'd a mind to.

"I saw only now that in the dimness beyond him Wilkins sat tinkering with the springs and coils of a dismantled clock, listening with both his big monkey's ears. He was working in almost complete darkness— either the cleverest clock-maker that ever was heard of, thought I, or else a man pretending to be busy as the devil when he ain't. I thought I knew pretty well which was right. Billy More, seeing Wilkins, had gone pale as a ghost.

IX

"I was bound and determined to penetrate the *Jerusalem*'s mysteries—the singing I'd heard that first night aboard (I'd heard not a whimper from those Negroes since) and, stranger still, that voice I'd heard, or dreamed I'd heard, of a woman. It was a voice that haunted me as once Miranda Flint's eyes had done—though Heaven knows it was no voice of a girl on the theater circuit, but a true-born lady's. (I understood the connection well enough, young and inexperienced as I may have been. As once I'd glorified poor commonplace Miranda—transformed her to an angel and sometimes devil in human flesh, till the playbill pictures, as Miranda grew older, made a fool of me—so now, on the basis of a faintly heard voice, I was constructing another unearthly being, a creature no more fit for our common actuality than the crowned Redskin maiden on the *Jerusalem*'s bow. I knew what I was doing but went on with it, meanwhile telling myself, all sobriety, that even if the lady had a wooden leg, her presence on the ship was a mystery, by crimus, and I was bound, for my safety's sake, to try and solve it.) I lay in my berth with my eyes not quite closed, listening carefully to the breathing around me and imagining the mystic face behind the voice. I was in love, it seems. A sickness of the blood, a misery of youth: a joy and a grave indignity.

"When I was confident that all the ship was asleep, except for the watches and, here and there, some restless grumbler, I sat up and crossed in darkness to the passageway. I stepped into it and moved quietly down it, groping sternward toward the trap through which, that first night, I'd seen the blocks. There was no light whatever: It couldn't have been darker in Jonah's whale. I came to the angling passage where last time

I'd seen that lamp-glow, and I continued to the state-rooms and past them until, strange to say, I came to a bulkhead of polished wood that sealed off the passage. I was baffled, torn between hurrying toward the place where I'd heard the voice, on the one hand, and, on the other, hunting further for the trap. I had passed no sign of a ring or lift, no spot of flooring that even faintly suggested the presence of a hatch. As if to prove my good sense, my sanity, I forgot about the voice and got down on hands and knees to listen for the music. The sea was calm, the *Jerusalem* as quiet as a moss-covered crypt. 'Strange business indeed!' I said to myself. 'If someone had laid new decking, I'd've heard the racket of it.' I toyed again with the thought that perhaps I'd dreamed the whole thing, but I knew it wasn't so, mere melodrama. (I don't say stage plays do harm to a man, but it's my experience, for better or worse, that they put a man in poses he never found in Nature.) The slaves were down there, that was the truth of it; and somewhere on this ship there was also a young lady—perhaps a captive, some beautiful unfortunate princess, say, or . . . I reined in, none too eager that the night should overhear me. On the doubtful chance that, in my pain and confusion, I'd gotten turned around on my former exploration, I followed the passageway bowsward—though I knew I had not been turned around. (Mere theater again.) I had already satisfied myself that this was indeed not the direction I'd come, that previous night, when my progress forward was checked by an open hatch and murmuring voices. Three men, common seamen I supposed from their speech, were talking in low tones about the Captain. Despite the emotion in all they said —fear and rage, I thought—their tones were so hushed I could catch no more than an occasional phrase, foul oaths, mainly, and once, I thought, the words 'Avenge him!' I had no idea who the speakers were, much less how the Captain had harmed the poor devil they were talking of avenging, but I guessed, from the anger in all they said, that I'd be wise to keep clear of them. I backed away from the opening and, rising to my feet in the darkness, hurried back toward the stern.

"At the companionway I paused and stood waiting for my heart to calm. The hatch above was open, revealing a serene night sky magnificent with stars— the first night sky I'd seen, as it happens, since my travels on the night that they'd hauled me aboard. Only when I saw how the patch of sky moved, yawing gently from port to starboard, then starboard to port, did I realize how accustomed I'd grown to the movement of the ship, how it had become for me a standard of landlike stability. I did not stand long in this reverie, however, but started immediately and silently up toward the deck. When I raised my head in the darkness, a breeze full of forest smells met me—a scent so distinct that I wouldn't have been much surprised to hear we were navigating the Amazon. But there was no land in sight. When I studied the sky to learn my bearings, I found nothing familiar, no star or planet in its accustomed place. Even the Great Bear had vanished. I could hardly make out, for an instant, the meaning of so strange a change in the normally dependable universe. I did not take long, however, to get my reason back. The wind was icy, and coming straight at us. We must be far below the Equator and bearing south, somewhere west, perhaps, of South America.

"I was less comforted by these deductions than I ought to have been. For one thing, I could no longer hide from myself the absurdity of my search for a girl I'd never seen, and who perhaps did not exist. For another—unless it's the same in the end—a queer emotion had begun to trouble me: My distance from all that defined me, so to speak—van Klug's butchershop, my chalk-dusty schoolroom—filled me all at once with a peculiar fright. A part of me longed to be seen and apprehended and thereby freed of this eerie unrelatedness. In the three crowsnests high above me there was no sign of life. Neither was there movement on the bridge. It was as if the ship were abandoned, plague-struck. I moved very cautiously out onto the deck and along the dark bulkhead toward the aft companionway. It was from somewhere up there, near the Captain's cabin, that I'd heard her voice.

No one saw me, no one interrupted me. I was still determined to pierce the *Jerusalem*'s mysteries, but the intensity of that conflicting urge grew by leaps and bounds—my perverse desire to be discovered, overthrown.

"Then came an emotion stranger still. I began to have an uneasy feeling—residue, perhaps, of my reading of Boethius—that my seeming freedom on the still, dark whaler was a grotesque illusion, that sneaking alone through hostile darkness I was watched by indifferent, dusty eyes, a cosmic checker, a being as mechanical as any automaton displayed in the Boston theaters. (I'd seen more than one of them, those mechanical dolls so ingenious at playing the piano or dealing out whist cards or walking back and forth on the stage, nodding their heads and pulling at their whiskers like Wall Street bankers, that you'd swear to heaven there was a man inside them, though some were no bigger than a three-year-old child.) Mad as it may sound, I had to concentrate with all my might to resist the temptation to shout or kick something over and force them to reveal themselves. The unfamiliar constellations above me might have been the heavens as seen from Jupiter. It was that that dizzied me, I told myself—made me populate the ship with a ghostly audience. Adrift in a universe grown wholly unfamiliar, I'd been suddenly ambushed by the dark vastness which suggests to the mind of a healthy man the magnificence of God and of all his Creation but suggested to me, and very powerfully, too, mere pyrotechnic pointlessness. Nor was it any help to keep my mind fixed on the immediate and concrete. When my questions were answered, the answers, I could not help but see, would be trivial and drab. The Captain was a madman, and the ship full of creatures less than human. Such stories are as old as Noah's Ark. Even so, here I was, poor involuntary fool, stealthily mounting the poop, with no better reason for desisting than I had for proceeding. Such was my anguish, sneaking like a thief toward the object of my desire, a girl I'd never seen. (Ah, the blood, poor blood! Let no man scorn it who's not felt its dark pounding!)

"When I reached the poopdeck and the window of the Captain's cabin, curiously curtained in what appeared to be red velvet, caught together at the sides with ornate golden rings—a mighty strange cabin to be found on a whaler—there came a sound that shattered my speculations and sent them flying to the depths. Before I could even identify the sound—it might have been the roar of a tropical lion, for the blast of terror it exploded in me—some huge black beast came hurtling from the dimness, toppling me at once and tumbling me—the animal clawing and snapping at my shoulders—to the rock-hard deck below. I lay still as a gravestone. I couldn't have moved or screamed if my life depended on it. The thing's wild eyes burned into me, its fangs laid bare. I gave a slight, convulsive twitch, and there burst from the creature's throat a new roar, like the falling thunder of the firmament. Then there was a light on the bridge above me, and a woman's voice called sharply, 'Alastor!' The growling changed—lowered and became less murderous—and an instant later the enormous dog (for dog it was, though the largest I ever beheld on earth) turned from me, gathered, and bounded up the companionway to its mistress. She stood perfectly still, gazing down at me, drowning my spirit in shame. Her presence made my vision of her paltry, ridiculous—a young woman so beautiful in the light of the lantern and the blinking stars that I blinked myself to make sure I was awake. The Captain stood beside her, looking down like a black-bearded toad, in silence. I tried to speak, perhaps beg their forgiveness, but not one word could I bring out. For perhaps a full minute they gazed down at me and never spoke. I couldn't get my breath, overwhelmed by a blush I had reason to hope might be my last. Then they turned, she leading him as if he were an invalid or a sleepwalker, stiff-legged, off balance—the girl as graceful and indifferent as a goddess—and passed out of my sight. I gasped in air.

"A familiar voice said, 'Ye'll be pryin' yerself into shackles, me lad. 'E's a devil when 'e's roused, is Captain Dirge.' I rolled my head back to look at him, the owner of the voice that had spoken to me that first night, down in the stateroom. He must have been there all the while, out of sight in the shadows. He bent toward me. It was difficult to make out his face against the night, but I saw that his hair streamed wildly out from his temples and ears and fell to his chest like an Indian's. The hair was snow-white. Another mystery, then! A man his age had as little business on a whaler as did a woman. ' 'Ere, lad, take a hand,' he said gruffly, as if amused by my foolishness, and he stretched a huge-knuckled hand toward me. That, too, sent a tingle of alarm through me. By the way he groped I knew that he was blind.

" 'Who are you?' I asked, pushing up on my elbows. 'Who are *all* of you? Where the devil are we shipping?' At the sound of my own grandiose theatrics—questions tinged, in my own ears at least, with dark metaphysical overtones—my fear leaped to new intensity. 'What ship *is* this?' I asked. I spoke louder now, the silence of the ship all around me like the silence of a black-draped hall when a medium begins, and my question self-conscious despite my urgency, as if I were delivering lines long rehearsed. 'Where does the ship put in? Where can I get off?'

" 'One thing at a time, lad,' the old man said. He caught hold of my hand and, with surprising strength, raised me to my feet. He put his hand on my shoulder and turned me toward the hatch. I took a step, then held back. He relaxed the pressure urging me forward. After thought, he said, 'Who I'd be is a lunatic, as ye may have grasped, by the name of Jeremiah, one-time first mate to Captain d'Oyarvido on the good ship *Princess* that found out the Vanishing Isles of the South Pacific. Who these others might be no man can be certain, except to affirm they're deadmen, risen saints.'

"I was suddenly aware we had company all around us, sailors watching through portholes or poking their heads up through hatches.

" 'And one dead woman,' I said fiercely, determined to make him tell the truth.

" 'Aye, that may be.'

" 'Where will they put me ashore?' I asked.

"The old man turned as if to study me. His eyes

were as white as two glossy stones. 'That's dubious, lad. Very dubious. Look there!' I looked where he pointed, and for a split second it seemed to me I saw something—absurd or not. (He was blind, after all, and the night was dark.) What Flint had begun in the theater, that sea-going mystic had powerfully improved on. I resisted with all my might, of course. Nevertheless, for days after that I had a curious notion that the ship was being followed by an enormous, pigeon-like bird as white as snow."

X

"Unheard of!" cries the guest. "I declare on my soul, in all my days and in all my travels, I never encountered a yarn more outrageous!"

The mariner throws him a look of alarm. There's a chill in the room, and a flutter of bats in the twilight outside the tavern window, over toward the barn. There's mist on the woods.

"It ain't altogether a question of truth against falsehood," says the angel; but his golden eyes betray confusion. He puffs more furiously than ever at his pipe.

The mariner is trembling from head to foot, sifting through his wits for some high-sounding justification. "There's truths and truths," says he, full of thunder. "If a narrative don't seem to make much sense, mine deeper—that's the ticket!"

But the angel is paling, no question about it, and the mariner's lips are turning blue.

(Shall I strip myself naked and cry out, shameless, to stone-deaf graveyards and children uncreated, Brothers, Sisters, it was like *THIS* in our time? Better the cover of my dungeon fiction—no less chilly and remote for its being mere fiction. Better the dealings of a cracked old sailor and his sensible guest, the angel's benevolent ministries raised up between them like Time and Space or the pages of a book.)

"A straw for yer levels!" says the guest with a snort

like a railroad engine, and he pours more drinks. "Never mind. So the ship had a woman on her!"

The fading angel miraculously brightens, and the mariner is suddenly stern and dignified with what might be high purpose and then again might be a careful disguise of glee.

(The dead pass indifferently, shuffling to the woods, but at sight of the mariner's eye they hesitate, considering.)

The guest has grown solider, kingly in his chair. He leans to one side, taps the table with his fingers, like a shrewd man considering. He snaps his eye to the mariner. "Tell on!"

The angel tips his tankard up, goes immediately light-headed.

XI

"Mr. Knight and Wilkins continued to keep an eye on me, and it seemed to me that they kept an eye, too, on my red-headed friend Billy More. Though I kept a sharp, somewhat sulky watch, the whole business had me thoroughly confounded. I could have no doubt that Mr. Knight and Wilkins were somehow in league and that Billy More was extremely uneasy, if not downright petrified, in Wilkins' presence; yet time and again I saw Mr. Knight and Billy More whispering like conspirators. (The *Jerusalem* was filled with conspirators, come to that. Such a crowd of eye-rollers, whisperers, and grumblers you never did see.) Moreover, for all his seeming innocence and seeming openness, there were things that greatly puzzled me about Billy. Like Mr. Knight and like Wilkins, he denied any knowledge that a girl was aboard, and when I told him I'd also seen a huge black dog, his face was so incredulous, or at any rate startled, that I wondered if *any*thing I saw with my eyes was trustworthy.

"There was another thing puzzled me. He came back again and again to questions about my life in

Albany with my grandmother, as if probing to find out if I really came from where I claimed I had. I disappointed him there. Mike Fink himself couldn't have answered more slyly or circumspectly or supported his contentions with more convincing fabrications. Since I knew very little about Albany, I confessed that really I'd come from Quebec, then later that I hailed from Arkansas. I told of my days as patent-medicine salesman and got so carried away I got an order from both Billy More and Mr. Knight for a case each of Dr. Hodgkins' Elixir. But mostly my mood was a good deal less cheerful. In fact, mostly I was profoundly depressed. Ever since the night that huge dog knocked me down, I was their laughingstock, in my own mind at least: the stupidest, silliest, most unworthy of men; also the angriest, the most hopelessly in love.

"It was just about this time—my eighth or ninth day on the *Jerusalem*'s heights—that I came within a hair of ending all miseries for good by a fatal accident.

"I was high on the rigging of the mainmast, almost to the beams of the crowsnest, where I was struggling to patch a damaged stay, when for some reason I looked down. I had learned before, at lower levels, what looking down would do to me. One moment I was staring with all my soul at the frayed bit of rope I was working on—I remember recollecting an old, dried braid, from an Indian squaw, that I'd seen one time in the Boston Museum—the next, I found myself thinking of the distance between me and the deck, and the dangerous mutability of rope, my ladder back to safety. In vain I struggled to be rid of such thoughts. The more earnestly I labored not to think, the more busily my mind went spinning toward disaster. In no time, the crisis was solidly upon me—the anticipation of the feeling of falling: the giddiness, the struggle, the headlong descent—and then the mysterious *longing* to fall, the hunger to sink into the absolute freedom of suicide. I could not, would not confine my gaze to the rope before me. With a wild, indefinite emotion, half-horror, half-relief, I cast my gaze into the abyss. The deck was unaccountably shrunk in size and lay some distance to my right, from the lean of the ship. I felt my hands slipping, my heart going suddenly pancrastical, and I glimpsed, as if out of the corner of my wall-eyed glance, the faintest conceivable shadow of some ultimate idea. I found myself suddenly not afraid. It was as if I had lost identity, become one with the mystic ocean at my feet, image of the deep-blue bottomless soul that pervades all mankind and nature like Cranmer's ashes. That instant Billy More slammed against me like a veritable lightning bolt, with a banshee yell that more filled me with terror than ever the thought of my fall had done. His stocky legs were clamped around my waist as if to drive out the last mote of oxygen, his bristly red beard pushed hard into my neck, his rough hands closed on the ropework around me like iron hooks that never till the day of dissolution would be pried aloose. " 'Whoo*ee!*' he cried, 'hang on there, mate!' Whence he came, Heaven knows, but come he did, with the persuasive force of the angel falling on Abraham. I couldn't speak, for lack of wind. Nor did he have much need of conversation, going down the ropes like a spider with his burden. I was given the rest of that day off, to lie on my back—my ribs on fire, more painful than before—and mediate my stupidity. Billy More, with hardly a word, but wearing a thoughtful look, went back up the rigging.

"That evening, looking sly, he came over to me, holding two bits of rope. He eased himself down on the bunk beside me, unconsciously tying and untying knots, grinning and awkward as one of my schoolboys, and at length he said, 'It's a common thing . . . up on the masthead . . . the step to Nowhere. Keep yer bearings, that's the secret.' He worked his mouth and screwed up his eyes, hunting for words that would express his thought. After a moment, he said slowly and carefully, 'Know in the back of yer mind where ye stand, whatever ye happen to think of the place, and banish all thought of Nowhere by keeping yer mind from belief in it. Exactly like a man going over a gorge on a highwire. Throw yer vision to the rim.

If ye *must* think, think of Faith itself. Sing hymns or tell yerself Bible stories. If ye think of that highwire inch by inch, if ye think with the front of yer mind where yer feet are, why down ye'll go quicker'n a boulder: whoosh! Faith, that's the secret! Absolute faith like a seagull's.'

"I thanked him earnestly for saving my life and told him I'd keep his advice in mind. He looked at his shoes, thinking about it, then back at me. 'Ye make terrible knots for a pirate,' he said. He winked. So he'd been working with them all along, I thought. Yet his face was like a cherub's. I began to wonder if I was right to fear Wilkins, ugly devil that he was, and feel safe as you would with a baby near Billy More. I'd learned one lesson from old Pious John. A man mustn't jump to conclusions about what's real in this world and what's mere presentation. Just to be on the safe side, I took up the habit of keeping a marlinspike close at hand, and, the first chance I got, I made myself a little hiding place in the bulkhead by my bunk, where I could keep my belongings a bit safer than they were in the foot-locker. It was the neatest hiding place you ever saw, achieved by a foot-long removable board, and no less ingenious for the fact that I had nothing to put in it except my empty purse and my waterlogged watch and gold watch-chain.

"I went up in the rigging again next morning and remembered Billy More's advice about Nowhere and focusing on Faith. Silly or not, the trick worked jim-dandy. Never again was I afraid of the highest sail-yard. Within the week I was taking my turn with the others in the crowsnest, on the look-out for whales.

"That, I might mention, was as mysterious to me as was anything else: Whatever his deeper, secret purpose, Captain Dirge, who'd formerly seemed so indifferent, was suddenly hell-bent on capturing whale. Perhaps it was the universal grumbling of his men, out all this while and still nothing to show for it. But I couldn't help but think that the turnabout came mighty abruptly, and hard on Billy More's remark that the Captain had been like a different man on his previous voyage. In any case, again and again, both day and night, we'd hear the Captain shouting to the mastheads—shouting from inside his cabin door, out of sight in the darkness—warning the spotters if they valued their noses to keep a sharp look-out, and not omit singing at even the shadow of a porpoise. The whole crew was visibly relieved that the Captain was himself again, or near to it.

"Captain Dirge did not need to wait long, it turned out. On the forty-first day, sixteenth day on the Pacific, came a cry out of heaven, 'There she blows! there! there!' and the first mate's stern echo 'Where away?' All the ship was suddenly in commotion, springing to lower the longboats, shouting. Or all but the Captain, who was deathly sick. 'There go flukes!' was now the crowsnest cry.

"But it isn't my purpose to tire you with whaling. Suffice it to say they made their catch—a sperm-whale monstrous and cunning of eye. He was long as the ship, with a tail that could've sunk us at a single whap, and teeth that would serve as Plato's form for the fall of civilizations. They made their catch—the Captain still keeping to his cave-dark room—and I, in a manner of speaking, made mine. The slaves I'd sworn to the existence of, despite all scoffing by Wilkins and the others, and despite the silent, implied denial of the first mate, Mr. Knight, now scuttled among us with clanking chains, slicing, hauling, draining, carting, droning their ominous *Go-down-Moziz*. So that's it, thought I: The old man's widened his margin of profit by the simplest, most ancient, most devilish device in the universe. It was no great wonder he'd kept them out of sight. They were freedom-lovers, the Yankee officers and sailors on the *Jerusalem*—even the far-gathered savage harpooners. One glance at Mr. Knight's troubled eyes or the manifest sorrow of my friend Billy More would be enough to convince Captain Dirge of the wisdom of saying no more about his blacks than need be. Even the evil-eyed second mate, Wolff, a sour little German with hair straight as wheat-straw, and no more compassion in his soul than a witch, had a look about the mouth of disgruntlement.

My friend old Jeremiah stood leaning on the starboard rail, gazing with his stone-white eyes at the rest of us. 'Deadmen,' he said, with that belladonna smile. I had a premonition as clear and firm as an insight into geometry that his words would prove prophetic. But even with Jeremiah, I was determined to be canny, ruled by Davy Crockett's dictum, 'If he don't know I'm up this tree, he'll look in Pittsburgh.' Jaunty as a cynical young barge captain, my fists on my hips and my hat tipped back, I says: 'It's a devilish thing, that singing. Yessir! That's where they bury their hist'ry and keep their schemes alive.' I gave a crafty laugh. Jeremiah appeared to be thinking mournfully of something else, something only a man with second sight could know. I told him some merry, foolish tale about buying and selling slaves in St. Louis, and how one time I was very near murdered by a nigger that was drunk on fermented molasses down in New Orleans. The old man drifted away and left me talking to myself. I pretended not to notice. I caught the reflection of Wilkins' red bandanna on the varnished rail, Wilkins watching from the shadow of the longboats, sly as Br'er Fox in the plantation tales. I chatted on, cheery as Br'er Rabbit, to the dreamy air.

"The next morning Mr. Knight came over to where Billy More and I were patching sail. He stood gazing down at us, neither friendly nor unfriendly, thinking his own lugubrious thoughts. I expected him to speak to Billy More. As I've said, I think, I'd frequently see them together, as if plotting. But Mr. Knight turned, instead, to me.

"'Mr. Upchurch, ye're wanted in the Captain's cabin.'

"I glanced at Billy More. He grinned; his tough, freckled cheek muscles bulged. 'Turn the conversation to the Occult,' says he. 'The Captain's a true cyclopaedia there.'

"When I glanced at Mr. Knight, his eyes were as gloomy and distrait as before, his thought honed down fine as a weasel's. I remembered myself and jumped to. Mr. Knight turned away, still brooding, to lead me to the Captain.

XII

"I wouldn't be surprised if researchers should find out, a hundred or two hundred years from now, that all mortal beings have second sight, a kingdom of the soul as serene and aloof—and as seldom visited, in the usual case—as Lapland. To talk about the ship's old prophet Jeremiah would be to complicate things unnecessarily, though it's true enough that not I alone but every man-jack on the *Jerusalem* would have sworn, if ye'd been there to ask 'em at the time of the events I'm telling you about, that blind and enfeebled as Jeremiah may have been, he was a man of more value to the Captain than the rest of us together. He knew by second sight, he claimed, where the whales was playing. And he knew more than that, or so I've ended up believing. He may have fooled us— there's always that suspicion. But if all his skills was mere showmanship, mere mirrors and tinsel, so to speak, like some Boston bunko-man's (he had plenty of bunk in him too, Lord knows), then all I can say is, that man was the slickest impostor that ever was created.

"But I mean to talk of more ordinary cases of second sight, the kind you encounter in gambling casinos and the kitchens of New England. I make no pretense of understanding these things, but I confess I've toggled, together out of string and nails and two mushrooms I had from a harpooner by the name of Kaskiwah, a kind of homespun theory.

"A hunch is a religious experience, an escape from mere intellect into reality, home of the soul. Put it this way: The mushroom- and root-eating savages of the South Pacific have queer experiences, learning out of conversation with lizards, or from the scent of wild-flowers, answers to questions which couldn't be answered by any means that old scoundrel Locke would countenance. Time and Space became impish, now ingenious and full of wit, like Ariel, now sullen and ill-mannered, like Caliban in a funk. Effect precedes cause, causes and effects which are spatially remote refuse to be sensibly separate in time. The physical world turns crepuscular, like the dreamings of a bat, the spiritual world walks stolid, muttering, or serene and stiff-backed as President Lincoln, emplanting foot-long footsteps. To those who were never attuned to such things—Paris rationalists, or Wall Street brokers busy adding up sums—tales of mystical experience are no more than childish fables, probably hoaxes de-signed (like their own grand schemes) to bilk the public. There is in all our societies, whether whist-clubs or whalers, a law of sufficiency which begins by dictating what things need not be speculated on, for efficient operation of the business at hand, and ends by outlawing and angrily scorning all thought not directly productive of firm, fat bank accounts. If the whole of the mind is a grocery-store in all its liveliness and flux—ants in the bread-bin, smell of brown paper and new spring onions, string coming down from the spindle above Mr. Primrose's balding, bespectacled head—then the intellect is a cash-register, and an expressible idea is the clang of its cheap iron bell. By specialization we vivisect reality till all but the head or the left hind leg of the universe is by someone's defini-tion industrial waste. But move the New York indus-trialist to Tallahassee, abandon him there to hold forth for three years on right and wrong, or move Stonewall Jackson to a Seneca village, return in six months, and you'll find them gravely altered men. We stake our lives on nice opinions; the globe makes one half-turn, rolling up the Southern Cross, and we clench our brains against madness.

"Whether or not there is more in this world than philosophy dreams of, I allow if I'd lived to my pres-ent age in the South Pacific, I'd hold confab with lizards and soberly take down the political opinions of the columbine. If I'd lived in Tibet, I'd sit in my corner, shortly after my death, and I'd thoughtfully reflect on the *Book of the Dead* being read to my corpse by my survivors. All we think and believe, in short, is foolish prejudice, even if some of it happens to be true (which seems to me unlikely). Or to make it all still more altiloquent: Human consciousness, in the ordinary case, is the artificial wall we build of perceptions and *con*ceptions, a hull of words and accepted opinions that keeps out the vast, consuming sea: It shears my self from all outside business, including the body I walk in but muse on the same as I do on a three-legged dog or an axe-handle, a slippery wild Indian or a king at his game of chess. A mushroom or one raw emotion (such as love) can blast that wall to smithereens. I become a kind of half-wit, a limitless shadow too stupid to work out a mortgage writ, but I am also the path of the stars, rightful monarch of Nowhere. I become, that instant, the King's Indian: Nothing is waste, nothing unfecund. The future is the past, the past is present to my senses. I gaze at the dark Satanic mills, the sludge-thick streams. I shake my head. They vanish.

"I had a kind of hunch from the beginning about Captain Dirge. There was something fundamentally unnatural about him, but whether I ought to be awed or revolted was difficult to say. Now that I'm old and have seen a few things, I'm aware that the world is full of men exactly like him: single-minded, tight-sphinctered, violent and unfeeling as thrashing machines. Extraordinary men. Seducers of megalomaniac youth. (What young man can bring himself down to the opinion that the secret of the universe is commonness, flexibility, plain goodness-of-heart, or that the highest ambition available to mankind is hard work at serious business in the morning, and in the evening a tipple at the public-house? Can all Time and Space have conspired to perfect this magnificent machine for no purpose more pythonic?)

"As I say, I had from the beginning a kind of hunch about him. I had no doubt that Captain Dirge was in some sense mad (a strange misapprehension, but I was young, inexperienced; I had no notion how brash and outlandish this universe can be), and I had no doubt either that the Captain's madness, long before they'd hauled me aboard, had already infected a majority of the crew. '—But madness, what's that?' I asked myself, waving at the sun like an auctioneer when I pondered these matters and others in the crowsnest, the following few weeks. 'Was Homer Mad? —raging against war, bemoaning the very foundations of his world in the name of a vision of life never tried before nor since? Was Tecumseh mad, murdered because he refused to sell Congress the air, the clouds, the sea? What is madness, after all, but overweening pride, the daring assertion, always mistaken, that man is God—a high office otherwise left empty?'

"At times throughout our voyage (though I'm getting ahead of my story), I would see the Captain standing at the rail in his gentleman's clothes—Captain Dirge was well-known among whalers as a dandy gazing out to sea toward whatever it was he had come here for, or studying his Bible, with a stern face, or praying at the bow, oblivious to the world as a propped-up doll, and I'd be overwhelmed by a pair of emotions more fit to be vented on ancient plays. What did they talk about, he and the girl?—his daughter, I presumed. Did they talk at all? Was the girl aware of the plain absurdity of her presence here on a whaling ship?— or was she, too, as crazy as a magpie? If she wasn't crazy yet, she'd soon become so. She spoke to no one, by all evidence. Never emerged—except that once— from her cabin, unless she crept out at night when the decks were empty. Did she know how many whaling vessels have spiraled down, broken-backed, unmasted, to hang in a limbo of dead green light, inhabited only by bones and prowling jewfish? Did she ever hear, wide awake on her pillow, the ominous hymning of the slaves and, like an echo, that further music, weird crying from the sea?

"Though I didn't know it at the time, of course— following Mr. Knight to the Captain's cabin—I was not the only man on board who was secretly half in love with her, or in love, rather, with a Dantesque image of beauty and gentleness untestable, unreachable, and no doubt ultimately unreal. The half-breed Wilkins, I learned much later, had more than once made bold to speak with her. In the end, there was the great-shouldered mastiff, with a growl like a tornado's, and Wilkins came out with his shoulder half torn away. Henceforth, she had privacy. True—this too I found out later—the first mate, Mr. Knight, sometimes spoke with her; but he wasn't much, lately, at casual conversation. With the Captain's daughter, as with the rest of us, when asked a question, Mr. Knight would smile, his mind still torturing that darker question that consumed him these days, and would shake his head, purse his lips, and in the end say nothing.

"Mr. Knight and I, I ought to mention, were more familiar now. In the span between kills, life is quiet on a whaler. Mr. Knight would come near where I was working and would watch me, and to keep him on his toes I'd chat with him. I told him such tales as would make an undistracted man's eyes pop out. Tales of pillage and murder and Lord knows what. He believed every word of it, of course, and none of it. He continued to bring books from the Captain's cabin, and at times we talked sober philosophy. I learned early in life that any man not fiercely committed to a single point of view is as apt a philosopher as anybody else. I learnt it from performers on the Boston stage— magicians, I mean, or bunkum professors like that old devil Flint—men secretly tying and untying knots, dropping mirrors into boxes, firing pistols, pushing levers, and all the while solemnly declaiming the opinions of Leibnitz or Marx or Winckelmann. Mr. Knight had a good deal of curiosity about things, for the most part on wholly unrelated subjects. He had a mind like sheepswool, not active or searching but capable of fixing like the devil on any little bur that might happen to land on it. He was puzzled by the ways of beasts and plants. He'd observed a good deal, in his random way: subtle alterations of beak and claw as one passed from equatorial latitudes north or south. He'd run across the curious theories of Goethe, in *Metamorphose der Pflanzen,* and the theory of "organic force" in Müller. He'd heard some strange theory that eggs feel terror, that plants can sense things and keep watch on a friend—a human being, a spider —from miles away.

" 'Ye don't believe that!' I said.

" 'It's a proven fact. Read this.' He extracted from his money-pouch, carefully unfolded, then handed to me a yellowed bit of paper from some science magazine. I read: *At a test at Prague University we introduced a gardenia to a spider, then took the spider from the room. We released the spider on a dark stairway and had someone try to find it. Meanwhile someone else watched the sensor device which we'd affixed to the gardenia, and whenever the sensor showed excitement in the plant, the observer would shout, 'You're close!' to the pursuer of the spider. In this manner, we were able to locate the spider every time.*

" 'Dogs,' said Mr. Knight, 'have been known to find their masters from a half a continent away.' He gazed off, troubled, at the horizon.

"Mr. Knight took an interest in astronomy, too, which he seemed to think somehow related. Whatever the subject, I held forth with the wisdom of the Man in the Moon, claiming I'd heard it from Goethe himself when we met one time in Zeeland. The first mate would pick at his chin and frown, staring, full of sorrow, at the calm night sea, and at times he'd heave a great sight like a man condemned. I knew pretty well what his trouble was. His natural science was scuttling his religion. Then more fool he! I might have felt sympathy, if I'd let myself, but that was a luxury I couldn't afford. It would make me one of them, one more helpless victim on that ship of slaves and prisoners. (Overweening young fool, ye may say; and I confess it.) However, I gave a bit of thought to his theories.

"I might mention he was interested in voodoo, too —an interest he'd no doubt acquired from the Captain. Old Dirge had books on the Hindoo occult and mesmerism and the transmigration of souls. He practiced experiments in thought transference, or so I was told by Mr. Knight, and he received, whenever a whaler had mail for us, letters and packets from the British Society for Psychic Research. Mr. Knight, whenever we touched on such subjects, was like a man at the end of his tether. He had facts corpuscular and facts crepuscular, messages from Newton and news from the company of table rappers, but the connector his Methodism longed for had vanished: the moral principle, the arc-flash, the man with the halo. Mere fact was killing him. His sighs got so deep they seemed to rise out of his shoes, and the way he would screw up his eyes made me fear for his vision.

"Tonight, as he led me to the Captain's cabin, I felt no temptation to converse with Mr. Knight, and, as for him, he was quiet as snow on a fencepost. I could form no opinion what manner of thoughts was molesting him, and I could gather from his long-legged walk no clue to the Captain's disposition. I'd had no idea, before this instant, of the extent to which I was afraid of the mysterious man who'd summoned me. I thought, without a smile, of Reverend Dunkel's talk, long ago, of Discipline, 'her subjects standing in the stocks . . . limbs swollen and lacerated . . .'

"At the cabin door, Mr. Knight stood listening, head bowed, for a moment. Then he knocked. The curtains on the windows were shut and I could see no light behind them. Mr. Knight knocked again and, at last, in a queerly muffled voice, the Captain called, 'Come in, sir!' Mr. Knight opened the door and swung it inward, then stepped back, allowing me to enter. As soon as I'd done so, groping a little, since the room was dark as an opium den, the door closed softly behind me.

XIII

"Take my word for it, you never in all your days did see such a room as was that one. From top to bottom the bulkheads was draped in dark red velvet—not for beauty, it was plain, but for some reason more sinister, or, at any rate, such was my immediate impression. The cloth was stained, cracked, creased, frayed, moth-eaten like a hundred-year-old theater curtain from a hall destroyed by fire. The Captain's furniture was equally abnormal: great padded dark-green leather chairs such as captains of industry might sit in—or might have sat in years ago, when they were new— and a black oak chart-table that might have seen service, a century ago, in some conference room. In the room's four corners there were tall narrow mirrors that it seemed to me could have only one purpose: They protected the Captain from any mortal man's sneaking up on him. I'd heard from my father tales of the oddity of captains of whalers—they're a fierce and arrogant breed, the whole lot of them, and more than one's gone mad out there cruising on his terrible business—but the oddity of Captain Dirge was a little beyond what I've ever heard mention of. There was only one lamp on, a whale-oil lantern suspended from a chain above the chart-table. It was there at that table that the Captain was sitting, and close beside him was the blind man, Jeremiah. They had their backs to me as I entered the cabin. The blind man turned his face toward me. As for the Captain, he showed no sign of awareness that I'd come. He sat humpbacked and motionless, bent over his charts, so still I'd have thought he was dead except for the occasional puff of smoke from his pipe.

" 'You sent for me, sir?' I said at last.

"The Captain gave a curious, belated jerk but otherwise ignored me. Old Jeremiah raised a finger to his lips and said, so softly that I could barely hear him —his face all lit up like a man just interrupted from ecstasy—'Speak quieter, lad. The Captain's a man of most delicate sensibilities. Too much noise, too much light, and he suffers like a man in hellfire.'

"I nodded, apologetic, and kept quiet. I'd have sworn those blind eyes were studying me hard, with the joyous fascination of a lion getting ready to come bounding off his rock, but I had, just now, no time to give thought to Jeremiah; my attention was fixed on Captain Dirge. He was a largish man dressed all in black, with a half-length cape of the kind you might see on a coachman down in front of the opera house. His hair was as black as the clothes he wore, but streaked with gray, and it was long and curly—

not hair to be vain of: coarse as the hair on a mountain goat or the stuffings in a sofa.

"At last, slowly, jittering like a man with delirium tremens, he turned his head and revealed his bushy black beard and his pockmarked, dead-looking nose. Because of his deformity—that hump like a whale's—his face aimed floorward, and he was forced to compensate by rolling up his eyes. It was clear the first moment you looked in those eyes that the Captain was a very sick man and, it could be, drunk to boot. I'd been aware from the instant I entered the room, though only now did I come altogether conscious of it, that the cabin reeked of whiskey worse than a distillery. He leaned forward a little, as if thinking of getting up, then thought better of it.

" 'Come over here, son, where a body can see you.'

"I obeyed instantly, moving around to the side of the table and standing with my hands behind my back, trying to meet his eyes. It was impossible. It gave me such creeps and crawls along my spine I blame near bolted. And his face was no better. A more wrinkled, more unsightly visage I never encountered in all this world. He had bushy black eyebrows as coarse and curly as the hair that rolled down off the top of his head or ramdiked out as his mustache and beard. But no doubt the thing that made it all so horrific was that the clothes the man wore was the soul of elegance, as if the Captain took pleasure in his foul appearance and meant to set it off the way you'd set off a first-class painting.

"He raised one silk-gloved, lace-cuffed hand to his pipe and kept it there, fingertips lightly touching the bowl, not really holding it. 'So you're the terrible pirate Jonathan Upchurch,' he said.

"I nodded. 'Yes, sir.'

"His eyes never moved at all, never flickered, never blinked. He was as still and remote from head to foot as a creature from a planet with seven times less gravity than ours, and his words, when he spoke, were as cool as an Assyrian god's, or a spider's. 'Jonathan Upchurch, yer a liar,' he said.

"I went red, maybe purple. 'Yes, sir.' The confession, for all its simplicity, brought a flood of relief I could hardly understand. I felt like a man who, by sudden impulse, has dropped a hundred dollars in a collection plate.

"Perhaps behind where the beard and mustache met he smiled—such was my impression, though Heaven knows how I could've formed it. His horrible face went on staring at me.

" 'Yer name, sir. Yer true name.'

"There was no escaping him, no way in the world to outbold those glittering eyes. I had, for that matter, no *desire* to escape. I rushed to the abyss as if I thought it my soul's last hope. 'Jonathan Adams Upchurch,' I said.

"He reached toward the whiskey bottle, then decided against it. 'Where d'ye come from?' he said.

" 'Boston, sir. I was a schoolmaster.'

" 'Ye telling lies again?'

" 'No, sir. It's the truth.'

"He lowered his head some and seemed to consider it, still as eternity, except for that trembling; he looked like a malevolent, hump-backed, black-whiskered Buddha. At last he said, his voice so muffled that it might have been coming from another room, 'There's some aboard this ship that maintains yer from farther west. Some claims ye got a particular knowledge of the Mississippi River.'

" 'Just from books,' I said. 'It's a place I meant to go visit someday.'

"He showed no sign of hearing. 'Ye *act* like a man from the Mississippi River. I never been there myself, but I've heard stories. I b'lieve yer a Mississippi flim-flam man.'

"Why it should seem to me important that I convince Captain Dirge that I was telling the truth, after all my pains to throw the others off, is difficult to say. His fundamental inhumanness, perhaps. I may have needed to strike from him some spark of humanity to answer and reassure my own. In any case, it was desperately important, or so I thought. I reached out and almost touched him, my face no doubt clownish with agony and appeal. 'It really is the truth, Captain.'

"He considered some more, then granted me a queerly formal little bow and changed the subject. 'Yer a Latin scholar, I'm given to understand.'

" 'I know some Latin, yes, sir.'

" 'And Greek?'

" 'No, sir.' I could feel myself blushing.

"He slid his eyes toward old Jeremiah as if not only disappointed but fiercely annoyed. However, he went on to other questions. 'Ye can cypher?' he asked softly. 'Ye know yer geography? The study of the Bible?'

"Weak-kneed, trembling, I answered all his questions with scrupulous honesty. He bore down with such energy on the interrogation—though neither his face nor his body ever moved, and his voice was just a whisper—that I began to be a little befuddled and confused, almost wondering if I ever really had, as I claimed, been a schoolmaster. Drunk or not—I was now pretty certain he was drunk—Captain Dirge's words came out relatively clear—though hushed and muffled, if not slurred—and his wits were as sharp as a lawyer's. What he had in mind I had no idea. His face showed absolutely nothing, not merely because of the dimness in the room, though that was part of it, but mainly because he was capable of masking all hint of emotion, if he felt any. He would've been a marvel of a poker player. (He had, on one side of his table, a chess game in progress.) It suddenly struck me he was quizzing me exactly like a prospective employer, minutely testing not only my acquaintance with my subject matter but my morality as well. The very instant that thought occurred to me, an incredible speculation began to tremble into life at the back of my mind. I felt the blush rising through my neck again, and a terrible excitement invaded my chest, such a turbulence of hope and dread that my voice became a quaver. Somewhere here on the *Jerusalem* Captain Dirge had a daughter—far from home, far from school—! The Captain noticed my agitation and immediately broke off his questionings.

" 'Ye must forgive me,' he said, sitting motionless as ever. 'I don't ask ye these things, as it may seem, from idle curiosity.' He turned and looked toward the door leading to his inner chambers. It seemed to me from the way he sat bent over, his head inclined toward the small, closed door, that he meant to call her, his daughter—the beautiful Augusta! I'd sink away in a deliquium at sight of her, I thought. My head became filled with the vision of her standing above me, with soft, blinking starlight behind her, and I felt a faintness coming over me even now. Would I dare to speak to her? Unthinkable! She'd laugh me to scorn, remembering that first encounter with me, Jonathan Upchurch laid out flat on his back, having gone down the poopdeck companionway head over heels like a bumpkin at the fair. Never in this world, after such an embarrassment, could I face my vision of feminine perfection, my soul's desire, Augusta. Yet now I was certain he meant to call her in, and my hope that he would was as boundless as my shame and dread.

"He turned to study me, expressionless as always. 'Ye seem very young to be a schoolmaster.'

" 'Nineteen, sir,' I said.

"For once what he was thinking shone clear in his eyes, or so it seemed to me: that nineteen is very young indeed, and that nothing on earth is more flatly ridiculous, more outlandish and tiresome, than youth. But he did not say it.

"I added, 'Almost twenty, actually.' A bold-faced lie. Yet my voice was firm, my stance, it seemed to me, casual. I amazed myself.

"The Captain touched blind Jeremiah's arm, feebly signaling for help, and Jeremiah stood up and assisted Captain Dirge to his feet. The Captain said, 'I have a daughter, Mr. Upchurch, that I'd like ye to act as a tutor for.'

"I pretended to hesitate.

" 'Her name's Augusta.'

"My throat went dry as cobwebs and locked up my voice.

"Captain Dirge, leaning hard on the blind man, went over to the door, opened it a crack, and called his daughter to the room.

XIV

"Augusta! Not the greatest of alchemists could have unlocked the mysteries of my dark Rosarium or explained her contradictions. She was as elusive and baffling as the world itself. Emblem of womanly generosity, yet spiteful and mean; honest as sunlight, yet devious, wily; soft, unbelievably gentle, yet ferocious. She was a place, a climate, a direction, but I could find no bearings. She was Arcadia and Sodom, the ideal pattern of Nature, the idea of Evil. I knew all this, with a part of my mind, from the first instant. It was as if we'd been acquainted for centuries.

"When she came through the door I glanced away, watching the monster who accompanied her, Alastor, her low-slung mastiff, dusty, heavy as a lion. He merely rolled his glance past me. The girl, without seeming to do so, studied me. I felt myself turning pure object, stulted—flatfooted and defeatured as a cider barrel—and then the next instant I was a riot of particulars, all ill-considered, flambuginous. I was dizzy with the awareness of the undue proportions of my hands and feet, and I was sickened with shame at the flaw I had heretofore suffered more or less philosophically, my eyes' misalignment. The room filled solid with her Edenic and unartificial scent, the delicate, slaughtering sound of her rustling skirt.

"The Captain stood bent over, puffing at his pipe, uglier than ever beside his daughter.

"'Augusta,' he mumbled, 'this is Jonathan Upchurch, who'll be yer tutor.'

"Old Jeremiah seemed to listen to something inside his mind, looking up at nowhere. He kept one arm around the Captain, supporting him.

"'I'm pleased to meet you,' Augusta said. She patted, half stroked the dog's head in a way that, by its very innocence, made my maleness quicken.

"I had no choice but to look up at her now. She curtsied—just perceptibly—and gave me her bewildering smile. I could think nothing at the time, could merely bow, as clumsy as a schoolboy reciting a poem; yet I later devoted many hours—nay, more like weeks —to study of that curtsy and smile. Lying on my berth with my eyes wide open yet blind as Jeremiah's, or balanced on a yardarm, one hand closed indifferently on a sial-hem or stay, I would summon back that tantalizing image, hunting its secret. It was impish, possibly, as if she were claiming already her inalienable scholar's right to mock the teacher; but it was something else, too—a suggestion that she knew things from which my kind of mind was sealed off for eternity. Yet the smile was also kindly, I thought, as if she had seen all my faults at one glance—even those buried deepest in my soul's abditorium—and had lightly, easily forgiven them. And she was, at the same time, perfunctory, formal, as if something in her father's tone had quite by chance triggered a response of automatic gentility. Because of the direction in which my thought had been inclined to run since Mr. Knight had first brought me Boethius (he'd since brought me Edwards and Spinoza on Free Will), I saw the impishness as Augusta's line of *necessity,* the kindness as *free,* the perfunctory quality as the random stroke of *chance.* Everything was suddenly clear as day. Yet the very next instant I was downright alarmed at how inadequate all my conceptions were for penetration of the mystery of Augusta.

"She was seventeen, her father said. Her hair was jet-black—as black as her apparel—with fiery glints of blue in it, flashes like those on the wings of a raven. Though she kept her hair discreetly ribboned, it was rich, luxuriant. Her complexion was not so much fair as pale, ghostly in fact, and had the strangest conceivable effect on me: It made me tremble for her safety, filled me with an ardent and fatuate wish to be near her, protective as her giant dog— though whether it was harm from without or some mysterious egritude of mind that I feared might threaten her, I had no idea. But it was in the *eyes* of Augusta that I found her chief beauty and the source of her impenetrability. They were the shining gray of storm-charged twilight, larger even than the gazelle eyes of the tribe in the valley of the Nourjahad; and when Augusta was excited—by a line of poetry, an astonishing sunset, the terror of longboats lowered away, or excited perhaps by graver terrors that lurked in some corner of her mystic brain—they had a beauty which can only be described as unearthly, as though her small and perfect body were the house of some Plotinian spirit come down from a paler world to spy.

"The Captain said, 'Perhaps ye'd give Mr. Upchurch a general idea of how far ye've progressed, Augusta.'

"She curtsied again. 'Shall I show you my books?' She was suddenly as innocent, as ignorant of the world of women and men, the terrible hungry expansion in my trousers, as a child of six years old.

" 'That would help,' I said, 'yes.'

" 'This way, then.' She smiled—rather foxy, it seemed to me, or perhaps scornful of my seaman's garb and smell, my crooked eyes. She turned away, leading us to the door. I followed, behind the dog, with the Captain and Jeremiah.

"The dimly lit room into which the door opened was like a genteel parlor back on land, except the larger furniture was bolted down and the chairs—dark-blue velvet with studs of brass, as near as I could tell in that somber darkness—had staying chains. Here all four walls were lined with bookshelves, interrupted only by space for two doors and the great, square ports—velvet-draped and as solemn as the chairs—two oil lamps that gave out just the barest little flimmer, and a badly damaged portrait, a mustached, wild-eyed man. As I stepped toward the portrait to examine it more closely, Augusta sang out in a voice filled with, I'd have sworn, sheer terror, 'Ah, here they are, Mr. Upchurch!' When I turned, she reached toward me an old leather-bound volume of Ovid, her hand violently trembling. From the dog's throat came a low, uncertain rumble.

"Baffled, panicky, I took the book from Augusta and opened it. I pretended to listen as she explained to me how far she'd got and what her difficulties were, but my whole attention was fixed, really, on the miraculous change that had come over her. Her words poured out in a wild flood, her bosom heaved, her gray eyes blazed, she was unable to hide the violent shaking of her fingertips. I couldn't for the life of me think how I'd frightened her or, indeed, how any mortal could so frighten another. It made me more shy, more clumsy than ever. I suffered a curious impression of *coldness,* as if we were standing at the border of the mediums' much-touted 'Beyond.' Whether the coldness was objective or merely an effect of my extreme agitation, something suggested by the books all around me—volumes on famous hauntings, visions, and other such matters—I was in no condition to determine. Nevertheless, I managed to bring out some expression of satisfaction with her scholarship, and we turned to her work on cyphering. She became somewhat calmer. (Was it sensual, quisquos old Ovid that unnerved her?) I turned with a nod to the Captain to impart my impression that all was sure to go well. He'd moved slightly, still leaning on Jeremiah, coming over behind me so that he stood directly in the way of my view of the painting. He responded with his curious, aloof bow, and I thought in the dimness that his face was distinctly pale. I returned my attention, what I could summon of it, to Augusta once more, and the business of determining where to take up her education was soon dispatched. I gave her lessons for preparation next morning, and we agreed that I would come to go through them with her the following afternoon. Our business finished, I suddenly became all self-consciousness again. She was looking at my chin in a way I'd got used to after nineteen years—the expression of one who is carefully not looking at my eyes. She smiled abruptly, flicked her gaze up to meet mine, then away. 'I'm dreadfully grateful to you, Mr. Upchurch.' I too smiled—a thing I couldn't have managed for mere politeness—smiled because I couldn't help it. I was enslaved. 'The pleasure's entirely mine,' I said, so formal I'd likely have burst out laughing if it weren't for her strange behavior earlier, that peculiar trembling, so that I gave the formality she seemed to require, gave it unthinkingly, as though it was the naturalest thing in the world.

"I turned back to the Captain, trying to steal one more glance at the painting, but he gave me no chance, tottering toward me, studiously ignoring my extended hand, subtly moving me backwards toward the door. In the outer cabin he remembered something, excused himself and, with the blind man's help, stepped back into the inner apartment for a word with his daughter. He returned looking morose and abstracted, as it seemed to me—still deathly pale—stood puffing at his pipe and staring at the floor, and told me without much animation what an excellent find I was on a whaler. Then, with Jeremiah's assistance he led me, or rather, subtly drove me, out onto the poopdeck. There, himself keeping out of the sunlight, in the doorway, he held me a moment longer with his eye—his eyes were as dead-looking as his daughter's were praeternaturally alive—and after an instant's hesitation, said: 'I appreciate yer breeding, Mr. Upchurch. I know pretty well how queer it seems to discover a young lady on a Nantuck whaler, not to mention my own . . .' He gestured vaguely, indicating, perhaps, his illness, then dully finished: 'I appreciate yer tact and discretion.'

" 'Thank you, sir,' I said.

"He seemed not to hear me. He was thinking, I supposed, of other things—some old and familiar matter of concern: the grumblings of his sailors, or some trouble on the far-distant planet he hailed from. It came to me that he'd ingeniously blocked me from ever inquiring about the ship's mysteries.

" 'Ye've made friends among the men?' he asked.

" 'Oh yes, sir.' I nodded.

"He looked at me with his beard behind his fist, his head lowered, so oddly like a great, black, hunchbacked bear that a shiver went through me. His eyes became unnaturally still, full of violence, or so I imagined.

" 'Good lad,' he said at last. 'The things of this world have their place, it may be. But keep a look-out.'

" 'I will, sir,' I said, considerably puzzled.

"Blind Jeremiah, standing just behind the Captain, gave me a nod, a hint that Captain Dirge should be subjected to no more strain.

" 'Good-night, sir,' I said.

"The Captain said nothing. He'd forgotten my existence, his eyes rolled up for a peek at the sky. His silk-gloved hands rested lightly on his beard, and his large, frail body was drooped on Jeremiah as if the life had all drained out of it.

"The next afternoon, when I went to hear my pupil's recitation, the Captain was fast asleep on his bunk—I saw him through the hatch. He was snoring horribly. Blind Jeremiah was nowhere to be seen. The painting they'd kept me from looking at had vanished."

XV

"What a tale!" cries the guest with a laugh like an explosion. "I swear, all the lightnings of Scheherazade can't hold a candle to it!"

"Ye think so, do ye?" the mariner cries, and gets an eager expression.

But the angel is staring out the window, blank. The woods have grown darker. There are crows in the trees, and even in the inn there's an autumnal smell. The hollow-eyed dead have begun to shuffle away again, remembering their business. They move, soundlessly, through fields of sheep.

The mariner notices the direction of the angel's look and grows sober. "It's always easier in the winding up than in the carrying on, of course," says he. "There's many a stagnating calm to slip past, that's the truth of the matter, and many a tedious obstruction to be circumnavigated."

"That's true, I'll grant," the guest confesses. He shows a flicker of distress and glances at the clock. But it's early yet, inside the room, or so he appears to persuade himself. His decision grows firmer. "We've got our work cut out for us, that's so." He chuckles sternly. But the guest looks increasingly dependable, determined. He forces a somewhat louder chuckle, puts one hand on the mariner's arm, and with the other he bangs the table. BANG! "You with the golden wings—more spirits!"

The angel gets up quickly, absent-mindedly puts the pipe in his pocket, where it continues to smoke, goes out and at once returns with a bottle. The guest and mariner lean forward, solemn as the devil, though smiling hopefully, racking their brains. The angel pours.

XVI

"So began the period of my joyful enslavement. Not a spar, not a scrap of sail remained from my jolly independence—young man's idiocy, I called it now—dressed up, bepowdered like a New York donzel, spiffed like a Frenchman on promenade. Wherever my thought turned, the world was filled with a delicious hope, as sweet with incense as Augusta's room. I looked back on Reverend Dunkel now with profound respect, as if his sermonizing by the cellar chute had borne up from the waters of chaos and unfolded into the universe petal by petal the Brahma Himself. 'Discipline!'—aye!—for me, too, now, it was a word wrapped in glory. No man can know what purpose the most trivial events may serve in the grand but for us inscrutable scheme of Providence. I might now thank God for having thrown me in with pirates and nearly drowning me that night, for cracking my ribs and once more dulling my wits on Latin, and driving me thence to the rigging, where . . . The purpose of this last was not quite so plain, God's plan for me being, presumably, not yet revealed in all particulars; but I did not specially worry the matter. The general design was clear and radiantly blessed.

"When I spoke of Augusta to Billy More he was astounded.

"'Preposterous,' he said. 'If there's a woman on this ship, I'll eat my hat. Yer up to yer same old tricks, I'll wager!' Though he smiled, he looked crafty, like Ebenezer Frye at the county fair when he considers he may have been horn-swoggled.

"'Think what ye please,' says I. 'What I know I know, that's all.'

"Wilkins was laboring at his low bench behind us, or pretending to—bent over like a monkey, till his eyes were three, four inches from the coils he struggled with. With every further hour he put in on those clock-parts, the thing he was constructing looked less like a clock, though it resembled nothing else much neither.

"'The Captain claims it's his daughter, ye say?' says Billy More.

"'So he introduced her,' says I, and continues my devilish careful shoe-shining.

"'Well I be damned,' he says, and shakes his head, grinning. He calls over to Wilkins—acting, just now, as if Wilkins and he was boon companions: 'Ye heard the latest from our pirate, Wilkins?'

"Wilkins tips up his wicked little frog-head—frog-mouth half-open, eyes like shaded lanterns.

"'He's deep, that Jonathan Upchurch,' says Wilkins, and he gives me a wink. What he uses for twiddling those screws like mites' eggs is a double-edge dagger about six inches long and lighter in his hand than a partridge feather. 'He'll come to no good, you mark my word,' says Wilkins, and gives me another good wink. 'If he ain't up to some kind of confidence game, then I'll be a bow-legged albatross.'

"'Tell us what she looks like,' says Billy More.

"I oblige him as well as I'm able to—I've never yet seen her except once by starlight and twice in the dimness of that inner room—and Billy More's face gets increasingly astonished. At last he breaks in on me, thumping on his big bony knees with his fists. 'I swear, the more I see of ye, Johnny, the more I wonder if ye really *was* a pirate once. Ye've set down the Captain's daughter to a *T*. I've seen her myself, fact is—though never on shipboards.'

" 'I hope ye got a spare hat,' says I.

" 'Ha, ha,' says Billy More, and sits watching my shoe-rag slap.

"If he was still uncertain, the fault wasn't altogether his, I confess. Despite all Augusta's good influence on me, I was too much the son of my yarn-spinning, card-forcing, tricky-footed father to make everything as plain as I might've done. There's a curious pleasure, for a certain kind of soul, in keeping a card or two tucked in his suspenders. (Even that palaverer Reverend Dunkel knew it, telling me that time that the part ye understand is 'irrelevant.') What I said to Billy More was the solemn truth, but something in my spirit—some wisdom as old as the Devonian fish, it may well be—made me frame it with a smile like Pious John the Pirate's. What we claim we desire in this vale of tears is resplendent truth, distinct bits of certainty that ring like dubloons, but that very claim is, like everything else in the universe, a skinner, a bamboozle, an ingenious little trick for out-sharping the card-shark gods.

"With the Captain's daughter, nevertheless, I meant to be as honest as the day is long, whatever my manner was with commoner souls. So I curled my tresses on my fingers and shined 'em with candlewax, nights, and polished my teeth till they glittered and winked like Hawaiian pearls, and I let no syllable fall from my lips that wouldn't be proper at a Synod meeting. There's honesty for you in the grand old sense!—foolsgold from Plato and the Bible (as journals for young ladies construe it). I was in love, in short. As instinctively cunning as the peacock displaying what he normally drags indifferently through dirt. And exactly like the peacock or the preening mouse, I was fooled myself, to the bottom of my soul, by my antics —and also by Augusta's.

"As I worked with her, almost every afternoon, what had struck me most powerfully at first began to have a lessened effect—her extraordinary beauty. Like the ship's darker mysteries, her beauty became familiar, and in time I hardly noticed it, as a rich man hardly notices his wealth. I would notice it, to be precise, only when Augusta betrayed what I swore was her 'true' nature.

"At times Augusta was the emblem of virginal simplicity and goodness. Smiling at her work and enjoying it, enjoying the roll of the sea, enjoying my company, too—reddened sunlight needling through the curtained, stained-glass ports and coming back to life in her coal-black hair, her ghostly features innocently relaxed, sweetly unguarded—she made me understand the medieval image of the Virgin Mary, and not as some vulnerary hope for the desperate but as an actual human possibility, a fleshed ideal. I reveled, at such moments, in the quickness of her mind, her uncanny gift for piercing to the heart of the most abstruse speculations, questions that should puzzle a woman three, four times her age; and I reveled in the sensibleness of her emotions, her ability for instance to write poems precisely descriptive of her feelings and poised precisely between over- and under-valuation of the emotion's place in the general scheme of things. My pleasure wasn't grounded in the fact that it was I who'd made clear what the metaphysical problem was, nor, in the case of her poems, that it was I who'd taught her the poetic means that freed her to make every poem her spirit's own portrait. My pleasure came out of the Truth itself, which I'd helped her to reach and which embraced us both and would outlast us both.

"She'd hone away at a poem for hours, until I began to fear that her father would be cross at my failing to press her on her other studies. It was more than diligence, that poetry writing, it seemed to me. It was as if, with a finely wrought lady's bower of decisions and spells, she was striving, superhumanly intense, to lock out the enemy who'd stolen already as near as her death-pale cheeks. With the instinctual wisdom of the frail, she meant to seize the good, know its value beyond mere convention, and raise up that value like an exorcist's cross against extinction. She gave me, for instance, this curious poem, which she handed over with a shy smile and the words, 'Here's a grave little love poem for you, Jonathan.' It was called 'An Invitation.'

> *After the last*
> *Grave bell,*
> *After the ghost*
> *Of the dead girl*
>
> *Returns to earth*
> *Like autumn light,*
> *And spades smooth*
> *The hollows out,*
>
> *Memories*
> *Will turn to rock,*
> *And carved words*
> *Become her clock.*

'Beautiful,' I said. She smiled, all-knowing, and the faintest possible glow came to her cheeks. She looked down at her pale hands, folded in her lap, and continued smiling. 'Thank you,' she said. And that instant my Virgin was transmogrified to the medieval Eve. *A love poem,* she'd said. *An Invitation.* I was blushing now. As for Augusta, she sat smiling exactly as before, all innocence, but with eyes gone darkling and lips slightly moist. Her hands rested on her waist in such a way that they tightened the material of her blouse and fiercely called attention to her breasts. 'Hussy!' they'd have said in the *Ladies' Repository.* But the elderly ladies and Doctors of Divinity who write for such journals would have no great need for their squawking rhetoric were not Eve as mysterious and rare as the Virgin.

"At her worst, if one can call it that, Augusta's wicked streak played mocking games with her nobler qualities. We had been reading the poetry of Crashaw one night, seated side by side at her ebony table, the dog's head inches from our feet. She said suddenly, with bright-eyed innocence, that Crashaw's devotion, and the humble simplicity of his visual fancies, had inspired her to try a poem in the same sincere and loving manner. I said, 'Might I read it?'

" 'It's very short,' she said.

" 'Do let me see it!'

"She hesitated. 'I'd really prefer to read it *to* you,' she said. 'It's not very good, actually.'

"I bowed my head, stretched out one arm. 'Then read away.'

"By a magnificent exertion of will she made her face—except for the luminous eyes—lambishly sweet. She took a deep breath and put the fingertips of one hand over her heart, then read:

> *Full teats of milk that cannot cloy*
> *He like a nurse will bring,*
> *And when He draws the promise nigh,*
> *O, how we suck and sing!*

"As she finished, cheeks bright, she glanced at me, then suddenly laughed, richly and beautifully, at my blushing discomfort. It was the laugh, you'd have thought, of a woman much older, much slyer than Augusta.

"I wrung my hands a little, wounded to the quick. 'That's an interesting rhyme, *cloy* and *nigh*,' I said. Upset or no, I was my father's son, crafty to the last.

" 'I rather hoped you'd like it.' She touched my arm, sweetly, childishly, and even as the shock of her touch went through me, I understood that she'd planned that move like a stage actress—had perhaps even written the poem to make it possible. I suppose my eyes widened. She blushed and withdrew her hand, knowing she'd been caught. 'Forgive me,' she said—a whisper of alarm. Suddenly she was weeping, and I was convinced, despite my perfect certainty an instant ago, that all my judgments had been shamefully wrong. She was an avid reader of the Bible, after all. Her father was a man as religious as any who ever sailed the seas. She jumped up from the table and fled to the corner of the room where she stood with her back to me. The image of the dunce-block flashed into my mind and I almost guffawed, but then, the next moment, I was on the verge of tears myself. I saw her sorrow as the sorrow and shame of all groping young-womanhood, our comic melodrama ancient and beyond our strength, monstrously unfair, a callous and tasteless joke by a weary universe. I stood up awkwardly, biting my lips, and went a few steps toward her. Five feet from her—the great dog between us—I stopped and reached out to her, over Alastor's head. 'Augusta, I can't tell you how sorry—' I began.

"She said nothing, her face in her hands. I leaned a little nearer. 'My poor, dear child,' I said, 'if in any way—'

"She turned suddenly, with an outraged expression. The dog leaped away in fright. 'Jonathan Upchurch, don't you ever call me that again!' Tears coursed down her cheeks and her small lips trembled.

" 'Call you what?' I exclaimed.

" 'And I want you to apologize.'

" 'For *what?*'

" 'For *everything!*'

"Instantly, for fear of worse, I did so.

" 'Shake hands on it,' she said. It struck me that she was not quite so furious as before, and that if I wished to implore her to be reasonable . . . Nevertheless, to be on the safe side, I held out my hand. She took it and shook it firmly. I had a faint and of course incredible suspicion that however earnest her tears, she was secretly gloating, a murderous, heavy-lidded witch enjoying the electric-storm power of her unreasonableness. When she'd finished shaking my hand, she said, 'We're friends again?'

" 'Friends,' I said, with a smile and a glance at her pet.

" 'Good. Then you may kiss me.'

"I drew back in astonishment. 'Augusta!'

" 'Jon-a-than,' she said.

"But surely somewhere there have to be limits.

'Augusta, you're a child only seventeen years old, and I am your tutor, which vests in me responsibility for your intellectual and moral—'

" 'I will never again ask you anything so improper, I give you my word, Jonathan.'

" 'Mr. Upchurch,' I corrected.

" 'Mr. Upchurch, then.' She smiled as if *she* were the one submitting.

"I sighed helplessly, then kissed her, aiming for the cheek—but Augusta was tricky. I recalled, as she moved her hands around my shoulders, once reading that kissing is a common cause of heart attack.

"That night I did not sleep, nor the next.

"As is, I suppose, the usual case, I was as sick with love and its complications when away from her as I was when I was with her. In her presence I was prisoner to scents and whispers, age-old drives, strange pressures invisible to the poor-fool naked eye. Away from her, I was the victim of my own imaginings, hour on hour of theatrical, deliquious lunacy. I stood at the rail looking down at the steadily rolling sea and tried futilely to understand what was happening to me. I was suddenly, because of one kiss, consumed. I could think and dream of nothing but Augusta, even high on the rigging where there was a certain advantage in keeping one's mind on one's position in relation to Nowhere. She was the wind, the sea, the motion of the ship. She was the sweet and unspeakable reality enclosing the narrow opinions of Plato and Plotinus, Locke and Hume and Newton. All my hours away from her were merely a burden I must endure . . .

"My mind paused, grapneled, on the word *endure*. Reverend Dunkel's word, the dark side of Discipline. I frowned thoughtfully, gazing out at the midnight ocean. The world I must endure in separation from Augusta—stars, dark water—had an aliveness I had not observed in it before. It was her counterpart, her extension. As I'd considered falling from the rigging once, I could now toy, unseriously, with sinking peacefully, even joyfully into the waves, my element, my brother. I had a fleeting memory of old books about Indians moving silent as foxes through moonlit forests, their souls at one with them.

"Somewhere below me, the slaves were singing. They, too, were her extension, not demonic tonight but merely part of the whole, their anger and weariness an element in Augusta's complexity, and an element as much to be venerated as the virginal goodness that defined the upper limit of the total gradation. Her most perfect poetry, it came to me, could never be achieved without that darker, more ominous music in the hold. It took, I told myself, abundant leisure to develop the utmost reaches of mind. Without slavery there could have been no Homer, no Pericles, no thousand and one images of the Goddess of Mercy in the temple at Kyoto. What were the pyramids, the books of Aristotle, the three-hundred-eight-ton Buddha of Nara, but hymns to the labor of literal or figurative slaves? Augusta may have been a natural genius; but her writing (thought I) was no mere warbling of woodnotes wild. She'd read—she had been *free* to read—good poetry all her life. Free Will was not as simple as I had imagined, then. It arched up out of enslavement exactly as mind blooms up from befuddled, tormented flesh—poor timorous green, if those experiments at Prague were right. One was, I thought, either a slave of purposeless ebb-tide and stormwind from the south, or the slave of some meaningful human ideal, like the secret purpose, which no one had so far imparted to me, of the whaler *Jerusalem*. Perhaps, indeed, they were the same in the end, both weathers and the winds of thought stirred up by the same omniscient Mind, archangel finger in the swirl of events. So we must hope, we metaphysicians. Better a bad but universal system than rootless good, occasional, floating like a derelict.

"The following day I went to her early, before I was expected—the Captain was asleep, lying still as a corpse—and though I could see she was embarrassed and flustered (pretending to be drawing when I was sure she'd been busy at something else when I knocked), I pressed my conversation on her. Leaning over her to look at the drawings she pretended to be working on (imaginary flowers), I was ambushed by a whiff of perfume, and I kissed her. She resisted for an instant, then returned the kiss with all her young soul, rising from her chair to press close to me. I closed my arms around her, frantic. There was a footstep at the door, and in panic—inspired by some angel, no doubt—I snatched up a pile of books, the first that came to hand, and fled.

" 'Jonathan!' she cried.

" 'Just stopped by for these books,' I explained to old Jeremiah, at the door.

"He cocked his head, brows lifted in astonishment, listening with all his ears as I hurried past.

"The books, I found when I reached my bunk, were of no great interest. One of those fraudulent deLaurence books on Hindoo snakecharming; a petty-form history book; a book of poems (religious); a book, with engravings, called *The World's Great Scoundrels*. I tucked them into the little hiding place I'd made (the removable slat in the bulkhead), intending to examine them more closely at my leisure (pore over them, treasure them—because they were hers!); then I hurried back up to the deck, where, drunk on the memory of Augusta's kiss, I forgot all about them.

XVII

"One thing there was about Captain Dirge that was stranger than all the rest. For all his sensitivity to light and noise and stench and excitement, he never let a ship pass by without hailing her and boarding. Even in a healthy whaler captain, that would've been mighty peculiar behavior. You gam with fellow leviathan-hunters—for mail, for news of where the schools have been sighted—but you don't haul in for every casual passer-by. What question it was that the Captain asked I couldn't surmise, nor why he went over, in every case, with an empty satchel and came back with a full one (a point Billy More first made me take note of); but I knew sure as day that when he hauled up to gunboats, merchantmen, and such-like, and lowered away with Jeremiah beside him and a crew of black oarsmen—the Captain hunched over and limp from his sickness—he must have some strong motivation.

"The visits meant as much or more, it seemed to me, to blind Jeremiah. From the time the stranger first appeared on the horizon, long before anyone had told him it was there, the old man commenced acting nervous and peculiar. You'd find him standing alone in odd corners, muttering to himself, and sometimes grinning, ecstatic, as if deep in conversation with the Holy Ghost. When the time came to lower the long-boat away to row over for the boarding, the slightest mistake or alteration of procedure and Jeremiah, though all gentleness at other times, would go suddenly zacotic, prepared to take a kick at whoever was standing near-by enough. He looked like an actor in a tragical play just preparing to strike into the stagelights—pulling at his gloves, twitching his lips to get his mustache right. But when they got to the stranger (I knew from watching through the crows-nest spyglass), it was suddenly the Captain, not Jeremiah, that looked like the actor, waving and jabbering, for once hardly leaning on the blind man.

"To Augusta, too, those visits were important occasions—occasions of terror, it seemed to me, though I couldn't make out why. All the time they were gone, if I happened to be alone in the cabin with her, she'd chatter nonsense, trying to keep her mind occupied, and sometimes she'd wring her pale fingers or give a great shudder.

" 'Oh, Jonathan, Jonathan,' she said to me once, 'what do they *do* over there? Why are they so *long?*' She was clinging to my hand, trembling as if with fever. (Things had by now progressed considerably between us.)

" 'Why, passing the time of day, most likely,' I answered with a laugh, to reassure her.

" 'It's criminal, a man in my father's condition!'

Augusta said. 'If only I could be a little bird and fly over and spy on them!'

"I laughed again and kissed her fingertips, though in the back of my mind I suspected there was something I was missing in all this. It was all just a little too finely turned. What *presence* there was in the hankie she clutched in three fingers of the hand clamped on mine with such abandon! With my cast left eye, I saw that she was watching the mirror, observing our performance like a critic.

" 'Augusta,' I said. And then, startled, 'Why, Augusta, you *love* this!'

"She clutched her heart, and her tears came gushing. 'Jonathan, how *could* you!'

"That very instant I had a clear intuition that there was something I'd known from the first about Augusta—some horrible truth her paleness, her trembling, her illness masked. But meeting her eyes, I believed I was mistaken and dismissed the matter. 'Don't be cross,' I said. 'Fear and joyous excitement have a similar look, and I was fooled, I fear.' I kissed her cheek. After a time, she forgave me.

"But that night, lying on my bunk in the darkness, no sound around me but the breathing of my fellow sailors, sleeping, I remembered that feeling and all over again got the same icy chill. I tried to pin down the cause of it. I could get very clearly the sensation of fright, but I could conjure up nothing to account for it—certainly nothing that had anything to do with that beautiful, pallid face, those luminous eyes. Nevertheless, my odd fear grew, as if part of a nightmare: a fear of dangers on every hand, all masked, hidden, but inexorably closing in on us.

"With a jolt I realized, or perhaps dreamed, that someone was there in the darkness beside my bunk, some person or thing reaching slowly toward my face. I cringed back, then impulsively reached toward the shape and, the same instant, shouted. My grip closed on what seemed a hairless monkey's hand, small, wet, as cold as snow. I released it, not shouting now but screaming; and now my companions were gathered around me, frightened, asking questions. Then it *was* a dream, I thought, vastly relieved; but then I thought I heard fleeing footsteps. 'Listen!' I cried out. The others insisted they heard nothing.

"It was about this time that the crafty ex-pirate Wilkins said: 'Curious how the Captain keeps turning, time after time, to the south.'

"I was manning the pump. We'd sprung a small, insignificant leak which was being repaired by the second mate, Wolff, and his longboat crew, and Wilkins was resting—spraddle-legged, like a demonic frog in a red bandanna, eyes alarming in the lantern light—awaiting his turn to relieve me. His hands twitched and jerked and he kept bouncing his knees. He said: 'No matter how far north or east or west we ship—put yer mind to this a minute, me pretty— the old man always tacks south again, heads for, if I ain't mistaken, latitude 52° 37′ 24″, longitude 47° 43′ 15″.'

"I twisted my neck to look up at him. (I had recently taken to insisting to the crew that what I really was was a grave-digger—Heaven only knows what drives me to these things. Sometimes I dug for churches, I said, and sometimes for physicians—it made no difference. All my former lies, I said, were mere feeble attempts to disguise my involvement with that ghoulish trade. (This with my head bowed, eyes rolled up; the living picture of a poor wretched sinner in an agony of shame.) To make my story seem a little more convincing, I frowned a good deal, and walked bent over, and now and then I'd let out a lachrymal chuckle.) Wilkins was leering, puffing at his pipe, and a great dark crease ran up from the side of his leer to his glittering right eye. Two rats in the shadows sat licking their fingers and watching Mr. Wilkins twitch.

"In point of fact, I had given some thought to the Captain's periodic returns to what seemed one same stretch of water—though I hadn't noticed the precision of his returns. I was no longer, I should mention, the innocent who'd looked up, some months ago, and hunted in vain for some recognizable quadrant of the heavens. I'd perched in the crowsnest hour after hour, or hung in the rigging conversing with my red-headed friend Billy More, and thanks to his instruction and the Captain's books, I was coming to be something of an astronomer. I could pretty well identify every glimmer or blink from the Andromedae to the Pegasi. I'd learned from the books about stars of varying magnitude, dark stars, twins, and the mysterious so-called wandering stars. My head was crammed to the beams with facts, and I carried them up a little higher with me every time I mounted the mast. There they ceased to be facts, became something more lively—singing particles in a sleepy-headed universe. I began to know things people don't know if they've never given up all private identity to a shore-less sea or a forest extending, arch on arch, the breadth of fifteen mountains. I began to comprehend time and space not by mind or will but by a process more mystical, like the process by which old married couples understand each other, or trees in a valley keep minute track of the wanderings of birds and spiders. It all began consciously enough, no doubt. I remember trying to make out exactly what time it was by the stars' positions, and laboriously adjusting for the whaler's changing locus. I never could seem to get a firm calculation, and I was stung by how cleverly Billy More could tip his red beard toward heaven and toss off, casual as a glove, our place and time. Then, one night, like a fellow coming out of a dream, I knew I too could do it. The whole universe moving around me, less like a clock than a huge, slow bird, the ship moving gentle and regular below me, my mind at the center of the gentle, seemingly random groping like the mind of God (I don't mean some judging, providential god but one who eternally rides and smiles)—the whole universe was my soul's extension, my ultimate temporal-spatial location, so that the roughly six cubic feet of air my fleshy inner shell displaced was as easy to locate in relation to the rest as the placement of my cast left eye in relation to my toenails. All this may seem purest gibberish to some. But it's a fact, as any crow can tell you, that the mind always knows where it is till it stops and thinks.

"I'd gotten comfortable with the flow of things. So I knew myself what Wilkins was slyly telling me, though not to the exact degree and second. (Nor did he, of course. That is, the pipe-puffing lizard knew because he knew what the Captain was hunting.) Thanks to Wilkins' hint, I too was soon informed, at least partly. I kept those bearings in mind (scowling, bent over like a man too familiar with shovels), and the first chance I got in the Captain's chartroom, I had myself a look. On the point signified, I found two words, if you could call them that: *Van Is.* I puzzled and brooded, then ventured a question to blind Jeremiah, where he sat at the Captain's chessboard fingering the pieces. He smiled, his cheek twitched, and he leaned over sharply sideways toward me. 'The Vanishing Isles, me boy! Hsst! Not a word!' and he threw a half-terrified blind-man's look toward the Captain's bed-chamber. That was all the old loon would say, and I knew, from the excitement the words stirred up in him —fear like Augusta's, so intense that it verged on manic joy—that I'd better ask nobody else.

" 'Game of chess, lad?' says he.

" 'Sorry, I never learnt the moves, sir,' says I. (As a matter of fact, my father'd won tournaments, and he never beat me in a game since I was seven.)

"Well, I kept, from then on, a more careful watch on the Captain's meanderings as he swept the seas for whale. We were cruising, at this time, north-north-east, bound due for Alaska; we were further north than we'd ever come formerly, as if the attraction of the south had lost its hold on Captain Dirge, and we were free now to visit the North Pole. Six hundred miles from the Alaskan coast, the ship tacked west in hot pursuit of a mighty school of sperm whale. It was a great kill and, except for the loss of a long-boat and two men of the second mate's crew, it was an incredible piece of luck. I half expected, despite all I knew, that the *Jerusalem* would sail for the Cape and home. We veered southeast, as if that were exactly the Captain's intention. By the fourth day, as if sucked along by an undertow, we were sliding perceptibly southward. The whole crew was aware of it, and not happy about it. We were loaded full, and heading for anywhere but home was plain madness. But still we slid southward, strewing the sea with skeletons of whales. (Birds flew busily, like gnats, above them, sharks thrashed around them, snatching what we'd left and from time to time snatching some absent-minded bird. From miles away you could see the white bones floating in the sun and the white spray heaving up skywards against it. 'Up goes the spray,' Mr. Knight said grimly, bending close to me, 'and straightway trembling fingers set it down— *Shoals, rocks, breakers hereabouts: beware!* For years navigation shuns the place. Aye, there's the story of yer obstinate survival of ancient beliefs . . .' 'Mr. Knight, I'm a Unitarian,' I said. 'Nothing you say, however so blasphemous, can offend me.')

"And still we bore southward. The grumblings and mutterings of the crew grew fiercer. Even gentle souls like Billy More grew sullen and intractable, huddling to themselves—and from more than the numbing cold, I could see. The sea and sky were gray as slate. The birds that took a moment's rest in the rigging were peculiarly formed, if you judged them by temperate standards. The Captain, sickly but ferocious in his cabin, would be obstinately silent when Mr. Knight or the second mate, Wolff, asked questions about the course we steered. What they said when I was listening in the neighboring chamber was elliptical, coded, but the fact of disagreement was clear as day. Even blind Jeremiah seemed dead-set against the Captain, though he ventured very little, remembering his place. Augusta, listening to those angry debates—loud enough to sound like thunder if the Captain's ears were as sensitive as he claimed they were—Augusta, I say, was pale, shivering; her large, gray eyes were like the southern sky before a storm. In the forecastle, nights, Bill More began mentioning, in a guarded way, the laws regarding replacement of a captain judged incompetent.

"Then, for complication, there where no ship but

a madman's should be, we met a stranger. As soon as the crowsnest cry went out, Captain Dirge and Jeremiah came tottering to the poopdeck, Captain Dirge hardly able to move without help, and the order was given to approach her. No sooner was the lunatic order sounded than Mr. Knight went striding aft. We went with him, every man on deck, hanging back, for fear of the Captain's fury, but eager to hear what Mr. Knight would say. We heard nothing, of course; Mr. Knight was too discreet. But we saw pretty well that, once again, Captain Dirge was indifferent to all wills but his own. What could make visiting a stranger so important—important enough to risk turning the *Jerusalem*'s crew to mutineers? It was past my imagining, and I decided then and there that this time when the Captain and Jeremiah went over, I'd be with them, come hell or high water.

XVIII

"To any man who casually passed my bunk it would've seemed that young Jonathan Upchurch lay sleeping as peaceful as a newborn babe. But if he tipped back the covers, I'm sorry to say (and sorrier because of what the sequel must tell), he'd've seen a poor black man, bound and gagged, misused and victimized beyond human toleration. I had no choice, as I explained to the fellow. He didn't look persuaded. He may have been told such things before, in Africa, maybe, by the blacks who trapped him, or in Boston by the Christian who purchased his wife. To be sure of his continued cooperation, I popped him on the back of the head with the blunt of my marlinspike. Away he sailed to dreamland.

"Then, mittened and wrapped and sou'westered head to foot, I waited by the rail with my fellow blacks, praying the spray wouldn't wash off my cork-black skin. Jeremiah was frantic with excitement, as he always was on these occasions, one arm supporting the Captain (in an irritable sort of way), the other arm waving like a tree in a hurricane, impatient to be into the longboat. Moving all around us but keeping their distance like grouchy wolves, the crew of the *Jerusalem* was muttering, just loud enough to hear, about Dirge's whims. Mr. Knight's stern looks had no effect, and the second mate, Wolff, was more with them than against them.

"If Dirge heard their grumblings, he showed no sign. Relaxed, almost limp, his face as still as a pile of old potatoes, his black suit majestic, he watched the heavy stranger. She flew no flag, which seemed to some of us an ominous business. But she was a cumbersome old tub and apparently unarmed—a three-master schooner, too lumbering and slow to suit a pirate—and her captain, at the rail, looked far from dangerous. He was a heavy old Russian or Slav or Pole in a seal-fur hat and a seal-fur coat, with a muff to keep his hands warm. He chewed at his mustache and kept glancing behind him like a man expecting trouble, but though he was puzzled and dubious, his peasant decency—or else our Captain's bullheadedness—gave him no choice but to receive us.

" 'Get the niggers in,' Captain Dirge commanded. His voice was more muffled than usual. Mr. Knight gave the order, reluctantly; and with his left arm—the arm not supporting the Captain—blind Jeremiah waved at us again, more angrily than ever. We went into the longboat as if there were ships raised to hurry us, and scrambled like monkeys for rowing positions. Then, with help, Jeremiah got the Captain in and sat down beside him. Ten seconds later, Captain Dirge gave the order to lower away. The longboat gave a jerk, as if to fall the whole distance to the gray, grinding waves, then caught itself and moved down slowly. Wilkins stood smiling, watching us go, his arms folded and his frog-face like a mask. Though he pretty well hid it, I had an idea he was as excited by the whole affair as was old Jeremiah. Then the first wave hit us. We went flying like a cork, thumped hard against the side of the *Jerusalem,* then sank like a pail into a well-hole. I was sure we were goners, but up we came two seconds later like a breaching whale, and I pulled at my oar the way the others were doing. In half a minute we were out in the wave-swells, flailing away like a centipede fallen in a cistern. Jeremiah, unable to see what was happening, clung to the Captain with both arms and shouted, maybe to Heaven, maybe to us, it was impossible to tell.

"The blacks around me were as frightened as I was, mouths gaping, sucking in air, eyes rolling. Only the Captain seemed indifferent to the sickening pitch and yaw, the dizzying leap and collapse of the horizon. He sat bent over, staring at his boots and puffing at his pipe, as motionless, I'd've sworn, as a man fast asleep. But I had no time for more than fleeting impressions. I pulled with all my strength, striking deep to get under the troughs between waves. And then I received a stranger impression. The black behind and to the left of me was different from the others. As soon as I could manage, I swung my head for another quick look. The impression came more strongly, though even now I couldn't get it clear. I studied the image I'd fleetingly snatched, and suddenly I knew. The black was small, far too small for an oarsman; but that was the least of it. The man's eyes weren't brown, they were gray as mist. When the truth dawned on me I could hardly believe it. The oarsman was—Augusta! That same instant a huge swell came under us, and I reached back to steady her. Her icy, furious eyes stopped me dead, and I at once put all my attention back on rowing.

"We'd now come to within yards of the stranger. They threw down ropes and we secured them to the rings, and up we went, swaying. When we came level with the rail, the Captain and old Jeremiah went aboard, Captain Dirge bowing and gesturing and muttering to the seal-furred captain of the stranger. They were already withdrawing toward the other captain's cabin when the rest of us began clambering out. 'Pleased to meet you, sir,' Captain Dirge was saying in a voice far more lusty than usual. He leaned as hard as ever on the blind man's arm, but the way he bobbed up and down and wagged his head made me wonder if he really was as doddering as he liked to pretend on the *Jerusalem*. When they came to the mainmast, they paused and admired a grizzly that was chained there, silent and mournful of eye as a Liverpool orphan. Now my cork-blacked Augusta was beside me, furtively touching my hand, guiding me portside, away from the others.

"When none of the *Jerusalem*'s Negroes was in earshot, though the stranger's common seamen were packed tightly around us, Augusta said, 'Jonathan, what have you done? This is madness!'

"I jerked my head, indicating the big, grinning sailors all around us.

" 'Nonsense,' she said. 'They don't understand a word of English.' Then, jabbing her face at the nearest of them—a small, darkish fellow with a nose like an onion and friendly brown eyes—she said, slowly and distinctly, 'Do you speak English?'

"He beamed and nodded, answering in gibberish, and she turned to ask all the others the same. It was soon clear that we could speak as freely as we pleased around them.

" 'And what of you?' I said to her, hurriedly whispering. 'Surely such a risk—'

" 'Don't question me, Jonathan! I assure you I have reasons.' Her small, mittened hands closed tightly on my arm.

"I could see that it was true. Her eyes shone with a wildness that alarmed me, and I knew that no arguments of mine could have the slightest effect on her.

" 'Well, if we're here to spy we may as well spy,' I said.

"She flashed her radiant smile and squeezed my arm again, fiercely and gratefully. Then, bowing with exaggerated politeness to the sailors around us, we slipped aft along the rail toward the poop, where the captains were conversing. A dozen of the strangers followed us, smiling a little foolishly, as if hoping even now that we might find some way to trade words with them. When we reached the poopdeck companionway I hesitated. The stranger's first mate (or some other officer—they wore no markings) stood at the door of the captain's cabin rather like a guard, though apparently not taking his work too seriously, since fur-coated sailors were crowded all around him, trying to peek in through the hatch and ports. Augusta started boldly up. He looked through her as if she were invisible, and after a moment I started up behind her. Any man looking at her hips and seat, I thought as I went up, would know in an instant that that was no oarsman. But then, if old Dirge were to get a good look at my cast left eye . . .

"I was light-headed with fear for both of us, but there was nothing I could do. Two of the stranger's common seamen came timidly behind us, still smiling. Even when we peeked in the cabin window, crowding in beside a man with a coarse leather eyepatch and sharp red ears, the man who stood guard seemed oblivious.

"Inside the schooner captain's cabin there was a crowd, mostly men we hadn't seen before, fur-coated like the others (one or two of them with ear-rings and one with a parrot, which gave me, let me tell you, one devil of a turn). Most of them stood with their backs to us. At the center of the crowd, across the table from the schooner captain, sat Dirge in all his finery, with Jeremiah, as usual, beside him. Billy More had misled me on one minor point. Dirge spoke nothing but English, and the other captain spoke nothing but whatever strange lingo he'd been born to. Yet both of them chattered with considerable animation, Captain Dirge fanatically puffing at his pipe and slugging whiskey down between bursts of conversation, the other captain laughing sort of strangely and hollowly and pouring and drinking, from time to time glancing at Jeremiah with a look of utter bafflement. Jeremiah, seated beside our Captain, was smiling like a man in a Hindoo trance, hearing not a word either one of them said, even when directly addressed.

" 'The Lord God is in his Heaven,' Captain Dirge was saying, waving three white-gloved fingers. 'Our redemption's as plain as the nose on yer face. I bear witness myself. The whole of this universe is a miracle.'

"The stranger-captain nodded, eagerly agreeing, though by no means clear, it seemed to me, on what it was he was agreeing to.

"Captain Dirge stood up, tottering a little, and walked a few feet—a thing I'd rarely seen him do before without the blind man's help—then came back, still chattering of God's holiness and power and blowing up smoke like Mount Vesuvius, and sat down again. Augusta, beside me, seemed strangely excited. I could make neither head nor tails of it all and resigned myself to the probability that I never would.

" 'There's no such a thing as Death,' Captain Dirge was saying now. 'I don't mean some fool resurrection in Heaven. Nothing of the kind. I mean this cabin is filled to the beams with the departed. Listen!' He pointed at the ceiling, stern as Reverend Dunkel when he talks about Love. 'Ghost of Elijah Brown,' he shouted, 'speak to us!' Everyone was still, squinting at where the Captain pointed, and suddenly, from the ceiling, came an agonized moan you never heard the likes of in all this world. The Captain swung his eyes and his pointing finger to a bare patch of bulkhead. 'Ghost of Hiram Billings, if ye can hear me, speak!' There came another moan, this time from the bulkhead. Their mouths were wide open—all those I could see. I glanced at Augusta. She was wide-eyed, shining like a sinner just converted. Captain Dirge was saying, 'We're in the region of the Vanishing Isles, ye see. Jeremiah, the charts!'

"The blind man blinked, coming out of his trance, and drew a rolled-up map from inside his coat. Those in the cabin crowded eagerly around him; the schooner captain stood up and bent close. As Jeremiah spread the map on the table, the huge, heavy-mustached sailor beside me gave a pull at my shoulder and whispered in English, 'He's not the real Captain —the Captain's dead. The man in control—' His face went contorted and he fell toward me, gagging. Augusta, on the other side of him, gave a scream, and the very same instant I, too, saw the spurting blood.

There was a dagger buried to the silver-virled hilt in the sailor's neck. I suddenly remembered the fat man with the patch and the sharp red ears, the other side of me. With all my might I shouted, 'Treachery! Pirates!' The huge man standing to the right of Jeremiah turned, and I knew him—my old friend Pious John the Pirate! 'Treachery!' I tried to shout again, but they were all over us, grabbing us, yelling like baboons.

"Right there the history of Jonathan Upchurch would have terminated, but suddenly a very queer thing occurred. Blind Jeremiah swung his arms out and caught Pious John's thick chest, and he whispered something in the pirate's hairy ear and Pious John staggered and blinked a time or two, looking baffled as the Devil, staring at Captain Dirge. Then he shouted, 'No wickedness!' and threw a look at Jeremiah. 'No wickedness!' he shouted again. 'Leave 'em be!' Jeremiah bent down to help our Captain up —he sat puffing at his pipe as if he'd been through such foll-de-roll a thousand times—and the two of them came walking out the cabin door, and the devils who had hold of Augusta and myself let their arms drop, meek as lambs. Like charmed beings we walked to the longboat and climbed aboard, and twenty minutes later we were standing safe and sound on the *Jerusalem*. Augusta pretended to be as baffled by the whole affair as I was, but I knew pretty well there was more going on in that crafty little head than she let on to me. Before she could slip away, I caught her arm and said, 'What's the secret, Augusta? I've had enough. Tell the truth!' I didn't mean the obvious and petty secret, that the Captain's carpetbag was for carrying the collection.

"'What secret, Jonathan?' she said. But her lip was trembling. I refused to release her arm, and it flitted through my mind that the cork-black skin looked as natural as her own.

"I squeezed her arm more tightly. '*Tell me the secret.*'

"Billy More stood watching us.

"She glanced at me, then away again in panic, and

I knew all at once that Augusta's sickness went deeper than I'd guessed. It was as if I was suddenly seeing her plain, without stagelights, without make-up. She was small, a mere child, and yet she was one of the damned—hopeless, remorseless, filled with terror. 'You'll learn sooner than you like,' she whispered. And then she was free of me, running for the hatch. Billy More stood frowning, examining his shoes.

"There was some unpleasantness when I reached my bunk. Someone had slit the Negro's throat from ear to ear, torn the blood-soaked bunk to bits, and scattered what little I had in my foot-locker. There was no one in sight. Sweating, shaking, sick from the blood stench that filled the place and sickened more by my own shameful part in the tragedy, I opened my hiding place in the bulkhead. The books were still there. With violently trembling fingers I lighted the lantern, pulled out the book on top, the volume of poetry. Where the book fell open, I found the poem—

> *Full teats of milk that cannot cloy*
> *He like a nurse will bring . . .*

The ship seemed to reel. When I reached out to steady myself I touched blood. I reached into the cubby for the second book, but a sound stopped me. Somebody was coming. I thrust the volume of poetry in, closed up the hole, and gulped in air for a blood-curdling scream. *'Murder! Heaven save us! Murder!'*

"Billy More came in blinking like a hoot owl, clutching his marlinspike.

XIX

"Who murdered the black we could not learn. Wilkins, the man I chiefly suspected—insofar as I could organize my reeling wits—could account, with witnesses, for every minute of his time. We dropped the blood-soaked bedding in the sea and soon after it the body. I was in a state, half-crazy. I listened to the Captain's mumbled prayer like a man in a daze. I wasn't guilty, not technically—and because of the damage done to my things, not to mention my plainly visible anguish at the poor man's death—no one suspected I'd had a part in it. Yet I *was* guilty, Heaven knows. I could remember with shocking clarity the indifference with which I'd popped that poor black devil on the head, reduced him to an object useful to me—helpless as a stone when his killer came. And the memory sent an emotion shogging through my veins that was easily as powerful as the emotion of a lover, though exactly opposite: guilt cold and boundless as damnation. I don't mean for a minute that I felt some great upsurge of moral principle, a feeling that according to some code, religious or otherwise, I'd acted wrongly; and I don't mean some ethical matter, either: What I felt was certainly not shame. What I felt, in fact, was the wordless and stark, metaphysical terror of the totally isolated. As casually as I'd popped that black on the head, the man who'd slit his throat could slit mine, and Captain Dirge would indifferently mumble, and the sea would sluggishly part to receive my fat and lean and bone. The men around me, every one of them—so my act declared—could be popped on the head, have their throats slit, and the world would adjust itself. Let the mast come crashing down on us, let the ship submerge into Davy Jones's Locker; the drifting, tottering universe would never bat an eye. No longer was I one with the wind, the sea, the motion of the ship. No longer were stars gone-out-long-since my ultimate skin. I was an object in a great bumping clutter of objects—every wave, every coil of twine, every nail, my enemy, cold-blooded Massuh. I knew now the madness of my former opinions, freedom arching up through enslavement, redeeming, reaffirming it. "The thralldom of love." What a lunatic phrase! The man powerless in a hostile land, there's your ultimate thrall—there's all of us! For Augusta had lied about writing that poem. Had probably lied about all of them. It was easy to believe that her love for me was equally a lie, as true to her feelings as a smile from Pious John. I felt no confidence, at any rate, that I could go to her, talk about the thing I'd done, this monstrous anguish of meaninglessness, and be sure of a sisterly, all-forgiving kiss that would bring the slain world back to life again. 'Guilty!' I thought, and clutched my head in my hands. Guilty all my life, though only now did I see the plain truth of it. Guilty of the same cruel indifference to my mother, because I, being young, had no knowledge yet of the odds against living forever. As stony-hearted as a flimflam man, as disingenuous as a theater magician—I thought suddenly of that lovely little child Miranda Flint, one moment tricking us, cunning as the friendly snake in Eden, and the next moment toppled to the maelstrom of life by a scream from the back of the theater. She'd stared straight at me, screaming, terrified by emptiness. '*Guilty!*' I thought. All poor miserable mankind, *guilty!* Pitifully tilting up grandiose ikons of the bears they slaughter or the corn they chop, and praying to the ikons in terror and anguish: 'O Lord, Dread Ruler of Life and Death—' (Aye, there's the story of yer obstinate survival of ancient beliefs! Love, sir! The love of man and bear and windblown wheatfields; love and the misery of killers!)

XX

"There was on the *Jerusalem* a harpooner by the name of, as near as I could get it, Kaskiwah. He was a short, powerfully built Red Indian who never spoke. In his trade he was second only to Ngugi, the black African with the bone in his nose, and like Ngugi, he took pride in his appearance of savagery, never wearing more than a buckskin shirt and trousers, even here off Antarctica, and never oppressing his feet with more than buckskin shoes. Around his throat he wore colored beads drawn up tighter than a noose, and from his right ear hung a feather on a silver ring. A man did not need to talk to him to know he was a kind of heathen saint. His gentle brown eyes looked steadily to sea and never blinked. They would gaze at nothing physical, neither man nor beast. I am willing to swear that never in his life, or at any rate never in recent years, did Kaskiwah experience anger, depression, guilt, or ordinary human delight. When he died, I'm told—died by stepping off into the ocean—he showed on his face not a trace of fear or bitterness. He was not mad, in any ordinary sense: In the prow of a longboat he was as alert as any other harpooner, and his throw was as calm and sure as Jim Ngugi's. Yet he wasn't sane, either, in the ordinary sense. He knew where he was, knew all that was happening around him, but he was—in the ordinary sense—indifferent. He was a walking deadman, and on that clear, cold morning just after our burial of the black, I learned why.

"Kaskiwah was sitting on the rail, one foot on the longboat, gazing at the ocean as usual, when, to take my mind off my guilt, my distrust of Augusta, and my fear that terrible events were closing in, I went up to him.

"'Fine day!' says I, and puts my hand on his shoulder.

"Kaskiwah gazes on.

"'Been two full weeks we been sliding south,' I continue—a man too desperate to be rebuffed. 'It's a mighty strange business.'

"He gazes on.

"I study him a minute, screw my nerve up tight and pass my hand before his eyes. No change.

"'You're a mighty silent man, Kaskiwah. I imagine you must have a powerful lot to think about.' I smile to show him he has my respect.

"Still no change.

"I lean toward him, frustrated, annoyed that the Indian denies me the secret of his peace, and I turn my head and follow the direction of his gaze. It comes to me all of a sudden that I know what he's thinking about; I too had once felt at one with all things living or inanimate. 'You got a squaw out there somewhere, that's it,' I say. Then, on second thought: 'Or you used to have. Aye! The world's gone meaningless, a gap between now and the time you rejoin her in the Happy Hunting Ground.'

"No trace of reaction.

"I blunder on, growing louder, tenser. I narrow my eyes, gazing seaward with him, and I say to him: 'It's a curious thing, Kaskiwah. We look at each other as furniture, or not at all, us human beings. Not till this moment has it struck me that you too, for all your strange ways and outfit, are a man. A man the same as me, the same as—' I hunt around the deck. 'The same as Wilkins there.' I am startled to think that even Wilkins is human. But I hurry on. 'A man could waste his life not noticing his fellow man is human. And waste his fellow's life too, no doubt. It can be a lonely world, this mote in the abyss. We've taken too little reflection on that.'

"Without a word, without turning his head, Kaskiwah moved his hand toward mine as if to take it in a silent gesture of friendship. I opened my hand to receive his. He dropped in two mushrooms. 'Eat,' he said. 'From the King.' I wasn't sure, the next instant, whether he'd spoken or I'd imagined it.

"I looked down at them, suspicious. If ever poisonous mushrooms existed, these looked to be the ones: Black, stiff, shriveled—with curious white specks all over them—they looked like the souls of two burnt-up lizards just recovered from Inferno. I could feel the skin of my face tingling. How could I know that it wasn't to kill me, silence my idle talk for good, that he handed me those toadstools? I squinted at him. He gazed at the sea. I had seen how calmly, how indifferently, he threw his harpoon at God's own benthal viceregent. Why, then, should the slightest flicker discomfit the man as he handed *me* my doom? Could I be sure it wasn't him that dispatched my Negro? But even as I was thinking all this, I remembered Rousseau and was ashamed of myself. I was cringing from possibilities higher than my own, and defending cowardice by base, degrading, white-man's argument. It was civilization—or at any rate, it reasonably might be—that darkened my mind with such wicked thoughts. They were thoughts perhaps foreign to an Indian, a man who knew that men and the land or sea they live on are one, an indivisible being. Men close to Nature killed for a purpose, not for sport, much less from whim. Surely the mushrooms were safe, then, a gift to be treasured! Quickly, before I could lose this happy optimism, this possible avenue of escape from deadly separateness, I popped the mushrooms in my mouth and gagged them down. Then, proud of myself, I patted Kaskiwah's shoulder. 'We brothers,' I said.

"We gazed out at the sea in companionable silence.

"As we gaze, a far-off voice calls out, 'Ahoy!' I smile, thinking about it, slightly alarmed that my mind is not what it usually is, and I glance at Kaskiwah. He gazes at the sea. 'Ahoy!' says the voice. I blink once or twice and peer in the direction of the voice more intently. I notice something troubling the water a hundred yards off, and I lean forward a little, with another quick glance at my comrade, who gazes on. To my surprise, an object comes bubbling up out of the ocean, a thing like a swordfish snout. As I continue to stare, it reveals itself as the bowsprit of a whaling vessel, because up comes the vessel, little by little, forecastle, decks, masts, sails, and all. Remarkable enough, the instant it hits the breeze it's as dry as a biscuit. 'Ahoy!' says the white-bearded man on deck, and waves at me. 'Ahoy,' says I, and waves back, still a little perplexed by the general direction of things. With a pair of reins such as coachmen use, he turns the ship towards us, and when he's twenty foot away, his bow tandem to our stern but his ship sailing comfortably backwards, he says:

" 'Even death may prove unreal at last, and stoics be astounded into Heaven.'

" 'That's so,' I call to him. 'Upon my soul!'

"He nods, delighted, and waves his cap, then cups his hands by his lips again and calls to me, 'Man, beast, grass, 'tis all one: Bearers of crosses—alike they tend, and follow, slowly follow on!'

" 'That's a fact!' I answer. 'By crimus, that may well be!' I feel queerly triumphant.

"He nods and smiles. Then, with a wave, he noses his ship toward the bottom again, and down slow and easy she goes, with the man still waving. The breeze was suddenly filled with music—harps, violins, pianos, pipe-organs—such a concert as never was heard of from Moscow to London. Great white birds came flapping silently out of the south, and for some reason —the music, it may have been—it did not impair their dignity in the least when they dropped shots of excrement, every chunk of it enormous as the White House and vastly more majestic. A pigeon-like thing twice the size of a man came flopping slowly, gently down and closed his crooked pink feet on the rail. 'Fool, retreat!' he tells me.

"I closed my eyes. It was all still there. With a cunning that pleased me, I deduced that it must be all in my mind—or, perhaps, in mine and Kaskiwah's. 'Kaskiwah,' I said thoughtfully, 'I'm going to bed.'

"He gazed at the sea.

"I got up, carefully, and made my way toward the forecastle. The enormous pigeon or webless boobie walked beside me, his wing on my arm.

" 'Thou teeterest on the rim,' says he, or something to that effect, and winks his eye.

"When I awakened, days later, Kaskiwah had left us and the world had become itself again. But ever since, I've had spells of otherworldliness. They come and go, like other pleasures, and they tell me nothing of any great significance, so far as I can see. They give me a certain comfort, of course. They fill a man's soul with a healthy, groundless confidence.

"Says Augusta. 'Why are you looking so strangely at me, Jonathan?'

" 'I was thinking about that sailor.'

"She looks worried, suspicious.

" 'That sailor with the knife in his neck. You were standing right beside him. How could the fellow who did it reach past you, without—'

" 'The knife was *thrown*.'

" 'Ah! Thrown!'

"She looked in alarm at the door leading to the chartroom, where her father and Jeremiah were at chess. 'It was horrible, Jonathan. Horrible!'

"I nodded thoughtfully. ' "He's not the real Captain," that's what the sailor was telling me,' I said. 'Your father's behavior was so strange, there on the schooner—so unlike him, I mean—that for a minute I thought—'

"She shot a wild glance at me, and her hand went to her mouth.

" 'Tell me the secret, Augusta,' I said.

"She stood rigid, not breathing, no color in her face, and I caught hold of her hand, snatching it from her lips to make her speak. The sensation went through me like an electric shock: It was the same hand I'd seized in the darkness, from my bunk—small and wet and as cold as ice. 'Alas, more's the pity!' cries the great white bird.

XXI

"We bore on south.

"I wrung my hands, a mournful spectacle, avoiding Augusta, avoiding all thought of the dark implications, till at last Billy More took pity on me.

" 'The Captain he's got a great dream,' says Billy, clinging like a bat to the crusted rigging. The sky was cloudless and bitterly cold, the sea such a mirror you could barely make out the horizon line. Our breathing made steam, and Billy's red beard was flecked with ice.

" 'Aye,' says I, too morose to care about encouraging him.

"He smiles like a leprechaun. His bluegreen eyes are so filled with twinkles I'd hardly believe him if he told me and swore on the Bible my name was Upchurch. My nose, when I look down it, is red. He said: ' "The fish beyond the whale," the Captain calls it. But it ain't no fish; it's men, Jonathan—or mebby ghosts. He's lookin' for his shadow.'

"I mused halfheartedly on the strange remark. He had, Billy More, a peculiar manner of expressing himself; I'd found by experience it was best to lay to and wait him out. He smiled down from his perch above me, his legs clamped tight on the stay from which he worked, leaning out to the yardarm. We'd suffered a good deal of wind damage, the night before. We'd been hitting storms almost nightly of late, and now and then it was touch and go as to whether we'd skirt the icebergs or take up residence with Davy Jones. We were circling around and around in the area of the Vanishing Isles. 'He ain't informed you on his business yet, I take it,' Billy More said.

"I sighed.

"He too was silent for a time, working, his tongue clamped between his teeth, his hands red and cracking from the cold. 'You won't believe it if I tell you,' he says, with that same easy grin that bunches the muscles of his freckled cheeks, 'so I'll tell you.'

"Sunk in gloom, full of unholy suspicions, I felt more dread than excitement, now that I was to learn at last—so I imagined—the secret that had put me off for so long. As I've said before, the greatest mysteries grow ordinary if you live with them. Sunrise and sunset, or the suspension of sunrise and sunset near the Poles. But also the day was the objective idea of frozen blue, if such a thing can be; the yardarm above me gleamed with iced varnish, and the frayed knots, gritty with salt and ice, and grained like oak, were solid enough to refute without a word the airiest dreams of Bishop Berkeley.

"'Tell on, if ye've a mind to.'

"He told me the story so casually, interspersed with the necessary grunts of his labor and now and then a remark to a bird (he spoke only to the dark, substantial ones; I alone was aware of those others, white as snow), that I hardly considered till after he'd finished it whether or not the things he said were possible according to my own humble scheme of reality.

"Four years ago, he said—the last time the *Jerusalem* had docked in Nantucket—there was a great commotion from the ship's owners, two wrinkled old salts long since retired, by the names of Tobias Cook and James T. Horner. Bent and bright-eyed as two owls they were, and as full of antique secrets, judging by their visages. Hardly was the gangplank firmly set before they were aboard and cloistered with the

Captain, whispering sometimes, sometimes guffawing, drinking their rum down like buccaneers after a boomer. Soon they emerged, along with the Captain, all three of them looking akilter and bewildered and chock-full of drunken hilarity, as furled and grandiose as gunboat flags; and, without a word to the crew, ashore they steered. It was from innkeepers, fellow whalers, and members of their families that the crew got word. The *Jerusalem* had been reported gone down six months ago, in a maelstrom in the region of the Vanishing Isles, and reported gone down by not just one ship but three, all trustworthy Americans. All three were familiar with the ship thought lost, swore they'd recognized the men in the longboats, and swore they'd seen clearly not only her name, painted large on the bow, but also the ship's painted figurehead. There was one thing more, a mystery impossible to fathom and equally impossible to deny: After everything was lost—the low-riding ship and every man of her crew—one memento bobbed up and was hauled aboard the whaler *Grampus*. It was a painting known by relatives of Captain Dirge to be aboard the *Jerusalem*. The rescued painting was still in existence—so Billy More claimed—and when compared with the painting still hung, safe and sound, on the *Jerusalem*, it was found to be squarely identical, except for a rip from the salvager's grapnel and the damage from its time in the sea.

" 'That's a very strange story to be telling a friend, Billy More,' says I.

" 'So it is,' he tells me with his cherub smile.

" 'Surely you never was fooled by such trifles.'

"Again, as innocent as a babe, he smiles. 'Ah, but I was, mate, and am to this day. When you come right down to it, I'm a superstitious fool.'

"I laughed. He too laughed. I'd put away, for the time, that nagging fear, and my doubts about Augusta. The day was wide and beatific, with no possibility of evil or ominous mystery in it. Even the diamond glint of icebergs, even the merely philosophical possibility of death had no trace of evil in it: The world was music—white birds around us—a hymn of natural process shading heavenward. 'But I saw the two paintings, ye see, Jonathan, and I talked with the mate from the *Grampus'* crew, only man of the lot who hadn't set off on another whaling voyage. More important, for the purpose, I sat with our Captain in his big white house, along with first mate Knight and the rest and three gentlemen the Captain brought down from Philadelphia. Scientists they were, or two of them were scientists. The other was a specialist in spiritualist trickery, a master swindler in his own right, some claimed. He'd taken an interest because the picture was of him. Dirge was a great admirer of the man, Dirge being, as ye know, a follower of things praeternatural. It was a picture supposed to have some curious power. It never occurred to me to doubt that the sinking of the *Jerusalem* had happened exactly as the witnesses said it had, in some way or other, nor did it occur to the others there neither—not after those men from the Society was through. All we ever wondered was how and why.' He blew on his hands to warm them, then went back to work. He seemed to have talked all he cared to, for the time. But I could hardly leave the matter hanging like that. 'So you decided, the lot of you, to come down and have a look.'

"He laughed. 'Not exactly. The Captain and the three from the Society went off to another room and talked. Sometimes they called in one or another of us to question. The rest of us, we joked about the thing, with a shiver of ice now and then along our spines, but no one suggested we search the myst'ry out. We joked and drunk rum and had a bit of hot soup the Captain's daughter cooked up, and we talked about it all in the Captain's big house looking down on the Cove till it's nearly dawn. It was the first time most of us had seen the place. It was lovely, I can tell you. A house to rule an empire from, so enormous you couldn't get warm in it, yet so crammed with brass and silver and gold it would keep a dead Eskimo sweating for fright of thieves.

" 'So dawn came, ye see, and because of the drinking, or Lord knows what, we begun to sink deeper in the weirdness of it. The Captain and the men from the Society came back to the parlor and joined us. Sober as judges, those three men were. We still had the paintings there, the real and whatever ye'd call that other, and that other one seemed to be rotting by the second, like a butterfly sent out of heaven to earth's heavy air.'

" 'Billy More, ye're a scoundrel and a liar,' says I.

" 'So it sounds,' says he, and smiles. 'Well, there was those that declared it was an omen—about half the crew, it was—and swore they'd never put to sea again. I was ready to join with 'em. It was a reasonable theory, the only half-reasonable theory we had. The Captain encouraged us to do as we believed, with a glance at 'is friends from the Society; and those of the crew that was certain got up and went home.

" 'I meant to leave with 'em, but I didn't—for no reason. The scientists was talking with them of us that stayed, telling all about the Society's work and how there was people that had a kind of sixth sense, as a man might say, and the Captain's daughter was one of them. They'd been giving her psychic tests for years. In the right situation—in a place where the kingdoms of day and night interpenetrate, as they put it—it was possible such a person might have perceptions far keener than the ordinary. I was only half listening. It gave me the shudders. I stood undecided by the Captain's front window, looking down at the harbor, and I got the strange idea the view had changed all at once. It was something like a dream. You know how suggestible a man can be, early in the morning with the mist on the wharves . . . In a kind of daydream I seemed to remember our ship's going down. The minute I realize what it is I'm dreaming, the dream evaporates like dew. "Billy More," says I, "it's time ye got home to yer Mary, ye drunk!" But I saw the Cove moving. The water was moving like . . . It's hard to say. Suppose the whole world was a merry-go-round, slowed down, as slow as the tumble of a nightmare. The land is the center, and the sea—the water off Nantucket—is the platform and horses. The sea's hard and firm, not like ice but like lead in a smelter's mold, and there's objects in it, maybe hulks of ships. The sea moves steady and firm and the land turns with it, like a hub, the sea lead-gray, dead-gray as the sky, the objects in it black, ships soulless and dead, long dead, being ground into nothingness, and above it, birds. . . .

" 'The Captain was saying in the room behind me, "As for myself, I won't be satisfied till I've tracked this thing down." "Ah, Captain," says Mr. Knight, "ye'd better leave it rest." But the Captain was adamant. He kept talking about it, talking about doom, despair, predestination, the inevitable fall of Assyria and Rome. The bunkum specialist kept watching him, pulling at his mustache and scowling as if any minute he'd see through to the trick in it, but the blasted insight wouldn't come. "Think of it," says the Captain. He was pacing, hands clasped. He seemed hardly aware of us. "Suppose it were possible that Time could loop back—suppose there were the barest shade of truth in the hocus-pocus of table-rappers, the mesmeric 'demonstrations' of men like Murdstone, the trickery of Swedenborg's clairvoyants! Suppose, that is, that by somehow passing through a crack in Time a man could discover his destiny, find out the manner and place of his death. You understand what I hint. What if these two distinct paintings here are one and the same—a single painting seen from different points in Time?" "Come, come," says one of the scientists—brown-bearded he was and as fat as a sea-cow—"we have no reason to hypothesize . . ."

" 'But the Captain's still talking, and the bunkum man watching him, chewing on his knuckles and pulling at his mustache fit to bust. "Is the explanation more strange than any other available? But the implications, gentlemen! How could such a man help but believe that what will be *must* be—in other words, that all our freedom is a ludicrous illusion? The idea's intolerable. It would drive a poor devil stark mad!" Now the bunkum specialist was pacing too, looking downright furious that he couldn't see through it. He looked to be suspicious of everyone in the room. There was talk of a scientific expedition, but it grounded;

the Society couldn't afford it. "But a whaling voyage," the Captain points out, "—a whaling voyage would pay for itself, and, as a kind of side interest, between good hunts . . ."

" ' "Why not just quietly accept what God gives? Why worry such questions?" says Mr. Knight.

" ' 'But the Captain's eyes was all aglint like when he lowers away (or like when he lowered away before his sickness). He nailed us with them. If he'd told me I couldn't move my hand—that trick of the animal magnetists—I swear to heaven my hand would have turned to stone. "One of two things is true," says he. "Either the future is predetermined, in which case, down we'll go, as we've done already, or anyway as our Shadows have done—down we'll go then and there no matter how we connive to shun those waters—or else we can escape it, even if we visit the place of our possible destruction a thousand times. It's a place of mighty strange sights and sounds, the South Pole is; everything south of the Vanishing Isles is outside corpuscular experience. It's made men prophets, visionaries." Again the fat one tried to interrupt, but to no avail. "For myself," says Dirge, "I mean to haunt those waters and know what there *is* to know."

" 'Before you knew it, what little was left of the crew was with him, the same as in the longboat, vowing they'd get to the truth of the matter if it's the last thing they do, which it would be, seemed to me. And there was I, mate, swearing my soul to perdition along with the best of them. Even the scientists got a little excited, even the specialist in bunkum, in spite of all he knew. Someone mentions a blind old seaman by the name of Jeremiah they'd like to see aboard. A man they say is downright uncanny. But Mr. Knight sits solemn in his polished chair and shakes his head and says, "Captain, ye'll never get a crew in this world." "I've got half a crew right here," says Dirge. His daughter pokes her head out from the kitchen and throws a look at Mr. Knight that'd wither a crocodile. "You get yourself a full crew," says Mr. Knight, "and I'll be the foremost of the lot!" "And Billy More too," shouts I, and so do some more of 'em. "You swear to that on yer immortal souls?" We swear and swear. He makes a mighty fuss of it, and before we know it we're shouting to the sky and drinking to damnation like maniacs—' He stopped abruptly, grinning, 'Aye, that was a night, lad. That was a night.'

"I believed him.

"He shook his head, looking out toward sea. 'But oaths, they shrivel. Words, whatever their sweetness and juice, turn prunes at last, and eventually ashes. This world was never built for oaths. Time passes, ye find yerself far from the place that stirred yer nerves, and ye don't know whether to laugh at the foolishness ye fell to before or play the madman and try to make foolishness sensible, come hell or high water, which they do.' He monkeyed upwards, blowing out steam, swung out over on the yardarm to the next strapped stay.

" 'You regret yer oath, Billy?'

" 'I don't think about it. Never let myself. Man of Faith, ye know. But look at Wilkins there. He wasn't one of us, that night—he'd never sailed with Dirge before—but he knew our arrangement. All Nantucket knew. "Oaths are for maniacs and fools," says Wilkins. The Captain never did get a crew together, took slaves instead—a desperate stratagem, to Wilkins' way of thinking. Since the Captain cheated, the project's off, so Wilkins claims. And Mr. Knight's more 'n half in agreement with him. He'd rather had a vote, cold sober, beginning with the question whether that painting was real or illusion. *Either* painting. . . .

" 'It's broken the ship, all things considered.

" 'Or maybe this: We were ready to sail into the dragon's mouth, slaves or no slaves, even with the Captain's daughter on board—a thing we liked no better than the slaves. So in we sailed—and nothing happened. So we turned back to whaling, harpooning and slicing the physicality of things, for the moment putting off that stranger purpose; and we did pretty well—filled vials with oil and spermaceti—exactly as the Captain hoped we would, not guessing where his own best interest lay. Distract 'em, that was the Captain's thought. Keep the energy flowing! And so we returned a second time, and again nothing happened, and we turned back to whale. There were one or two who commenced to mutter about the Captain's great purpose. It had been a long time ago now, ye know, since we'd set there like equals in the Captain's big house. And, of course, we got less and less equal every day. The hold got richer. We all—some more, some less—took note of it. We could turn back early and collect small fortunes, especially considering that the slaves would get nothing, even less than the common seamen do when the owners and officers have lugged away their share. There got to be more talk about a hoax. Say it's this: What we wanted was to do something BIG—make use of big energy for a big purpose, and do it fast—big speed—and do it, like Jesus Christ himself, at a mighty big cost. But the bigness drained out, that's what happened, Johnny. The dream became merely the Captain's dream. Our purpose changed, as purposes will, like any other thing in Nature. The big success had been too long coming, and the cost was beginning to seem absurd—our freedom to be each his own man, not cogs in a machine which is doing some job we've got no use for.'

"I could have asked him a number of things. I asked: 'Ye've mentioned all this to the Captain?'

"He smiled, nodded sadly. 'But the Captain's got all the books.'

" 'The *books?*'

" 'Books, charts, theories—it's all one thing. If we argue, the Captain makes fools of us. The swabs begin thinking: Then no more listening to reason, lads! Blind assertion is all. If it's illogical, hurrah!'

" 'Ye've been listening too much to the grumblers,' I said.

"He smiled. 'I've been talking to them too, ye know.'

"I said, 'Captain Dirge knows that?'

" 'Everybody knows.' His smile brought suddenly back to mind his telling me to remember where Nowhere was. I saw that he was there.

"But his story had given me worse than that to worry about. I said, 'How much did you see of the Captain's daughter, that night?'

" 'Oh, she was there with us most of the time—
working in the kitchen. Or it may be she went up to
bed for a while. I remember she brought out soup.'

" 'That's all you saw of her—when she brought out
soup and when she looked out to make that face at
Mr. Knight?'

" 'I suppose we saw her two, three times.'

"That was, of course, what I'd been afraid he'd say.

"Mr. Knight said later, gazing straight ahead in the
forecastle dimness: 'I can tell you only this, Mr. Upchurch. That phantom painting should never've been
believed. Whatever man found it should have burnt
it up at once. There are things we're not meant to
think about. The world was created sufficient for
our needs. Understand things merely physical—that's
what's required of us. The questions asked by that
hellish Society—'

" 'Seems to me,' I said, 'that both are mere questions of Natural Mechanics.'

"His jaw worked, the line at the side of his mouth
cutting deeper. 'That's a risk,' he said. 'The assump-
tion that the world's mechanical—since otherwise it
can't be studied . . .' He nodded, stern. 'That's a risk.
Aye.'

"The ship was grumbling. Billy More stood shaking
his head at the sea. 'Three things will sink us.' The
men sat silent, listening to him.

"The slaves were singing. Strange, darker voices responded from the depths.

"Later that night (that is, what would've been night
farther north), after I'd gone through her lessons with
her, I talked with Augusta on the poopdeck. Her hand
laid gently on mine, she said, 'Jonathan, you couldn't
believe the truth if I told you. I beg you not to ask
again. I implore you.' But I was silent, cool as an
iceberg, waiting. The icy breeze had strange scents in
it, the smell of fields, though the ship was thousands
of miles from living land. Augusta was pale, more
chilly than the breeze accounted for. She meant to tell
me, I knew by her trembling, though how much of
the truth she meant to tell me was any man's guess.
The cold made her more beautiful than ever, her coal-

black hair blowing free around her white, white face, the world all around her deathly still. I half expected to hear organ music.

She turned to study me, her eyes just perceptibly widened, her lips slightly parted. It was studied, professional. She drew another deep breath, closed her eyes, and tightened her grip on my hand. 'Oh, Jonathan,' she whispered. On the maindeck below us, old Jeremiah gazed blindly up at us; but it was not his listening, the sightless gaze on that bearded, homely face that had drawn that cry from her. Was there any honesty at all in my little entertainer? I wondered. Was the virginal side I thought I'd seen in her merely a measure of her thespian cunning? She drew my hands to the sides of her waist, put her hand on my hips and moved her mittened hands around to the back. So we stood for a moment. Then I took her in my arms, poised, desiring and suspicious, my whole soul teetering, as usual.

"At last, calmly, Augusta said, her voice oddly raised, 'Jonathan, believe if you can that there is a ship—a ship filled with ghosts—called the *Jerusalem*.'

"I squinted, waiting.

" 'She's been seen many times, in many places.' She turned away from me to look at the sea. Then, voice far away, like that of a medium possessed by a child from the kingdom beyond: 'She's appeared, off and on, for many years. Always my father, and you and I, and all of us . . . There's some tragedy connected with her. There's a painting—I'm forbidden to show it to you . . . It's all that remains from a ship that went down near the Vanishing Isles, the place where a hundred years ago . . . But the painting . . . the painting—' She caught her breath, as if frightened of saying what she'd meant to say. She began to tremble and caught her lower lip with her upper teeth. I held her more closely, eyes averted, to calm her. 'It was the portrait of a famous theatrical man. A man named Flint.' She bowed her head. 'Oh, Jonathan,' she whispered. She was shaking violently.

"I said, 'You hung this thing in your *room,* Augusta? You stared at that horrible fiend every day—

and became at last so inured to his evil that you even forgot to hide the picture when I came in to talk, that first afternoon?'

"I felt her muscles tense against me, trembling like fencewire. But she said, 'I never looked at it, Jonathan. I had no need to. It was burned like a retinal scar into everything I saw. We kept it on the wall in order to learn to live with it, because . . .'

"At the look of horror that leaped through her features and stiffened every muscle, I spun, still holding her, to look behind me. The Captain stood ten feet from us, a form materialized from nowhere. He merely stood, humpbacked and silent, for all the world like a deadman, staring at his shoes. Despite the violent pounding of my heart, I said, 'Tell me the rest.'

" 'We have come to find him, Jonathan.'

" 'But he's drowned long since! The painting, the ship . . .'

"Crazily, staring at the motionless old man, her eyes wide, full of what might have been terror and might have been barbarous, rackety glee, Augusta said, 'We've come to find him, to meet him, if possible understand him, understand . . . *everything.*'

"The smell of land was all around us, solid, real —trees reaching out to us from a thousand miles away, as eerily still as a megalithic door, a blind stone eye against darkness. It made the world heavy. The ship rode low in the water, a great dark casque of murdered whale.

"I asked: 'How many on the ship know your purpose?'

" 'Just the commoners, of course.'

" 'And they approve, you think?'

"She was silent a moment, still trembling, her fingers clamped tight to my arms, but the look of both terror and glee was still there. 'Jonathan, *trust* me. Trust *us* —Father and me. *Believe* in us!' She tipped her head up as if in conscious imitation of some woodcut figure in a Saint's Life.

"I said nothing.

" '*Believe in us!*' A whisper. Her expression—face lifted, eyes rolled down to watch me—was so desperate, so filled with fear that I might not believe, that at last I nodded. Jeremiah had groped nearer.

"The Captain said, 'Augusta!'

"She made a move to go in with him, then glanced at me, hesitant, and the next instant, as if on a sudden, defiant impulse, kissed me on the lips. When she drew back she was blushing and frightened, on the verge of a swoon. I held her. As she recovered, I released her and she turned away, eyes closed. She moved toward her father slowly, feeble and trembling, as if her fear, her betrayal of us both, had made her ill. She took her father's arm. Turning slightly, the fingertips of her right hand on her heart, she said, 'Jonathan, God's will is inexorable!'

"I stood alone, shaken. The music of the slaves in the hold below was a hum low and steady as the rumble of some animal awakening from centuries of rest. I went back to my quarters, directly to the hiding place in the bulkhead.

"In *The World's Great Scoundrels* I found her picture, as I'd known I would—though in the picture she hadn't dyed her shining, golden hair or transformed her expression to make herself resemble the Captain's poor gudgeon of a daughter. She was Miranda Flint, offspring of the infamous Dr. Luther Flint, magician, mesmerist, bunkum-man extraordinaire, known from Shanghai to Joplin, Missouri, his birthplace (and Miranda's), for tricks both benign and malevolent. That was why it had worried old Dirge when he heard, by way of Wilkins, my claim that I'd once been a riverman. Well, I had to hand it to him. Even now that I knew, I could hardly believe that, behind the disguise, he was the incredible Flint.

"When I turned the page I got another surprise. There stood Augusta's black mastiff, 'Wonderdog,' and across from the dog sat 'Swami Havananda,' Flint's assistant—inventor of illusions, piano player, personal bodyguard, cut-throat. It was Wilkins.

"The history of that crowd, if the book could be believed, was enough to make a man's blood curdle. They were gypsies to the core, the pack of them; tricksters by maniacal compulsion. Flint might have been one of the greatest of stage illusionists, but the urge to deceive was boundless in him: The rabbit in the hat, the levitated lady, the mesmerized child that a man could drive nails in, all those were mere taps at the jalousie of the madman's boundless ego. He must bamboozle churches, steal fortunes from crafty, perspicacious old brokers, steal the chief ship from the daring and bloodthirsty pirates of China Bay, and, soon after, the golden, emerald-studded crown from the King of Sweden. His present whereabouts, the book said, had been unknown for years.

"So now I knew everything—or so I thought. The trouble was, what could I do with it? Because sure as her name was Miranda Flint—and sure as that dagger in the sailor's neck was none other than Miranda's—I'd been in love with that murdering vixen all my life.

"'Ah, well,' said the huge, partly visible pigeon, and sadly shook its head, 'something may come of this queer business yet.'

"'Never,' I said bitterly, and closed the book.

"It was the next morning that Billy More was flogged for mutinous agitation. Mr. Knight, looking miserable, managed the whip. 'In the name of the Father, and of the Son, and of the Holy Ghost!' old Captain Dirge mumbled, staring at the planks. Jeremiah's face was white, his blind eyes wide. 'Repent, Captain Dirge! The heavens have turned their face! I implore thee!'

"That afternoon came the mutiny."

XXII

"Mutiny, ye say?" says the guest, uneasy.

The mariner looks troubled. He knows himself that the tale's overblown, too pleached and twisted for an evening's entertainment. The dead have been gone from the fields for hours, and the sheep as well (it's midnight now). The angel is fast asleep, dead-drunk.

For the living there are roads to be gotten down, and in the morning, pigs to feed, cows to milk, children to be gotten to the schoolbus on time. The ticks of the clock ring loud and ironic on the fireplace stones.

"Having come so far—" says the mariner's eye.

Halfway to the mountains, in a white house with towers, a fifty-year-old sculptor with a terminal disease sits painting with infinite patience and total concentration a pale yellow lemon on a field of white. With each light stroke added, the lemon shows more its inclination to vanish. Oh, all very well for a man like Flint to play tricks on the world, void his span on mere lunacy! The man in the tower has a son to raise, a wife whose life's meaning is tottering even now. His hand grows steadier, severe as steel; in his mind all reality expands toward white.

A knock at the public-house door; the door opens. Lo and behold, it's Luther Flint, with eyes like fire, one arm reaching inward; behind him a terrible, ravaged Miranda! He snatches off his top-hat, makes a grab at her arm. Their faces are gray, as gray as the faces of newly drained cadavers at the mortuary. He stretches his arm out once more in supplication. Mere fictions, cartoons, though more real than the stones of my dungeon room, the gallows in the square. Surely some truth can be found for these creatures, some church-hard solidity, salvation of phantoms!

Beyond the barn, old trees stand listening, reaching through the darkness toward snakes and toads, toward the sleeping sheep, with anguish like a mother's, listening in a terror of concern for the footsteps of spiders gone astray. Say no more of the thousand-mile animal, philosopher! I gave you an animal large as the world, blind and full of terror, purposeless, searching.

"Aye!" says the mariner. "Mutiny. *Aye* sir!"

And now the guest, too, feels the trees groping inward, dark, age-old, mute inglorious Miltons, hungry as the heart of the sculptor, the sculptor's dog.

The guest glances at the clock. "Tell on."

XXIII

"Captain Dirge sat freezing—silently, motionlessly raving in the hold—his fine clothes crumpled and squeezed where the heavy gray cords cut in, and his eyes were shut tight, his fingers as still as a deadman's. Wilkins had gagged him with coarse rope lapped three times and knotted wet, so that now that it was frozen stiff and contracted, caked blood-chips glinted on the Captain's lace collar and matted his great black beard. At the end of an hour, his jerking stopped, as if finally he'd understood he was not to be resurrected. Mr. Knight was dead. Billy More was dead. Jeremiah had vanished. The mutineers had spared me—had put off reaching a decision about me. I'd rolled my eyes and knocked my bony knees together and insisted in the voice of a Gold Coast man that I was really a black; mad scientists in Zurich had transmogrified me. Scoff as they might, or bang their heads with their knuckles in frustration, the white mutineers couldn't risk the displeasure of the slaves they'd freed. And Billy More swore that what I claimed was true. After Billy More was dead himself—killed with Mr. Knight, and for the same mistake—the mutineers forgot me, left me there lashed to the ice-crusted foremast and didn't remember my existence till the violence was done with.

"I watched the executions. The mutineers, who'd begun with only axes and axehandles, had rummaged the staterooms and equipped themselves with muskets and ammunition. Then, back on deck, they proceeded straight to the forecastle, which was fastened down and sealed shut with ice, two mutineers standing one on each side of the hatch with axes, and two more by the main hatch. Below were the men who'd held loyal to the Captain—some from true loyalty, no doubt; most from conviction that the mutiny would fail. Mr. Wolff, the second mate, cracked the seal of ice with his axe and called out, 'D'ye hear there below? Tumble up with you, one by one. Come now, and no grumbling!' It was several minutes before anyone appeared—at last an Englishman who'd shipped as a raw hand. He was weeping piteously and beseeching the mate to spare his life. Wolff split the man's forehead with the axe. The poor devil fell on the deck without a groan, his bright blood steaming, and the Chinese cook lifted him in his arms and tossed him to the fishes. Mr. Knight went pale. It had happened too fast for human interference, but he leaped forward now, angrily protesting, trying to take Wolff's axe away. Billy More was right behind him. Two blacks with muskets were on them in an instant, jabbing them back with the musket barrels, and Wolff flew toward them with the axe slanting back past his shoulder. Mr. Knight stared, cringing, but it was a blast from one of the muskets that killed him. Billy More screamed, outraged. The second musket hushed him. 'You will interfere with me no more,' Wolff shouted. 'You're not in power here!' He was dwarfish, bespectacled; his straight blond hair fluttered around his shoulders as if terrified birds flew inside it, and he foundered like a drunk in the fur coat he'd stolen from the Captain. The two shattered bodies lay reaching for each other. They'd neither approved nor disapproved; they'd allowed it to happen, true democratic hearts, and when the thing had turned murderous (who could have imagined that Wolff would suddenly assert himself?), they were powerless to stop it.

"The ruckus had alerted the others below; and now neither threats nor promises could induce them to come out. Then Wilkins said in his loud, reedy voice, bending close to the hatch, twitching, leering, his puffy, slanted black eyes like needles. 'Why not smoke 'em out?' A rush ensued, and it seemed for a moment that the ship might be retaken. But the mutineers managed to close off the forecastle after only six had reached the deck, and seeing themselves outnumbered, they gave up hope and submitted. Wolff spoke them fair, knowing all he said would be heard below. Within minutes the rest had emerged on deck.

They ascended one by one and were pinioned and thrown on their backs—fourteen in all.

"Then came the butchery. One by one the bound seamen were dragged to the gangway, where the cook stood waiting with his axe, clumsily striking each victim on the head as he was forced to the rail by the other mutineers. I shouted against it, inside my gag, but my shouts went unheard, mere whispers beside the anguished bawling of the victims. When seven had gone over the side in this way, the black harpooner with the bone in his nose went silently up to the cook and said: 'No more.' The cook looked at him, furious but frightened, then looked at Wolff for orders. The same instant, with the same deep calm with which he'd fire at a whale, the harpooner struck the cook on the ear, his doubled fist like a blacksmith's hammer, and the cook sank to the deck, jerking. In a minute he was dead. Four slaves, two in shackles, joined the harpooner and stood prepared to try a new mutiny, though armed only with axe-handles. Wolff and Wilkins, looking startled half out of their wits, changed tactics at once. 'Enough,' Wolff said. 'Throw the rest in the hold with the Captain!' I watched, bound and gagged, while mutineers and the slaves they'd freed dragged away their captives. Jeremiah, all this while, was nowhere to be seen. I assumed they'd killed him.

"And now black Ngugi again showed his surprising humanity. As Wolff and Wilkins and their detail of mutineers came back up through the hatch, most of them expressionless, one or two smiling like mules gone crazy, the black harpooner—he'd remained above—strode toward them. He held his axe at waist level, one fist at each end. Wilkins held a musket, casual but ready. The big black spoke to him, then pointed at me. The fire was still in his eyes, but his tone seemed harmless. Wilkins and Wolff talked, too low for me to hear. The air, motionless, was full of the smell of land, though there was no land. My hands, tightly bound in icy cords, had no feeling in them. My eyes stung.

"Wolff came toward me, Wilkins a few steps behind. Wolff said, polite as a traveling preacher but without much conviction—more like a stage automaton than like a living man—'Mr. Upchurch, you will see to the Captain's daughter.' Without another word, he cut away the ropes that held me to the mast. I couldn't move, for a moment, my feet like stones. He waited. Wilkins, behind his shoulder, smiled and winked and twitched his lips. I rolled my eyes, still playing poor black (on the chance it was that that had rescued me), and, as soon as I could move, I sidled loose-jointedly to the poopdeck and into the chartroom. I found a lantern, oil, and phosphursticks and soon had the room a good deal lighter than I'd ever before seen it. Nothing was disturbed. The Captain's chess game was waiting on the board.

"I will not dwell on what my lantern found in the Captain's inward chambers. I had never before been beyond the dim parlor where I worked with Augusta —Miranda—on her lessons. Two rooms, not counting the chartroom, opened off it: the Captain's sleeping quarters and the girl's. The Captain's bunkroom had been torn to shreds. The bunk had been cut to bits with axes, the locker smashed, and the Captain's belongings scattered from bulkhead to bulkhead. On the floor beside the Captain's berth, half-hidden under feathers from the ruined mattress, lay the painting of Flint. The staring eyes, the straight, fierce mouth below the black mustache, gave my soul a shiver. If I'd ever been mesmerized by that devil Flint, I believe I might've been mesmerized again. Was that why Flint kept it in Miranda's parlor?—a device to control her? The head glowed, like those pictures of Jesus, except that the pictures in a church are more mannerly—eyeballs rolled up, apologetic, arms raised straight-at-the-elbows in prayer, as if lifting an invisible veil to shield the viewer, make no undue demands, respectful as a still-life, a bowl of pale lemons. I picked it up, not looking squarely at the picture even now. I felt a queer numbness coming over me and threw the picture down again, dropped it as you would an adder.

"In the second room, I found Miranda. She lay stiff

and furious, in a dress like torn and bloodstained moonlight, her small hands clenched to fists under her chin. She was bruised and swollen. Her eyes were wide with fear.

" 'Miranda!' I breathed, forgetting myself, kneeling beside her.

"Her eyes widened more. She whispered, 'How long have you known?'

" 'From the beginning,' I said. It was partly true.

" 'Where's Jeremiah?' she said.

" 'Vanished. No doubt murdered.'

"She closed her eyes, fleeing inward, terrified, the remorseless Miranda Flint made guilty at last. I squeezed her hand. She refused to awaken.

XXIV

"Wolff stood at the Captain's chessboard as if thinking of completing the unfinished game. He said in his burred, stiffly upright English: 'The Captain had no understanding of power.' He grinned, looking over his spectacles at the pieces, two fingers sharpening the end of his moustache. Wilkins beamed, enjoying the performance, though I was doubtful how much he agreed with Wolff's opinions. Wolff hooked his thumbs in his vest, still studying the pieces, and continued, professional: 'He used his power ruthlessly— there he was right—but he did not recognize that one must appear to use one's power for the welfare of the ship. The ship, one must make one's crew believe, is of greater value than the life of any crew member. The ship is a creature with a purpose of its own, beyond our understanding, and each of us is merely a cell in that creature. The Captain is, perhaps, the brain—so he should have told them—but even the brain is subservient. The duty of every part of the ship—this he should have made clear—is absolute submission. The ship is the Father.' He began to speak more sternly, biting off his words. 'The ship's needs are our orthodoxy, and to any dissension from that orthodoxy we must respond with rigidity and *no imagination*. That surprises you, Mr. Upchurch, Mr. Quick-tongued Trickster. But mark my words. Given enough imagination, a man may come even to sympathize with the whale. "How grand he is!" imagination cries. "How vast, how majestic!" ' He smiled.

"Wilkins smiled too, more heavy-lidded than usual, thanks to the Captain's wine.

"Wolff shook his finger, immensely stern, immensely pleased with himself. 'Whatever the cry of imagination, my friend, the whale is the enemy of the whaling ship. Aggression is the meaning of life on earth, the only freedom. Because I am clever, and more powerful than you, I am the Captain of the *Jerusalem*. I grind you under my thumb if I please. That makes you, you think, a mere victim? Not so! By the nature of the case, I leave you free to oppress those beneath you, as they, in turn, oppress those beneath them, and so on down to the feeblest spider who tears the wings off flies. You do not especially like this system, I can see, Mr. Upchurch—nor you, Mr. Wilkins. "Elsewhere perhaps," you say. "Not here, not on the *Jerusalem*!" But I tell you: *Everywhere!* Be comforted; I did not make the system up. Mother Nature did. She lays down the code for all things living.

1. Distrust Reason
2. Deny Equality
3. Succeed by Lies
4. Govern by Violence
5. Oppose All Law but Biological Law

Under Wolff, my friends, the *Jerusalem* will have order.' He smiled again, fiercely, showing all his square and perfect teeth, then bowed, about to leave. He lifted the black knight from the board, seemed to reconsider, then put it back where he'd found it. In fact, there was no move the knight could make. It was empty posturing, this pretense of shrewdly examining the board.

" 'Heal your patient well, Mr. Upchurch,' he said,

and looked away toward Miranda's room. 'She's the only female on the ship, and we have our needs.' He chuckled, more like an actor playing the part of a villain than like a villain. Wilkins looked up at the ceiling and smiled. I knew, watching Wilkins, that Wolff was not by any means the strongest or cleverest on the ship.

XXV

"I lay in the darkness on the floor beside Augusta's berth—or Miranda's, as I must call her now. I'd sealed the ports against the everlasting twilight. The ship wasn't moving, stalled by a calm I'd never seen the likes of, unless it was the present stall of my brain, or the stillness of Miranda. She breathed without a sound—I could tell she was breathing only by placing my hand on her stomach. It was as if her whole being were listening for something—as if, like the sentient trees and flowers Mr. Knight used to speak of, all the functions of her mind had flowed together to one desperate channel, her absolute, terrible listening. Such was my impression, or faint intuition. I did not pursue it. I was not at my best, to say the least. I must think and plan, I told myself; but my mind was still crowded with nightmarish images—the cook's axe rising, then slashing down, the twitching and jerking of the murdered men, the blood-steaming deck, the limp, bloody figures of Billy and Mr. Knight . . . But the image more terrible than all the rest was that of Miranda Flint as I'd found her, raped, ruined, in her cabin. I felt as one feels at the death of a child: stopped, unable to believe the thing. Again and again I reached up to touch her. She slept on, like an innocent—slept or went on listening, if my intuition was right. Listened, waited in the absolute dark of her unconsciousness, like an ancient, iron-jawed trap. Each time I touched that chilly flesh, my hand shrank back as my mind shrank back from the recognition that sooner or later I must face: She was no longer beautiful. The swelling might go down, the bruises fade, but the ugliness would stay—missing teeth, stooped shoulders, the beaten, cunning look of old beggar women. Inescapable. And I must face, too, the fact that what I'd deemed terrible and unholy in Miranda would also be gone forever now: her pleasure in deceit, her monstrous cold-bloodedness. Foul she might be, but never again evil. And that was, suddenly, a dreadful loss. A trickster's virtue—nay, friend, his *glory*—is that he says what sounds true, says it ringingly, convincingly, believing he knows for the moment what's false. But a man whose house has been burned to the ground in an electric storm can never again be an accurate judge of lightning. The murderer's virtue is that he thinks himself God: perfect, indestructible. Pity his victims, but pity more the murderer converted to belief that his weight is a burden on the earth. I hoped, in short, that Miranda Flint would die.

"I heard not a sound, for all my care—neither in the chartroom nor in the parlor nor where Miranda lay. I knew he was there only when he said, 'It's Wilkins. Be still.'

"I obeyed. I did hear him then, or felt him, rather, coming through the darkness toward me as if he knew exactly where I was. 'After Mr. Wolff, you and me,' he whispered, just inches from my ear. He gave a voiceless laugh. I was so startled by his nearness— the stink of his breath was suddenly all around me— I could give him no answer.

"With the subtle skill that marks all true masters of the confidence game, he quickly insinuated his way into my sympathy. He asked about 'Augusta.' I gave him no hint that I'd discovered the truth about all of them. He was careful not to mention that he himself was the man who'd raped and beaten her; and he did not pretend that he thought the thing shameful. But he observed, objective as a family doctor, that it would not be an easy thing for 'Augusta' to get over in her mind. He talked of her feeling of God-given superiority, the mistake in self-appraisal that would make that rape a catastrophe.

" 'She's proud, that's true,' I said, stalling against something.

"He chuckled exactly as a snake would chuckle. 'I used to go in there and tipple with the Captain,' he said, 'along with Mr. Knight, God rest his soul. Ah, how she'd put it to us, pious little whore! Swinging her hips out, bending down so her pretties would dangle. And any time she could find a way she'd put that together with her holiness trick. "God bless you, Mr. Wilkins!" says she, and claps her hands together like a lady at her prayers, and draws her thumbs back hard against her chest so you'll get a good look at her pirate's guns. "God bless yerself," says I, and I gives her a wink, most fatherly. She lured me back into her bedroom one time—I'd known her a good long while, understand—and there I am standing erect as a bowsprit, and next thing I know I've got dog in my shoulder. Yet I wish her no harm, Mr. Upchurch—no more harm than she's made other people suffer.'

"If I hadn't known the truth, nothing in his tone would have led me to suspect. But I did know, and so I heard more than he said. In dressing rooms from Indianapolis to Bangkok he'd pursued poor Miranda, and she'd teased him on, cool manipulator, image of her father. Not even by rape had he brought her down off her snowcapped mountain. *Believe in us*, she said with every swing of her hips—*Believe in us!* —cry of every fraudulent outfit from the first bullshit government to the last bullshit religion—*Believe in us, Wilkins!*—and the poor fierce idiot had believed.

"He got around now to what he'd come to say. 'Ye've answered not a word to Wolff's theories, Mr. Upchurch.'

"I said nothing.

" 'Even when he spoke of his reason for wishing Miss Augusta well, you were quiet as a mouse.'

"I still said nothing.

" 'Very well,' he said. He sounded calmer than I'd seen him before. He said, flat-voiced, just above a whisper. 'I've watched you from the day we first hauled you aboard. Yer yer own man, Upchurch. Yer idea of a chat is to listen and smile, with one eye peeking out the window. Very good. Listen:—'

"And now, all at once, I was hearing Wilkins' version of the story Billy More had told me. I showed no sign that I'd heard it before or that I knew that, the night of the meeting, Mr. Wilkins wasn't there. He told of the vows, a whisper full of anger, exactly as if he really had been there and felt he'd been betrayed.

" 'Listen, listen well. Wilkins is a villain, says Jonathan Upchurch. He murders with a smile, plots mutiny, scoffs at God, scoffs at beauty. Well, howl and rage all you please against Wilkins, you can't out-howl the howl in Wilkins' own spirit, sir. But I'm past despair, though not out of it. Despair's my foundation. The world's what the mind of Wilkins makes it—my hand, my head, the ocean, that wretch on the bunk. Today I'm the Devil. Who knows, perhaps tomorrow God! You understand?'

"I kept silent.

" 'Do you understand me?' The whisper was intense, forking out like flame.

" 'No,' I whispered. Miranda's fingers moved a little, and alarm went through me. Wilkins, too, must've heard something. He held his breath, listening, but there was nothing to hear. The ship sat quiet as a boulder.

"He said: 'My acts add up to nothing. No Heaven, no Hell, mere chain of events neither guilty nor glorious. I may murder again, or I may give away all my goods to the poor. I vow nothing. Nothing. There are no stable principles a man can make vows by, and there are no predictable people, only men like myself. A whole world crammed with cringing half-breeds unfit for the woods or the gabled house. Take Mr. Knight. Once there was no man on all this ship more loyal to the Captain. So I vow nothing. I have come to warn you: Do the same.' He fell silent, breathing heavily, waiting for my answer.

"He wasn't asking, I had a hunch, what he'd come to ask. He'd come to ask me to rebuild the universe, undo his murders, his attack on Miranda—understand him, and like a god, forgive him, confess that I too was a cosmic half-breed, connected to no one and nothing, despair my foundation and his similar despair my shred of hope. Upchurch the purifying whirlwind, all-equalizing Flood. The road to Paradise, no doubt. But a wise man settles for, say, Ithaca. Miranda was still as a corpse, listening, and he too was listening, hunched in the darkness, listening with all his soul. Wolff's voice, far away; some Negro, singing. It was nothing like that that we listened for. We listened . . . It would not come clear to me.

" 'I can make you no promises,' I said.

"After a moment, Wilkins laughed. Without another syllable, he rose and left us.

"When he was gone, I got up, felt my way over to the ports and undid them to let in light, then went back to Miranda. The eye not swollen shut was opened a little, staring nowhere. A tear ran down the side of her face onto the bolster. I moved my hand to brush it away, and Miranda stiffened. 'It's Jonathan,' I said. There was no response. I couldn't tell whether she was in pain or not. I discovered, kneeling beside her in the dimness, looking at her mutilated face, that I couldn't even talk, though talk might help. A ruin. My mind went back to that scene on the poopdeck, when Miranda tried by those queer half-truths and then by that kiss, with her father looking on, to secure me once and for all as her captive, make me accept her magic-lantern show as peasants accept theurgic tales of healing water, celestial visitations, the raising of the dead. I could understand. She was afraid. On this weird, mad ship, she needed a protector more keen than Alastor, Wonderdog, now buried in the ocean, his brains blown away by Wilkins' musket. But how could I forgive her for the wreck of my hopeful fantasies— for going after me not from love but from faith, stupid faith, that her trickery, like her knife, could never fail? Wilkins' boast again. *I vow nothing.* So with Miranda, but worse; because Wilkins at least could hate himself, mourn the ideals he'd turned against. Miranda was no idealist lapsed or otherwise: mere girl, mere woman, humanity's showpiece, trans-

formed by nineteen centuries of pampering to a stage
creation, tinseled puppet painted, taught speech by
troubadours—championed by knights who knew her
lovely and probably unfaithful—philosophized by
painters and jewelers and poets—and now the theater
had collapsed on her, ground her to the staddle, revealed what she was. In the gray light I looked hard
at her tear-streaked face. Not a woman's now; a mutilated child's, a monkey's. I remembered the night on
the wharf by the abandoned lumberyard, Pankey's
failure—remembered the betrayal of my friendly
pirates, my ludicrous desire to pursue my dearly loved
daddy to sea. I did love him, yes, old drunken howler,
and however foolish my behavior with the pirates, I
was good at that time, an innocent; they couldn't have
tricked me otherwise. And I remembered golden-
haired Miranda-as-child, no doubt eager beyond
words to please ferocious Daddy Flint. It was then,
maybe, that she'd learned the smile, the trick of
catching the sunlight in her hair and trilling it like
moonlight reflected in a pail. So all things beautiful
come crashing down: Comes mindless ebb tide, wind
from the southwest, and the poor ridiculous smiling
independent goes down, like all poor barques before
him. . . . Alas, poor Miranda, poor Jonathan! Incredible, the clarity with which I remembered the
pretty little fraud in that Boston theater, lisping out
by rote the tragedies of man from the beginning of
Time. How lovely we were then, the Flint girl and I
—and how ignorant! All at once, without warning,
my chest filled up like a drowning man's and I began,
despite all I could do, to bawl. The welling tears
came driven by a power that I hadn't realized I still
possessed, a pressure as magical and baffling as the
root pressure of the tomato plant, which can push
a one-inch column of water—so my science book
claims—nearly two hundred feet in the direction of,
possibly, God. As if the earth had burst open, letting
dinosaurs out, dark wall-eyed dragons, I whooped
and gasped. I couldn't breathe, couldn't check in the
least the violence of my childish, humiliating woe.
Miranda's hand moved, closing on mine with a grip

as firm as my dear, good mother's, many years ago, when I awakened from a nightmare of my father's being eaten by a whale. I sobbed harder and tried to pull my hand away. She turned her face, lips trembling, and looked at me, gripping my hand still more tightly, her whole soul silently bawling as mine was, bellowing for no more illusions, no more grand gestures, just humdrum love such as children and plants feel, and poor whining mothers, or angels treading air.

XXVI

"So Wolff fell in his turn.

"I have no time to speak of Wilkins' machinations. Before every successful mutiny there's scheming and talk, an idea that seems true enough to universal law as the universe appears that moment to convince free-thinking men that the order of the moment is contrary to Nature and therefore certain, if given a nudge, to come toppling. So Billy brought the Captain down, though he had no intention, with all his talk, of unleashing a full-fledged mutiny. So Wilkins stood on the deck triumphant, the back of Mr. Wolff's head blasted off, Wilkins shouting with what I took at the time to be rackety glee, but it wasn't; I'd not yet begun to understand his sorrows: Shouting and laughing like a mad crow, the murderer again, beginning to suspect that his theory was nonsense, he was no more free than the ship becalmed in a smell of land where there was no land, the ship's decks humming prime-evil with the shouts of his fellow worldmasters, comrade slaves, until sorrowfully, though he'd hated him, the black harpooner with the bone through his nose, Ngugi, gentleman, lifted Wolff's body like a child's and carried it gently to the starboard rail and let it fall. The Negroes and whites of the crew fell silent, bowing in spirit to the big black king of some universe built more enduring, more sensibly disciplined, than ours.

" 'Come out, Jeremiah!' cries Wilkins. 'It's safe now!' And he laughs. If I hadn't been persuaded before that he was crazy, that laugh would have done it. 'Brothers, sisters, I did it all for you!' cries Wilkins now, and laughs again. I took it for obsequious whining, at the time, but I believe now I was wrong again. He could prove he was human, one of us. There are no divisions, no dualities, only monstrous mirrors, the existence chain—even in the hour of our final dissolution: We hang in the balance 'twixt the Bear and the Southern Cross, and follow on. He was, if imperfect, a thinking animal caught in awareness of his imperfection, and as tortured by it as he would have been if he'd had some god he could stand back-to-back with for measurement. It's never required enduring forms to make the world Platonic; it requires only inescapable pain. So Newton teaches. *Every atom, of every body, attracts every other atom, both of its own and of every other body, with a force which varies inversely as the squares of the distances of the attracting and attracted atom.* If I venture to displace by even the billionth part of an inch the microscopic speck of dust which lies on the palp of my finger, I have done a deed which shakes the moon, and causes the sun to shudder in its path, and alters forever the destiny of the myriad stars and planets that roll and glow in the majestic presence of our insatiable desire. Like Gilgamesh of old, or like mad Achilles, Wilkins had decided he'd strike a blow for love.

"And so Wilkins, in his turn, fell.

"In the dimly lighted oil-stinking hold, talking with bound, gagged Captain Dirge as if the old man could answer him, or would if he could, black Ngugi and I looking on, saying nothing, never guessing how dark the farce would turn, Wilkins laughed, half-sob, half-rage. The Captain was like a deadman, inwardly struggling—or so I imagined—to hurl from his beaten soul some hint of his former animal magnetism, but no muscle in all his seated, tightly bound body stirred.

"Wilkins drew his pistol, waved it at the Captain. Ngugi, unarmed, took one step closer.

" 'What would it mean,' Wilkins said, "if I blew

yer mighty brains from here to Java?' 'Wilkins,' I said. But he raved on. 'If Creation is nothing but blind chance—mind this, milord—then the highest thing I can aspire to become is an impulse, a mindless whim, whether terrible or lovely.' Wilkins laughed, wet-eyed. 'So it is, milord. Seamen, engendering spirit, unite! Follow me, lads! Rise out of civilization, the cool marble halls of mere reason, convention, the sickness of orthodoxy.' He bent closer to the Captain, still waving his pistol. 'We've cut ourselves off. That's the secret, Captain. Ye've said so yerself. Our skulls seal out the universe. Very shrewd, sir. Shrewd observation!' He suddenly tensed, like a man struck by a whip. 'Ye'd have liked to change that, if ye could —you and yer Society. Ye're a fool, Captain. We're all of us fools. Yer glorious project—would ye hear about that?' He gave a crazy laugh, and Ngugi flinched back, afraid again that the gun would go off. Wilkins howled, ' 'Twas a hoax, yer lordship! A ridiculous hoax! 'Twas a hoax put together by two antic devils by the names o' Tobias Cook and James T. Horner— aye! and a sailor who'd put in time with the *Grampus,* by name of Willie Burns, and a fourth man, fourth devil, the sly insider, a whimsical maniac known to the world as—Swami Havananda! Aye, sir. Himself! It's him slipped the painting ashore for the copying— and as fine a copying as ever was seen to the west of the Paris forgeries. And no trouble, that, the forger being the same man as painted the original.' He threw back his head, theatrical, and laughed. Ngugi moved. Wilkins swung the pistol at Ngugi, and he froze.

"Now Wilkins looked at the Captain again—the Captain still as death. Wilkins hissed: 'And *why?* ye may ask me. *Why* this monstrous, unfriendly hoax? I have asked the same question a thousand times, yer majesty. Asked it every time I set down my foot on a spider's back, and every time the sun rose fiery and lovely. Aye! And given a thousand answers, all contradictions. Because ye were absurd with yer talk about God and yer Society—outrageous with yer praying in the dark of the sea, and yer Bible-reading and yer hymn-singing, and yer deigning to preach to us lesser men that was kindly invited t'ave brandy in yer cabin and be told of the undisciplined and ignorant rabble and the aristocracy "not closed to men of genius"—which was not us, sir, ye made that clear!—absurd with yer mumbles of ghosts and yer beautiful daughter's "impressions," and no wonder, half-dead already of yer pale theosophy. Ye set yerself up as our better and gave us no choice but to tumble you—and not just me, the very owners of the ship, milord.' He laughed, gone pale. 'So I says to myself, "That's why we done it." But no sir, not so. I'd fain have believed you. That's why. Aye. But I lie again. It was only from whim, sir. Monumental whim! Artistic impulse, the urge of the Creator. Eight million years ago, humpbacks tell us, fish took a notion to depart from the sea. Fearfully, Captain, glancing in alarm over scaly shoulders; but on they walked, our slimy gill-flopping grandfathers, lords of whim. They learned the strange trick of breathing air, separating one from the elements four, in defiance of God (*Thor* he called himself, and willed his fins into mammoth's legs, then called himself *Woden*, and willed his crisp fish-head to brain-packed skull)—by *whim*, Captain, by meaningless whim, because nothing in the universe was firm. No, I lie again. I hoped ye'd outsmart us, prove yerself a leader. There 'tis. The hell with us! Ye were only a man, and it ain't sufficient. We've cut ourselves off, sir. *There's* the secret.' Suddenly he was shouting, bellowing like a bull. 'Now hear this, me glorious ship and crew! This is Wilkins speakin'! We've sealed out the world with our thinking about it, our lies and philosophies and grandiose fictions. I'm determined, as a worshipful Christian, to leak it back in!'

"Quickly, as if in fear of losing his nerve, in fear of another instant's change of purpose—at the same time drawing his second pistol (but it was a joke, all of it, his last, most spectacular theater trick, and we his dupes, except that, finally, Swami Havananda was leveling with us)—Wilkins aimed and fired, and the Captain's head flew open. The rest of him did not move, not so much as a twitch, but sat calm as a dead Tibetan, listening. There was no blood. Ngugi and I jerked our heads in amazement. The Captain's head was full of springs and coils, and tubing for letting out smoke when he puffed on his heavy black pipe. A walking puppet, huge ventriloquist's dummy —Wilkins' own creation, or, rather, Swami Havananda's. Even the blood on his beard was false—more trickery. Whim indeed! Then it came to me:

" 'Jeremiah!' I shouted. '*That's* who old Flint is! No wonder he was always at the Captain's side!' It was all clear as day to me now, at last—Jeremiah's wild excitement when he went with the Captain to visit other ships (no mean feat, that trick he played on them, just to keep his hand in—though he came back with sacks filled with money, his collection). 'The devil!' I whispered as the thing came still clearer, 'why the God damned arrogant maniac!' Wilkins must have known that, I understood then, must have suffered for years Flint's icy scorn, and must have hated him. At last he'd gotten even, had slashed what little heart Flint had left by raping poor Miranda.

"But Wilkins said, 'Devil! Ye make me laugh. Poor weak, slavish mortal, poor dupe, that's old Flint. He's hunted all his life for some holiness past magic. That's what brought him here, out to the region of the Vanishing Isles. Oh, his power's magnificent, no doubt about that, and his cynicism's the highest quality, I can tell ye from long experience.' He sneered. 'It's true he had a feeling it might be a hoax, and partly he came from professional interest: If somebody's tricking him, his arrogance demands that he spy out who. But at bottom he came here believing, sir. Fact. Gullible and desperate as only the greatest magicians can be. "Surely not *every*thing's mere illusion!" cried he. He made men his slaves with his bunkum religion ("Ghost of Hiram Billings, speak!" Har, har!), but religion it was, in the end, that undid him.'

"He gave me a wink. 'Flint murdered the Captain 'fore we ever come aboard, and the Captain's poor foolish daughter too. I assisted him, of course; and assisted him again when certain crewmen found out, God rest their souls.'

"He was about to squeeze the trigger and dispatch himself—for no earthly reason, so far as I could see. Little as I liked him, I was horrified, sweating. My mind raced, and it occurred to me to say: 'Wilkins, where's he now?—the blind man, Flint.' (Miranda had asked that in the cabin, I remembered—'Where's Jeremiah?' in terror but hiding to the last his identity. Cunning past cunning, a thousand times more wily than any Indian.)

" 'Blind, ye think?' says Wilkins. 'You'll see who's blind! Tell him when ye see him I was busy to the last. Faithful assistant, manufacturer of tricks. Can a man become one with the universe, undo the separation that makes sinners of us all? Impossible, ye say. Yet, behold, I seem to!'

" '*Not shoot!*' Ngugi shouted, and leaped at him, but not fast enough. Wilkins' face exploded, dark blood in the bandanna, and it was over, the repercussion still booming, deafening, in our ears. The *Jerusalem*'s tragedy was finished, or just begun. I could suddenly see things far away, like the mind of a tree. Miranda in her cabin sat up in the lingering twilight, knowing, and believing like all of us the thing was her fault—overweening lunatics, all of us—and screamed, and the scream like a lightning bolt slammed down on us and we looked up, chilled. Back in Nantucket the two old men, sly practical jokers, looked startled, went ashen, but the next instant couldn't remember what it was that had startled them. 'Yer move,' said Tobias Cook, though he wasn't certain of it, and frowned at the old worn checkers as black as midnight and red as blood.

"Wilkins lay bleeding, motionless, above him the ventriloquist's dummy he'd built, blown faceless, at his shoulder on the bulkhead the crudely carved but ornate memorial of some mortal presumably dead long since, returned to the universe (as Tibet's book tells), paroled forever from Discipline, word full of hardness: A. G. P. We carried up Wilkins' body and lowered it away.

XXVII

"There was no breeze. It was the eighteenth day of that eerie calm. The smell of land lay all around us. We waited for change, any kind of change. Even that maelstrom we'd heard about would be better than this endless hovering. As for Flint, we hunted the devil in vain. We dared not hope that he'd discovered some means of abandoning us—preferably Wilkins' way, and Kaskiwah's. But we saw no sign of him, and no sign he'd been into the galley biscuits. We were not easy in our minds, for all that. I was certain now that Miranda wasn't merely asleep in the ordinary sense of asleep. She was listening, and what could she be listening to but Flint? We searched the ship from top to bottom, again and again. Not a trace. We worried on.

"On the eighteenth day of the calm, as I say, black Ngugi and I stood on deck, waiting, listening for wind. The plan was changed now, barring accident. We'd steer for home as soon as the sky remembered us. Icebergs glinted in a circle around us, and the water was full of a strange music, choral, like the singing of sunken angels.

" 'Whales,' Ngugi said.

"His head was tipped. He was listening the way men who love symphonies listen. 'Mighty singers,' Ngugi said. 'No one believes but those who have heard. Have many songs, all with many parts. They sing to live, like the Negro, someday like the white man.' The ship was ringing like a violin.

" 'What are they singing?'

" 'Joy,' he said. 'Sorrow.'

"I studied him. 'Then how can you kill them?'

"He touched his lip as if the question had troubled his mind before, then smiled, slightly baffled. 'How else come hear them? Everything very expensive, this world.' I couldn't help but think of Mr. Poe's *Ligeia*.

"We listened. Whatever else might be true or

merely imagined on this ship of absurdities, it was true that the whales were singing—to each other and to us, or so it seemed. On the other hand, it was also true that there were huge white birds on the yard-arms. I could see straight through them. I felt some word tugging at me, deep in my mind, demanding my attention. And then, suddenly, Ngugi touched my shoulder. I smelled it myself the same instant. Fire.

"We flew to the deck but we couldn't reach Miranda before she'd set the second blaze, candle in tribute to her father's grand purpose, Death or Absolute Vision among the Vanishing Isles. She was in the same torn rags, her flesh still horribly bruised and swollen. She seemed drugged, or sleepwalking—perhaps drawn to this cruel last trick by some telepathic command from Flint. Ngugi seized her arms and gave a cry of anger and frustration like a child's as she scratched and bit him. He threw her down on the deck; we heard the thud of bone. The aft sails and mainsail were sheets of yellow flame.

" 'Cut 'em off,' I shouted. "Save the masts and yards or we'll never see Nantucket!' Already they were going up the rigging, slashing at the ties, leaping and swinging from the yards like gibbons, the burning sail sagging, collapsing towards the deck. If the flames reached our cargo of oil and wax we'd last about three seconds. There was no possibility of shouting out orders against the roar of the fire. But they knew. You don't sit a whole year on a ship full of whale oil and fail to guess what a spark might accomplish. They were there, reaching up with their bare, dark hands, all hatches closed, my lordless crew, and no sooner had the burning sail crashed down than over they went with it, a dozen seamen, down into the ice-cold sea to swim it away from us. So the masts stood bare, dangling rope, and every stay was smoking.

" 'Woman!' said Ngugi, bright tears on his cheeks. Then, to the others: 'We find more sail.' They turned instantly to search the ship for something to make sail of, but before they'd gone a step they were stopped by a voice booming, *'Stay where ye be!'* We turned like one man, and there on the poopdeck, where a minute ago there'd been no one at all, stood Luther Flint in all his grim, satanic glory. He looked as he'd looked in his theater days, great gleaming triumphant stovepipe hat and majestic tailcoat, his arms reaching out like an orchestra conductor's— except that his hair was wild as a rooster's and as icy white as snow. 'Get him!' I shouted, 'get him while there's time!' But it was already too late.

" 'Cover Upchurch, lads,' cries old Flint, and behind my left shoulder comes the voices of none other than Swami Havananda, that is, Wilkins, that we'd buried in the sea: 'He's covered, sir,' and he lets out as evil a laugh as was ever yet heard on earth. I couldn't catch my breath.

" 'You with the bone in your nose, put yer hands on yer head,' Flint tells Ngugi, and Wolff's voice comes from close to the black harpooner: 'You heard 'im.'

"My rabble of a crew was staring all around, confounded and shuddering at those voices of deadmen from the empty air. On the deck Miranda was beaming, triumphant and crazy as a loon, as if it was her eyes she'd set on fire. Meanwhile, Flint's voice is mournfully intoning, 'Yer sleepy, very sleepy . . .' and he's swinging his eyes from man to man, and it comes to me by heaven he's out to Mesmerize the pack of us, and it's working, too: I can see them weakening, slouching a little, tipping their heads like a man that's beginning to hear the mumble of a dream. He swings his evil eye on me now, and he strains so hard his eyeballs bulge. Beside him on the poopdeck stands my friend the white bird, shaking his head, looking weary and disgusted. It strikes me that Flint looks a little perplexed. He's overstraining, as if meeting some curious resistance. And at last, of course, it comes to me what his trouble is. He can't decide which eye to look in!

" 'Very sleepy . . . sleepy . . .' says Luther Flint.

" 'The devil in hell I am,' says I. Which is true, it strikes me; I'm wide awake, old wall-eyed John, though I'm the only one left, all the others are standing there like statues with clothes on—including (it comes to me) Miranda.

" 'It ain't working, Doctor,' says Wilkins' ghost.

" 'Then kill him,' says Flint, just as cool as can be.

" 'No!' shouts I, and my mind all the sudden is busy as thunder with pictures of those sailors being axed on the head. I go down on my knees like the Englishman. 'I'll do what ye like, sir. Ye don't need to put me in a Mesmerized state. The fact is, I'm Mesmerized already, been Mesmerized for years. I've learned to, you might say, compensate—act normal, don't ye know, though in fact I'm a walking deadman. God's truth. It happened one night in Philadelphia—'

" 'Hush yer tongue!' says Flint.

" 'Yessir. Yer wish is my command, sir.' Crying like a baby.

"Now Flint drops his arms down, and slowly he pulls his right hand over, still scowling like a grizzly bear, and rubs his chin.

" 'I still say kill him,' says Wilkins, at my back.

"The bird's still shaking his head, disgusted.

" 'A point to consider,' says Flint, still scowling, 'is, a fellow as quick with his tongue as young Upchurch might be useful if a man could just depend on him.'

" 'I'm yer servant!' I cry, and I wring my hands, crawling toward him on my knees. The bird's still shaking his head, sometimes rolling his eyes up as if praying for patience. I think about it, meanwhile bawling, 'Let me be yer disciple! I'm an eager learner and devoted heart and soul to yer daughter—if I have yer approval, that is.'

" 'Yer a good groveler,' says Flint, and give a nod. 'Yer a real professional.'

"The big white bird is getting furious now, moving back and forth like a parrot on a perch, and I strain to read his mind. It pops into my head: *There IS no Wilkins. Flint's throwing his voice.* My eyes widen and the bird spreads his wings out. *I thought ye'd never guess!* thinks he, and I read it.

"I'm weightless, suddenly. As free as the bird. I

can rush the old man—big as he is, he's no match for me. I'm already tensed to do it when I think: On the other hand, for most of my life I've been walking around scared to death of him, and now suddenly he's a humbug, an impotent old goof hardly better than the puppet he scared me with before. My heart fills with joy and I can't resist.

" 'I'll work hard, sir!' I say, and crawl toward him some more. 'I'll shine yer shoes and brush yer top-hat and feed the pigeons and rabbits, and I'll learn to play blackjack for when you need some amusement, or chess, if ye prefer, if ye've the patience to teach me.' But then I hesitate.

" 'There's just one thing,' I say, and crawl toward him some more. I stretch one arm up pitifully and I make my fingertips tremble. 'It's not for me to say, but if ye mean to make me yer lifelong slave, you ought to *win* me, seems to me. It would make me more valuable, so to speak. Ye should win me fair and square, by yer own honest wits, and not by these magical powers—yer command of deadmen. Send away the ghosts, and let us contend in some honest test of ingenuity, as long as it ain't chess.'

"Flint smiled—a terrible thing to see. Without hesitation, he said, 'A chess game, or nothing.'

"I widen my eyes. 'Chess, sir?' I say. I look terrified, pitiful. 'Chess is a difficult business, I understand.'

" 'Chess or nothing, my friend. Only dumb farmers give even odds.' He smiles, benevolent, and puts a point on his mustache.

"I ponder the question, and at last I bring out, 'I don't think lightly of my cunning, as ye know. Show me the moves and I believe that even in chess I might stand some chance against you.'

" 'Done!' says Flint, and with a snap of his fingers brings Miranda to. She blinks her eyes. I have a curious feeling she's faking it, never was asleep at all. As for the rest of them, they stand there asleep like a field full of horses in October. She opens one eye wide now, with a befuddled look, and, remembering her ragged half-nakedness, she covers her bosom with her hands and turns away.

"Her embarrassment touches me, makes a fool of me, and I suddenly blurt out: 'Since yer taking such advantage, let us raise the stakes higher so if I win, by some fluke, I win big, just the same as you would.'

"Dr. Flint cocks his eyebrow, puts his hands on his hips.

" 'Say if I beat you—by some miracle—I win . . . Miranda.'

" 'Never!' cries Flint's daughter, with a horrified look.

"He glances at her. She's misshapen as a gnome, lumpy as a kitten that's been mauled by a dog. It tickles his fancy. 'Done, my boy.' He smiles, looking sly. 'Yer a mighty confident young fellow, seems to me. If I didn't know better, I'd swear ye were secretly acquainted with the game.'

" 'I'm a whiz at checkers, sir, *that* much I'll say.'

"Dr. Flint gives once more his benevolent smile.

"So off we go to the Captain's cabin where the chessboard stands waiting, and we seat ourselves, Miranda peeking out from behind the door. What she's thinking, is more than I can say, but one thing's certain: Whatever it is she thinks of me, it stands to reason she's looking at her daddy with brand new eyes. He'd trade her away to captivity for a chess-game—his own daughter!—after all she's done for him! The door's behind Flint's back; he can't see her look. I muse on it, pretending I've got all my attention on the moves he's explaining, and it comes to me she might not be wholly opposed to being traded into Upchurch captivity. Flint asks me, sly, if I follow the explanation. He's been purposely confusing. I fumble with the pieces, show my ignorance. She watches me, whether in delight or alarm I've no sure way of telling. He explains again, more confusing than before. The ship lies as still as the solid land. At last, I allow I'm ready. With minimal chicanery, I happen to draw white. Perspiring, fingers trembling,

I begin the game. Quick as you please we've played six moves each.

"Then, like a wild man, Flint leaps up. 'That's no game of a beginner!' he bellows. 'You've opened with the damn *King's Indian!!!*'

" 'Ambushed!' cries Miranda, and her face goes wild.

"The old man went white, reaching over toward me. Before I could move, he had his hands around my throat. I pulled away from him, yelping—his hands on my throat were like seething fire—and I raised my fists to defend myself but, alas, no need! Before my flabbergasted eyes—God's own truth—his face went from chalky white to yellow, from yellow to a terrible, blood-dark red. Sweat came washing in rivers from his forehead, his eyes squeezed shut, his temples bulged, and all of a sudden he was smoking like a pile of old rags, and belching steam. The room filled solid with unearthly stench, and before I could even cry out, he was on fire, a great black furnace on legs, flaming, the top-hat sending up smoke and bits of soot like a railroad-engine chimney.

" 'Spontaneous combustion!' I gasped, and in horror turned my face away. But even as I did so, I leaped toward him, knowing by instinct what I had to do. I tore down a curtain to shield myself, then hugged the bubbling, curdling mass, dragged it through the hatch and across the deck to the rail and pushed it over. It sank into the ocean with a snaky hiss. The sailors on the deck below me slept on.

" 'Flint's dead,' I cried, and waved my arms. There was no sign of life from them.

"From the cabin behind me came a terrible mournful laugh, and I ran to Miranda."

XXVIII

The end is upon us; I admit it, honest reader. The inexhaustible supply of tricks is exhausted—almost. Dr. Luther Flint has been raised from mere artifice—

a ventriloquist's dummy!—to a touching spokesman
for all criminal, all pseudo-artistic minds. His death,
though perhaps not unique in all literature, is one that
should drive more ordinary villains to a jealous rage.
As for Miranda—but that's a ribbon not yet tied. She
sits observing the ancient mariner with thoughtful eyes.
She has half a mind to take control of things herself,
and she may do it, too. We know her kind. And the
angel will support her (whatever, exactly, that may
mean). So will the guest.

But I haven't interrupted this flow of things imagined
for mere chat about the plot. This house we're in is
a strange one, reader—house or old trunk or circus
tent—and it's one I hope you find congenial, suffi-
ciently gewgawed and cluttered but not unduly snug.
Take my word, in any case, that I haven't built it as
a cynical trick, one more bad joke of exhausted art. The
sculptor-turned-painter that I mentioned before is an
actual artist, with a name I could name, and what I
said of him is true. And you are real, reader, and so
am I, John Gardner the man that, with the help of
Poe and Melville and many another man, wrote this
book. And this book, this book is no child's top either
—though I write, more than usual, filled with doubts.
Not a toy but a queer, cranky monument, a collage:
a celebration of all literature and life; an environmental
sculpture, a funeral crypt.

The guest looks embarrassed. The angel disapproves.

"Tell on, Johnny!" the old mariner cries, and throws
his head forward and slaps his knees.

"No, *you* tell on," says I, "I just thought they'd like
to know."

XXIX

Says he:

"Then this, sir.

"Miranda lay face down on the berth, refusing to
turn to me or speak. Though she'd heard me coming,
she hadn't bothered to pull the cover up. She lay half-

bare in her ragged dress, her skin mottled and clouded like marble, wide milky veins between the green and plum-blue bruises. 'Miranda,' I said, 'now you listen to me.' When I touched her shoulder she twisted away, lightning fast, rolling over on her side and straight up on one elbow, not bothering to hide her buttonless, torn-open front, and glared at me with one eye, like Odysseus' Cyclops. Her face was more swollen than before; not a trace of its former beauty. Her smile was scornful—cunning and superior. I shook my head, and she pretended to laugh, a laugh identical to Wilkins' —or so it seemed to me—full of rage. Her face, all at once, went revoltingly coy. With a gasp of pain as great as mine, she threw away the cover to show the rest of her. The blood, where the dress was ripped away, was dry and peeling. I stood up, turned my eyes from her. 'Miranda, see here,' I said sternly.

" 'I gave myself to you,' she said, violent, '—wrote you beautiful love poems, shamed myself—blessed Heaven how I loved you, Jonathan!—but even then I was nothing. And *now*—'

" 'Be still and listen,' I said. Love poems indeed. And yet it was impossible not to believe her at least partly. I turned back to her, and it did not check me that she refused even now to cover herself, reveled in her destruction, flaunted her shame as she'd flaunted, once, her supposed nobility. Ah, pride, pride! No end to it!

" 'I'll take care of ye, Miranda. But from now on, because of yer criminal nature, ye must give up this willfulness and obey me absolutely. Otherwise I'll clap ye in irons and that's a fact.'

" 'Take care of me!' she sneered. 'Jonathan, yer too kind.'

" 'And love you, that too.' My voice was shaky, and where the words came from, Heaven knows.

"She laughed again, her face filled solid with what might have been hate; then, fast as a cat's paw, she snatched the cover up and lay rigid, eyes clenched shut. I was helpless, viciously slapped back for an instant, then suddenly I understood and could have laughed. In her place, I wouldn't have pulled up that cover but for one reason: uncertainty, a crack in my wall of despair. Her dyed black hair was coarse and scratchy, but at the roots it was yellow and delicate, a coming of spring.

" 'Ah, ah, wicked Miranda,' I said. She would come to love herself again, in time. She would preen in the broken piece of mirror on the wall, smiling in such a way that she did not show her broken teeth, coyly batting the lash on her damaged eye. I could have told her what Wilkins said: *There are no stable principles.* I put my hand on her shoulder and a queer shock of excitement went through me. I would tyrannize her back to health. She trembled, but didn't turn away. 'You'll be all right, Miranda.'

"For a long time she was silent, bristling, or so I thought. Then suddenly she raised up a little and turned her face toward me. 'Fool,' she whispered. 'I brought my father to the deck for you. You couldn't find him, for all yer tricks. The whole lot of you couldn't make him show himself.'

"It stopped me for a moment, thoroughly confused me. I remembered that motionless listening. I said: 'And the sailor you murdered? That was a kindness for me too, Miranda?'

" 'The knife was *thrown,* Jonathan. Ye must've been looking at the sailor at the time. If ye'd been looking into the cabin ye'd've *seen* it thrown.'

"I laughed, wishing it were true and half believing it. 'And when you came to my bunk, the time I caught your hand?'

" 'I was looking for the books, to keep you from learning who I was, keep you from despising me. Have you any idea what it's like to be—' She paused, too proud to let her humanness slip out, if that was what it was. '—Anyway, the books were *mine,* remember?'

" 'Yes, of course. And the time you told me that ridiculous ghost ship story? *"Believe in me, Jonathan!"* That, too, was for my sake?'

" 'The story's *true.* Not even my father could find a flaw in it.'

" 'A hoax, a trick by Wilkins. He said so.' I watched her eyes.

" 'Wilkins is a liar!'

"I shook my head. 'Miranda—poor desperate Miranda!' I said.

" 'Fool,' she whispered again, and drew back from me. The cover, where it hung from the edge of the berth, stirred a little. 'Poor desperate Miranda. What do *you* know about poor desperate Miranda?—what does anyone know—even poor desperate Miranda herself?' She'd be crying in a minute, but not from self-pity, from an overflow of anger that arched beyond me to all the universe. 'I lived with that tricky-brained devil all my life, and maybe loved him—just a child . . . Never mind, never mind. He was my father, and fond of me, whatever you may say, though also of course he was a devil. Never mind. I too learned magic —the child-bride stage-smile for when Daddy was in a rage, and a smile I really meant, but identical to the first, for when Daddy was in jail, or drinking and talking about suicide. "Be real, Miranda"; that's what you ask. But theater curtains are my outer skin, and my soul is the sound of the piano player. You hoped perhaps I'd grow up pure and innocent, untouched by my surroundings, some mysteriously engendered precious jewel in the forest, or your friend with the bone in his nose, Nigger Jim. But there is no purity or innocence in theaters, or in forests, or in oceans—and no wickedness, either. Only survival, only cunning and secrecy. The tortuous opening of theater curtains, the deep, deep breath, then—God help us!—the terrifying dimming of the lights. *Innocence,* Jonathan! You poor desperate fool!' She turned her face away. I did not notice, for a time, that tears were washing down her cheeks. 'I was beautiful,' she said.

"I thought about it, studying her bruises. They had become—quite suddenly, perhaps because for an instant she'd forgotten her secrecy and cunning—no longer repulsive. They'd become outer wrappings, mere theater curtains, as Miranda said. Particular encasements of the painful universal desire and fear.

" 'I'll be back,' I said abruptly. I left her, then quickly returned, bringing water and towels.

"She drew back in fright. 'Jonathan!'

"I ignored her. I sat on the berth, beside her, and gently dabbed away the blood at the edge of her lip. I rinsed the cloth and moved on to her neck, then her shoulder. She was trembling.

" 'Don't be afraid,' I said.

" 'Please, Jonathan!'

"But I'd discovered something. I knew every flicker of thought that went through her, because her nature, however deadly, was like mine, like Wilkins', like wise James Ngugi's: Whatever the age and continent that framed her, she housed no fear, no hope, no shade of opinion we ourselves had not also housed. I made my mind a blank. I could control her body as surely as could any Mesmerist. I could soothe away shyness, self-hatred, support her against a flutter of guilt, eighth and most deadly of the deadly sins. If I tyrannized, seduced her, it was by becoming her, not a cry of *Believe in me!*, but *I believe!* Her right hand touched my shoulder, stopping me. With her left she tried to hide the swellings on her face. 'Jonathan, don't,' she whispered. Age-old withdrawal of the female into shadows, the secrecy and cunning at the heart of things. I gazed at her, thinking nothing, drowned in sensation, desiring her. At length, Miranda closed her eyes. When I pulled my shirt off she said nothing and did not look at me. I took off the rest of my clothes and lay down beside her, carefully not touching her. I knew what she was thinking, watching her with my vague left eye. The splendid possibility of life without flesh, love without tyranny.

" 'You must come with me to southern Illinois,' I said. 'It's a whole new geography, beyond philosophy and stabilizing vision. Terrible tornadoes, unbelievable winds. In the springtime the hills are more green than emeralds, the sky more blue than cobalt, with clouds of unthinkable white. No dangerous animals high or low, except the Harpe brothers and the Baptists, and we can outwit them, wait and see.' I touched her breast. [*She blesses him unaware.*] She reached to me suddenly and pulled me to her. 'You're so *wall*-eyed!' she whispered. I saw on her face a wild, unintentional idea. 'Jonathan, I love you,' she whispered. 'You're grotesque.'

"I was alive, all at once. It seemed to me the whole ship was alive. My hands stopped moving on her shoulders, understanding ahead of my mind. 'Wind!' I whispered. She stopped breathing, listening. 'Wind!' we said, both of us at once. Outside the ports, the sky had changed. There were blooms of lightning. 'Sleep, Miranda. I'll be back when I can.' Without waiting for her answer, without stopping to dress, I left her, ran out on the poopdeck. 'Ngugi! There's wind!' I shouted. Ngugi snapped out of his sleep like a puppet jerked upward, and the rest of the crew came awake the same instant. 'Wind it is!' he shouted back, his eyes popping open, his smile as wide as the Milky Way, as full of strange joy as the black-green sliding Congo. The heavy air echoed mysteriously, *Is!* Our skeleton crew was all on deck, waiting for someone to give or take command. Charlie Johnson stood clapping, ready to start running—a smiling little black in spectacles. 'Sails!' I yelled. 'Stitch sails together—sheets, shirts, hankies, anything the wind can get its fingers in!' They went scampering down through the hatches to tear the beds apart, rip seams out of clothes, clamp sails together with thread, rope, nails, knives, marlinspikes. I stripped the Captain's cabin, tore away the covers from Miranda, 'A thousand pardons,' I said, and began on her dresser. 'Jonathan!' cries she, white arms over breasts. Her good eye was wide with indignation.

"The stirring ocean and the gentle wind were moving our sailless hulk to southward, edging us down toward sullen darkness and a milky sea where a strangely luminous glare arose, a kind of vapor that shifted here and there like a theater curtain. Ngugi had already a man at the helm, a man who knew no more of guiding ships than we did. Gigantic, pallid white birds were now flying great circles around us, emerging from behind the glowing veil. I went up with six men to lash on sail, snatch a little wind and put on such distance as we could toward the Cape before the weather turned. I shouted to our helmsman, 'Tack

alee!' The sky rang with echoes. *Tekeli-li! Tekeli-li!*
The *Jerusalem* yawed and leaned, then righted herself.
From my perch on the yard I saw ships in the distance
—two of them, then three, sent as witnesses. Far
below I could see, like mechanical toys, our orphan'd
crew running back and forth, each taking orders from
all of us. Them too I understood. Rankless, ruleless,
they were learning to be a community of sorts on the
mutilated ship. No more geniuses, no more great kings.
Only wild pale-faces, contemplative Apaches. They ran
about crazily (but gentle, sure-footed) like children
eager for Mama's praise. Miranda peeked out the
cabin door. 'Hooray!' she yelled. The wind came
steady, we had all the time and space of the wise
Chinese, though not their dignity. The whiteness of
the sea to southward darkened; a huge sad man rose
up from the water, standing on newly emerged dry
land, his arms laid out lightly on an oak tree's limbs
and his antique garb as white as snow. I addressed
him, shouting: 'So it's thee our Captain came to hail!
God bless you and good day!' I kept my right eye
steady on the bowsprit, the solemn white monster
blurry in my left. 'Tack hard alee!' I shouted. The
pale white birds were as large as the three ships circling us. 'Homewards, my sea-whores,' I shouted from
the masthead. '—Homewards, you orphans, you bandy-
legged, potbellied, pig-brained, belly-dancing killers of
the innocent whale! Eyes forward, you niggers, you
Chinese Irish Mandalay Jews, you Anglo-Saxons with
jackals' eyes. We may be the slime of the earth but
we've got our affinities! On to Illinois the Changeable!'
I stood on the yard, letting go with both hands, below
me a sail of shirts, sheets, trousers, rain-slickers, under-
wear, and below that my shimmering fellow Cains.
At the Captain's door, for inspiration, stood our blushing wild Sister. Perched like a bird, an archangel
teetering on Nowhere's rim, I intoned, dramatic, orbic-
ulate: 'Discipline, lads, is a World full of hardness,
abounding in disagreeables, till we've learned to chew
through to the eternity hidden in its pits.'

" 'Tack alee!' the Holy Ghost exclaims, disguised as

a sea-boobie sitting by my shoulder. His head hung down, disgusted by rhetoric.

" 'You better hang on there, bird,' says I.

" 'Hang on thyself,' cries he, 'thou fucking lunatic!' "